PRAISE FOR I DIED TOO, BUT THEY HAVEN'T BURIED ME YET

'Nobody writes grief better than Ross Jeffery.'

Josh Malerman, New York Times bestselling author of *Bird Box* and *Daphne*

'Deep, dark, and dire - Ross Jeffery plumbs the depths of grief.'

Ronald Malfi, bestselling author of *Come With Me*

'The longer we are on this earth, the more we are shaped by the experiences that expand and contract our memories. Ross Jeffery knows this well. In his latest, I Died Too, But They Haven't Buried Me Yet, Jeffery demonstrates how grief doesn't just wash away with the passage of time. Here we are witness, or rather concerned bystanders, to Henry, a father that has lost his child and in tragedy has lost part of himself. It's tragic and yet also endearing in its fragility, a sorrowful balancing act that walks the lines between solemnity and horror. This novel, like grief itself, will leave readers changed.'

Michael J. Seidlinger, author of *Anybody Home?* And *The Body Harvest*

'A compelling exploration of emotional complexity and dread. I Died Too... reaches from the grave forcing you to take its hand.'

James Ashcroft, Award-winning Director of author *Coming Home in the Dark*

'Atmospheric and disturbing, I Died Too finds Ross Jeffery scraping his knuckles through gravesite dirt to explore all the ways grief is just another word for possession. A wicked and twisted journey into a father's nightmare where each new revelation brings more blood.'

Tyler Jones, author of *Burn The Plans* and *Midas*

'Ross Jeffery is bold. He writes about the very worst and the very best parts of people, proving how ugly and glorious we can be.'

Priya Sharma, British Fantasy and Shirley Jackson Award Winning author.

Also by Ross Jeffery

The Devil's Pocketbook

Only The Stains Remain

Beautiful Atrocities

Juniper (The Juniper Series)

Tome (The Juniper Series)

Scorched (The Juniper Series)

Milk Kisses and Other Stories

Tethered

CLASH Books
TROY, NY
www.clashbooks.com

I DIED TOO, BUT THEY HAVEN'T BURIED ME YET

ROSS JEFFERY

CONTENTS

For Josh Malerman,
A true master of the genre and a dear friend.

&

For all the fathers and mothers who fail to see their children for who they
are... there's still time.

'Do not judge, and you will not be judged. Do not condemn, and you will not be condemned. Forgive, and you will be forgiven.'

Luke 6:37

'She wanted nothing that he could offer her, except perhaps his absence.'

Clive Barker, The Hellbound Heart

PROLOGUE

Henry was burying his daughter: again.

He was waist deep in the ground. The cool October air tickled his exposed and sweat covered flesh with icy fingers, and as the wind picked up and blew across the darkened pit it felt as if some unseen phantom had tousled his thinning, lank hair.

Henry, and the earth around him, were bathed in the harsh red glow from the rear taillights of his rusted-out Ford, which he'd backed up to the foot-edge of the freshly dug grave once the encroaching stygian hands of the night had strangled out the last rays of light from the day.

The vehicle sat precariously at the lip of the pit. As Henry continued to dig he wondered if at any moment the weight of it might cause the walls of the grave to collapse around him.

The rear lights of the car afforded him just the right amount of illumination in an otherwise pitch-dark scrubland, it was a blessing really, because he didn't want to be seen and he certainly didn't want to draw any unnecessary attention to himself.

Not now, anyway.

Not when he was so close.

He paused in his digging.

A Barn Owl's screech echoed through the trees, a sound which was more akin to someone skinning a cat than being attributed to those feathered angels of the night. He peered in the general direction of the sound but his eyes were instantly drawn to the wing mirror of the car, the glass throwing back a hideous reflection.

It took him a beat to recognise himself, his hands clenching tightly to the shovel in fear.

But the apparition was him. Washed in the red, rear lights; his face muddied from his diligent work, he appeared more ghoul than human in that moment, and maybe he was.

Turning away from the haunting image, he dug the head of the shovel into the moist soil and continued his furious digging.

This was the twelfth grave he'd dug for his daughter, Elsie; but still he hadn't managed to successfully bury her yet: she just kept coming back.

Henry had pondered many times on nights like this – waist deep in another of his daughter's graves – if the ground he'd toiled upon these past twelve years would ever finally welcome her home or if it would regurgitate her once more.

Lifting another shovelful of dirt from the ground, he proceeded to dump it on the ever-growing pile which now ran the entire length of the grave. To the side of the exhumed mulch, his gaze alighted on his previous, desperate attempts at laying his daughter to rest.

Eleven markers shone in the dark, each with a small, handcrafted cross and pile of stones at its base, every one of them were tinted red.

Henry had dug a grave for his daughter every year since her disappearance and with each one he still struggled to let her go. Maybe it was that innate tethering, how he fathered her in death better than he'd fathered her in life, which kept bringing her back.

He'd promised himself each time he stared down at a freshly dug burial pit at his feet, that it would be the last, but how many graves would ever be enough. As he climbed out of the twelfth grave and clambered to his feet, he knew he couldn't stop, wouldn't stop;

because as far as he was concerned he was only just getting started at making his peace with Elsie.

It had taken him twelve long years to finally realise he was to blame for everything, and if he had to dig a grave every year for the rest of his sorry life to atone for his callous actions, then he would.

Henry moved to the boot of the car, pulled it open and leant the shovel against the bumper at the rear of the car. Peeling back the blue tarp within, he revealed his latest offering, one which he'd soon inter to the soil for all of time.

The sight of her backpack almost dropped him where he stood, his legs were suddenly not his own, he shot a hand out quickly to the edge of the car to steady himself.

The backpack was the one Elsie had been carrying the day she disappeared, the one the police found stuffed into a bush near the playground he'd used to take her to, back when she wasn't ashamed of him, before he became an eyesore of her contempt.

He removed the denim backpack, held it within his shaking hands, turned it over reverently to observe the patches she'd sewn onto it: The Rolling Stones, The Beatles, Fleetwood Mac, AC/DC, David Bowie, Iron Maiden and Kiss. He smiled in that moment, when all he wanted to do was cry.

Elsie had been fourteen when she went missing, an abbreviated life if ever there was one, but however short her life had been, Henry knew, unquestionably, as he stared at the patches on her bag, that he'd been able to imprint some of his love of music onto her before she distanced herself from anything and everything to do with him.

Turning the backpack over to carry it by the arms, he saw the bloodstain, it was twelve years old now, a shitty-brown instead of the dark-maroon it had been when the police brought it to their house, sealed in an evidence bag. The presence of blood and the torn strap – which Henry fingered now – were signs to him at least that Elsie hadn't run away from home as they'd presumed, but she'd been abducted. The blood on the bag a stark indication that she wasn't taken peacefully either, there'd been a struggle, one that she'd inevitably lost.

Henry gripped the backpack by the good strap, let it dangle by his side as he picked the shovel up with the other hand before skulking across the blood-tinted ground towards the head of the grave.

The cross and pile of stones were waiting for him. The number twelve had been scribbled in his chicken-scratch on the largest pebble at the base. Elsie's name had been carved, as all the others, into the wooden crossbeam.

He held the backpack out, over the grave.

"Elsie, I'm sorry."

Henry dropped his offering into the pit where the darkness swallowed it whole.

Turning to the side, with shovel in hand, he thrusted the business end into the pile of loam at the graveside. Pulling a shovelful of dirt from the accumulated mound, he swung it out and held it aloft the gaping maw of the pit, but he couldn't bring himself to soil her memory, not yet anyway.

He held the shovel over the grave for some time, his heart unwilling to offer another morsel of his daughter's memory to the cold ground.

His arms began to shake with the exertion, an ache quickly forming in his lower back which slowly radiated through his core. He was frozen in place. His eyes pleaded longingly with the soil on the head of the shovel to stay put, but as his arms began to cramp, clumps of mud began to tumble free from its edge and fall into the grave.

He couldn't delay the inevitable any longer, the ground was finally calling this piece of her home. Henry succumbed to the call of the grave and turned the shovel in his hands, the soil tumbling into the darkness, the only sound that returned was the dirt landing on her bag, which in this desolate scrubland sounded like rain hitting a canvas tent.

After the deed was done and his daughter had been successfully interned for another year, Henry climbed into his battered Ford and checked the time on the dash. He still had time to get home, wash himself, eradicate the stench of the grave and drive across town for his meeting.

He turned the keys in the ignition and the car roared to life.

Peering into the rearview revealed Elsie's grave marker, bathed in red behind him. He attempted to speak but the lump in his throat trapped his words and flooded his eyes with tears.

He wouldn't leave this place until he said what he needed to say.

Slowly his words found their way past the blockage, what he'd planned as being a bold farewell ended up sounding weak and feeble.

"I died too, you know...the day you disappeared, they just forgot to bury me!"

CHAPTER ONE

Henry was sitting in group, a session which was supposed to help him channel and deal with his grief, but today his heart wasn't in it. He'd left it at the graveside of his daughter, whilst the rest of his sorry corpse was here, slouched in his chair with soulless eyes.

There was a reason the heart was made to love, for if it were to ever stop, we'd die.

Elsie would always have his heart, now more than ever; but it was the fact that she'd not wanted it all those years ago which plagued him the most.

Henry rubbed at the ache in his back. He didn't know if it was from his recent exertions at the gravesite or if it was down to the plastic monstrosities that passed for chairs in this godforsaken group which was causing him his latest bout of discomfort. As he reclined further into the chair and instantly found his answer, the damnable contraption offered no support whatsoever; if anything their torturous hold made baring one's soul – when it came to it – unbearable.

Unable to get comfortable, he began fiddling with his hands

when he discovered, in his haste to get here on time, he'd forgotten to scrub under his nails. Each finger was crowned in a sickle of brown and he set about picking the dirt from beneath them without anyone noticing, because if they did, they'd ask questions, and Henry hated nothing more than questions about how he was coping.

Because quite clearly he wasn't. But he wasn't about to volunteer that information, because in his humble opinion, being open and honest was for sissies and he was anything but a sissy.

"Every time I treat myself to an orgasm, I feel like I'm cheating on him. But he'd want me to be happy right... right?"

At Harriet's remark, Henry peered up from harvesting the grime from under his nails, dropping a sliver of brown to the floor.

The room and the assembled group of grieving misfits remained silent.

Harriet began weeping and Henry couldn't work out if it was due to her infidelity to her dead husband or the group's lack of a response with regards to her wanting to pleasure herself.

He couldn't look away from the broken woman before him: her hair was dishevelled, there was dried egg yolk on her cardigan, her eyes were red and bloodshot and snot dribbled from her nose like a leaky tap.

The silence in the room grew heavy, members of the tribe were either staring at the filthy tile squares at their feet or inspecting the cobwebs billowing lazily in the corners of the ceiling. Everyone was trying their damnedest to avoid eye contact with Harriet, mainly Henry assumed through fear of having to answer her lurid question.

From the corner of his eye Henry enjoyed a rare moment of voyeurism, he didn't have to talk right now, Harriet quite clearly had centre stage for the evening. He quickly became both horrified and fascinated by the slug of green mucus which slid from Harriet's nasal cavity and inched its way slowly towards her lip; he winced inwardly at its trajectory, but he was also curious as to whether she'd tongue it?

She didn't.

Instead Harriet wiped it away with the back of her hand, smearing it across her face. Henry hadn't realised he'd been leaning forward, inclining his body towards her, desperate to see what would transpire, because tracing that mucus down her face was a far better prospect than trying to answer her questions about flicking the bean whilst your husband's in the ground.

"Grief's a trawler's net Harriet," the voice came from his left, it was Roger; Roger was leading the group this week and he was always one to serve up a platitude to show his superiority and how well adjusted he was with his own grief. His truisms were usually completely out of context, just like this one, but it was his week in charge and so Henry let him have his moment.

"It grows ever burdensome with time." Roger continued. "So, if you wanted to get a little frisky beneath the sheets, I'm sure Shane wouldn't hold that against you, you're only human."

Although what Roger had said didn't really make sense, Henry couldn't help but muse on it as he leant back into the unforgiving embrace of his chair, as if it were an iron maiden.

A flash of Elsie's backpack appeared in his mind, the red font on a black background, AC/DC. As that memory which was now five feet below the ground began to fade, his thoughts turned swiftly to what Roger had mentioned: a trawler's net of grief.

Henry pondered how heavy the net of grief he dragged around with him was, and how much sorrow was left to haul up from the unfathomable depths of his aching personal despair; because he was tired of it all. Grief had wasted his muscles and weighted him down for twelve long years, and if his net – as Roger had eloquently phrased it – was still trawling the bottom of his grief, how much more sorrow would it discover in the dark depths of his mind and heart? He had a hard-enough job coping with the catch he'd hauled in already, most days he could barely walk without dragging his shoes along the pavement and it didn't matter how much sleep he got, he was always exhausted.

He didn't want the totems of pain he'd done well to forget over the years being pulled to the surface, their weight being added to the crushing burden he already had to carry. It wasn't fair. He shouldn't be forced to carry them around with him for the rest of his stinking life because of some dumb platitude Roger had espoused that rang true. And so Henry cut that imaginary net Roger had planted in his mind and watched his ladened catch fall into the sea of his personal despair.

As he watched his imaginary net disappear beneath the surface of his frothing grief, Henry was forced to observe all the things he'd buried in those twelve graves over the years bubble up to the surface before finally sinking beneath the waves.

The biggest question he was left with, now that he was free of that stinking net, was if he'd have anything substantial to show for the unending trauma of reliving the worst day in his sorry life again and again?

He was quite sure the answer to that last question was no.

Harriet who was smeared with snot had picked up another thread of her grief and was gently pulling on it.

"What I don't understand is why it doesn't get any easier." Harriet uttered weakly as her eyes scanned the group once more. "I'll be making Bovril on toast and when I turn around he's right there with me, like he never went away. Just sitting at the kitchen table with a twinkle in his eye. But then when I look away he vanishes. It's all consuming isn't it, how their lives touch our lives in more ways than we know whilst they're with us, as if they've stained it somehow..."

Henry glanced down at his watch. Harriet had been blithering on for half an hour in total and showed no signs of letting up.

The usual time permitted for members of the group to share was ten minutes, something Henry was adamant about and tried to keep to it religiously when he was leading the sessions. Twelve minutes was a maximum. The sweet spot was between eight and ten and if you could bring your trauma in under five, well that was just dandy. They could all just pack up their shit and be gone within the hour and thirty-minute time limit that came with renting the community centre.

The sooner they were done the better as it afforded more time at the pub afterwards, and that was where Henry's true therapy was found.

Henry had good intentions when he'd set up the group eleven years ago, a way to help others with the gut-wrenching and soul-destroying questions he was asking himself.

Over the years though, that sparkling idea he'd put into motion had become rusted and tarnished with the unrelenting grief which was scraped up alongside its hull. He realised after the first year of the group's inception that prolonged exposure to another person's trauma had become a bitter pill to swallow at the best of times, and today – because of Harriet – that pill felt as if it had been bejewelled with razorblades.

Harriet continued prattling on, her eyes scanning the group for a weak link, but there wasn't one to be found because they were all hardened, grief-riddled husks.

Henry caught her eye briefly, but quickly looked away, returning his gaze to his Converse, the toes of which showed signs of his antics earlier on in the night. He couldn't shake Harriet's eyes though, puffy and dull, like worn pennies, the skin around them red like an infection. Although he was looking at his trainers, he could still sense her head moving, her haunted eyes desperately beseeching those in assembly, hungry to latch onto someone: anyone.

Henry noticed that around his seat, on the carpet squares were dried diamonds of mud, which must have fallen out from the tread of his shoes; further incriminating evidence of his time spent in his daughter's latest grave.

Tearing his eyes away from the slivers of compacted soil, he checked his watch for the fifth time in five minutes. Hoping Harriet would notice and take the bloody hint, he didn't want to have to be the bad guy again, it felt as though he'd spent his life being *that* guy.

And with that thought percolating in his mind, he knew he

couldn't intercede, although he desperately wanted to; instead he knitted his fingers together and squeezed, throttling his own hands until his fingers turned white.

He wanted to shout at her to shut up, but he needed to prove to the group that he wasn't the soulless monster they'd all had him pegged as from the start.

He settled back into his chair, hands knotting together in his lap, knowing that letting Harriet talk herself out – exhaust herself – would go some ways to demonstrating to the group that he still had at least a shred of empathy left for their unifying cause for being here.

Henry chewed it over, pinched his lips closed, could feel the fuzz on his tongue and the bad taste his apathy left in his mouth, but he knew he couldn't do anything, because at the end of the day, how can you deny someone the time to share the worst moment of their life? He didn't like it – not voicing his frustrations – being subservient to a woman, any woman, grieving or not; but he knew he didn't have to like it, he had to endure it, and so he grimaced and swallowed the bitter taste of emasculation from his tongue.

Henry crossed his legs at the knee, his foot spinning circles in the air at the ankle, frustration or boredom, it was for the room to decide.

He was a conductor in that moment, his black and muddied trainer the baton which controlled the peculiar orchestra before him. Harriet's voice had taken on the whine of an out of tune violin, a depressing and all-consuming tune of despair which assaulted everyone in attendance and put Henry's teeth firmly on edge.

"My dog sometimes sees him you know, my Shane..."

Harriet was back to sharing the exact same story she'd shared every three weeks when it came to her time in the 'grief seat'. Her words never changed a single iota. It was as if her trauma was a scratched record which the group was forced to endure every three weeks, once it rolled around to her time in the spotlight again.

Just when they thought she was done, she'd flip the record and it would be the same tune, the same mournful song, skipping and jumping and they'd be forced to listen to her tale of woe about how her husband talks to her through her Pomeranian all over again.

If he wanted to, Henry could cut in and quote her miserable monologue verbatim, but he wouldn't.

He'd learnt over time not to pretend to know, or even attempt to understand, someone else's trauma. It was personal to each and every one of them, tattooed permanently and often painfully onto each person's heart and mind and soul, so they'd never forget, or be allowed to forget: its presence.

If ever someone thought they'd worked through it, conquered grief, if that were even attainable; they'd only have to look inwards to discover the stinging reminder waiting for them to pay it attention. And when they did, they'd be back at the foot of the mountain which would call them ever-onwards to climb and conquer it once more.

Henry had always cut Harriet a little bit of slack with her oversharing because she brought the donuts to each meeting. Little doughy pieces of Heaven in a place that felt like Hell most of the time. But today she was pushing her luck and testing Henry's resolve with her recurring malady about her late husband using her dog to speak to her from the grave.

Henry shot a glance across the circle to Josh, with whom he shared a look which communicated: *how do we get her to shut the hell up?*

Josh was in his early forties and the closest thing Henry had to a friend.

He'd come to the group after his wife passed away a few years back. They'd been trying to conceive and nothing was happening, so her doctor ran some tests and discovered the reason: stage four ovarian cancer.

Turns out, Josh's wife couldn't grow life, but she could apparently grow her own death.

Henry had seen Josh at his weakest, but there was no denying he was a strong man, both in brawn and intellect, attributes that lent themselves perfectly to his job as a carpenter.

Since Josh's house had become a mausoleum for the memory of his dear, dead wife Amanda; he'd committed himself to flipping houses instead of spiralling into depression. He bought them cheap and after completing the painstaking work of turning those hovels into homes he'd then sell them high. Josh would spend all his spare time away from his own abode which had quickly become a graveyard for his burgeoning dreams of fatherhood, but he'd never abandon their memories, he'd tend that plot until his dying breath.

For Josh, his occupation had given his life purpose once again and Henry hoped that's what they'd all find one day; a purpose to keep on keeping on. Josh gave all of himself to the group and in doing so he became the light they gravitated towards; both in the chitchat after the sessions had concluded, and at the pub across the street when the lights were finally turned out and the door locked behind them.

They'd all drag their weary carcasses to the pub in search of escapism, a way of fending off the start of another day and the looming holes that would be revealed in their lives if they stopped, and more times than not, they'd find some semblance of their elusive escapism at the bottom of a glass or at the end of a bottle.

People hung off Josh's every word, enjoyed his stories and his natural thirst for life, a life he was now living according to his rules and not under the stringent reign of tyranny, of misery and of grief.

Josh, in his short time attending the group – compared to the many that made up their number – had even ascended to the lofty heights of '*second in command*' at the grief support group.

The Circle of Caring Souls or as Henry liked to refer to their group as: '*The COCS*'.

Henry nodded towards Harriet, urging Josh to intercede, to put a halt on her outpouring before they all drowned in a stream of snot and tears. Josh was the only one who could get away with it, and that was why Henry was imploring him on, pushing him under the bus.

Josh rolled his eyes at his friend before he leant forwards in his chair, his strong fingers knitting together in front of him as his elbows rested on his knees.

Henry watched on, willing his friend to end this torture. He observed Josh's mouth open, he was seconds away from cutting Harriet off and sending her dead weight plummeting into the precipice of insurmountable grief she hung over.

Josh let out a held breath, he was going to do it.

Suddenly Roger stood up, marched across the circle and presented Harriet with a tissue. Henry thought he was going to feed her a knuckle sandwich by the way he strode confidently across the circle and thrusted his hand towards her face.

In some dark part of his soul Henry wished he had.

But that small act of kindness was enough to bring her back to the room and end her crazed mutterings about dogs being vessels for human souls. Henry noticed that the interruption had thrown her off, her face suddenly a mask of confusion, disorientation; Henry wondered if she even knew where she was.

'Where was I?' A look of deep confusion creased her brow. Again the group remained silent, leaving her to her befuddlement.

Roger had shuffled back across the circle and sat down. The group trained their gaze on Harriet, observed her desperately trying to find herself, centre herself, but all of them – Henry assumed – secretly hoped she'd remain lost, because if she did, it would mean this hellish night was one step closer to finally being over for another week; Henry wanted nothing more than for this recurring anniversary – nightmare – of a day to be over.

Roger glanced up at the clock that hung above Harriet on the wall before quickly, and loudly slapping his thighs. The sound cracked so loudly that it made a few of their number snap awake as it echoed around the room, it was as if his hands were gavels and his legs forged of oak. He was their master of ceremonies this week and he had declared their court officially adjourned for the evening.

Henry was grateful for Roger's swift interruption and intervention as it saved him the job of bringing everything to a close again.

He knew many of the group members believed he didn't have a heart for wallowing in other people's grief, and the little empathy he did have would fit into a thimble; but he didn't give two shits. He never gave much credence to people's opinions of him because as he'd said to Josh one evening after the beers had been flowing and Josh had tried to enlighten him about the higher power he'd discovered: *'Life isn't always tidy and God's plan isn't always easy to understand, but he'll make beauty from the ashes of our lives, just you wait and see,'* Josh had said. Henry had waited a beat before he replied with a witticism of his own: 'Opinions, my dear friend, are like arseholes; everyone's got one and I haven't found one yet that didn't stink.'

That refrain had become somewhat the motto of his life.

But Henry's grief was deeply personal and just as inescapable.

If only those that cast aspersions on his character knew the places he wallowed in during the cold nights when sleep was just a word, a word he could never will into action; or the waking nightmares that kept him company and whispered to him about his part in the tragedy that bound him to the graves he dug each year. If they knew the personal hell which awaited him each night, maybe – just maybe – they'd cut him some slack.

But he understood enough about this cruel world to never let his guard down or to let others see into his private seething Hell, because if he did they'd discover quite quickly that he did have a soul after all. Albeit a tattered and withered one; and that's why he kept everyone at a distance, the truth – which he hid so well – was too much to bear others discovering.

As Henry sat there silently judging Roger, the man quickly stood up, folded his chair and placed it on the rack before walking away from the circle.

He was apparently done for the evening.

Henry hated that bastard with a burning passion.

Henry's hate was more deep-rooted than his annoyance of the

man's platitude spilling lips because Roger – holier than thou Roger – was in charge of providing the refreshments for each meeting. It wasn't much of a spread, because all that bastard provided for the group was coffee, plain old coffee. The lack of refreshments though had become a long suffering bone of contention and a constant thorn in Henry and Josh's side, a silly thing to grouse over, but they did.

Coffee was all the irritating man provided. Ordinarily, it wouldn't be so bad but he'd leave it to percolate for the length of the meeting, which made the coffee insufferable. But what pissed Josh and Henry off most, was that if you weren't partial to coffee there was sod all else provided, although other refreshments had been requested on numerous occasions.

There was however a water fountain down the hall but you'd probably develop Legionnaires' disease or something far worse given the neglected nature of their surroundings.

Henry had heard from the landlord of the community centre that a few kids from the Scout group that used the hall on a Wednesday evening had been hospitalised with dysentery a few months back, they'd traced the illness back to the fountain, but still the thing was in commission.

The community centre was falling apart around them and Henry couldn't help but laugh at how perfectly the sparse space mirrored each of their own lives, as they each sat in their uncomfortable chairs and watched each other's lives crumble down around their feet.

One of the reasons Henry believed they'd got such a deal on the rental price was because whilst they were using the place, it was another night the building was in use. The lights being on and the foot-flow they generated to and from the building on a Tuesday evening was a deterrent for potential squatters.

The coffee though, tasted like warmed up piss. Bitter and unpalatable - but they'd all still drink it; choke it down with their tears, because after all, it was better than the alternative.

Roger headed over to the refreshments table. To call it that you'd think it was something special: it wasn't, it was just a pasting table with a cheap, stained, paper tablecloth on it. Henry kept forgetting to get another one, so week in and week out they'd pull the same tired table covering out and carry on like normal.

As the group herded towards the lacklustre refreshments table Henry set about collecting the few remaining chairs, their previous occupiers keen on getting to the donuts before all the ones with crème filling were scoffed by Jacob, who was eating his way through grief, one cake at a time and letting out his belt one notch a week. Henry was sad to see him go that way, but each of them had a cross to bear and Jacob's way to cope was food, whereas Henry's was grave digging.

"Where the hell's Erik?" Henry said as he took hold of the chair next to him and collapsed it before peering over his shoulder to Josh.

"Erik?" Josh replied as he carried a chair over to the rack on the wall.

"Yeah, I thought we delegated chair stacking duties to him last week?"

Josh hung a chair on the wall rack, turned to face Henry. A smile broke out across his rugged, handsome face.

"Man, you're one lazy bastard," he chuckled. "He's gone away with his wife, said they were going to try and get some space, retreat for a while from the world; work stuff through..."

"Where'd they go?"

"Some place called Polperro in Cornwall, said he'd do some painting and stuff when they were down there, try and do a bit of healing too."

"What a load of shit–"

"Pardon?"

"You know, that arty-farty, fairy bullshit. Painting, how's that work?"

"You know people do that as a job right?" Josh took the folded chair from Henry's grasp, placed it on the rack with the others before turning to collect the last remaining chairs.

"It's called art therapy, helps people process their trauma–"

"Daylight robbery more like it," Henry uttered under his breath, stifling a laugh at his own witticism as he carried the last of the chairs across the room, shaking his head all the way, a wry smile on his lips.

Josh caught up with him at the rack as they both slid their chairs onto the growing stack.

"What's so funny man?" Josh said.

"Just the things people do to try and make themselves feel better. Art-fucking-therapy?" Henry chortled at the mere mention of those words hardly believing they made sense strung together.

"Man, laugh all you want, but it's probably more constructive than pickling yourself with booze each night, and don't think I haven't noticed your shoes; you know that if you keep picking that scab it ain't ever going to heal?"

Henry stood straighter, his jaw set.

He glanced down to his Converse, took in the muddied toe before returning his gaze to Josh, silently appraising his second in command. Back when he was younger he'd have punched someone's lights out at the slightest signs of disrespect but at fifty and having the fight pulled out of his life; not to mention being a good many years Josh's senior, he let the comment slide because he knew he couldn't be without a drinking buddy, tonight of all nights.

"You're probably right," Henry uttered.

"Well, blow me down..."

"I said probably."

Both men laughed suddenly and stood there watching the mingling throng of damaged souls devour the donuts Harriet had provided for the evening. Their laughter, a fragile moment of joy in a place full of sorrow was something Henry hadn't known he needed, but it was something his soul had been desperately craving since he'd woken up this morning.

"Shall we go join them? Sooner we do, sooner we get out of here, right?" Henry nudged Josh with his elbow before slowly setting off to join the assembled group.

"Hey, Henry." Josh called out before Henry had ventured too far.

Turning back, Henry noted the smile which had been on Josh's face moments before was gone, in its place was a look of concern. Josh twitched his head back, a *come here* gesture. Henry stepped towards him and they huddled together as if conspirators.

Josh peered over Henry's shoulder at the group, before his eyes focused on his friend again.

"How you holding up?" Josh whispered.

"Yeah I'm great, I–"

"Don't bullshit me man, I know what today was–"

"Hey, look, I'm cool. It's just another year, in a long line of years..." Henry trailed off, not wanting to over-share.

"I'm just worried about you is all."

"You going to try and kiss me or some shit?" Henry chortled, before throwing an arm around Josh's shoulder and turning them back to the group.

"I'm just messing with you," Henry continued. "But if you try that shit well... it's your funeral."

They chuckled together as they walked towards the thinning group of dejected and sorry looking souls. Henry observed the sad faces in the distance, each one riddled with pain and he wondered if he looked the same to them.

As they neared, it hit him in a moment of clarity that this group – *The COCS* – wasn't a support group for grief, it was an everlasting memorial for the dead.

"It's her twelfth anniversary Henry."

"You say that like I don't know." Henry's tone was abrupt, cold: numb.

"Look, I didn't mean anything by it, I *know* you know. I understand you've been living with it for twelve years, I just want you to know that if you need to talk about it, process it in some other way than those graves, I'm here for you. Twelve years is a long time to bury that hurt man, one of these days you're going to need to talk about it or you'll end up burying yourself instead of whatever it is you bury on these nights."

Would that be so bad? Henry wanted to say, but didn't.

As they approached the refreshment table Henry lifted his hand up and motioned for two cups of coffee. Roger gave him a nod and proceeded to pour two steaming puddles of shit into polystyrene cups.

"Josh, I appreciate you looking out for me man–"

"Two coffees!" Roger's voice was a clanging symbol, one that Henry wanted to smash to pieces for the interruption.

Josh turned, thanked him for the coffees, passed one to Henry.

"But listen, I've got things sorted. I'm going to drink this shit, no offence Roger," Roger shook his head at the remark before continuing to clear up for the evening now everyone had one of his delectable beverages. Henry noticed him diligently putting everything back in the plastic box marked DON'T TOUCH COCS.

Henry wondered as he read the label what the Scout group made of their box when they had to get equipment out of the shared cupboard, he hoped they had a sense of humour at least.

Smiling to himself he turned back to Josh and continued from where he'd left off.

"So, after this, I'm going to head over to the Yeoman and sink a few pints before going home, where I'll get my head down and see what tomorrow brings, you still coming right?"

"To the Yeoman?"

"Yeah."

"Of course, I can't leave my buddy in his time of need. If Hannah were still around I'm pretty sure she'd disown me if I left a friend's side on the anniversary of his daughter's–" Josh paused.

"Death. You can say it man. It's fine, it is what it is."

Josh appeared as if he wanted the ground to swallow him before smiling meekly at Henry, nodding his head in response.

Henry lifted the coffee to his lips. His hand was shaking, just the mere mention of his daughter and her death had rattled him more than he thought it would.

Still, after all these years, he felt guilty for what he'd done and as he watched his hand shaking, he hoped Josh didn't see the guilty tremor. He took a quick sip and instantly regretted it, grimacing at its foulness.

Peering over Josh's shoulder, to ensure Roger wasn't looking, he quickly threw his cup and the contents of it into the bin before quickly snatching the cup from Josh's hand before he could take a sip and dumped it too.

"Thatta boy, shall we?"

Both men headed for the door because misery loved company after all.

They left Roger and Jacob – who was still busily hoovering up the crumbs of donuts from the box – to turn the lights off and lock up.

There was drinking to be had and sorrow to be celebrated and a little girl to be drowned.

CHAPTER TWO

They were a few beers deep by the time the topic of Elsie's anniversary inevitably permeated their conversation.

The trauma of that day had never truly faded for Henry, but over the years, and usually around this horrid time of the year, today's date loomed large on each of their individual calendars (*Henry's because it was marked with a large, black X and Josh's because he needed to be there for his friend in his hour of need*).

The events that had transpired on that day long ago were tangible on the evening that Henry found himself in another grave for his daughter, as if the pain and trauma of the day she went missing had bled into the present.

Josh was staring at his beer, his fingers tracing the condensation, his heart hammering inside his chest with the words that were forming in his mind. He took a deep breath and let the words out, however painful they were, Henry needed to hear them.

"You know you got to bury Elsie once and for all and let her go right?"

Josh glanced up from his beer, wondering if his friend had heard him over the clamour in the pub.

Elsie. Those five letters weighed as much as an anvil once they'd left Josh's lips and instantly soured the mood, whilst also crushing his friend beneath their weight as he watched Henry's shoulders sag.

Josh knew her name would come up tonight whilst they drank to forget, but he had no idea he'd be the first one to mention her.

"I don't want to, but I got to, right? It's not like I've not thought about doing it once and for all, but I just can't bring myself to say goodbye to her for good, it feels as if I'm letting myself off the hook for what I did. I don't dig those graves for her you know, I dig them for me, it's selfish I know."

Henry took a sip of his beer, holding his finger up to Josh so he wouldn't interrupt before he continued on his train of thought.

"It's all my fault Josh. She died because of me, because of what I said to her that day. You probably think all this grave digging is a charade to make *me* feel better, to prolong my wallowing. But the whole *one grave* thing you mentioned just seems kind of...selfish. The thought that I can just do it once and forget everything I did which led up to the moment she died is a fucking pipe dream, because there isn't a day that goes by that I don't think about what I did and how I'm responsible and the one grave for all of time thing isn't going to change that... it isn't going to change me, however selfish it looks to those looking in."

"There's nothing selfish in grieving,"

"I know, but a grave without a body's just a hole in the ground, and until Elsie's body is interred for all time, I'll keep burying her."

"Don't get me wrong man, I understand what you're doing, where you go on her anniversary, it's a sacred space, your sacred space. Markers to help you channel those feelings you've got swarming in that ol' noggin of yours. I know you need it, I just don't feel you deserve to relive it each year."

"But I do deserve it. After what I did, it's unforgivable, I shouldn't be allowed to forget it–"

"Here we go again," Josh couldn't help but roll his eyes, he'd heard it all before.

"What's that supposed to mean?"

"Nothing, just forget I said anything."

"Don't pull that shit with me Josh, come on; out with it?"

Henry was always argumentative after a few pints. Josh should have known to keep his opinions to himself, especially tonight. Henry's eyes were wide with anger, his brow deeply furrowed.

"Look, I don't want to start anything, now's not the right time, but how long have I known you man? How long have we been having these meetings? Not once during those times do you open up, you bottle everything away, you're scared to–"

"Bullshit–"

"Let me finish. This is typical of you, this..." Josh used his finger and encircled it around Henry's face. "This, right now, it's bloody typical. You don't want to hear what others are trying to tell you. You just shut them down and shut them out, when all we're doing, all we're trying to do is check that you're okay, I care about you buddy..."

"Don't you go getting all queer on me," the way Henry said queer was laced with venom. It appeared that just speaking the word he despised so much left a bad taste behind. Josh knew about Henry's homophobia, shit, everyone did.

Josh watched on as Henry quickly picked up his drink, desperate to eradicate that foul-tasting word from his mouth with a slug of beer. Unfortunately, at that moment they'd run dry and so Henry was forced to suffer the taste a little while longer. Josh smirked as he watched how uncomfortable his friend had become.

"And there's the deflection. Congratulations for being the cliché I expect of you."

"I'm just shitting with you man, what's wrong; you on your period or something?"

"Look. Listen to me, can you keep quiet for just a moment? Let me say my piece and then you can laugh it off or insult my manhood further when we're done... does that sound fair?"

Henry lifted his hands in a placating gesture; a pissy, prissy smile crested his lips. He waved his hand as if permitting Josh to continue before lifting a few of their empty glasses up to the light in search of dregs.

"You're scared to be real man," Josh said, "trust me on that. I've owned my grief. I don't dare to assume you haven't, but you gotta be real with me, and above all else with Elsie. I've owned my pain, spoken about my heartache, purged its misery from my soul, become a blubbering mess more times than not, for your viewing pleasure, and the COCS."

Henry sniggered like a school boy at the use of their acronym.

"But you, you've kept it all bottled up for what... twelve years now?" Henry shrugged his shoulders, a petulant move that infuriated Josh more than he let on. "The thing is Henry, if you bottle that shit up; all that pain and suffering, it's only going to get stronger, it'll ferment and end up corrupting the very thing that keeps it locked inside... that's you man. It'll destroy you."

"Ouch..."

"What?" Josh peered over the table, concerned for his friend.

"I think I just hurt myself on your point."

"Funny."

"But are we getting to your point? Drinking time be wasting..." Henry said before glancing over at the bar.

"Yes, we are! The point is, I think that you having that time and space with your daughter is a good thing. Is it the best thing for you? I'm not so sure. You might not see the worth in one grave, and that's cool, but there's only so much ground to dig up, and with your obsession about it you'll be digging that ground of your past your whole life unless you start looking inwards, that's where the true healing takes place Henry. Start digging up your hurt, your shame, your perceived culpability in what happened and start burying that instead of the memories of Elsie. Or at least open up about it in group. I'm not forcing you to do anything you don't want to man, if digging those graves helps you process shit, then cling to it, own it.

But there will come a time when you'll need to bury your own hurts or they'll end up hurting you too, and when that time comes buddy I'm here for you, the COCS are here for you as well. I don't dare to know your pain, or why you feel so responsible for what happened, but I do *know* you and I can see you're hurting. What happened was a tragic accident, you need to understand that, forgive yourself for whatever you said or did. Elsie would want that for you, I'm sure of it."

"Hmm..." Henry peered over the table at Josh, a look of deep thoughtfulness on his face. Josh was almost relieved because he'd imagined a fist flying in his direction, knowing full well Henry's temper had a hair-trigger, but it appeared he might've finally gotten through to his friend.

Henry's next words proved he'd been pondering something indeed, but it wasn't what Josh had hoped.

"Right, drinks? Does the queer want an umbrella with his drink or would a manly beer suffice?"

Josh felt himself flush with anger at how easily Henry had brushed him off again. Just when he'd thought he was getting through to the belligerent man, Henry had just crammed it all back down in the pit of his soul again. Josh had often wondered if Henry's dad was one of those *don't show your feelings* bastards. Henry calling him a queer was expected. That's what Henry did. He said what he thought and he didn't care how it made him look. In fact, sometimes he'd stare straight at Josh and say something cruel or gross, just to see how Josh would react.

"A beer would be great." Josh said, as Henry staggered to the bar.

Josh watched on as the bar literally held his friend up. As Henry swayed in place Josh began to reappraise their surroundings. The Yeoman was a shit hole, but one they both felt at home in. Their drinking sessions in here had, over time, become legendary, especially on Elsie's anniversary. These nights were a habitual affair that allowed them to drown their sorrows and forget the worst days in each of their lives.

Josh glanced at the vacant booth, usually there were more of them, a gaggle of broken people trying to survive the pull of the grave, but not tonight, they'd learnt to stay well clear of the Yeoman on Elsie's *death day* because Henry always became the worst of himself, and usually dragged someone into his self-destructive tendencies.

Henry had decided early that to fully earn your place at the COCS table, a night at the pub was a rite of passage – a strange initiation, for want of a better word – which inevitably brought you in to the inner sanctum of the group, where you were trusted and you felt as if you belonged. It also served as a chance to learn who this strange amalgamation of people was, away from the ghosts they'd drag with them to group each week. Behind the tale of woe was always a person desperately trying to hold their shit together, some managed to do that, others failed miserably, but *all* were welcome. The drink that flowed helped in some way to mask the pain, allowing each of them a brief moment of respite, and when their guard was down, it was possible to peek behind that curtain of mourning which cloaked their usual personas; affording those in attendance a rare glimpse of the person who they were before their grief had pickled them.

For a few hours each week, in the Yeoman, they were more than the assembled broken parts who sat snivelling and sobbing on uncomfortable plastic chairs; chairs which were a torturous endurance task in themselves, adding to the pain and suffering they trawled through on a weekly basis.

Josh pondered that comfort was a commodity they could ill afford and if they were all honest with themselves, would never be blessed with again.

Henry wobbled back to the table, hands laden with drinks. Two more beers and two shots, all held precariously in his grasp. The night, the anniversary, Elsie's death day was about to get very messy indeed.

The way the two of them were collecting empties, a passing patron would imagine there was a bunch of COCS in attendance

28

rather than a solitary two. Josh's head was beginning to swim, he didn't know how much longer he'd have control over his faculties or the leash that kept his drinking buddy in check.

Henry slammed his hand onto the table, the liquid trembled in their drinks.

"Here's to swimming with bow legged women!" He hollered before extending his glass across the table, they clinked glasses, sloshing beer all over their hands, Josh noticed in Henry's haste to consume his poison, beer trickled from the sides of his mouth and hand where it dampened his trousers.

"Jaws right?" Josh said before taking a sip.

"You bet your arse it is!"

His exclamation brought the attention of an ageing couple sitting nearby. The elderly man's face was sunken, his dentures were too big and pushed his jaw out like a bulldog. His eyes were like stagnant pools of scummy water, but the look of disdain glistening in them was easy to read. Josh watched on as the man's wife, he assumed, put a calming hand on her partner's arm to pull him back to her and away from a possible confrontation.

Josh thought the woman looked like a poodle. She had a purple rinse in her hair to mask the grey but it only served in making her look older than she actually was. Her blouse was buttoned up to the neck where the skin was all dangly and loose, it wobbled as she uttered something that neither Josh nor Henry could decipher. The old man turned around, whispered something to his turkey necked wife, before turning back to facedown Henry again, fixing him with a hard but pathetic stare.

Henry leered back at the pensioner.

The man shook his head and tutted loudly at both men.

'Why don't you take a picture, huh? It'll fucking last longer.' Henry leaned forward, rested his elbows on the sodden table and continued eyeballing the old coot until the fossil finally realised he was dealing with crazy, and you can't reason with crazy; and so, he twisted back around to his wife where they continued their conversation which had been rudely interrupted by Henry's outburst.

Josh couldn't help but feel that Henry and himself were an eyesore to those in attendance. Some weeks it felt like they were a circus freak show that had just rolled into town, and the patrons had all bought tickets to watch the new attractions.

Each week the COCS presented a new oddity to stare at, their pained presence jarring the mind and drawing the eye. Josh often thought it was similar to the way a birth deformity calls out to an inquisitive child to pay it attention, their need to know forcing them to raise a stubby finger – much to their mother's consternation – and declaring in a loud voice: 'Mummy what's wrong with that person's face?'

The old folks a few tables over weren't the first to find offence with them being there and they certainly wouldn't be the last, but Josh prayed diligently that they'd be the last to poke the bear that sat opposite him tonight.

God help the sonofabitch who steps out of line with Henry ready to pounce he mused, *because something wicked this way comes.*

"I'm not too sure about that new girl, Sian," Josh said, to change the subject.

"Who now?" Henry's head snapped back to Josh, but his eyes still roved over the crowded pub looking for the person to sharpen his axe on.

"Sian, you know her. Been coming for a few weeks now, blonde hair, blue eyes, big–"

"Tits–" Henry mimicked hanging breasts in front of his chest, sloshing more beer on his already wet top.

"No, well maybe. I was going to say big personality. She's got that laugh like Harriet's Pomeranian's yap."

"What about her?"

"Well she reminds me of that other guy, Michael; the writer?"

"Oh, that prick. Can't believe someone would be as shallow as to fake losing someone to attend the group, just so he could get the inside track for his next book. Why do you think she's like him?"

"Well, it's probably nothing, but she hasn't come here yet, has she?"

"Nope."

"And when we're talking, sharing–"

"Speak for yourself..."

"Well, when we're sharing and you're quietly stewing in your own way, she's always playing with her phone, I swear I saw her take a selfie a few weeks back when Jacob was blubbering on about his weight gain..."

"That's millennials man, ever since the internet arrived people have been obsessed with feeding that thing a bunch of nonsense, like anyone gives a shit about what someone had for lunch."

"I think she's live tweeting our talks, uploading not only her account but ours too."

"Like a bird?"

"Man, you are such a troglodyte, where's that cave you've been hiding in all these years, maybe we can hook you up with some broadband or something?"

"I'm just shitting you, I know what Twitter is; I'm not as detached from the world as some might think, although sometimes I wish I was – you were saying?"

"I just think we need to keep an eye on her, you know... What's mentioned in the group needs to stay in the group. What do we have if we don't have trust?"

"I'll keep an eye on her."

"I bet you will," Josh said with a smirk before winking at his friend.

They dropped into a long silence, the kind of quiet shared by friends who were both comfortable with each other's company. Some evenings at the Yeoman they didn't even talk, they'd just sit there in long stretches of silence nursing their drinks.

Josh sipped his drink and thought more on Sian as Henry picked at the mud under his nails, watching the crumbs fall onto the table before brushing them to the floor. The sight of those crumbs reminded Josh of the day Jacob was sharing, boring them all about how much weight he'd put on and he couldn't understand why. Josh would have been paying attention to Jacob if he believed the man was sincere about his problem and willing to change; face his demon of comfort eating head on. But Jacob had been sitting there bemoaning his weight-gain with a fist deep inside a pack of Cheese Puffs, orange powder having stained his lips, chin and fingers in a carroty-orange. 'God helps those who help themselves' he'd wanted to say, but he'd never voice something so spiteful, he wasn't Henry, people liked him and he wanted to keep it that way.

Josh remembered peering down at Sian's bag, the screen of her phone had been facing him. He'd sat there transfixed as her phone lit up and then faded with each incoming notification. In the brief time he observed her flashing phone he must have seen near to a hundred notifications tumbled onto the screen. A never-ending tide of interruptions, motivational quotes and condolences from well-wishers across the globe. Josh guessed she'd ruminate on each reaction to her distress flare of 280 characters later; where she'd find her healing, value and place in the world through the short-lived popularity of her grief-riddled tweet.

Sian's need for connection and self-worth had been reduced to the paltry accumulation of likes, retweets and shares, the road to recovery took many forms but Josh struggled in seeing any hope down that particular path. It was no wonder she'd never joined them at the pub, Josh had assumed her evenings were taken up getting back to all those faceless avatars. She'd reached people that evening, there was no doubting that. But Josh just hoped that someday she'd find the belonging and happiness that she undoubtedly craved from someone that could love her back for who she was and not what she projected to the world.

Recalling that moment and how Sian was hurting and there was nothing they could do to reach her made Josh sad as the silence continued to thicken around Henry and himself. 'Pity support' was the worst kind of life raft to cling to, because once it deflated, once you became irrelevant, once people had moved on; the support network you'd built your recovery on would sink faster than a lead balloon and it'd take you down with it.

Josh thought about inviting Sian to the Yeoman the next time she turned up to one of their meetings. He took a swig of his beer and placed it on the table, his eyes rose and he found himself staring at his friend. Henry appeared to be adrift, lost but in the presence of others. His eyes were peering intently at something across the room. Josh followed his gaze and through the crowd he spotted what held his friend's undivided attention. Henry was a creature of habit after all, and that helped Josh know when the bad times were surely due to strike.

Across the pub, in the far corner; shrouded in darkness was a pay phone.

This element of Elsie's *death day* was the same each year; his dear friend would drift off, willing the phone in the corner to ring. Josh knew how absurd it all was, because who would be calling to speak to him here? His wife? Maybe, she knew about their after-session drinks at the Yeoman. But Josh knew unquestionably – not that Henry had ever voiced it, because he was a closed book in that respect – that Henry was holding out for the ghost of a phone call that never arrived all those years ago. He was pining to hear the voice of his daughter, it was a fool's errand because both Henry and Josh knew it would never come, but that wouldn't stop him willing it to ring and Josh would never rubbish his friend's hope.

For Josh, his own pain reared its ugly head every time he closed the door to his house and called out to his wife, Hannah. His shouts would always go unanswered, as he knew they would; but it never stopped him hoping – however fruitless the ritual had become – that one day she might answer.

The comfortable silence had in the blink of an eye now turned into an awkward one.

Josh's eyes roved over their booth whilst his friend yearned for the phone to ring. He smirked when he thought about their table, because although there was never a sign stating the table was reserved; this booth – their *grief altar* – on a Tuesday by happenstance was always vacant, but there was a reason for that which they'd discovered after it became their home away from home. It was next to the restrooms and was therefore perfumed with an ammonium rich bouquet which wafted across their table after each patron made his liquid deposit.

They'd assumed for a while that the smell was just Ethel.

Ethel was the eldest member of their group at eighty-two. She'd been known to leave a puddle of piss on her seat after their group sessions, which was something Erik had brought to Henry and Josh's attention a while back. It was Erik's job to wipe down and sanitise her chair after each session, having been bestowed with the lofty title of *'chair monitor'*. Henry had told Erik that "The first rule of successful management is delegation" as he nudged the younger man in the ribs, and so from that day on it was Erik's cross to bear.

Ethel was a good sport and a breath of fresh air to the group if you could get over the choking odour of urine that hung around her like a cheap perfume. Henry and Josh both adored the time they spent with her because she was one of the most vulgar octogenarians they had ever met. She didn't give one sod what people thought of her, she'd swear and curse and be as politically incorrect as she wanted. If she ever had to explain her brashness, her answer was always the same.

"My husband had fought in the war for the freedoms you dandies have today."

Josh mused often about Ethel and how freeing it would be to be so old and not give a single shit. But as he smelt the piss waft around them as another patron exited the toilet, he wondered if the cantankerous Ethel was still with the living. They'd not seen her since she came down with the flu, and that was about two months ago; he smiled and hoped that she'd finally been able to follow her Stanley to the place beyond, maybe she was sipping on martinis with her Stanley in the clouds somewhere, but Josh knew for certain, wherever she was, she was cussing her heart out.

Henry finally pulled his gaze away from the phone, which still hadn't rung and found his half-drunk drink on the table, he raised his glass to Josh but didn't utter a word before gulping it down. Josh couldn't help but think his friend was desperately trying to drown the anger which was bubbling below the surface of his sombre disposition.

Sometimes these sessions in the Yeoman, for Henry at least, gave him a chance to vent his frustrations and unbottle his rage on an unsuspecting individual; usually with words, but Josh had also seen him opt to use his fists, taking his drunken frustrations out on some unsuspecting individual in the carpark. The issue Josh had wasn't Henry's use of excessive violence, it was that those nights usually occurred on Elsie's anniversary and it fell to him to ensure his friend stayed out of a cell for the night or heaven forbid find Henry in the gutter with a broken bottle stowed in his eye socket.

Josh lifted his beer and realised he'd fallen a few beverages behind Henry. Putting the glass to his lips Josh felt his stomach broil and he knew he'd reached his limit for this evening's drinking. He placed it on the table before taking in the countenance of his drinking buddy and dare he think it; best friend in the whole damned world. He laughed inwardly at the thought.

Of all the people he had in his life, the one person he'd gravitated towards and could count on the most was a man almost twenty years his senior; who liked to drink and every year buried pieces of his daughter.

There was something in the air tonight and it wasn't the piss or the damp carpet that had that faint stench of vomit. It was heavier, oppressive; and Josh could see its alluring dance displayed in Henry's eyes. He was somewhere else, with someone else in a place only he could see.

Josh peered down at the table just to remove his friend's troublesome eyes from his vision. The table was littered with empty glasses. He'd done a good job matching Henry's thirst, but he knew now as he glanced over the empties that tomorrow's job would be a late starter, if it ever got started at all.

The house renovations on Petherton Road would have to wait another day, because tearing down plasterboard and removing the stud wall to the lounge didn't appeal to him right now; and when he thought about wearing his respirator to protect himself from the dust he'd rather shoot himself in the head with his nail gun. If he had to wear that infernal contraption on his face, feeling the way he did now; he knew he'd be liable to upchuck in his mask and choke on his own foulness.

Henry was fussing with something on the table.

Suddenly he spun the object with his fingers and Josh watched on as a perfect golden circle appeared from thin air and began to whirl around on the table like a dervish. It was a truly arresting sight, a thing of absolute beauty as the light shimmered on its surface, and in a place usually devoid of such beauty it was mesmerising.

He'd initially thought it was a coin until it began to slow, it was then he noticed its hollowed middle. Gradually the golden disc lost its momentum and it rattled down to the table where it finally presented itself; it was Henry's wedding ring. Quick as a flash Henry snatched it up from the table and slid it back onto his finger where he proceeded to worry with it, flicking it up and down using the nail of his thumb in a well-practised routine.

Henry was still lost in thought and so Josh felt the need to break the silence before Henry broke someone's jaw.

"You see that new guy tonight?" Josh offered.

Henry continued to thumb his wedding ring.

"Henry?"

"Huh?" Henry managed before bringing the dregs of another pint to his mouth.

"The new guy? Arrived late and left early; emo looking fella, black skinny jeans full of holes, mop of black hair, some band T-shirt, could have been Sabbath or AC/DC, thought you would have noticed given your taste in music."

Henry pondered that for a moment, his mind clearly elsewhere. Suddenly he sprung to his feet, the empty glasses chimed together on the table and Josh had to quickly catch a couple before they tumbled to the ground.

"I gotta call Kiera. She'll be worried," Henry stated, eyes wide, breathing quickly. The way he'd blurted it out was as if they'd been talking about Henry's wife just moments before his declaration.

"You sure that's—" but before Josh could finish, Henry was halfway to the pay phone, stumbling into the many patrons between their table and the phone; Josh didn't like this one bit.

He observed Henry barge past a rather rowdy group of students who were enjoying spending their student loans, and appeared to be enjoying the lifestyle of no responsibility and the luxury of not having to get up in the morning with a hangover and hold down a job. *Their time would come though,* Josh mused.

One of them number threw his hands up in Henry's wake and yelled something about his spilled drink, caused by Henry's bull in a china shop routine.

"Don't," Josh whispered and hoped his fragile voice carried to the young man who was poking the hornets' nest of rage that was his friend, who wouldn't bat an eyelid at stinging that kid to death, especially today.

Henry kept moving with a singular purpose and had obviously not heard the student's remarks, because if he had there'd be blood on the floor, Josh was sure of it.

Henry had the receiver to his ear, his shaking hand pressing the numbered keys before he began smashing his fist into the keypad when one of the buttons became stuck. As the conversations in the bar rose, the atmosphere balanced on a knife edge. Josh noticed Henry talking on the phone, a hand placed onto the wall keeping him upright. One of the merry students obscured Josh's view again, it was a fleeting obstruction but as they stepped away again Josh discovered Henry yanking at the receiver and smashing the head of it into the keypad; sending shards of plastic into the air which littered the floor around him in slivers of red plastic, from where Josh sat they looked like red petals.

This isn't going to end well, Josh mused. For him, Henry or the poor bastard that unquestionably stepped into the firing line. He needed to get moving before Henry did. As he slid along the booth's chair he peered back up and Henry had vanished. All that moved where his friend once stood was the swaying, broken receiver that hung by its silver cord. Josh stood and as he did the room spun around him. He reached out a hand to steady himself, waiting for the room to stop swaying. He spied Henry barrelling his way back across the room, bodies moved out of his way as if he were Moses parting the Red Sea.

Henry was halfway across the room, with a face like thunder, when Josh began searching for the nearest door. He decided that if he could intercept Henry on his way back and swiftly make their exit, it would spare those in attendance the bloodshed that was duly bound to follow if they stayed a moment longer.

As Josh got moving one of the students stepped back and stood in Henry's path.

"Shit, shit, shit," Josh uttered as he shook his head, making the room spin all the more. He lumbered towards his friend and as Josh came around the bar he noticed the young man was wearing a skirt; nails painted, red lipstick smeared across his mouth like a wound. The rest of their face was done up like a drag queen. Josh knew in that moment that this person was a visual representation of every-thing Henry despised, and he knew without a shadow of a doubt that the shit was going to hit the fan.

"Sorry pops... but I think you spilt my friend's drink?"

"So–"

"So, I think you need to buy him a new one petal."

Josh trundled closer, he was on intercept mode and he might just get there in time to stop everything before it had a chance to develop.

"No, I don't," Henry spat, as he brushed aside the student in the dress.

As Henry passed, the man reached out a hand and gripped him by the forearm. Henry glanced up quickly and caught Josh's eye. Henry winked at Josh before letting out a held breath as his lip curled up into a snarl, an expression that said: *oh no you fucking didn't*.

Josh shook his head at Henry, his eyes pleading with Henry to not do what he was about to do. Henry smiled back, nodded calmly before he raised his hand to say *stay there I've got this* and Josh stayed put, as if he were an obedient mutt at his master's feet. Henry turned slowly before staring at the student's hand which still secured his arm; revealing a perfectly manicured set of nails, pink shellac adorning their surface.

"Look pops, just buy my friend his drink and we'll forget about it."

Henry leant in, his face so close Josh was sure the student could smell all four lagers, three stouts and the shots of whiskey on his breath.

"I ain't your pops," Henry growled. "But if I was, I'd be ashamed of... of... What the hell are you anyway?"

"We're Terry and we're–"

"What a load of shit," Henry exclaimed for all to hear. "Every-one's got a label these days, I'm tired of it all. It's just something to make you feel part of something, it's pathetic. I own my sorry state; you just hide behind a bunch of pronouns looking for belonging, you lot are to blame for everything you know. Everyone nowadays is pandering to make sure everyone's feelings don't get hurt and I tell you what, all this *we they* bollocks is giving me a fucking headache... so go cry me a fucking river you faggot."

"Excuse me?" Terry placed their hand with splayed fingers on their chest; visibly shocked at how they'd just been spoken to.

Josh wanted to step in, tell them to leave it well alone but before he could another voice called out over the din of the pub.

"Just leave it Terry, it's fine, honestly," Terry's friend was already at the bar getting another round of drinks.

Josh jolted forwards, the chains that had bound his legs moments before had been loosened and he shuffled towards Henry. He was within earshot as Henry peered past Terry before his gaze returned to them.

Henry's teeth were bared as he whispered, "Now if you'd kindly remove your disease riddled hand from my arm, I'll be on my way," Henry snapped his arm free from the manicured grasp of Terry, turned and began to make his way to the door; stepping past Josh as if he wasn't even there.

Josh was left standing opposite Terry like a deer in the headlights before he raised his hands in a placating and apologetic manner.

"I'm so sorry, he's just... he's got some—"

Terry didn't even acknowledge Josh, they bowled straight past him, grabbed the departing Henry by the shoulder, spinning him around before landing a gristle crunching blow to Henry's nose. Josh heard the crunch and then saw the blood running down his friend's face as he stumbled backwards before tripping over his feet and landing on the pavement outside the entrance to the Yeoman.

A few regulars pulled Terry back. Whether they were trying to protect Terry from what was to come, or if they were protecting Henry from biting of more than he could chew, Josh hadn't the foggiest idea. But Josh knew there was nothing more dangerous than a wounded animal.

As Terry was pushed back into the pub, Josh began to skirt around the rabble at the door, praying he wouldn't be tarred with the same brush and get a clout for his troubles.

Josh was squeezing his way out of the throng of bodies, but paused on his escape when he noticed Henry had gotten to his feet and was rocking from side to side, his knees slightly turned in. The crowd hushed when they noticed his looming figure, but instead of storming in to claim his pound of flesh, Henry just smiled back at the numerous faces watching him, his teeth covered in red as the blood continued to trickle down his face.

Henry turned on wobbly legs and walked off into the night.

Terry raised their voice from the momentary quiet.

"Oh, I get it you Neanderthal... yeah that's right, you keep walking away before I finish you off, or call the bloody police and report you for homophobia... that was a hate crime you know?"

Josh wanted to tell Terry to be quiet, wanted to hush them down before Henry changed his mind, but he was sure any attempts to tamper the situation down would end with him leaving this place in roughly the same state Henry had. He was already guilty by association, so Josh just turned, bowed his head and followed his best friend out of the pub.

Terry continued shouting long after the door closed, the last things Josh heard as he trotted up the path after his friend were words full of anger and disgust.

"Who are you to judge me, you ageing sack of shit. I guess you think that because we look like this... you think that means we've got AIDS. You're lucky we don't..."

Terry's voice faded to nothing as Josh crossed the road and approached Henry who was sitting on the curb by the bus stop outside the kebab house. His face was a mask of red, which was almost black in the night and he was peering back at the Yeoman and the bastard was smiling his bloodied, crazed smile.

"Good night huh?" Henry said as Josh approached and sat beside him.

"Henry, you can't go around spouting that shit at people, it's not right. You can't just say whatever vile, shit that pops into your head like that, even if that's what you believe. What do you think Elsie would think if she could hear her dad speaking like that?" He wanted to say *she'd turn in her grave is what she'd do* but Josh bit his lip because he liked his teeth where they were, thank you very much.

Henry shrugged his shoulders, a sulky gesture but one that Josh knew meant he'd gotten through to his friend. Josh could tell there was an inkling of shame swirling around somewhere in Henry's head right now, but he'd never let Josh see it, he was too proud a man for that.

"Go home, get your head down and grieve your daughter."

Henry stood up sharply and swung an arm at the still seated Josh, who flinched as he feared a flying fist, but soon relaxed after realising Henry was placing his hand on his friend's shoulder.

He gently squeezed Josh's shoulder as he walked past.

"Thank you," He uttered as he staggered off in the direction of home.

"Don't mention it," Josh called after him, standing up and dusting off his trousers.

Henry lifted a hand in silent recognition. Josh turned on his heels and headed in the other direction knowing what awaited him once he stepped into his house and closed the door behind him.

"Hey Josh?" Henry's voice rang out from behind him.

Josh spun around but Henry was still walking away into the distance like some outlaw from a western.

"Yeah?" he shouted back, thinking his friend would stop.

He craned his neck over his shoulder before shouting his reply.

"You're a prick, do you know that?"

Josh chuckled to himself before bellowing back.

"Prick, would seem to be the common refrain of my life buddy!"

Both men laughed as Josh turned and walked the lonely path home.

CHAPTER THREE

Henry stumbled up the path to his house at the arse-crack of dawn, rummaging in his pocket for his keys.

It shouldn't have taken him long to stagger back to his decrepit dwelling, but being three sheets to the wind and harboring the inescapable urge to destroy something – to make him feel less emasculated – he could have been dragged, or blown anywhere but home.

He had murder on his mind. The axe he'd wanted to grind all evening was still sheathed and blunt after his less than satisfactory confrontation with Terry. He'd wanted to see the bastard bleed, but it turned out he'd be the only one bleeding tonight.

He'd been desperately hoping to find someone on his way home to ruin, but when no willing sacrifice offered itself – either staggering from another pub, or out of one of the many Indian restaurants that lined the main road – he'd eventually charted his course for home and his bed, although sleep – for tonight at least – would be another matter.

As he slid the key into the lock, his fourth attempt, Henry heard Josh's sobering words afresh, as if he was hiding in the hedges that lined the path to his door.

'*What do you think Elsie would think if she could hear her dad speaking like that?*'

Henry's hand was shaking, his keychain rattling into the eerie quiet of the night.

He was utterly crestfallen at the thought, because: *what would she think of him?*

His breath caught in his throat as the keychain rattled even louder in his trembling hand, as if Jacob Marley's ghost were approaching from the other side of the door; but it wasn't Jacob Marley, it was *her.*

Everything in his being told him to run, but he'd spent his life doing just that, and he was dog-tired; not to mention completely shitfaced. He observed the looming silhouette within the house shrink into focus as it approached the glass, gradually swimming into clarity, as if it were a beast rising from the dark-depths of the sea.

He was grateful for the frosted glass, which at least obscured her features slightly, making the sight of his dearly, departed daughter's face bearable, but only just. His mind filled in the pixelated version of his daughter the glass had conjured; a faceless, ominous, revenant who'd come to welcome him home.

His mind superimposed Elsie's features on the blank canvas of a face that stood behind the glass; she looked exactly the same as the last time he'd seen her, beautiful and full of life. She smiled back at him now and he wondered how many hearts she'd have broken if she'd been given the chance at a fuller, longer life.

He always pictured her as she was on that fateful day, because it was a fool's errand to imagine her any other way; there was no way of him knowing or even contemplating the woman she'd have grown into if she hadn't been torn from their lives so soon; to do so was a torturous act in and of itself and so he imagined her as she was, four-teen-years-old and full of teenage attitude.

Henry closed his eyes, waited a painstaking beat before braving another glance at his daughter – the heart wants what the heart wants after all. She was still present in the glass when he looked, but the sight of her now filled him with dread; her expression had changed. The sweet-smiling face he'd imagined had been replaced by something all the more sinister. A deep scowl furrowed her youthful brow, her eyebrows were pinched together around a deep crease between her eyes which almost cleft her head in two, forcing her glare to become narrow, her gaze cold.

From the depths that lingered behind the door she raised a with-ered hand to the frosted glass, where her pointed index finger touched the pane which currently separated their two worlds. Henry focused on the accusing finger – which pointed directly at his trou-bled heart – because he wanted to do anything in that moment to tear his gaze away from Elsie's spiteful scowl. He knew he was the one to blame for what had befallen his daughter, but to see that knowledge etched on her face pained him gravely.

"You–" Elsie's voice came softly to his ear, as if it were a dying breath.

Her utterance pulled his eyes past the accusing finger, as if her voice were a magnet and his eyes were filled with metal filaments, where they drank in her spectral image imprisoned behind the glass, or did the glass itself house an echo of her image?

Her image faded momentarily, as if she were permitting Henry to witness what she was observing through her long-dead eyes. Reflected in the glass was his ravaged bloodied face; his possibly broken nose and haunted eyes. Every inch a middle-aged man who'd let himself go, one who'd become obdurate to change, who'd been clinging on to his bigoted and outdated views the way he'd been clinging to the bottle these past twelve years - for dear life.

Elsie's image swam back into focus again as if she were appearing in a crystal ball.

"What's that smell on your breath daddy?" she whispered, before a childish laugh spilled from her lips, echoing into the night around him.

Henry shook his head, frantically trying to dislodge the taunting vision and accompanying sound.

"If Mummy was still here, she'd be mad... but she isn't, is she? Because everyone leaves you in the end, don't they?"

"Stop it... stop it... STOP IT!' Henry screamed at the apparition.

He finished turning the key in the lock before flinging the door open in disgust and horror. It banged against the wall of the hall before slowly swinging back in place with a rusted whine; the image of Elsie in the glass, gone. Henry knew the veil between his world and wherever Elsie had gone to was thinnest on her death day, when his guard was well and truly down, today's visitation wasn't the first, and he knew it certainly wouldn't be the last.

He placed his hand to the door, noticed some of Elsie's grave dirt still under his nails, persistently clinging on – like his daughter's memory. Henry wondered why she couldn't stay gone; forgotten, interred, but the realisation as to why she never stayed gone came to him via Josh's wise words: *'You know that if you keep picking that scab it ain't ever going to heal?'*

He gently pushed the door until it rested against the wall, and he peered into the stygian darkness which welcomed him home with open arms. His breathing quickened as he edged forward, because he knew that, within the enveloping darkness, lurked his daughter who refused to stay buried; especially on nights such as these and he knew she wouldn't welcome him home as freely as the dark.

As his eyes grew accustomed to the darkness, he flinched; Elsie was standing in the thickly shadowed, draughty hallway of the house. From where he stood, the doorway appeared to him as a huge, toothless, screaming mouth. His daughter swayed deep within its throat, on the burgundy rug which ran the hallway's length, as if it were a tongue waiting to swallow her. In that moment, Henry wished it would. Anything to take her away, to end his guilt at seeing what he'd turned her into, furthering his culpability in her disappearance and most likely, her death.

She was crying. Her bewailing reached such heights that Henry stepped back, conceded ground to the apparition, fearful that she'd rush at him from the dark, burst past him in a flailing of limbs; screaming obscenities at him like she had before, on the day she left this home for good.

The only thing which moved in the darkness was her dirty, blonde hair which billowed around her face as if she was underwater: *maybe she was?* Henry pondered.

Standing resolutely before him, Elsie's gaze found his and he shuddered under the weight of it. There was a gritted determination in her countenance, one that wanted to make her father – and mother, at the time – suffer. She existed now as a visual echo from the time before, when they'd been a family; a broken one, but still a family, still together.

Her hand snapped to the strap of her rucksack, the same one Henry had buried hours prior to this meeting of the past and present. His thoughts turned to its contents on the day she'd vanished, it had been hastily stuffed with what she believed to be her worldly possessions, the things she couldn't be without, but she could be without her family apparently, especially her father.

Little did she know, in the moment which was playing out before Henry now – as if it were a grisly re-run of how much he'd failed her - that the momentary suffering she'd wanted to inflict on her parents that day, would inevitably last much longer than she'd ever intended, the wound she struck them on that day he'd carry to his grave.

A hellish scream tore through the night behind him, forcing Henry to sever his momentary connection with the ghostly apparition of his daughter. He spun around to the sound of dustbins clattering to the pavement somewhere in the night. A neighbour shouted something indecipherable at the racket before Henry observed a mange-riddled fox skitter past his gate, its tail so bare it looked serpentine.

He snapped his head back to the house quickly, realising he'd let his guard down for far too long, as he turned he half-expected Elsie to have advanced on his position. He let out a breath as he searched the darkness for his daughter, who'd appeared to have vanished yet again into the folds of shadow that hung throughout the house. With her gone, he gingerly stepped towards the silent house, boldly reclaiming the step he'd conceded to his daughter moments before.

"Get your shit together," he uttered as the entranceway loomed before him, deep and dark and cavernous. He wondered if Elsie hadn't vanished after all, rather she'd just moved deeper into the house, only to crawl out from somewhere shadowed when he'd least expect it, only to haunt him afresh again.

Inching over the threshold he paused. Turning away from the vacuous hallway, he set about closing the door, inevitably sealing himself inside the tomb which his home had become. With the door closed, he rested his forehead against the cold wood and breathed deeply, battling the fear and shame which was holding him a prisoner of the moment.

He knew he had to turn around and face his house of horrors, because rising above the fear that wrecked his mind and spoiled his stomach was impossible; he knew he needed a drink, something to calm his nerves, whilst also knocking-him-the-fuck-out. His brain was already damp going on wet and his back teeth were swimming, but the need to drown himself, and the memories, were far too alluring to pass up.

He slowly peered over his shoulder towards the kitchen, knowing the tool for his drowning resided in the room at the very end of the hall. He half-expected to catch a glimpse of Elsie's backpack disappearing into one of the vacant, lightless rooms off the hallway. But nothing like that greeted him and so he turned boldly into the empty house, a house which had once been a home until it had its soul gutted from it.

He flicked the light switch in the hallway, watched on as the darkness scurried away to find a new dwelling place. The kitchen tempted him onwards, its door opened slightly, the bottle of whiskey glinting at him from the table by the light thrown from the bare bulb in the hall, as if it were winking at him, begging him to taste and see that it was good.

All he had to do was stumble down the corridor to where his reward awaited him, a drowning in amber fuel. The only things giving him pause and rooting his feet to the spot were the numerous rooms that lined the hallway, where hands could easily reach out and claim him; however, it wasn't the ghost daughter from his past he feared: the thing – *or things* – he feared most were what had set up residency in those rooms, those things terrified him like no other.

Each darkened room was filled with inescapable memories; trinkets, photographs, numerous finger paintings which Henry didn't have the heart to throw away. But amongst all the clutter in those chambers, there was something else, something worse; it was imbedded in the very fabric of the sofa, bleached into the faded wallpaper, soaked into the threadbare carpets and rugs of each room. It was the cloying sadness which had permeated the very atmosphere of each room, manifesting wickedly over time from the prolonged absence of laughter and love these rooms once held in abundance.

He'd have to run the gauntlet to get what his flagging soul craved most: his whiskey, and the escapism it brought. He peered once more down the hallway, counted to three – which ended up being more like ten – before his feet became unstuck from the fear that held them in place. He soon found himself stumbling into the kitchen as if he were being chased, and in a way, he had been; pursued by the memories that clamoured for his attention from each room he'd passed.

Flicking the light switch revealed a kitchen in all its past glory. The place was a shit hole, crockery and cutlery were piled high and balancing precariously in the sink and across the draining board; unopened mail was strewn across the table, rotting food hung out of the bin and a number of empty bottles and cans littered both the table and floor. His mobile was where he'd left it, on the table; an archaic brick of a thing, an envelope was flashing on the screen.

Henry picked it up and opened the message. It was from Josh and he smiled as he read it.

> Just checking you got home safe?

Henry thumbed out his reply, taking a temporary solace in knowing someone still cared he was breathing.

> Safe and well, you coming to tuck me in, you big fairy?

Henry chuckled at his retort, but the sound was humourless given the fear still pervading through his body. He threw the phone onto the table which inadvertently caused a landslide of accumulated paperwork; bills past-due, correspondences with family, and all manner of scribblings tumbled to the filthy floor. Grunting his displeasure and placing a hand on his hip, he stared at the mess and contemplated his next move.

"Fuck it," he said. "I'll pick it up tomorrow," but he knew full well they'd remain there until he got around to it, which would most probably be never, because now was a time for drinking.

Peering around his squalid surroundings Henry recalled telling Josh on numerous occasions that the place was missing a woman's touch. Josh of course had chided him each time for being a misogynist arsehole, and he was probably right.

'Maybe that's why she left you?' Josh had said. Henry's drink addled mind couldn't help but hear a ring of truth about his friend's jovial quip as he stood in his kitchen, observing the chaos around him. *Maybe it was?* He mused sadly to himself, but he rubbished the thought because he knew it was much more than his slovenly nature which had driven her away.

Henry loved Josh, although he'd never tell him that. He'd turn in his grave before a declaration of that magnitude spilled from his lips about someone of the same sex. But if he had to admit it to himself, what he loved about his friend the most, was that over time he'd become a voice of reason in a world full of unanswerable questions. He couldn't deny that Josh was usually right about matters of the heart and mind, and that got him thinking about what he'd said at the Yeoman.

'You know you got to bury Elsie once and for all and let her go right?'

Henry scrunched his face up, he knew his friend was right about that too, but he wasn't ready to give her up so easily. He grabbed the bottle of whiskey, twisted the cap free, let it tumble to the floor where it joined the other detritus around his feet. Lifting the lip of the bottle to his mouth, he took the first of three deep glugs, desperate to free his mind of the intrusive thought Josh had planted there, desperately trying to taint the very soil of his mind so nothing could grow from that scattered seed of truth.

Holding the bottle by the neck and now fuelled with Dutch courage, Henry turned back to the hallway, ready to face whatever the past and this damnable house threw at him. The memories of his failures didn't hold back, quickly assaulting him as he sauntered from the kitchen with each family photograph he witnessed, and the smiling faces that taunted him, imprisoned behind glass for all time; reminding him that they'd been happy once – before everything changed.

On a table in the hallway, where the key bowl sat, Henry noticed Elsie's fabric bunny; a tatty old thing which she'd cuddled to death. It had been her comfort blanket of sorts, but the sight of it now held no comfort at all. As he observed it resting there, all forlorn and discarded by its owner, he could do nothing to stop the tears that formed in his eyes but never fell; he was instantly glad he'd spared the bunny from the soil for another year, having removed it from the backpack before this year's burial, but he knew its time would come.

Josh's words of truth repeated in his mind again.

'You know that if you keep picking that scab it ain't ever going to heal?'

"Fuck you Josh, who made you the oracle on grief, you don't know shit!" Henry spat, before picking up the bunny and lifting it to his nose, inhaling its scent. It still smelt of Elsie, after all these years; and the tears he'd successfully held back began to fall.

Tilting his head back and taking another glug from the bottle, his eyes fell on the darkened staircase to his left. He shivered, half-expecting to see his daughter's face peering back at him through the spindles, as she had been prone to do after he'd yelled at her, retreating to where she felt safe and protected; her eyes wide with disgust and mistrust of her father. Seeing the coast was clear, he gave thought of climbing the stairs and jumping beneath the covers of his double bed, where he now slept single.

A sly smile graced his lips as his thoughts turned briefly to Harriet. He wondered if she'd be awake and up for a tumble beneath the sheets, but he quickly rubbished the thought, when he glanced down to the hand holding the bottle and saw his wedding ring; he wouldn't mix the business of grief with pleasure, although he was desperate to feel something other than the agonising pain and insufferable guilt that wracked his body and made him walk stooped on a daily basis.

Deciding a double bed didn't have the same pull without company to enjoy it with, he lifted Elsie's bunny up by its ears where he stared into its worn, button eyes.

"Looks like it's just me and you tonight Bunny," he said as he stumbled towards the lounge. "I hope you can handle your–"

Henry stopped dead in his tracks at the threshold of the darkened room.

In the far corner was a large, hunkered shape, a single red eye pulsed from within its mass. He reached out his hand holding the bottle, using the heel of his hand to hammer at the light switch; never once taking his eyes off the monster that lurked in the corner of the room. The light clicked on.

The sudden illumination wiped away any possible beast lurking before him and revealed the answerphone to his landline nestling upon a bunch of cardboard boxes labelled: **Elsie's Don't Throw Away**.

He made a beeline for the machine, stumbling over more clutter strewn across the floor but managed to stay upright before collapsing arse first onto the arm of the sofa. He placed his bottle on one of the boxes to free up one of his hands, the whiskey would be the trade for now as he didn't want to let go of Elsie's bunny just yet. He pressed play.

A shrill voice greeted him.

"I told you not to call here anymore," it was Kiera, and she sounded pissed. Henry anxiously thumbed his wedding band, which suddenly felt as if it was constricting around his finger. "Especially when you're drunk, and *especially* on today of all days; I'd thought you'd have more respect for her memory..." Henry thumped his leg with a balled fist, furious that his wife wouldn't even acknowledge their daughter by name anymore.

"But I guess I was wrong to think you were somewhere near a decent human being. I know you're hurting, but the things you said, the things you accused me of, it's just spiteful Henry, especially when we know you're to blame for all of it."

Henry peered down at Elsie's bunny only to discover he was throttling the poor thing. His fingers were bone-white with the pressure he was exuding, its head sagging in his grasp; if it had a neck made of bone it would have been well and truly broken. A muted conversation was happening on the other end of line, as if Kiera had placed her hand over the receiver. Heated words were exchanged before she returned like she'd never been away.

"You don't you have a shred of decency left in you, I swear to God you don't. Matthew said if you call here again he'll change our number. Stop calling, I mean it Henry, get yourself some help or another shoulder to cry on, because we're done, we've been done for eight years now; and you calling here, it's disrupting our family life. Just let me grieve her in peace. I don't want to hear from you again, just let her go Henry, she's never coming back."

"Bitch!" Henry shouted at the beep which ended the message.

He grabbed the bottle from the box, necked what remained and took aim at one of the many family photos hanging on the wall like a gallery for the dammed. The bottle and frame were instantly obliterated, glass and wood raining down over the carpet, another mess he'd never get around to tidying.

He could still hear Kiera's words in his head, as if they were stuck on loop: *'disrupting our family life'* and *'she's never coming back'*. Anger and drink were coursing through his veins now as he pondered how easy it'd been for Kiera to say goodbye to all they'd built; turn her back on their family and start over.

Bitch has got herself a new husband, new home, new family. Fuck, she even made herself new children to replace the old, Henry mused; his mind was a kicked hornets' nest of rage.

He stomped around the sofa before collapsing into it, where his eyes fell on the coffee table where some of the rejected offerings for this year's burial sat: a baseball cap, a brush (which still had strands of Elsie's hair stuck in the bristles), jewellery and a small box – full of her baby teeth. Each item was a taunting totem of how much he'd lost and how little he'd gained since she'd gone. On the floor near his muddied Converse was a small cardboard box, the mouth of it gaping open to reveal another treasure trove of horrors. Scribbled along its side in Kiera's deft script was one word: **Police**.

Everything inside that box was related to Elsie's disappearance and the protracted case which followed. Crime reports, evidence found and later returned in plastic pouches, interview reports, photographs of locations of interest and a great many newspaper clippings were all stuffed inside.

Henry dipped his hand into the box as if it were some macabre lucky dip, his fingers sifting through the nightmares of his past, a self-flagellation of the mind, body and soul. He pulled his hand from the box sharply, as if the memories it contained had grown teeth over the years and nipped at his hand. Held within his grasp was a laminated photograph of Elsie. Tears wet his face again because he knew that Kiera was right; he was to blame for it all.

The photograph was one Kiera had printed from her phone and

handed to the police when Elsie failed to come home, and they'd finally reported her missing. If they'd known it would have been the last photo they'd ever take of her, maybe they'd have made it a family one, or paid it more attention, rather than it becoming just another photograph in a camera roll of snatched moments in time.

As Henry scanned the now dog-eared, laminated picture he realised that all the clothes she'd been wearing on that day were now finally in the ground, and he was glad of it. That outfit, and this damned photo had haunted his every waking moment for the last twelve years; it had been on the news, on missing posters, stapled to noticeboards and handed out as flyers at the local shopping centre as they desperately tried to find their missing daughter.

He'd buried the clothes she'd worn in that photograph with the hope it would lessen its crippling hold on him. With today's offering, her backpack, the last piece of that particular puzzle firmly in the ground; he hoped that now, interred piecemeal by piecemeal into the ground, he'd be free of that ghastly memory at least, but he knew there were many more willing to take its place.

"I'm sorry Elsie," his voice was a simulacrum of sorrow and regret.

"Please... I beg you, forgive me; I'm sorry, I'm sorry, I'm sorry."

Henry dropped the photo into the open mouth of the box which had birthed his latest misery before reclining on the sofa. He pulled Elsie's tattered bunny to his chest and hugged the raggedy thing for dear life; and the smell of his daughter leaked from the one thing that had given her so much comfort over the years.

In that moment, it was as if Elsie were in the room with him, and as he closed his eyes and his lips whispered his regrets; he wished she was.

CHAPTER FOUR

Josh had given considerable thought to killing himself when his world imploded after the death of his wife. His contemplations around suicide – of which there were a great many, and as he discovered quickly, the innumerable ways of carrying out the deed – came flooding back as he sat on the bare wooden stairs of his latest fixer-upper, staring up at the missing spindle.

The house had come into his possession when the previous owner hanged herself, right above where he was sitting, with a length of electrical wire. It wouldn't have been Josh's chosen method of suicide, and he'd given a great many methods much thought during his dark days; but death by hanging seemed far too grisly for even his grief-riddled mind to comprehend.

He'd narrowed his choice of death down to two: overdose or asphyxiation, and asphyxiation had become the front runner in that macabre race.

He'd read horror stories about overdoses, where the right mixture and quantity of drugs taken, unbeknownst to the desperate soul seeking an end on their terms, didn't kill the user; instead it left them in a vegetative state, braindead but still clinging to a life they'd wanted to cash in. He didn't want to end his days like that, plugged into a machine and having it breathe for him, just because he had no family left to do the decent thing and extinguish his life with the flick of a switch. Getting it wrong would only prolong the torture he'd wanted to end, increasing the agonising wait until he'd be with her again, his dear Amanda.

Asphyxiation became his obsession in a world of possible outs.

There were so many choices, but being a neat freak in life, he'd wanted his death to be the same – neat and tidy. And so, on a cloudy Tuesday afternoon, he'd chosen to gas himself, not in his house, where most likely his decaying body would have been found weeks later, a puddle of decomposition spreading across the hardwood flooring he'd spent a great many years getting just right. No, that wouldn't do at all, because in his line of work he'd had to polish, buffer, sand down, paint over and scrape away a great many stains of those that had taken *'the coward's way out'* as Jacob had shared in group once.

Jacob's father who still lived with him, and who Henry had teased: 'still probably shared a bath and a bed with', had taken his own life by throwing himself down the stairs. Apparently, he'd attempted it many times before, but this last time worked a charm; he'd broken his damned neck and his head had split open on impact like a rotten watermelon.

Josh, unlike Jacob's father, didn't want to leave a human shaped mess for whoever took over his dwelling to buffer out of existence, and so he'd settled on an industrial estate carpark at night, when the place would be abandoned. He'd end his life breathing in the fumes that choked the world, he'd found a poetic justice in that.

He bought the hosepipe, the tape, even topped his car up with petrol for fear he'd only partially finish the job. But the two things he'd failed to bring with him on that fateful day were his courage and the conviction needed to follow through with his exit plan.

On the night of his scheduled suicide, Josh sat in his rusted-out, burgundy coloured, Ford Escort; which looked more scab than car and waited. The industrial estate carpark was deserted as he'd expected, his vehicle the only sign of life in that desolate wasteland as the darkness of the night faded into the early light of the coming dawn. The engine was running, but the headlights were off, ensuring he'd remain hidden from the world he was choosing to leave, he didn't want some '*have a go hero*' pulling him from the car.

He wasn't alone as he marched towards death's door because on the dash, was a picture of Amanda, in life and in death she was with him. The image had become harder to make out the longer he'd sat in the car revving the engine, each depression of his foot allowed more poisonous, noxious exhaust fumes to find their way into the car; trickling through the hosepipe which hung limply through the window. The other end of the hosepipe was securely fastened to the exhaust with duct tape, which he'd also used to make the gap in the window airtight around the hose which brought his slow, creeping demise.

As the fumes clouded around him, filling the car with a poisonous fog, he looked on lovingly at his wife whilst he could still make out her angelic face. It was a piece of her frozen in time, before the cancer made her eyes cavernous holes of ruin and her skull a sunken monstrosity. As his body, mind and lungs began to surrender to the pull of the grave, he recalled, from where he could not remember in his current predicament, that suicide was a sin.

He'd never had a faith, or believed in a God for that matter, and after what had happened to his wife, he doubted one even existed. If God was willing to allow what had happened to his wife to happen, he didn't want to know a God like that.

But towards the end of his wife's life, he'd latched onto the ardent faith she professed, albeit with weak fingers. It had been to appease her mainly, ensuring her transition from life to death would be as comfortable as possible, but he still had his doubts.

She was at peace in the end, knowing she'd see him again in

heaven.

It was that thought which pulled him out of the fog that was slowly killing him. More than anything he wanted to see her again, and the realisation soon struck, that if he killed himself, would that *unforgivable sin* mean he'd forfeit his chance of ever seeing her again?

He hadn't a clue of the complexities he was mulling over as the gas swirled around him and entered his lungs, but he'd much rather believe God existed – if it meant he could see his wife again – and be called a fool, rather than deny God ever existed only to be proved wrong when the time came, having already forfeited his soul to whatever hinterland awaited those who'd chosen '*the coward's way out*'.

It's where understanding ends that true faith begins and, from that day on, Josh pursued a God he knew nothing about. It was this higher power that Josh had discovered swirling in the exhaust fumes in his car that Henry ceaselessly mocked him about. But who'd be the fool at the end of the day; that was something he'd never know until the time came, but Josh prayed earnestly it wouldn't be him, for the sake of being with his wife again.

The damn spindle needed replacing, that was for sure. Josh guessed the woman's pendulous weight had snapped it free, from her weeklong trip on the wire, or from where the emergency services snapped it off when they tried getting her down – but her echo of death was still in this space thanks to that missing post.

That job would come, like all the others; he'd need to whittle it himself though, due to the ornate filigree in the wood, but his first port of call, for today at least, was stripping the wallpaper from the staircase, which he was planning to get done before the COCS reformed for their evening group session.

It had been a week since Josh had last spoken to Henry. His friend had sent him a garbled text in the early hours following Elsie's death day, drinking session and broken nose, and Josh was relieved momentarily that he wouldn't be buffering another human stain from the floor, or wall or tub; but the messages caused him pause due to his friend's fragile state of mind.

> I saw her last night. She was here, in the house.

Josh had let out a tired breath before he'd fired back his reply.

> Who?

He knew all too well whom the '*who*' in this situation was, but he knew that to entertain it gave it meaning; made it almost real, and Josh knew there was no meaning, or truth for that matter, to be found in a paranoid, drunken delusion.

> Elsie.

Josh rolled his eyes after he'd read the name.

> She was waiting for me.

Knowing the answer to the question already, because whenever Henry gave himself over to drink, especially on Elsie's death day, he seemed to will and welcome these visions of his daughter with open arms; but Josh had to ask, to make sure he was right.

> Were you drunk when you saw her?

This question had been followed by a long pause.

> No. Well, I might have been last night, when she came for me; but she was here, in the house, like before...

Josh had let out a flabbergasted chortle, his head had been

banging all morning and he'd taken a personal day; his hangover had been monumental, and he'd drunk less than Henry. He was surprised his friend even had the ability to text so early following a night of such heavy pickling, because even Josh was struggling to not come across as incoherent.

> Trust me, you were. Completely rat-arsed. It was just your mind playing tricks on you, also your nose, if you hadn't guessed already, is probably broken, you'll want to see someone about that... you got into a fight Henry, you were wasted. Hell, you probably still are.

It had happened many times before, Henry seeing his daughter. This was just another drunken conversation in a long line of drunken anniversary conversations, spanning a great many years; where Henry's heart had wanted what it couldn't have so badly, he'd just imagined the whole affair.

When Henry didn't reply, Josh had text him again.

> You know she's not coming back right?

Since that truth, Henry had dropped off the face of the earth. It wasn't uncommon for him to do so, Josh had been friends with him long enough to know that his bouts of euphoria and delusions about Elsie '*coming for him*' were quickly followed by unsettling and deeply troubling spells of anxiety and spiralling depression.

Josh pondered for the rest of the week if he'd been too harsh with his final reply, but he couldn't – wouldn't – pander to his friend's temporary madness, Henry needed to know she wasn't coming back, and if Josh had to be the arsehole to keep reminding him of that fact, he'd wear the crown and take the scorn.

Picking his scraper from the step beside him, he stood up and ascended the wooden hill of stairs, ready to strip this house of the life that once flowed through it. Grabbing the sponge from the bucket at the top of the stairs, he pressed it against the wallpaper, smearing the dirty and now gummy water across the wall. Rivulets of brownish liquid began to run down the paper before landing on the wooden boards. It was as if the house were weeping about what would soon transpire once Josh began stripping back the years, shredding the memories stored within these porous, nicotine stained walls.

As he unburied the past he couldn't help but think of Henry, and how he'd been trying to bury *his* for the last twelve years. But until Henry had forgiven himself, Josh mused, there was nothing he could do or offer or say to help his friend carry his cumbersome burden; and so he'd resigned himself to just being there when Henry needed him.

Josh knew all this heartache was because Henry had tried to bury her, forget her, but what he'd buried in those shallow graves, he'd buried alive, because unless he could forgive himself – *for what,* Josh had never really found out – he'd be a hostage to the past.

His friend had always been very guarded about what had happened, but as Josh had learnt over time, lonely people built walls around themselves instead of bridges and Henry was walled in because he was unwilling to face his part in this tragedy, like that body in Poe's story. Unforgiveness would always be Henry's master, keeping him a slave to his past and his mistakes, and in turn, keeping him a prisoner to the graves that called him to turn their soil to make his yearly offering. Josh was adamant that without an intervention, those graves would keep stacking up, and his friend would be tending a graveyard in years to come, instead of the small memorial he currently tended.

Josh grabbed a piece of torn wallpaper and tugged on it, the tear spread across the wall, revealing the plaster and to his surprise, an entombed stick figure family. It had been drawn in black marker pen, by what he presumed was the hand of a small child; the proportions were all out of sync – a strange thing to note in the moment, but he did. Dropping the torn paper to the floor, where it joined the detritus from his diligent work, before he set about scraping the rest of the gum and persistent pieces of paper that remained; excavating slowly the family from its grave of dust and time and wallpaper.

It wasn't the first sketch he'd found behind a house's façade, but it was one of the oddest. A small child, held the hands of two – what appeared to be – parents, the adults' legs were unnaturally long, but it wasn't the legs that caused him concern, it was how they seemed to grow taller and loom threateningly over the child, as if the child were a potted plant withering in their ominous shade. One of the adults, the mother Josh presumed – given the spaghetti like hair which crowned its head, sticking out as if they'd stuck their finger in a plug socket – had a huge smiling mouth. When his eyes passed to the other looming presence – the father – he noticed the arch of an upturned smile and fangs protruding from the line in two sharp triangles, the hair atop its head a mess of squiggles, as if they were snakes.

Josh scratched at his head, before tilting it, trying to see the meaning of the picture. His eyes quickly discovered the hands, which were drawn almost like bows, tying the child to the parents. He felt a pang in his heart observing that small slice of beauty in the some-what crazed drawing, how child and parents were tethered together with bow-like hands for all of time; it caused a stinging reminder to resurface in his mind. The thing he'd never have, but wanted most in the entire world. A family to call his own.

His phone buzzed, pulling him out of his spiralling despair. He checked his pockets reflexively, before remembering he'd left it on the table in the dining room. Dropping the scraper on the landing and turning his back on the distress signal from that little girl, either long-gone or long-dead, he began to slowly descend the stairs in search of his phone.

He loved his job and was always fascinated by the little time capsules he discovered when stripping a house before flipping it; in some way he felt as if he were a strange archaeological-anthropolo-gist, discovering the long-since hidden humanity at the heart of family life. But what he enjoyed most about these discoveries, was scrubbing those reminders of family life – good or bad – from existence. Through their eradication, the wound he'd been struck – by his dead wife and her infertile womb – remained shut; if he couldn't make memories, adorn the plaster of his own house with declarations of their familial love before wallpapering over it, why should the dead or gone be allowed to leave their taunting and teasing reminders of how good they'd had it.

The one reminder of a happy family life he enjoyed removing the most, and which he'd found in nearly every family home he'd flipped, were the height charts. Sometimes they were drawn on a wall in pencil, but most of the time they'd been etched into the wood or carved into the paintwork of a doorframe. Josh would rub out and paint over every pencil line and name and sand down each notched doorframe, taking great delight in his meticulous work of eradicating the past. He'd never been given the chance to chart his unborn baby's growth on an app, comparing it to various fruits and vegetables – which was apparently the norm – because there'd never been a baby; the womb which was to carry it had been declared a hostile one by the cancer which had grown there and he had no wife left to carry a baby to term.

All of those possible memories had been stolen from him by the cancer that ate his wife's pelvis until it had its fill and which didn't just stop there, it ate with abandon and left him a widower – and he'd be damned if he left a house he was flipping with the mocking reminders of all he'd lost, every house he flipped would be a blank canvas for its next inhabitant.

He picked up his phone from the table, one new message, from Henry.

"So, you're still alive, you cantankerous bastard," Josh chortled as he opened the message.

> I've been to the Doctors this morning... I've not been feeling right.

Josh rubbed his stubbled chin, as he took in his friend's admission, which in itself was a big thing for Henry to admit to, needing help; *maybe he isn't feeling right?* Josh mused. He quickly typed a reply.

> Shit man, hope everything's okay?

The reply came back almost instantaneously, his friend clearly in need, Josh imagined Henry sitting there, watching his phone for a reply to his distress call; wondering fleetingly if this almost manic back and forth is where Sian got her kicks from, when she sent out her flares across social media during and after each group session, and Josh couldn't help but admit that it felt good to be needed, however briefly that need lasted.

> Doctor said I need to stop drinking the hard stuff and masturbating.

Josh scrunched up his face and raised an eyebrow before his fingers went to work.

> 'Why'd he tell you to stop those, the drink I can understand, but making the bald man cry? Is it your heart?'

He hit send and walked to the bottom of the stairs, as he began to ascend his phone vibrated in his hand. He glanced down, read the message and let out a huge belly laugh.

> He said it was because he was trying to examine me :)

Josh's laughter was a tonic he didn't realise he needed in that moment and it echoed around the empty rooms of the house. His joy soon soured however, because although it was funny, he couldn't help but think this was just another of the many diversion techniques Henry employed, masking the root cause of his problems with humour. It was just another way for him to cope with his sad, bloated, grief-filled experience.

Josh knew he could lead a horse to water – *an intervention* – but he couldn't make it drink, and if Henry was ever going to change, to heal, to mend his fragile life, he knew he'd have to keep dragging his friend to the well and pray that one day he'd finally take a sip.

Josh climbed the stairs, still chuckling from the message as he tapped away on the screen.

> 'You dumb shit, I thought you were serious, I thought you were ill, dying even. But it's good to know you're still with the living. Where've you been this past week, I tried calling? Are you still coming to group tonight?'

Josh exchanged his phone for the scraper, resting it on the landing before getting back to the job at hand. He'd finish scraping this wall and then head home; shit, shave and shower and be out the door early to help set up the chairs for group, knowing that Erik was also still missing in action.

Just as he started scraping again his phone vibrated, bending over the screen he used his free hand to swipe at the message.

> Just been licking my wounds. I've always had a Roman nose, but now it's roaming all over my face thanks to that faggot last week. I'll be there, also had a call from who I can only assume is that new guy you mentioned seeing last week. Said he'd popped by to check us out, happy with what he saw and wants to come along. I told him to turn up this week. Strangest thing though, he said he'd found us through Sian's social media account and she'd told him to turn up... guess there's some good that comes from her incessant tapping after all, huh?

Josh turned back to the wall where the eerie stick-figure-family stared back at him. This time he noticed the child's face and his brow knitted, how he'd not noticed it before was a mystery he couldn't understand. He wondered if the child's face had always been like it, or if it had morphed into this grotesquery since he'd gone to reclaim his phone – *once his back was turned* - but that was a madness he didn't want to entertain given the sudden unease he felt coiling within his stomach at the sight of it. He also knew the type of paranormal shit he was considering only existed in the crappy horror films his wife loved so much, it never bled over into real life, or did it?

One of the first things Josh thought as he gazed upon that cruel depiction was that he'd need to buy some filler. The eyes – which were two black X's – had been gouged into the wall above a squiggly mouth, a classic cartoon face representing the dead. He placed his finger to the eyes, felt the roughness of the scored plaster. He wondered, as his fingers traced the black X's which had corrupted the wall, of what had befallen the little girl who'd draw this portentous family portrait.

There was something about how the eyes were rendered that unsettled Josh the more he stared at them, they appeared to suggest the girl was trying to remove the things she'd seen or possibly the things she might soon witness in this place.

He put the unnerving etching to the back of his mind as he set about his next few hours of work. If he didn't put the etching in the fuck-it bucket, he'd never get the wall stripped in time, meaning and he'd be late for their group session, and he'd have to deal with the shit Henry would give him for having to put the chairs out again, it was a berating he could do without.

A few hours later, the walls to the stairwell were completely stripped and Josh downed his tools. Picking up his phone he began to descend the stairs, his mind ticking off the things he'd need to pick up from the hardware store the following morning: filler for that godawful depiction that graced the walls, and a spindle which he'd need to whittle and carve to match the others.

His eyes went instinctively to the missing spindle and his mind filled with dark and brooding thoughts. *Death certainly doesn't discriminate* he mused darkly; old, young, rich, poor, born, unborn, oppressed or free – it was inescapable.

It was how you chose to live in death's approaching shadow that counted, Josh had found his purpose – flipping houses – he just wished Henry would someday find his.

CHAPTER FIVE

When the COCS converged en masse there was always the unmistakable sense of dread which permeated the air; Josh likened it to a heavy and filthy blanket of grief being strung up across the room and they'd take their turns beating the living shit out of it. Each had stained it in some way and each took part in its thrashing – when the time was right – in the middle of their '*circle of caring souls*'; and from that beating, the spores of grief hung thickly in the air as if some deadly pathogen had been released.

But it wasn't the imaginary blanket which had caused tonight's more than gloomy affair; there was something all the more tangible. Josh cast his eyes to the ceiling and noticed two of the overhead lights had blown since they were last here, and of course, no one had bothered to fix them – *you can't polish a turd*, Josh mused wryly.

The gloomy atmosphere afforded by the missing bulbs had swallowed half the circle, causing those who sat at the edges of the void to be there and not be there at the same time. He'd half expected to find Henry in the centre of the darkness, hiding in plain sight as usual, but he wasn't, he was sitting directly in front of him, gnawing on whatever remained of his nails. Henry spat the harvested crescents – which he savoured briefly in his mouth – onto the stained carpet squares at his feet. Josh could tell Henry was stewing, and his friend's countenance perfectly matched the mood lighting, *despair* was the word that came to mind.

The air felt alive, charged and heavy like the onset of a thunderstorm; one which would soon break and they'd be floundering in the eye of the storm. In part it was because Roger had the floor and Harriet, who was running this week's session and couldn't fight her way out of a wet paper bag, had let Roger off the short leash Josh and especially Henry had him on. He was spouting off for all to hear. *Henry was right. Roger loved the sound of his own voice and could talk shite all day and say absolutely nothing of value.*

Josh watched on as between each chew of a nail, Henry's mouth uttered a string of unpleasantries at the man he despised more than himself, which was a hard task in and of itself. Josh glanced over at Roger, who was carrying on regardless of the words that bubbled away in the silence between his many words, if he could hear the hushed curses or not, he was doing a great job of ignoring the raging ball of hate which sat three seats over.

"When God closes a door, he opens a window," Roger offered to the room with a sweep of his open hands, his eager eyes desperately hoping to latch onto one believing soul in a room of burnt out husks; every inch a lay preacher trying to win a congregation.

Josh lowered his gaze to his work boots, but the hook Roger had cast into the abyss of grief-addled souls was lodged in his brain and each time he tried to tug away, swim out into deeper waters away from that door and window, it felt as if Roger's sentiment kept reeling him back in.

Josh didn't see it the way Roger had intended it to come across, he doubted anyone in the group had either, but as his mind thrashed to get away from the hook which had snared him, he just couldn't sum up the energy, it felt as if that hook had been laced with poison.

God had indeed closed a door, a great many doors for that matter; each had been slammed shut in his face after his wife's diagnosis, leaving him stranded outside, whilst his wife suffered in the many locked rooms of her own suffering.

The last door Josh had been running towards, but was never able to reach – as if he were running on a floor made of treacle – swung achingly closed, the sign on that door read: Family. As Roger continued to ramble on about his sanctimonious cliché, Josh had fully visualised the door, could hear the rusted whine of the hinges echoed in Roger's sanctimonious voice. As he desperately cantered towards that door he heard a voice from within utter: 'Six months, a year at most.' He watched the light behind the door extinguish as the door finally clicked shut and he was once again stranded in that netherworld, a room full of locked doors of which there was no escape. There was a window in the room of doors, quite possibly the one of which Roger had spoken, but it wasn't open, the damned thing was nailed shut; and so this room Josh found himself in, on cold nights when sleep became nothing but a word, had become a private, seething Hell.

Josh was going to intercede, but as he cast his eyes around the group, he was shocked to discover the rapt attention Roger was receiving from those in assembly. *I can't believe they're buying this shit*, Josh mused. They were hanging on his every word.

Josh decided to bite his tongue and wait for Henry to inevitably blow his stack at some point down the road. Where he'd more than likely cover the room in an ash cloud of rage because the longer Roger was left unchecked, the more Josh could see his friend fidgeting in his own skin. It was only a matter of time, and so Josh choked down the words he wanted to say, knowing that when Henry finally erupted – and erupt he would, there were certain assurances in life; death, taxes and Henry losing his shit – Josh would be able to swoop in to save the day, being the perfect foil for Henry's outbursts.

They each had a role to play. Henry was the enforcer and executioner, whereas Josh was the voice of reason, a knight in shining armour and he preferred not to muddy those waters.

Josh turned to Henry and was surprised to see his friend staring back at him, instead of shooting daggers at Roger across the circle. His friend looked like death warmed up. The black eyes which were a result of his run in with Terry had dissolved into yellowish-greenish bruises, which had blanched across his already jaundiced complexion; his nose – which looked more like a flamingo's beak – was downturned and hooked, a ghastly looking, twisted mess of a nose.

Henry rolled his eyes at Roger's constant droning. Josh widened his and raised his eyebrows in a *can you believe this guy* gesture before slowly shaking his head at the shit that poured endlessly from Roger's mouth.

"I guess heaven needed another Angel," Roger continued.

Josh felt himself tense at the remark. He could also tell that Henry wanted to reach across the circle and strangle the self-righteous bastard; Henry's knee was bouncing up and down on the floor in frustration. Each time the heel of Henry's Converse lost contact with the carpet, Josh could have sworn it made an audible squelch from where it became unstuck from the filthy floor. Henry was a rabid dog waiting to bite, snarl and tear flesh from bone, maybe he would. Hell, even Josh felt like marching across the circle and ripping out Roger's tongue, shoving it down his throat and having him choke on his self-serving, greeting card clichés.

Fortunately, neither of them needed to lift a finger or raise a voice to end Roger's verbal diarrhoea, because from the dark side of the room – the shadowland afforded by the blown bulbs – came a gloom-clad figure who shuffled towards the gathered COCS with a purpose.

As the figure stalked closer to a vacant chair, Josh and Henry shared a brief glance before snapping their heads back in the direction of the rising, mocking, laughter which ebbed and flowed through the room like a foul wind. The pearl of laughter earned the whole group a temporary respite from Roger's odd, holier-than-thou sermon, because the cackling had silenced the insufferable man instantly, as if someone had reached out and slit the egocentric, bastard's throat.

Josh watched the figure fall into the shadow-clad chair; dumping their rucksack to the floor by their tattered trainers before leaning forward. The light revealed them as if they were a villain from an old noir film, a living representation of chiaroscuro.

The laughter petered off as they placed their elbows on their knees and after tenting their fingers – the nails lacquered black, the polish chipped – rested their chin on the supporting bridge of digits; where he coldly observed the troubled souls, one after the other before him with eyes as piercing as a shark's.

A smirk or grimace – Josh couldn't work out which – had graced the stranger's lips. Josh observed a fuzz of pubescent facial hair sprouting in random patches on the new attendee's face, as if they'd been desperately trying to grow a beard but had only been rewarded with a few patches of wiry, pubic hair like growth. It was an odd sight to behold given the man's quite obvious, follicle dominancy, exemplified by the deftly coiffed, Styx-black, mop of hair atop his head.

The stranger's predatory eyes fell on Roger where they remained for a long while.

Josh watched Roger squirm on his seat as the silence stretched.

"Bullshit!" the stranger said sharply.

The group remained silent. Roger was on his own, no one was coming to his aid, if this stranger was a bus, he was sure there'd be a few people lining up to push him in front of it, to save themselves. Josh suddenly became aware of the half-hearted, stifled chuckle from Henry, who it appeared when he turned to face him, was taking great delight in the less than conventional interruption to their evening session. The man loved chaos and aggression and this was right up his darkened alley.

"And you are?" Roger said, trying desperately to cling on to his superiority, as if brewing the shit he served up as coffee gave him a seat at the table.

"Rowen. And you are?"

"Roger–"

"Like the rabbit?" Rowen retorted quick as a whip before cackling directly into Roger's smug looking face and slapping his knee at his remark. *If this guy had any more wit, he'd be a half-wit* Josh mused, but he also couldn't help but admire the guy's spunk; his devil may care attitude, which reminded him of the other devil in the group, Henry. Either the joke was lost on Roger – who appeared to be the only soul in attendance who hadn't found Rowen's witticism the slightest bit humorous – or he was doing his utmost to not let the little runt get one over on him, which Josh presumed was probably the case when he saw the sternness etched on Roger's face, as if he were a headmaster staring down a petulant child.

An awkward silence fell over the group as the titters dissipated, Josh noted that Henry's chuckle was the last one to subside, as if he'd wanted Roger to know the complete lack of respect he had for him and the pig-shit coffee he served up each week.

Roger began scanning the group for someone to come to his aid, and in that moment as his flustered eyes beseeched someone, anyone to step in and help, everyone – including Josh – cast their eyes to their feet, hands or ceiling. Josh felt a pang of guilt for his own silence, because he knew if he'd been running the session he'd have intervened a lot sooner, explained the rules of the group to the newcomer; but he wasn't in charge, Harriet was, and she was as much use as a chocolate tea pot.

He glanced over at her now, only to discover her staring off into dreamland, biting on her lower lip, her cheeks flushed with heat. Josh wondered if the sheer mention of a rabbit in group had her recalling a recent lonely night with a rampant one, her battery operated lover's lance supplying the orgasms she craved but those of which her departed husband *apparently* despised; often using their dog to convey his annoyance at how frequently she was parting her legs since he'd been in the ground.

Josh knew that no man was an island, but in the excruciating silence which had impregnated the room, Roger appeared to be a forgotten one; and he couldn't help but feel sorry for him. He hated seeing people be made to feel less than they were, but there was nothing he could really do, there was nothing any of them could do but wait the silence out.

Josh peered around the group wondering where Roger's help would come from, because for the first time in a long while, they were all in attendance, barring Erik, who was still on his jaunt in Polperro; and when he was due back was anyone's guess because no one had been able to contact him.

Jacob was busy stuffing his face with a share box of doughnuts, which from the way he was mushing them into his mouth, spilling the jam down his chin and onto his corduroy jacket, it was quite clear he had no interest in doing what the box said.

Sian was busy tapping away at her screen, seemingly oblivious to what had and was still transpiring in group.

Ethel, who'd not been to the last few sessions, had made a rare appearance – which Josh was delighted to see – but as she reclined in her seat; her jaw slack, spittle dangling from her chin which had trickled out of her gaping mouth. She'd been snoring and farting her way through the session and the delight he'd felt at seeing her soon turned sour when he thought of the little, warm and wet deposit she'd leave him to clean up when this was all over.

"Talkative bunch," Rowen uttered, letting out an exasperated breath before reclining in his seat and crossing his arms over his chest. Apparently whatever devilry he'd come to inflict on them hadn't been as exciting as he'd at first thought, he'd clearly underestimated the room, because no one had any fight left in them to challenge him; or so Josh mistakenly thought.

"So, tough guy, what's with the nails? You some kinda queer?"

"No, but if I was would that be a problem old man? Because judging by your face, your lips are writing cheques your body can't cash... who beat up on you anyway, your misses?"

"She left me."

"Oh, is that why you're... here?" Rowen tittered, feigning concern.

"No, the bitch just left, started her own family... after..."

Josh couldn't believe what he was hearing, were they about to witness a confession?

Would Henry's need to save face crack him wide open to the possibility of oversharing? Josh could almost hear a collective intake of breath from those in assembly as the members of the group – those who were paying attention at least – leant forwards, eager to hear the long held secret of Henry's grief spill from his loosed lips.

"After what?" Rowen questioned.

"Hey kid, I don't know you from Adam, and hell you ain't even bought me a drink yet... so let's just leave that for another time, once we get more acquainted."

"No harm intended, was just curious is all. You're all such open books, but you, you're dark and twisty, a bit like me I guess, blood calls to blood if you catch my meaning; him though..." Rowen pointed a black tipped finger at Jacob. "Clearly he's eating his way out of losing someone close to him, and judging by the share box of donuts he's snuffling down, it ain't going too well. No offence." Rowen offered the 'no offence' to Jacob as if it were some magical caveat that would gloss over his spite-filled words.

"Num faken," Jacob replied. He had a mouth full of doughnut and his hand was dipping back in to claim another.

"Judging by his clothes," Rowen continued to talk as if Jacob wasn't in the room. "I'd say it was the death of an elderly mother or father. Doesn't have a wedding ring, so there's no wife in the picture, or girlfriend for that matter if we take into account the state of his hand-me-down clothes, which I'm sure went out of style, what, ten years ago; not to mention the DIY haircut, what they do your folks, put a bowl on your head and cut around it?"

Henry sniggered at the remark and seemed to be delighting in the cruelty on show. Josh couldn't help but see an affinity between Rowen and his friend, a dark one at that, as if they'd both been cut from the same mean cloth but thirty years apart.

"Am I right tubs?" Rowen added.

Jacob nodded like a bullied school boy who just wanted the mean words to stop; his eyes were downcast, observing the half-eaten box of doughnuts in his lap as if he were seeing it for the first time.

"Now that's enough," Josh said, the words tumbling from his mouth before he realised what he was saying. He needed to intercede, the meeting was getting away from them and because Roger was *clearly* no help, Henry was enjoying the show and Harriet was still in dreamland imagining her next roll in the sack with her battery operated friend; the task for bringing this to an end fell squarely on his shoulders. The main reason he'd spoken up was because he couldn't abide bullies, and Rowen was just that, and he needed to be stopped.

"Ahh, he speaks!" Rowen clapped his hands together before placing them between his knees, his eyes pinpointing on Josh for the first time this evening, they looked him up and down, silently appraising their latest target.

"This is a safe space Rowen and if you don't start–"

"Who are you again? I don't think we've been introduced?"

"Josh. Look if you don't–"

"Ahh okay, nice to meet you Joshy–"

"It's Josh, trust me you'd do well to remember that, listen–"

"Ooo... someone's a little tetchy aren't they, but okay. Josh. What is it you do here, Josh; you run the group or something?" Rowen removed a hand from between his knees and cupped it to the side of his mouth before mockingly whispering, "Or are you the enforcer; should I be scared right now?"

"I kinda run it, yeah. I'm the deputy–"

Rowen took a sharp, loud intake of breath which cut Josh off. He placed a splayed hand mockingly to his chest.

"Oh, I'm so sorry officer," Rowen thrusted his hands out in front of him, wrists together and pouted, he blinked his big blues at Josh before talking in a mock feminine voice. "Is the big bad deputy going to arrest me for being cruel? I was only stating the obvious, I'm just trying to make friends, my parents didn't teach me too well you see."

Josh turned his attention briefly to Henry, hoping his friend would lead into the conversation but Henry was too busy observing the young upstart in front of him with a mixture of awe and prideful-glee on his face, as if he'd discovered a diamond in the rough – an equal to his vulgarity – and the sight of such a thing was too captivating and alluring to pass up.

"Why you looking to him?"

Josh turned his head slowly back to Rowen and as his eyes panned the group, he realised that everyone – even Sian who'd finally put her phone down – were watching on raptly, as if they were rubbernecking on a horrific accident they'd stumbled upon and couldn't look away. Even Ethel was awake; her power-nap cut short by the raised voices but judging by the glazed look in her eyes - Josh assumed she had no idea where she was.

"Oh, that's right..." Rowen continued, "He has all the power doesn't he? He's the sheriff to your deputy. And seeing as he seems to be enjoying this little session of home truths as much as me, why don't I carry on with my observations, because I got you pegged too–"

"Really, I highly doubt that." Josh said nonplussed.

"I saw how your jaw clenched up, when Mr. I-Swallowed-A-Bunch-Of-Meaningless-Greetings-Cards said about Heaven needing another Angel – you lost a child right?"

"No. I lost my wife, but I don't see–"

"But you wanted nothing more than to be a dad right?"

Josh didn't know how to react, he wanted to show this young upstart what happens when you started messing in other people's grief, but he also knew he needed to show decorum and the caring attitude the COCS had grown to admire and trust. It pained him to swallow his anger, but he choked it down, because he hadn't a clue what baggage this guy was carrying around with him under all his bravado. He was about to speak when a voice sliced through the momentary pause in proceedings.

"I think that's more than enough..." it was the gruff baritone of Henry coming to his aid. Hearing his friend enter the fray, at the final hour, when he was about to lose his way, filled him with a strange, deep-rooted peace which warmed his soul. They were still a team; when one hurt they both hurt, it was something Josh would never confide in Henry, knowing he wouldn't be able to judge what offhanded, bigoted reply he'd get back, but in this dark moment, he was elated his friend had found him and come to his aid.

"Oh, is the big boss man angry that I've overstepped, I was just trying to help. It was about time you all heard some startling home truths, you know you can't wallow in shit without getting dirty, right? So, why don't you all just—"

"I'm not angry, trust me you'd be the first to know if I was."

"Oooo... kinky, what you going to spank me?"

"Nope, but I think I got you pegged too?"

"Really? Care to enlighten this terribly misguided soul?"

"You quite clearly don't have any respect for your elders..."

"What is this, a church group or a grief group?" Rowen chuckled at his own retort.

"I'd say dysfunctional family? Overbearing father," Josh watched on as Henry's verbal jab landed, seemingly winding his sparring partner. It was the slightest of tells, but the corner of Rowen's mouth twitched, the shit-eating grin he'd been wearing since sitting down had faltered, it was as if he didn't know whether to acknowledge the remark – which Josh felt he desperately wanted to do – or brush it off. That little twitch displayed for Josh the first chink in Rowen's battle-worn armour of ripped jeans and a faded band T-shirt. Josh knew Henry had him against the ropes and he wouldn't stop swinging until he'd pulverised him; Rowen didn't have anyone in his corner to throw in the towel to stop the savagery and Josh wondered if he was now regretting all the choices that had led up to this moment, because it was clear to see he'd severely underestimated his opponent, this could quite easily turn into a bloodbath.

"Distant or weak mother?" Henry offered.

"Don't you talk about my mother," Rowen shouted, spittle flying from his mouth. "Or so help me god, I'll get out of this chair and slap the taste of her out of your mouth..."

"Seems like I touched a nerve, mummy's boy-" Henry delivered another verbal jab.

"Keep pushing it grandpa I might just realign that nose of yours."

Henry cackled, he could smell blood, he was on self-destruct and there was nothing Josh could do to stop it, it was a feeding frenzy now and he knew his friend wouldn't stop until he got to the squishy stuff; he was gearing up for the kill.

"So, it's a daddy complex we're dealing with? What he do, kill your mummy?"

"You piece of shit," Rowen shouted across the circle. He went to stand but quickly sat back down as Henry bolted to his feet, never one to back down from an altercation, especially one he'd win. In his haste to get to his feet, his legs knocked his chair backwards where it clattered to the floor. Josh was primed and ready to spring into action at a moment's notice; Henry would tear the poor sod apart if it got to that and so he slid to the edge of his seat and balanced there precariously, ready to run into the fray at the first sign of aggression.

Suddenly a voice broke the standoff between the rutting stags.

"How about we all just calm down and get some coffee?" Roger said as he timidly got to his feet and moved behind his chair.

"SHUT. UP. ROGER!" Henry and Rowen shouted in unison.

Josh observed Henry and Rowen as they stared at each other down; they were so similar in that moment, each a raging ball of hate and pain, belligerent and uncompromising; neither willing to concede any ground to the other for fear of coming off weak.

From the corner of his eye Josh noticed a whirl of motion and turned to see what was happening. Harriet was finally getting to her feet, moving into the circle, which now felt like more of a slaughter-house now, a killing circle. She slowly and apprehensively approached the hulking Henry, his barrel chest rising and falling with each laboured breath he took. Josh wanted to warn her, tell her to stand down, that you never approach a wounded animal, especially if that wound was its pride; but he was too preoccupied in ensuring he was ready to pounce if need be that by the time she'd reached out and touched Henry's forearm it was too late to intervene, he just had to sit back and watch the fireworks.

At her touch Henry turned to face her. He appeared lost for a moment as he took in the woman standing next to him as if he didn't recognise her, which was impossible given Harriet had been in group longer than most.

Henry's momentary befuddlement caused Josh to wonder what darkened corridor he'd been running down. He knew there were two types of runners in the world: those running away from something, and those running towards something. Which of those Henry was varied somewhat depending on the day; some days he was running away from his daughter's ever-present shadow, others he was running full tilt towards total self-destruction. Right now it appeared to be the latter, and who knew what tomorrow held. Harriet had reached him though, pulled him from the dark place he was traversing with a single touch of human kindness.

"I think it's probably best if we call a halt on tonight's meeting, it's gotten away from us wouldn't you say?" Harriet's words poured sweetly from her lips. She tapped Henry's forearm lovingly, as a mother would a crying child after they'd grazed a knee, it was a move which could have been construed as condescending, but Henry took it with all the love and sensibility it was intended – an act of loving concern.

Henry glanced down at her hand, then back across the circle to Rowen.

Those in attendance began to get up from their seats before shuffling away quietly towards Roger who'd already made his way over to the refreshment table, already pouring his foul tasting coffee into polystyrene cups.

Harriet had spoken, their master of ceremonies had declared their meeting adjourned and not a moment too soon, *who knew she had it in her?* Josh mused.

"Yeah okay, meetings over. But me and you," Henry pointed to Rowen, who was still quietly stewing in his chair, all skinny arms and legs like a daddy longlegs. "We're going to have a little chat, a clear the air discussion, you got big balls let me tell you that, but this shit," Henry span a finger around in the air, referring to all that had gone before. "It ain't gunna fly, especially if you wanna keep coming back. You got that?"

"Crystal," Rowen said, holding his hands in the air in supplication, as his mischievous smile returned to his face, a grin so broad it was as if butter wouldn't melt in his mouth.

"You want me to fetch you boys some coffee?" Harriet said as she reluctantly stepped away from Henry.

"Yes, please." Rowen said.

"No," Henry cut in sharply. "We'll be over in a few, keep it warm for us, okay?"

Harriet nodded and shuffled her way over to the group who were congregating around the refreshment table. Josh noticed that every eye in that place was directed at the three remaining souls in the circle, and he couldn't blame them, people were drawn to chaos like flies on shit.

"Trust me, the coffee tastes like warmed up piss," Henry uttered as he lumbered across the circle towards Rowen. "I'm doing you a favour, least you could do is say thanks!"

"Thanks," Rowen offered sheepishly at the approaching bear of a man before flinching when Henry thrusted his hand out. Josh assumed Rowen was expecting something other than a hand of peace. It hung there between them for a moment.

"How about we start over?"

Rowen eyed Henry's hand as if it were handing him a snake, when none presented itself he reached out his manicured hand to shake the olive branch which had been extended, seeing the meshing of two very different worlds by two very different hands made Josh smile. There was a welcomed oddness to it, Henry shaking the hand of a man with painted nails, Josh wondered if his friend was indeed turning the corner of his hatred and derision of the LGBTQ community, and if he was, that was good for everyone, especially Henry; he hoped it was the first tentative step in helping his friend recover his life and discover his purpose, both had long since been on hold given the noose of shame which had been slowly strangling his life since Elsie disappeared.

"I'd like that," Rowen uttered and patted the seat next to him. "Sorry about all that, I'm just working through some things. It's a lot easier to point out the stick in someone else's eye than focus on your own, if you know what I mean?"

"Makes perfect sense, you remind me of me, you know, back when I was working this stuff through, when it was raw and gaping."

"How'd you get through it?"

"I'll tell you when I get there," Henry chuckled and nudged Rowen's shoulder with his closed fist.

"Why don't you pull up a pew, I don't bite, these..." Rowen flashed his nails at Henry. "Are just for show, I ain't no queer as you eloquently put it, I like the ladies. But, if I was, queer, you ain't got no problems, a grandpa who probably needs a pill to get it up ain't ticking any of my boxes, if you know what I mean, no offence!"

"None taken," Henry said as he sat down next to Rowen.

Seeing as the two didn't look as if they'd be throttling each other any time soon, Josh got to his feet.

"You two gunna play nice whilst I tidy these away," Josh pointed to the chairs.

Henry nodded. Rowen winked at him before waving a dismissive hand in Josh's direction.

"Knock yourself out petal. I'm talking to the organ grinder not the monkey!" Rowen nudged Henry and they both began to laugh, it was refreshing to hear after all that had transpired, but being the butt of the joke spoiled the mood slightly and Josh turned away from the two men, who appeared as thick as thieves as they began talking.

Josh picked up the chair next to Rowen first and as he pulled it away it caught on Rowen's backpack, tipping it forwards onto the ground, the sound and motion drawing Henry's attention.

"My daughter used to have a backpack like that."

"Is that so," Rowen said, leaning down and reclaiming his bag, stuffing it securely under his seat. "She must have good taste."

"Had," Henry replied, his face screwed up in pain at his utterance. As Josh carried the chair away he couldn't help but feel that one word – *'had'* – was the cruellest word he'd heard uttered all evening and there'd been a great many to choose from.

"Oh, I'm sorry for your loss."

"Don't be, she ain't dead, that I know of. She's just missing is all," his attention was drawn back to Rowen's bag. "That's a nice bag though," Josh knew it was a weak attempt at deflection, to move the subject on, Rowen however failed to pick up on that delicate thread which needed to be left alone; instead, unwillingly or not, he pulled on it.

"How long's she been missing?"

Josh folded another chair and carried the two of them across to the rack.

"Twelve years last week," Henry uttered, but it was the silence that followed which was worse than the statement of fact, it seemed to deepen, growing to unfathomable proportions. Josh took Rowen's sudden and uncharacteristic silence as a contemplative moment, weighing up the statement: *missing for twelve years* – and the unsaid undertones it conjured to any rational thinking person, *she's gotta be dead*.

"Oh, right." Rowen offered, what else was there to say to such a declaration.

The two men sat in somewhat of a sacred silence for a time, neither wanting to elaborate further on the elephant which had been dragged into the room.

Josh returned to pick up another few chairs only to discover Ethel's latest deposit.

The sight of the yellow puddle in the depression of the seat made

Josh shudder, he inwardly cursed the still AWOL Erik, his eyes rising to the ceiling as he placed his hands on his hips. With Erik gone, cleaning that mess had fallen squarely on his shoulders; puffing out his cheeks Josh cut across the depleted circle to grab some paper towels from the refreshment table.

He almost stopped in his tracks as Rowen broke the shared silence.

"You ever thought of contacting her?"

Josh continued on but at a quicker pace, he didn't want to miss a word of this most recent development, returning sharply with towels in hand he caught the end of Henry's reply.

"... if I could. She doesn't have a phone, or didn't when she went missing–"

"No, not like that; I mean actually *contacting* her, like a séance or something,"

"I don't know? I've never bought into all that mumbo jumbo shit."

"But you want to exhaust every avenue don't you? If you did this, at least you'd know for sure, if she's passed..." Rowen's words were full of enthusiasm.

"Does it even work? Only experience I ever had was with an Ouija board. Like the thing that kid used in the Exorcist to speak with Captain Howdy; me and Kiera, that's my wife, or I should say *was* my wife. Anyway, we tried it but it was just a waste of time."

"It works man, I've done it before, I'd be more than happy to help, if you'd let me."

Josh was busy wiping the seat clean, he didn't need to look in their direction to know Henry's pause meant he was giving serious credence to considering Rowen's proposal, which Josh thought was sheer lunacy given they were about to tear each other to ribbons not moments prior. With a handful of sodden paper towels Josh turned and marched across the circle to the bin and when he caught sight of Henry rubbing his chin, his brow drawn in deep thought, he couldn't help himself he needed to intercede for his friend, because if he didn't, who would? He couldn't help but think that this proposal, from somewhat of a stranger felt predatory, as if he'd manufactured the whole evening for this exact moment.

"You sure that's wise?" Josh said as he dumped the paper towels in the bin and turned to face the conspiring duo, wiping the dampness from his fingers on the arse of his jeans.

"What are you his mother?"

"I'm his friend," Josh replied as he pulled up a chair and listened in on their conversation.

Rowen shook his head at Josh's interruption.

"It'll work, trust me, I've seen it work, dozens of times."

Henry had gone quiet, his hand now massaging the back of his neck, whatever he was thinking was weighing on him greatly.

"Look, what have you got to lose? If we hear from her, which we might do; you'll know for certain that she's gone and you can grieve or be at peace or whatever it is you wanna get from this, and if we don't then either she didn't show, and we can try again; or what's more probable, is she's still out there somewhere... missing, but not yet found.

"This is ludicrous, have you even heard what–" Josh began to argue before he was cut off by Rowen, who talked directly over him, petitioning Henry again as if he were a devil on his shoulder and Josh the pleading angel of rational thinking perched on the other.

"What's the harm in trying right? Are you scared or something? Big guy like you I'd thought you'd have the balls to at least try, if not for you then for your daughter, guess I was wrong about you."

Henry was deep in thought, he was peering down at his Converse as if all the mysteries of the world were lurking down there.

He let out a tired breath, whatever war he'd been battling in his mind had seemingly tired him out. But as he lifted his gaze, Josh knew what was coming from the sly smile on his friend's face, Josh shook his, praying his friend wouldn't say what the smile suggested. Henry didn't notice Josh's fear because he only had eyes for Rowen and Josh knew his friend had been duped by the oldest trick in the book; being called in no uncertain terms a chicken.

Henry wouldn't let that slide; he was too proud and too manly to be called out by a young upstart. When he uttered his reply, the bottom of Josh's world fell out, because he suddenly realised things would never be the same again, there were no winners in this scenario, only losers and Henry had a lot to lose.

"Let's do it, tonight."

CHAPTER SIX

"I ain't doing that," Henry said, staring down at Rowen's outstretched hand.

They were seated around an old table, which from where he was sitting looked scratched to buggery and he pondered if Josh was having palpitations, knowing what a neat freak he was. He peered over at his friend now, half-expecting him to be staring at the table, wondering what buffing tools and polish he'd need to get it looking ship shape, but he was staring at Rowen's hand and listening intently to his instructions.

On the table were a bunch of tall candles, the type you'd see in a church, these though appeared to have been robbed from a Satanist's altar, red and black things with snakes carved in the wax. They flickered in the cool evening breeze that snuck through the open window, the curtain lazily billowing into the room with each gust of air; Henry was watching the wax dribble down the candles, crawling slowly over the coiled serpents as if it were blood.

Spread out before them on the table were various items; incense was burning in a bowl, there was a photo – pulled from Henry's wallet – of Elsie, various crystals, a marker pen and an upturned tumbler.

"I wasn't asking," Rowen replied as he thrusted his hand out again.

Henry ignored Rowen's reaching hand because his focus was solely on his own fingers which were fiddling with the deep grooves carved into the table's surface. As his finger moved up and down, he realised it had traced a word: No.

"If you want this to work, we gotta hold hands, don't ask me why but it's better that way a truer connection with the spirit realm."

Henry glanced across the table; in the opposite corner was another gouged word: Yes. He suddenly realised that hovering above it was Josh's hand, already holding Rowen's, it looked awkward, but more than anything else it felt like a betrayal. Henry observed the 'Yes' below their joined hands and he knew he had to do it, but he'd put it off for as long as possible.

"We didn't come all the way here not to follow through. Hold the man's hand, it doesn't mean anything; he already told you if he was queer, you wouldn't be his type, if that's what you're worried about?" Josh lifted Rowen's hand in his as if to highlight his point. The dainty hand of Rowen's, full of painted nails and slim fingers, holding Josh's *workman's hands* looked like one of those United Colors of Benetton adverts, a symbol of unity, for persecuted queers all over the world, he could see it emblazoned on jackets, printed out and stuck to walls, handed out on flyers at a protest for equal rights or whatever bollocks they were protesting against next.

"Come on, stop being a dick," Josh uttered light-heartedly, before holding his own hand out to Henry too.

He glanced firstly at Rowen's weak looking, feminine hand, which must have never seen a hard day's work in its life. He then peered at Josh's calloused, bear mitt of a hand, sighing deeply and knowing he'd have to take both of them to get what he needed; he decided it was a sacrifice he was willing to make.

He stopped fiddling with the inscriptions of numbers his fingers had found on the table, which sat above two arcs of letters and pondered Josh's sudden urge to get things moving. It struck him as odd, because on the way over he'd been hell-bent on them turning around and finding another way – whatever that was, or looked like – to getting Henry the closure he desperately longed for.

There'd been desperation in his voice and Henry could tell by the way Josh was carrying himself, his awkward, shuffling, sulking demeanour he'd wanted to be anywhere but where they'd soon end up; it was as if something didn't sit right within his soul, and maybe it didn't. Henry knew that if he *did* manage to make contact, it meant that Elsie was dead; which would be a soul crushing revelation in itself, but it seemed more palatable in its definitiveness, than knowing she was alive, but just didn't want to come home.

Henry had realised as they approached the building why Josh was so apprehensive about making contact, because if Elsie did indeed answer Henry's call, it would leave him with doubts about the Heaven he was banking on and the reunion with his wife.

Doubt was a cancer that more often than not proved fatal – and Henry could testify to that. Henry knew that Josh had given his life over to Christ instead of taking it that night in his car filled with exhaust fumes, it was something he'd shared with reverence in group more than once; he'd spoken about relinquishing his own desires to end his pain for the eternal promise that he'd see his wife again in paradise.

But if Elsie was here, could Amanda be found too, wandering in that hinterland of the dead? And if she was here, roaming around with the other spirits, Henry knew the first two questions on his friends' lips would have been: 'Was Heaven full?' and 'Did it even exist?'

Henry knew that what they were about to do in this hovel of a flat in the arsehole of Bristol, along Lawrence Hill Road, went against everything Josh had come to believe in. Instead of feeling guilty for dragging his god-fearing friend along to a séance, Henry felt a huge swelling of hope – or was it love – in his flagging spirit. Josh was willing to stand by him even if it wrecked him in the process of getting Henry answers, his friend was ready to walk through Hell with him and hold his hand all the way.

As he looked up from Josh's hand to his friend's pleading face, he realised Josh was an island of sanity in the choppy waters of his maddening grief. Josh gave him an encouraging nod and lifted Rowen's hand for good measure, showing him he could do it, if he really wanted to, all that was stopping him was his own narrow-mindedness.

"I ain't happy about it, but you dicks won't be happy unless I do, so fuck it, give me your bloody hands; remember I'm doing this for Elsie," he relinquished his grip on the edge of the table and took their hands.

"See, that weren't too bad, was it?" Rowen said.

But it was. Henry wanted to snatch his hand back from Rowen's immediately, it felt wrong, there was something about how dainty his fingers were, how cold and wet his hand felt in his that made his gorge rise. There was an acrid tang in the back of his throat which soon coated his mouth; the taste of shame and he knew its subtle flavour intimately, he swallowed the rising foulness back down because he knew the ends of this outweighed the means.

He glanced down at his hand holding Rowen's and shivered at the sight of it.

"It'll be okay, don't worry, I've done this many times before... are you ready?"

Henry just nodded; not knowing if he could trust his voice in that moment.

"You know, if this doesn't work–" Josh started before Rowen cut him off.

"It will," Rowen snapped.

"But if it doesn't," Josh continued, "you haven't lost anything man, it just means you've gained the knowledge that she's still out there, waiting to be found, there's still always hope!"

"Anyone ever tell you you should write that shit down so you don't forget it? I mean it's just so heart-warming and informative, I wouldn't want you forgetting it," Rowen spat.

"Fuck you Rowen, I'm just being a realist, I think there needs to be at least one person at this table who's thinking logically about all this," Josh nodded at the table. "Smoke and mirrors bullshit, I'm just looking out for my friend, protecting him from charlatans just like you, preying on those you can see hurting, you're a cancer you know that?"

"I can assure you, there ain't no smoke and mirrors–"

"What the hell's that then?"

Henry lifted his gaze to see Josh nodding his head to the cut glass pendulum hanging above the table.

"That's a crystal you tool. It helps spirits find their way to–"

"But what if it does?" Henry's voice cut through Josh and Rowen's childish game of tit for tat as if it were a scythe felling a field of unruly corn.

Both turned to him, they were still holding his hands and he wondered if they could feel them trembling.

"What was that Henry?" Rowen offered, before squeezing Henry's hand encouragingly.

Henry ignored Rowen's address and the reassurance of that squeeze, instead he turned to Josh, his port in the storm he was facing. He quickly wished he hadn't. It was as if Josh's face had become the mirror he and Rowen had been childishly bickering about moments before. His friend looked exactly how he felt in that moment; confused and concerned and his eyes were wide with fear, there was no comfort to be had in that face.

They were both deeply troubled but for completely different reasons.

"What if it does?" Henry said again.

Josh stared at him, a puzzled look screwing his worried face up even more.

"Does what?"

"W...w...work." Henry had to force the word from his mouth, as if his gut wanted to hold on to it, but he eventually spat it out as if it had been a lump of gristle trapped in his throat, constricting his breathing.

Henry continued when he noticed both staring at him blankly.

"I mean. If she contacts us... that means she's... that she's dead, right?"

Henry peered between the two men, observing their differing demeanours he couldn't help but see them as a visual interpretation of his battle-worn conscience; an angel on one side of him, and quite possibly a devil on the other. Josh's face was downcast, as if he couldn't bring himself to state the obvious and tear the wound Henry was holding together wide open. Rowen on the other hand held his gaze with a maniacal glee, nodding his head with such enthusiasm it appeared to Henry as if his neck was made of a spring, like one of those bobblehead toys his daughter had on her now dust covered shelves.

Clarifying out loud what they were about to do, and what it would mean if she answered was a sobering moment indeed, one Henry wasn't prepared for. At group he'd thought it'd be a bit of fun – in for a penny in for a pound – but in the space of an hour, that off the cuff decision had turned ugly and spoiled his mind like a bowl of fruit left in the sun.

Elsie being dead, her body becoming worm food had always been a possibility lurking at the back of Henry's mind, but after tonight, after the séance; if she showed herself and conversed with him, it might just become a reality and there'd be no way he could deny his part in it any longer. He'd know unquestionably that he *was* responsible – for killing her.

"Look, we can leave now and not come back," Josh said, and Henry couldn't work out if it was for his benefit or for his friends, both of them were treading the tightrope of losing their sanity.

"I'm not keeping you here," Rowen uttered from across the table. "But if you leave, you'll never know, for sure I mean... if she's still out there. Don't you want some closure, to feel the unburdening that answer will bring? Surely knowing is better than not – however the coin of fate falls."

Rowen let go of their hands momentarily. Once the link was broken each pulled their hands away, Josh put his in his lap, Henry rubbed his sweaty palm on his jeans before cracking his knuckles and knitting his fingers together in front of him, resting his arms on the table. Rowen though lifted his in the air, one on each side of his body, Henry thought he looked like a plane, but when Rowen spoke, he realised he was making himself look like a pair of weighing scales.

"Dead," his left hand sunk low.

"Or alive," his right hand rose.

"Let's just get out of here man, what you say?" Josh's voice was threaded with panic.

"But if you leave now," Rowen tilted his arms, the scales balancing out. "You'll have nothing, you'll go back to your miserable, insufferable life and continue to perpetuate what you've been doing all along; you'll just keep burying it–"

Henry's eyes snapped up to Rowen: *how does he know about the graves?*

"–all until the day you die."

He doesn't know, that's good Henry mused.

"It'll rot you from within, trust me, unhealed hurt is the root of all suffering, it curdles the brain; bitterness chokes the heart."

Henry nodded.

"You've got to know if you want to heal, if you want to move on and doing that starts with finding out if she's breathing air; or choking on dirt."

"You're such a prick, why would you say something like that? Your mother drop you on your head in your formative years or something?" Josh said sharply.

"Don't you dare bring my mother into this, she's worth ten of you!"

Their voices continued to bubble around Henry as he pondered

Rowen's words – *breathing air; or choking on dirt* – because he needed to know.

"I've heard enough, let's get out of here Henry, this was all a waste of time and energy, he's clearly delusional, touched in the bloody noggin." Henry glanced up as Josh leant across the table, thrusted a thick finger in Rowen's direction. "If I were you, I wouldn't show your face back at group, you're not welcome there anymore. I'm not a violent man, but if I see you sniffing around that place, or us, or any other members of the group again; I swear to the almighty that you'll be spitting teeth and pissing blood for a month, you got that?"

"Oooo... I'm quivering in my little boots over here!" Rowen spat as he reclined in his chair, Henry noted a sardonic grin had stretched across his face.

From the corner of his eye, Henry observed Josh stand up and shuffle away from the table, retreating, but soon stopped at Henry's shoulder when he didn't move to stand. He couldn't even contemplate moving, because he knew Rowen was right. If he got up and left he'd be back where he was, and that was no way to live, he could see it now. He'd spent far too long being chased by her memory and he was bone tired; the not knowing had and continued to ruin him, piece by stinking piece.

"You seem to have forgotten something," Rowen uttered as he flicked a finger at Henry, as if he were a King holding court over his subjects.

"Shut up Rowen, just you stay out of it, you're toxic. I knew from the first moment I laid eyes on you that you were bad fucking news I should have–"

"Sit down." Henry's voice came abruptly into the conversation.

There were tears rolling down his cheeks which he quickly swiped away with his hand.

"Hey man, is everything okay?" Josh's concerned voice.

"You need to sit down man, I can't do this alone. I need my friend right about now."

"Of course, I just thought," Josh quickly sat back at the table.

Henry turned to him.

"I need to know, it's the not knowing that's killing me; I need to know if it was me?"

"If it was you what?"

Henry stared down at the table, he couldn't bear the weight of his friend's gaze.

"Who killed her." Henry said. His eyes never left his hands, which were clamped together like a vice. Henry could tell in the silence that followed his declaration – confession – that Josh was mulling over his words. Rowen too seemed equally shocked at his words, because for what seemed like the first time this evening, since he'd burst onto the scene – with his vicious tongue and his obtrusive devil-may-care attitude – his weasel like voice was suddenly absent.

"You're sure?" Josh asked.

Henry nodded, lifted his gaze and turned his face to Rowen.

"We gotta hold hands and shit again, don't we?" Henry uttered in a voice like gravel.

"I'm afraid we do, it works better that way, in the summoning spirits. If it helps any, once we start, after I've asked them to show themselves, we can all let go, it's only necessary to start proceedings, to be unified in our purpose. Unless you wanna keep holding my hand?" Rowen winked at Henry before holding out his hands to both of them, beckoning the others to take them by wiggling his black-tipped fingers in the air in anticipation.

"Well let's get this over with," Henry growled before taking their hands.

"Once we start, we can't stop, we have to see it through. So, are you ready?"

"Is the Pope Catholic?" Henry said.

"I believe he is, then let us begin," Rowen closed his eyes and bowed his head.

Henry glanced at Josh who was staring back at him. Josh nodded his head and mouthed '*Are you sure?*' Henry nodded back as Rowen brought their attention back to him as he spoke with authority to the shadowlands of lost souls.

"Tonight, we are here to contact the spirit of Elsie Clark. If you are here with us please make your presence known. We also welcome any good spirits to aid in our search, come forth... we welcome you to this place."

There was a pause, Rowen kept his eyes closed and head bowed.

"Is that it?" Josh whispered after a time.

Rowen's head snapped up, his eyes shot open. A knowing smile began to stretch across his face, it grew so wide Henry thought his face would split open.

"No. Now we wait."

And wait they did.

———

THE CRYSTAL WAS SWINGING BACKWARDS AND FORWARDS IN HUGE PENDULOUS swings. It showed no signs of stopping.

The glass which had been on the table was shattered against the far wall.

Henry had seen it slide over and cover the word HELLO. No sooner had it encircled that word it was thrown from the table by an unseen force, where it barely missed Josh's head.

They were no longer holding hands, which Henry was happy about, not because he thought it was rather queer to be holding hands in the dark with two guys, but because now he knew they couldn't feel his hands shaking with fear.

A candle blew out.

Then another.

Henry turned to look at Josh. He was breathing heavily, his eyes desperately imploring the remaining candles to stay aflame.

"Elsie, are you with us?" Rowen cried loudly into the room to be heard over the howling wind that had picked up outside the open sash window.

Something banged in the far corner, deep in a pocket of shadow, Henry turned his head but couldn't see anything.

His head snapped around as books tumbled from a dresser to the floor.

Something brushed past him in the dark and he flinched.

Josh flinched next.

Whatever it was appeared to be moving around the table.

Next up would be Rowen.

The floorboards creaked.

Something was stalking them in the shadows.

"Use me, I will be your vessel, speak for your servant is listening!" Rowen shouted as he held out his hands and turned his face up to the Heavens; Henry thought there was something odd about how it looked, but a sudden crack shattered his thoughts as a lamp toppled over and landed on the floor.

Another candle was snuffed out, Rowen's face was now swarmed by the shadows.

Henry heard Josh whimpering next to him.

He reached out a hand and clamped it over his friend's shoulder. Josh was shaking uncontrollably. His friend turned to him slowly in the half-light from the remaining candle. He couldn't see his friend's mouth clearly but he was sure Josh had said: 'God help us'.

No sooner had Henry read Josh's lips, his friend's head snapped away and Henry observed his eyes grow wide and his lip begin to tremble.

Henry followed his friend's petrified gaze.

The pendulous crystal had stopped swinging. No one had touched it. It hung over the centre of the table as if it were a plumb line, there wasn't even a tremor in the cord that bound it to the ceiling, nor a single rotation of the crystal on its end.

It was utterly still.

Or had it been stilled by something unseen? Henry mused gravely.

A muttering rose from across the table, a strange amalgamation of vowels and chattering teeth.

Peering into the gloom which had feasted on the features of Rowen's face, Henry could just about make out Rowen's lips, they were moving. Unintelligible words which sounded as if he were trying to speak many languages at once grew louder in the room.

"Even though I walk through the valley of the shadow of death," Josh's voice rose above Rowen's babbling, as if both men were competing to be heard above the other, and Henry mused that they'd been doing that all evening in some way or the other.

An ear-splitting shriek came from the other side of the table.

Josh stopped his prayer instantly.

Rowen's head snapped back and his arms went slack at his sides.

His body began to convulse in the chair.

The legs rattling a bedlam into the room as they clattered against the hard, oak floor.

"I SHALL FEAR NO EVIL, FOR YOU ARE WITH ME!" Josh started where he'd left off once he'd peeled his eyes away from the twitching Rowen. Josh buried his head in his hands and began rocking himself slowly back and forth.

Henry was about to comfort his friend again when his eyes alighted on the crystal.

It was beginning to revolve in small circles, slowly at first, but as he watched on, the arcs gradually grew wider as its speed increased.

It was flying now.

The twine suddenly snapped and it flew across the room, smashing through a pane of glass and into the night beyond the window.

Rowen was still fitting in his chair.

The wooden legs rattling maddeningly against the floorboards.

"YOUR ROD AND YOUR STAFF, THEY COMFORT ME!" Josh screamed; eyes closed, hands firmly pressed over his ears, desperately trying to drown out all that was happening around them.

Rowen suddenly stopped fitting.

His head snapped forward at such sickening speed that when it stopped Henry heard his teeth clop together. Two wet orbs reflected the light from the candle, Rowen was staring straight at him from across the table.

"Rowen? Are you okay?" Henry uttered, as he leant closer.

Josh opened his eyes, removed his hands from his ears and peered in the same direction as Henry.

"Rowen?" Henry asked again, concern threading his voice.

Rowen stared back at Henry with a blank expression before edging forward into the light which stole the feasting shadows, revealing his face afresh.

Rowen's mouth was a dark crescent, which inched wider and wider, displaying a maw full of teeth that seemed too many for a mouth to contain.

"Rowen isn't here anymore," the smiling Rowen uttered, his voice had changed, it seemed feminine, a few octaves higher than his usual voice. Henry and Josh both recoiled as a hideous stench poured forth with his utterance, it smelled to Henry like flyblown meat.

Josh pushed his chair away from the table and began to rise.

"Sit down!" Rowen demanded. The smile was gone in an instant.

Josh collapsed back in his chair but pushed it further away from the thing that sat opposite him.

"So, who are you?" Henry's voice was steady, although every fibre of his being was rattled.

"Don't you recognise me?"

Henry shook his head.

"It's been a while, I don't blame you," the smile was etching itself back on Rowen's face again.

"Who are you?"

"You know who I am."

"Just tell me, I'm about two seconds from standing up from this table and walking out of this whole shitshow-"

"I'm your abomination, that's what you called me once!"

Henry flinched at the remark, he braced himself to flee the table.

"Don't leave, why don't you stay a while, we've so much to catch up on."

"Then tell me who I'm speaking to?"

Rowen inclined his head slightly, as if he were taking great interest in inspecting the specimen before him.

"If I wasn't wearing this skin, you'd know who I am, but needs must when the Devil's driving right?"

"And who are you?" Henry shouted across the table.

"Filthy dirty whore!" Rowen spat before giggling.

"Out with it, I ain't playing!" Henry's voice was emboldened but where that strength came from he couldn't tell, because inside he felt as if he had ice in his veins.

"Isn't it obvious?"

"Tell me goddamnit, I need to hear you say it... I have a right to know, I deserve to know who I'm talking to!" Henry slammed his hand onto the table.

Rowen slammed his hand onto the table which was louder than Henry's.

Josh jumped in his seat.

They observed each other for a moment before Rowen leaned across the table, towards them, inching ever closer to the candle, closer to Henry and Josh.

"Hello daddy," Rowen uttered sweetly before blowing out the remaining candle.

The room went black and a hellish cackle erupted in the dark.

Henry felt something grip his shoulder.

It pulled him from his chair and began to haul him away, to where he had no idea.

Henry tripped as he was forced backwards, fell to the ground with a hard thud.

He heard something approaching from where Rowen had been.

Loud padding footsteps on the ground that sounded like many legs, as if whatever was coming was running on four legs.

It was coming at him fast.

But he was being dragged even quicker, enabling him to stay just out of reach.

There was a great crash, Henry assumed it was the table being upended.

Suddenly there was a sliver of light which cut through the stygian darkness.

The room was now divided in two.

A door had been opened.

Henry was hauled from the room into the stairwell.

Peering through the door he saw a shadow-clad figure.

Was that figure still Rowen, or were they now Elsie? Henry mused as his legs kicked at the floor to find purchase.

He couldn't tell, they stood half-in and half-out of the light.

They soon slipped into the welcoming darkness.

Their presence extinguished in a single moment.

There was suddenly sobbing.

Loud.

Awful.

Gut-wrenching sobbing.

It was his.

Henry was still sobbing when he was pulled to his feet unceremoniously and pushed down the corridor.

Soon he was running.

Running away from his daughter again.

As they hit the street he stopped dead in his tracks, bent over and threw up.

Josh stood next to him, hands on his knees, out of breath.

He was as white as a sheet.

Henry glanced up to his friend.

Translucent cables of snot and sick dribbled from his chin.

"I killed her Josh; she's dead!"

CHAPTER SEVEN

Henry was on his hands and knees, crawling his way over broken glass.

The room was as dark as pitch but still he lifted his hands to inspect their ruin.

It was a fruitless affair.

However close he brought his hands to his face, he couldn't see a thing.

But he *could* smell them.

The iron-rich, ripe tang of blood.

He winced as his racing breath wafted over the shredded remains of his palms.

Holding his hands aloft, as if imploring a higher power to intervene, he felt the warm trickle of blood run down his forearms, snaking its way lazily to the creases of his elbows.

In the now quiet dark, where before there'd been utter chaos; Henry heard his spilled blood, which had pooled at his elbows, drip to the hardwood floor.

Tap. Tap. Tap.

He shifted position and in doing so he heard the crunch, before he felt the glass shatter beneath him, puncturing his knees. The pain forced him back down on all fours where he tried desperately to distribute his body weight over a larger surface area which, in doing so, he hoped would alleviate the sudden burst of agony which had suddenly flared and laid claim to his knees. He knew the glass hadn't finished with him yet and as his hands came down on the splintery shards he winced, but could do nothing to alleviate his pain as the unforgiving glass feasted with a renewed vigour on his already damaged appendages.

He felt his blood pooling quickly underneath each palm, warm and wet.

He began to crawl – he hoped – away from the carpet of shards, but it was hard to tell in a room with no light and nothing in the all-consuming blackness to orientate himself with, so he helplessly and haplessly struggled on.

His fingers led the way, dancing over the glass like a blind man reading Braille – if the book he was reading was called 'pain and suffering'.

Placing one hand in front of the other he hauled himself over the clinking, snapping, crunching surface which, for all he knew, could cover the entire floor. His groping, tacky hands felt weighted down and they were; they'd collected glass like honey does bees, each raking movement, each forearm pressed into the ground which dragged his body ever forwards, drove the collected shards deeper and took his pain to new unfathomable heights.

But soon his diligent quest for comfort in a room full of pain came to an end.

The floor beneath his fingers changed, it was soft and thick, and it felt like home.

Henry hauled himself onto the rug before turning onto his back, laying his shredded hands across his chest, how someone would more than likely arrange a body in a coffin.

Suddenly, the thing he was fleeing made its presence known once more.

"Aren't we going to finish our game?" Elsie's voice asked from the void.

Henry rolled over onto his chest, he needed to keep moving, to stay motionless was to give in – surrender – so, he lifted his aching arms out, grabbed tufts of the rug in each hand and pulled as if his life depended on it, and in a way, it did.

In the stillness that had presided before Elsie spoke, he'd had time to orientate himself. The rug, which had become his temporary refuge was in front of his dresser, the door to his bedroom should be dead ahead, but he hadn't a clue which way was he facing. He cursed himself for drinking so much when he'd got back from Rowen's, but he'd needed it because he desperately wanted to drown himself and the truth he'd come to know that night; he just didn't know how successful he'd been in achieving that goal until now, floundering on the floor not knowing which way was up or down, or which direction led further into the darkness or which path would take him into the light.

All this glass, it must have been the bottle. Did I throw it at her when she appeared?

Henry relinquished his grip on the rug and reached out a shredded, trembling hand into the darkness to his right. It was trembling not with pain but fear.

He had visions of his inquisitive hand coming into contact with a face, Elsie's face; hiding next to him in the dark, watching him suffer, *how she loved to watch me suffer* he mused. He didn't have a choice; he had to know. He needed to get away from her and so he extended his trembling, fearful hand into the dark.

He couldn't reach as far as he needed and so he shuffled his aching body across the rug to gain a few extra inches of reach. His searching fingers soon alighted upon the dresser and he realised with relief he was indeed facing the way he needed to be.

With a renewed hope of escape, he frantically set about grabbing tufts of the rug and heaving himself away from the thing that had followed him home from Rowen's.

"Don't you wanna play with your *sick* little daughter?" Her voice came again from the dark.

With each inch of the ground he covered, his hands screamed out with pain. His feet had entered the fray, scrambling to find purchase but failing due to the pain which flared in each of his busted knees when he tried to extend them thanks to the shards of glass which were keeping him a prisoner of the ground. But he slithered onwards like the snake he knew he was; desperately hoping Elsie's boot wouldn't stamp the life out of him. He wouldn't hold it against her if she did – she had every right to, especially after what he'd done.

He remained quiet throughout his struggles, in the vain hope he'd remain hidden.

"Filthy whore," Elsie uttered menacingly, she sounded closer.

Henry scrambled, ignoring the pain that wracked his body; she was coming for him.

"Delusional dyke," Elsie was closer still.

He felt the rug disappear below his hands, his fingers resting on the coolness of polished floorboards.

"ABOMINATION!" she screamed and Henry heard the glass rattling behind him from the timbre of her shriek.

He continued on. His hands rising in large raking motions – as if he were swimming – before slapping wetly on the ground, driving the stubborn shards of glass further into his palms. His blood seemed to be congealing now and it aided him in finding much needed purchase on the polished wood as each sticky hand slammed down on the floor and pulled him to safety, he thanked the stars for small blessings in a room which housed many curses.

He was pulling away from her, edging ever closer to safety.

Suddenly there was a thud behind him, quickly followed by another, then the unmistakable sound of lumbering footsteps; she'd had enough of playing with her food, now Elsie was coming to finish him off and he knew she was ravenous.

Thud. Thud.

"Where are you going?" she teased as Henry continued to drag himself closer to the door, feeling like a bird this prowling cat was toying with before she finished him off.

Thud. Thud. Thud.

"You know you can't escape me, right? You carry me with you wherever you go..."

Henry threw another arm out and it hit the door.

I've made it, he mused, but he still needed to open it.

Thud. Thud. Crunch.

She was closer now, she'd entered the glass fields, and Henry knew it was now or never.

He pulled himself closer to the door, curled his broken body up at its base as if he were a child shielding themselves against an approaching, vengeful parent. He reached up blindly and after a few inquisitive swipes his bloodied hand wrapped itself around the doorknob, but he couldn't find any purchase, his blood-slick palm slipping around the metal as if it had been smeared in grease.

Crunch. Snap. Crunch. Snap.

"If you leave don't you ever come back!" Elsie's voice had become deep and gravelly.

Henry thought she was warning him and he pondered in his rising panic that if he could ever open this door, he'd run until he coughed up his lungs, coming back here was the furthest thing from his mind.

But he soon came to realise that Elsie wasn't speaking about his current plight, or the room he was desperately trying to flee; she was speaking *at* him, with words he recognised, words he'd memorised, because after all they were his words, his final words, which he'd regretted every day, week and year that had passed in a miserable blur.

"You sent me away," she uttered again and paused.

Henry could hear her laboured breathing in the dark and it sounded animalistic in nature.

Henry frantically began wiping his hands on his jeans, wincing as the shards of glass caught in the fabric, where they were imbedded deeper into his raw hands with each wipe. He lifted both of them to the doorknob, found the slightest of purchases and began to turn the handle.

"STOP!" she screamed. Henry heard the door rattle behind him in its frame from the force of her outburst.

His fingers were clinging on, the handle was turning; if he let go now he knew he'd fall into the abyss and be lost forever.

Crunch. Crunch.

There was an eerie silence which seemed to stretch on for eternity which was suddenly broken by a sound that made Henry's heart skip a beat.

Thud.

Henry's hands momentarily stopped with their fussing, his head turned to face the darkness.

The recent *thud* meant Elsie had traversed the glass and the rug, which meant she was mere feet away from him, but the darkness kept her hidden as if it were a garment she was shrouded in, and for that Henry was grateful; he didn't have the heart or the courage to see what he'd caused her to become. He let his arms fall and placed his palms on the ground on either side of his body, pressing down and grimacing against the stabbing pains that traversed his arms in waves of shooting pain he hoisted himself into a seated position; his back firmly against the door, there was no escape for him and so he wanted to face his demise head on.

He could smell her foulness, her *decomposition.*

The same awful miasma which had appeared at the séance was filling the room.

How he wished he could have remained ignorant to her fate; *ignorance is bliss* he'd heard people say, and they were right, because what Rowen had brought back was an unvarnished, hellish truth.

Thud. Thud. Thud. THUD. THUD. THUD. THUD.

Henry shrunk back from the onrushing sound of hammering feet.

The air suddenly stirred as something – two things – hit the door either side of his head. This close to whatever was veiled in the dark smelled atrocious; he felt his gorge rising as the stench of rotten fish and putrefied meat washed over him. It took him a moment to realise that Elsie had him pinned up to the door, the stench which washed over him, made his eyes water and brought bile to the back of his throat was her foul breath.

She was face to face with him now, and still he could not see her.

"You did this to me," her voice was a whisper.

There was movement and he suddenly felt her cold, dead, hands crawl on to his shoulders.

She pulled him closer and he let her because there was no fight left in him.

He could feel her breath at his ear, whatever she was about to say she didn't want him missing it.

"I'm going to enjoy making you suffer, daddy."

THUD. THUD. THUD.

Henry could hear someone or something else in the room.

THUD. THUD. THUD. THUD.

Elsie relinquished her grip and he felt her hands climb slowly down his body.

THUD. THUD.

She was at his ankle now and he feared she was about to drag him back into the room.

He felt her relinquish her grip and then she was gone.

THUD. THUD. THUD.

Where's that sound coming from?

Henry craned his neck, pressed his ear up to the door.

RIIINNNGGGG. THUD. THUD. RIIINNNGGG.

Henry bolted up in bed.

Someone was at his door. He peered around his room but it was dark, not as dark as the place he'd just left, but still it took him a moment for the world to gain a semblance of clarity, haphazard shapes he recognised began to solidify in the gloom. He scanned the room briefly, desperately trying to see if she'd followed him here, into his waking world. Turning up nothing he swung his legs out of bed and winced at the pain coursing through and from his hand.

He held it up in front of him and noticed a deep cut across his palm.

He glanced down and from the dim glow of the streetlight which crept through his parted curtains he noticed below him, on the floorboards, where he was about to place his feet, was a shattered bottle of whiskey – once again he was thankful for small mercies.

He shuffled up to the head of the bed where the floor appeared to be clear of glass and hit the light on his bedside clock: 5:30 am.

BANGBANGBANGBANG.

Someone was desperately trying to get his attention, hammering at the door like the police with a search warrant. He knew it wouldn't be the cops, and so Henry wondered, *who the hell cares enough for me to be hammering at my door at 5:30 in the fucking morning?*

His mind was still groggy from the whiskey and the dream but the answer found its way through his brain-fog quickly enough: *Josh.*

He'd left Josh in a state, that was for sure, pondering life's big questions and if the Heaven he believed in was still real or a fairy-tale made up to lighten the catastrophic blow of death's finality. If Henry's dream had been anything to go by, he wondered what monstrosity had been waiting to ambush his friend once he got home to his own empty house full of memories.

"I'M COMING!" Henry yelled as he got to his feet, the room spinning around him.

He shuffled slowly towards the door, taking great care and attention to stay upright but stopped quickly in his tracks when he noticed blood slicking the doorknob and dribbling down the face of the door.

"What the fu– ?" He began to say before the thudding recommenced at the door.

"I SAID I'M COMING! STOP YOUR BLOODY HAMMERING!"

CHAPTER EIGHT

Cradling his cut hand which was throbbing like a bitch, Henry took his first faltering step down the darkened staircase.

He paused after a few steps, peering through the spindles at the darkness pooling below. His eyes then scanned higher, observing the dark corners of the landing he'd just left. Every inky void was a place where something could hide and he couldn't shake the feeling that something *had* followed him back to the waking world from his nightmare; and its name was Elsie.

The words she'd uttered rose in his mind: *I'm going to make him suffer.*

THUD. THUD. THUD.

"I'm coming. Don't go getting your knickers in a twist!" Henry yelled back before dangling a foot over the next step. When nothing reached through the spindles to grab his ankle and pull him to the ground, he lowered his foot all the way; and before he knew it he was halfway down the staircase, moving at pace.

Goosebumps broke out across his flesh as he neared the last few steps.

The air down here was frigid. He shuddered and almost lost his footing. His good hand shot out and grasped the bannister where he almost pulled it back from shock; the glossed paintwork was like a block of ice.

He glanced down to discover it was covered in a fine layer of frost.

"What the—" Henry's words died in his throat at the sight of his breath clouding around him. He hurried down the final few steps and paused when he was on surer footing. It was as if he'd descended into a walk-in freezer instead of the ground floor of his house; he half-expected to find sides of beef strung up by great ruddy hooks running all the way down the corridor, the pink, reddish meat turned a dull shade of blue from the cold.

He glanced down at his hand, since the light afforded by the glass in the front door and the outside streetlamp enabled him to see the wound more clearly. It was deep and about three inches long. He stretched his fingers wide and the wound on his palm winked open like a bloodied eye, but there was no flow of fresh blood, which struck him as odd.

Am I still asleep?

He lifted his other hand and pushed an inquisitive finger into the wound.

"Damn it to fuckity fuck!" Henry screamed, the pain was a special kind of hell reserved just for him, as he shook out his damaged hand before quickly stuffing it under his armpit where he hugged it to his body using his other arm.

Definitely awake. So, why's it so damned cold?

A cool breeze stole through the house and tickled his neck, he flinched and quickly spun around; it reminded him fleetingly of the breeze he felt at Rowen's as the entity, the ghost, his daughter – Henry didn't know what the hell to call it – had worked its way around the table before entering Rowen.

Possessing him Henry pondered darkly as he searched around him for the fleeing presence, but the draft which he came to realise – and not a person – was coming from the kitchen.

He shuffled towards it now, fear slowing his steps considerably. The door was a black void to what could have been another dimension, a gateway that housed every shred of darkness the world possessed – *that word again just a subtle difference.* He scoffed at his own musing before all humour left his mind when he caught sight of the back door which was hanging wide open.

THUD. THUD. THUD.

Henry snapped his head towards the front door.

An ominous figure stood the other side of the frosted glass.

It was clear to him that they weren't going to leave without talking to him, if they were anything, they were persistent. He watched the looming figure raise their hand to bang at his door again.

"I'm coming!" he spat angrily and they instantly lowered their hand.

Henry peered over his shoulder as he skulked away from the kitchen, wondering if whomever had gained entry was still in there, crouched in the shadows; or were they somewhere else in the house. Fear of the unknown slowed his pace to a crawl as he inched past each darkened doorway that lined the corridor as he lumbered his way inch-by-inch to receive his visitor.

He reached the door and placed a hand on the lock, paused.

"Who is it?" he said.

"It's me," a feminine voice replied in a raised whisper.

Henry shook his head, turned the lock and began to open the door.

"Kiera what the–"

The slap cut his words short and sent him careening into the open door. He was pretty sure if he hadn't been holding onto it, the blow would have sent him sprawling across the floor on his arse.

"You're sick in the head... do you know that!" she unloaded on him.

"Bloody hell Kiera, you hit me in the fucking ear," Henry uttered through gritted teeth as he righted himself and stared at his ex-wife.

"You deserve that and more, but I can see by your face that some-one's already given you a good going over, deserved it too no doubt," she stood there staring at him. "Well? You going to explain your boat race?"

Henry loved the way his wife slipped back into her cockney roots when she was angry, it took him a moment to recall the slang, but then it fell into place. He lifted up a hand and framed his face.

"Occupational hazard," he said coquettishly before winking at her.

"Only if your occupation is being an utter prick!" she tilted her head at him. "You do know you're bleeding, right?"

"Yep," Henry said nonchalantly, hiding his hand behind his back. "Cut myself doing the gardening."

Kiera peered at the overgrown front garden and then back at him.

"In the back, the back garden, I've decided to let this one become a bit of a wild meadow–"

"I haven't got time for this shit Henry, why'd you do it?"

"Do what?"

"You know what, don't play all innocent with me, just tell me why?"

"Look Kiera I've had a shit day, a worse night and I don't have a clue what you're talking about, you haven't been in here have you?"

"In the house?" her face screwed up at the thought.

"Yeah."

"Henry, I wouldn't set foot in this house if you turned up dead and they needed someone to identify the body."

"Harsh," Henry uttered back.

Someone coughed in the distance, and Henry peered past Kiera where he found Matthew leaning against their car; two children were sat in the back looking at him, misting up the glass with their breath, one of them had drawn a smiley face, but the condensation had started to run and the mouth had dissolved into something menacing.

"I see you brought the nonce!" Henry nodded in Matthew's direction.

"Henry, please. Play nice."

"And the kids, what is this a family outing?"

"We're going away for a while... I was coming to... I wanted to tell you..."

"Just spit it out would you."

"We've changed our number."

"You drove over here at six in the morning to tell me you've changed your number?"

"Yes, and we're going away."

"I know you already told me that."

"No, far away Henry, somewhere where you won't be able to bother us any longer, we're moving–"

"Bothering you, I barely talk to you anymore, you never answer my calls."

"Exactly, you call, and when you do it's a bother. You need professional help..."

"So, you're leaving me? Us?"

"I left you a long time ago Henry, and let me make it clear, there's no *us*, she's gone..."

Henry held on to the door for dear life, his legs felt as if at any moment they'd collapse from under him. He couldn't help but think that everyone he'd ever loved was leaving him, and the common denominator was him: *it's all my fault.*

"So, what did I do now then?" he offered with a petulant shoulder shrug.

"Don't play dumb with me Henry, you know exactly what you did; it's unforgivable!"

"I don't have the foggiest–" he paused as Kiera leant forwards, his heart skipped a beat as she drew closer, her face swimming into clarity, he imagined her kissing him like she'd done countless times over their years together, before he'd finally driven her away with his obsession. She stopped an inch from his face and having her so close but still so far away was torturous. Kiera sniffed the air between them and pulled away sharply.

"Thought so," she said with a knowing smirk.

"What?"

"You're drunk or you were drunk, either way it doesn't excuse what you did. Who'd you put up to it?"

"Up to what?"

"Stop playing games with me, it's too damn early and I'm too damn tired, if you won't tell me who you had do it, just tell me why you did it?"

"FOR CRYING OUT LOUD WOMAN," Henry shouted back. He saw movement by the car; Matthew had instinctively pushed himself up from his leaning position, readying himself to come to his wife's aid at a moment's notice – *smug prick* Henry mused.

"It's okay," Kiera said over her shoulder and Matthew stayed put.

"Tell me what I supposedly did or get the fuck off my step."

Kiera rummaged in her pocket, pulled out her phone before swiping it open where she commenced furiously tapping at the screen. She thrusted it at him but kept it firmly clamped between her fingers and Henry noted the shellac, brown nail polish that adorned each finger; reminded him of dirt, grave dirt.

"Here," she said, the phone was trembling in her outstretched hand.

"What is it?"

"I recorded it from our answering machine, two hours ago, don't go pretending you don't know!" Kiera used her other hand and clicked the play icon on the screen and held it out again where Henry was almost felled by the voice that greeted him.

"Hello mummy," it was Elsie's voice, like she'd never been away, alive; not dead.

"Congratulations on your new family... and might I just say, they look good enough to eat," Elsie tittered her little laugh and the sound broke Henry's heart afresh as well as chilling the marrow in his bones.

"Samuel has your lopsided smile and little Rachel she's got your almond shaped eyes, not to mention their colour... those deep dark blues you could drown in. Who knows, maybe one day she might, drown I mean; when you're not paying attention, like you were this evening... when you were doing the nasty with your new man about the house, Matthew isn't it?"

Henry glanced at Kiera who'd averted her eyes; he noted though as she tried to look anywhere else other than at her ex-husband that her cheeks were flushed red with embarrassment.

"You looked like you were enjoying yourself; he seemed to be giving it to you hard, pleasing you deeply like daddy never could. The way you moaned and screamed and raked those luscious, brown, fingernails down his back... I thought you were fighting for your life... but you were just enjoying being fucked." Elsie tutted on the recording, "You were making the beast with two backs whilst your children, my dear siblings; were sleeping *alone* and unprotected in the next room. Anything could have happened to them and you'd have been none the wiser as you moaned and writhed in ecstasy."

Henry peered past Kiera, observed the children in the car; they were both present, no signs of harm, they were safe – for now.

"Don't worry, I watched over them whilst you got your *fill*... they didn't even know I was there; I'm not surprised though, you and dad didn't even see me when I was alive, so there's no chance anyone could see me now I'm dead."

"Kiera I'm–" Henry started to speak but Kiera cut him off by swiftly lifting her hand, her watch jangled on her wrist as she placed an index finger to her lips, her pain-filled eyes flaying him where he stood.

"You all seem so happy together," Elsie continued. "Happier than I ever made you, that's quite clear, looks like you've been sleeping with a coat hanger in your mouth, or was that Matthew's doing?" Elsie tittered again. "I've seen how you mother them, coddle them, kiss them good night after you've read them a bedtime story; and how you cook your darling children pancakes on lazy Saturday mornings at the kitchen table."

"It's good you've found a way to find a semblance of joy in all this chaos, really and truly I'm happy for you... but I can't say I'm not disappointed in how quickly you've moved on or how you've even forgotten you carried me in your body and brought me kicking and screaming into the world. I've seen how when someone asks you how many children you have when you're at the checkout making idle chitchat; that you smile sweetly and demurely as you pull their photograph from your purse and reply with 'two' – thrusting your children in their faces. I've observed you countless times repeating the same actions but every time you do, you fail to mention me, your first. Your dear, dear, Elsie."

"I don't need to listen to–" Henry started again.

"Oh, you do, trust me, it gets better," Kiera replied sharply before Elsie's voice returned.

"Daddy hasn't forgotten me, although he's tried numerous times, but he can't quite shake me, unlike you!" There was venom in her voice now. "Have you seen the graves he's been digging, there are twelve of them now, each one holds a piece of me, the pieces I apparently left behind; and he tends those graves with such great care and attention."

It was Henry's turn to look sheepish now as Kiera's eyes found him at the mention of the graves. He knew it was one of the many things that pushed her away, their presence something she despised, and as he stood there, having her judging eyes rove over his forlorn demeanour again was too much for him to face head on, so he stared at his aching, bloodied hand.

"If only he cared that much for me when I was with you both, maybe I'd still be there, still breathing; maybe we'd enjoy pancakes on lazy Saturday mornings? But it'll never be like that, will it? It can't, because daddy stole that from me, and from you; he's the one who sent me away, who demanded I go. And so I did, and well, you know how that panned out don't you?"

Henry felt guilt wriggling in his stomach, a pit of snakes snapping at his softest parts.

"I know you hate him as much as I do, but what I could never understand is: why you let him ruin me and send me away like he did. It was daddy who caused all the heartache and anguish you've tried to cover with a new family, a new life and a new home; as if I were a blemish to be concealed and not a daughter to mourn." There was a sound on the recording which seemed like a choked sob, but it was gone as quickly as it arrived.

"But for all his culpability, his guilt, his failures as a father and no doubt a husband, I can't ever forget that he's also responsible for calling me home, back to you... and now I'm back, I've got work to do. Dad ruined me, and for that he'll pay, and for you remaining silent, for giving up the fight – I'm going to take delight in ruining you too, by the end I'll have taken everything you both hold dear."

"I'll be sticking around for a while, I might even pay a visit to little Samuel and Rachel tomorrow, they'll be at the park I guess, well that's what's written on your calendar; I'm sure they'll be delighted to see their big sister..." Elise descended into a fit of giggles. "Don't think I won't. There are lots of places to hide in the park, and I'll know when they've strayed too far from your watchful gaze, I'll know when they're alone, when you're distracted, we'll have ourselves a long-overdue family reunion, I promise; I won't bite, or maybe I will."

Kiera lifted a hand and brushed away a few tears that had spilt down her cheek.

"Was I not enough for you to hold out for, for you to fight and grieve for?"

Henry could feel his own tears cooling on his face too, he had no idea they'd fallen.

"You're both as guilty as sin... and I'll continue to make you both suffer, the way I've suffered, the way I still do... suffer!"

Kiera pulled the phone away, tapped the screen and held it in her hands. Henry noticed Kiera's hands were trembling but couldn't work out if it was because of the cold, anger or fear; he wanted nothing more than to bury them in his and make them stop shaking, but he couldn't, she was no longer his to comfort in such a way.

"Who you put up to it?" she said resolutely, tapping her foot, staring him down.

"No one, I... I..." Henry was still too busy trying to compute what he'd just heard to be able to come up with a response, he knew his answer would have been '*no one*' – but his silence and apparent apathy at answering such a straightforward question caused Kiera to rage on him all the more.

"Have you been watching the house? Watching us? How could they know those things, if they hadn't been?" She was spitfiring questions at him, not even waiting for a response.

Henry felt a rage rise within him, it was one-part anger at being accused of something he didn't do, one-part the distressing message from Elsie – who'd *actually* come back; the recording was proof of the fact – and the rest of his rage was made up by imagining his wife and Matthew – who'd gone back to leaning against their car – who'd been *giving it* to his wife, and apparently better than he ever had.

"It wasn't me Kiera... I swear," Henry stepped forwards, Kiera stepped back.

"It's too much Henry, we're going... and you're not, I repeat NOT going to try and find us, if you do for whatever reason happen to track us down, Matthew is going to call the police."

"The police?" Henry questioned incredulously.

"I already had to talk him down from calling them tonight, after the message you left; he's serious, and so am I, if you try to find us, contact us again... you'll wish you hadn't–"

"Is that a threat, are you seriously threatening me right now?"

"It's not a threat, it's a promise. Get some help... just looking at what you've become, the depths you've gone to just to cause me pain is spiteful Henry. And getting some other deluded soul to call our house and impersonate our daughter, to threaten my kids, having them spy on our lives... it's... it's... insane is what it is."

"But, I–"

"I can't even believe I loved you once. Looking at what you've become just sickens me... to my very core, goodbye, have a good life!"

Kiera turned and began to walk away. Henry rushed forwards a few steps like a man possessed and grabbed her wrist before tugged her back. Kiera wouldn't budge. As Henry continued to jerk on her arm, pull her around to face him, he noticed Matthew push himself up from the car and hurriedly charge towards the busted gate at the end of Henry's path.

"Look at me," Henry was pleading as he shook her arm by her wrist.

Matthew was through the gate now, plodding down the path towards them.

Kiera tried to pull her arm free, not willing to turn back to the man she was leaving.

"Let her go Henry, you've done enough tonight already, you want to end up in a cell?" Matthew's voice came loud and clear, another firm threat.

"Look at me Kiera... please?" Henry pleaded a final time.

Kiera stopped struggling and lifted her other hand, holding it palm out to the advancing Matthew, he slowed at the silent command and stood at a short distance; Henry was momentarily glad she'd stilled her husband's advance because he didn't know if he could take him in a brawl, not in his current state.

"Please, just look at me and I won't ask anything of you ever again."

Kiera turned and as she did Henry released his grip on her wrist.

She took her wrist in her other hand and rubbed at the ache, Henry noticed the red finger welts already present, he had no idea how much he didn't want her to leave until he noticed those marks ringing her wrist, which would become bruises in the next few days, a final reminder of him on her skin, but it would fade in time along with her memories of him.

Kiera folded her arms and tapped her foot again; the picture of impatience, before fixing him with a glare that could curdle milk.

"Well?" she said with a head shake.

Henry was busy processing what to say. Should he tell her what he'd been up to tonight? How he'd brought their daughter back and how she'd spoken to him already the previous night, through the *possessed* Rowen? She already thought he was losing his mind, how would throwing a séance into the mix work, she'd probably call the men in white coats and have him dragged off into the night like some lunatic – he shook his head, no; that wouldn't do at all.

As he took in the utter disgust she held for him in her eyes – where there used to be love – he knew everything he'd hoped to reclaim was lost. There was no point hurting her any more than he already had, and so he stayed quiet.

Now was her time to heal, and his time to suffer alone; completely and utterly alone.

So, with tears welling in his eyes, Henry did the first kind thing he'd done in twelve long years.

He let her go.

"I'm sorry... *truly* sorry for everything I ever did to you and Elsie, and for what I've become. You deserved better and you got it... in the end." Henry nodded past Kiera to Matthew who was still lurking a few feet away. Kiera turned, observed who Henry was referring to and when she turned back she was smiling, but there was no warmth in it, it was a sad smile, full of pity and good riddance.

"Enjoy your life," Henry said, "and don't ever take it for granted; the love you have... like I did..." his voice broke into a sob, the rest of the words he wanted to say died in his throat, but he felt he'd said his piece and now he could let her go, knowing she knew he'd loved her once, but the truth of the matter was he still loved her.

Kiera didn't respond, she just turned slowly and meandered up the path to her new husband who wrapped a comforting arm around her shoulder – how Henry wished that arm was his, so he could hold his wife one last time – before ushering her to the car where they'd soon drive away into their new happy lives, devoid of him and the memory of their daughter.

As Henry closed the door, he pondered about love; a true love, a selfless love, and how it trumped the ravaging feeling of grief; in a way love was the most pernicious emotion of them all and it didn't care who it ruined.

He leant his back against the door as he fiddled with his wedding band.

He gave thought about taking it off, right there and then; closing that chapter of his life for good. All thought of removing it, of ending that promise he'd made to his wife when they were young and in love and life was full of endless possibilities for those who loved one another, fled his mind when he noticed the muddy footprints leading from the kitchen to the foot of the stairs.

As he stared in abject horror, he realised there were no returning footsteps.

Whoever – whatever – had made them was still in the house.

Henry heard Matthew's car accelerating away, taking the only thing he had left in this world that meant something to him with it into a life that finally excluded him. He contemplated turning around, throwing open the door and fleeing the house, chasing after them, begging them to stop and help him. But he couldn't. For one, he was too proud to beg and secondly, doing so would mean turning his back on whatever or whoever was lurking in this hellish, shadow-clad place he called home.

Edging his way forward, he took time to navigate the narrow corridor, peering intently at each darkened pool of shadow and each open doorway he passed.

The yellow glow from the streetlamp offered only a dim luminosity as he crept further away from the safety of the front door. He'd opted not to turn on the hall lights, some things were best to remain in the dark, and whatever was here, in the house with him now, although he was searching, he willed it to remain hidden – out of sight, out of mind.

If it was Elsie – which he assumed it had to be – he didn't have the strength left in him to see what he'd turned her into, of what had come back from the place beyond, and so he'd continue moving deeper into the darkened house. But he knew whatever came for him wouldn't be pretty, she was dead after all; and given the muddy footprints, it appeared she'd just climbed out of whatever muddy grave had held her captive these years; *is she more ghoul than ghost*, Henry mused, *or something much worse?*

As he neared the bottom of the stairs he noticed that the single track of footprints spread out, they appeared to almost walk in a circle, but as he observed this apparent strange dance of the dead, he noticed the muddied prints didn't have any tread, they were made by bare feet. *Cold. Dead. Feet.*

Crouching down on his haunches, he observed the tracks closely, he pointed his finger and placed it in the muddy track; it was cold and wet and when he removed his finger the mud clung to the tip. He brushed it off on his trousers and turned his attention to a few prints which moved across the corridor to the table in the hallway.

There were only a couple of items on the table; his phone and Elsie's toy bunny.

It looked different in the half-light and it took Henry a beat to realise what was so different about the bedraggled comforter, then it hit him; its fur was slicked with mud. Half its head and one ear were caked in the stuff, wet and brown, the soft fabric matted with moist sludge, as if it had been picked up, inspected by the intruder and discarded.

Henry couldn't help but think of it as a desecration, and after seeing it, knowing that something dead had touched it, he knew he'd never touch it again. If he picked it up he was sure he'd only smell death and loam; any small comfort that bunny had offered him recently was now lost because instead of his daughter's life which had impregnated its soft innards and of which he'd inhaled deeply; the stale, sweaty aroma of her skin, would now be forever tainted by the bouquet of death.

CREEEEAAKK.

Henry's head snapped to the ceiling at the sound, he'd located it instantly as it was a sound he knew intimately. It was the loose floorboard just inside Elsie's room.

Kiera had moaned at him for longer than he'd care to remember about fixing the creaky board; the one they'd hear moments before their daughter would climb into their bed and tell them that she'd had another nightmare. He'd successfully dodged that thankless job for years, and after Elsie disappeared, there'd really been no point.

Her room had, over time, become out of bounds, a mausoleum for the dead.

Henry smiled; his slovenliness had finally paid off, because now he knew where the tracks which ascended the stairs led, although it wasn't a comforting realisation he at least knew that's where he'd find his home invader. His smile faltered as he rose to his feet. He didn't know what he feared most in that brief moment as he weighed up his option; following the muddied footprints and discovering his dead and decomposing daughter at the end of them, or stepping into Elsie's room which had become a tomb.

He grabbed his phone from the table, stuffed it hurriedly into his pocket, knowing it was better to be safe than sorry and he felt comforted by having a means to call someone if shit hit the fan.

He glanced at the bunny but the sight of it made him angry and he knew that next year, if he got there, he had the next offering prepared and so he walked away from it and it watched him leave with its button eyes and soiled face.

He stepped gingerly around the circle of muddy footprints before reaching for the handrail; it was still cold, he scraped a thumbnail through the accumulated ice and watched slivers of it rise and then fall away into the dark. He shook his head at the sight, still unsure of how it was possible and began to climb the stairs, one aching step at a time; following the soggy and dirty footprints all the way to what he assumed was the wolf's den.

As he climbed higher he wondered how he'd missed them on his way down. *Your mind was elsewhere*, he told himself, *you were more concerned if something had followed you back from that nightmare than looking out for someone leaving great ruddy footprints on the floor.*

Following the muddied footprints higher and higher, he soon wondered if he was right in being concerned about something following him back all along.

He was three steps from the landing, which returned on itself at the top towards Elsie's room. He craned his neck and peered through the spindles, half-expecting to see glistening, onyx eyes, staring back at him in the gloom and below it a mouth, teeth like a burnt fence. His observations turned up nothing and so he steadied himself for what was to come next with a few deep breaths before taking the final steps up onto the landing.

He peered down at the footprints, which never faltered in their resolute and determined stride, all the way to Elsie's door, and so he followed their lead. He pressed himself up against the wall in the narrow corridor, there was something about the footprints that unnerved him and he didn't want to stand where the once dead had.

"Step on a crack, break your back," he murmured nervously to himself as he navigated the landing and followed the muddied path his daughter had left for him to follow.

As he neared the door another creak rang out.

CREEAAAAKKK.

The sound was quickly followed by bare feet padding frantically across the floor, away from the door; the rusted screech of bed springs soon followed, giving credence to something heavy clambering on to his daughter's bed.

Henry felt the sudden urge to run, but not away this time, he wanted to run towards his troubles, get it over and done with, face whatever resided on the other side of that door head on and the fate that awaited him. But his main reason for bursting into that tomb of a room was that he needed to explain to Elsie that he was desperately and hopelessly sorry for what he'd done, he needed to beg for her forgiveness; whether she'd accept it or not, he had to try.

He prepared to run at the door and fling it open, but as he took the first step, his courage fled him instantly as his legs threatened to crumble beneath him.

His daughter's muted sobs found him from behind the closed door.

But soon his daughter's muted cries had risen to a deafening, damnable cacophony which swirled around him, forcing him to clamp his hands over his ears to drown her sorrow-filled weeping out. Her bawling turned quickly to a throat-shredding scream, which although dulled substantially by his hands, weedled its way through the cracks of his fingers and into his ears which caused the fillings in his teeth to rattle and ache; he soon realised it wasn't his teeth, it was his whole body shaking from the force of her lament.

The floor soon began to tremble from the unrestrained resonance of her suffering.

Closing his eyes against the pain and keeping his hands firmly planted over his ears he began to shuffle blindly towards the door. He bumped into the wall shortly after setting out but righted himself before staggering onwards, the sound seemed to be pushing him back but he wouldn't let it. He couldn't – wouldn't – turn away as he'd done so often before, he needed to face this nightmare and own his mistakes, however much it would pain him.

He'd found his way blindly to the door, his forehead was pressed up against it and he could feel the door shaking from the aural tidal-wave that crashed against it, rattling it on its hinges as if something was desperate to get out.

"I'm here Elsie. Daddy's here... I'm coming in!" Henry screamed over the commotion.

No sooner had the words left his mouth, the wall of sound which threatened to tear the flesh from his weary bones died instantly. In the silence that followed the auditory assault, he felt as if something had released its grip on him, as if the unwelcome presence in his house had fled at his declaration of facing his fear.

Although the sound had vanished, it had quickly been replaced by something else. A sickening miasma assaulted his nose, a filthy reek which Henry recognised because it was the same stench that had been present at Rowen's and now it crept from under Elsie's door like some deadly gas; a sickly bouquet of decomposition, of meat left in a bin during the height of summer, thick, cloying and heavy. It was so offensive it even had a taste, a foulness which coated Henry's tongue as the nauseating odour found its way to the back of his throat and made him choke.

Henry opened his eyes as he coughed and spluttered with his head still resting against the door and his eyes alighted on the door handle. His hand was instinctively poised to reach out and turn it but he paused with revulsion as his eyes took in the ruin which covered it.

He knew it was mud, it had to be, but as he observed it in the half-light it could quite easily have been offal; a thick clod of dark mess rested on the top of the handle whilst some of the offensive substance had dribbled from the brass, streaking its foulness down the face of the white door as if it were a scene from a dirty protest. As his eyes fell lower, he realised he was also standing in a soiled, soggy patch of carpet, where the mud or blood or whatever the hell it was had dribbled down or possibly even seeped out from under his daughter's bedroom door.

He listened intently for any movement on the other side of the divide. All he could hear were his indecisive feet squelching on the muddied carpet and with that he knew what he needed to do. He boldly took hold of the handle, it was cold, ice cold and the mud squelched through his fingers; he imagined this was what it would be like to shove a hand inside the body cavity of the long dead.

He grimaced but didn't relinquish his hold of the brass handle, instead of letting go – which he desperately wanted to do – he turned it in his shaking hand, the latch clicked first and then the door began to creak open. The godawful smell that had been present before wafted out with a renewed strength; as if he were cracking open a crypt which had held the putrefied remains of the long dead, the smell bringing tears to his eyes. There was a dark symmetry in his thoughts and what was playing out before him, because this room had become a crypt of sorts, and Elsie had been long gone – *and a long time dead*, he mused.

He pushed the door open, relinquishing his grip on the tacky handle, he let it swing wide. He remained at the threshold, his courage to step into the room was still absent like the light to see by, without illumination the room appeared as a black hole of misery, one he knew would soon suck him in and spit him out.

The overpowering stench of death soon dissipated, replaced now by the subtle aroma of wet soil; it reminding him fleetingly of the twelve graves, each holding a fragment of his daughter's life and memory, but as he stood at the threshold, he was overwhelmed not by the freedom he'd sought from his yearly offerings, but by the guilt of trying to wash his hands of her ever-present shadow which had been cast upon his life since she left.

The guilt was engrained in his skin, it had become a part of him over the years, and as he reflected on that smell, on its cloying nature; he realised maybe for the first time in his miserable life that no amount of washing, scrubbing or burying would cleanse his sin-stained hands or ease his broken heartedness – because he was to blame for it all.

He knew what he had to do to end this current torture, he had to turn the light on and reveal what was waiting for him in the pregnant, ominous dark; but it was the thought of what had lingered and manifested in her room for the past twelve years which threaded his heart with panic. The memories this room housed would have no doubt grown crueller over time and through his wilful neglect; the thought of those memories being dragged into the light was almost as worse than what he imagined was waiting patiently for him on her bed.

He reached into the darkness, stretched his hand across the wall; the hallway had been cold but in that grave of a room the air was frigid, and as his arm disappeared into the vacuous black it looked as though it had been amputated. The momentary fear subsided when he felt his disappearing limb prickle with an outbreak of goosebumps as his fingers continued to rove across the wall. He felt the glossiness of a band poster tacked to the wall, the roughness of the wallpaper, then the smoothness of the plastic light switch. His fingertips caressed the button as his mind prepared to let in the memories this room held and the nightmare which had crawled in there to roost, Elsie; or what was left of her.

She's come home, at long last.

Taking a calming breath Henry clicked the switch. He shielded his eyes against the sudden brightness and stumbled, momentarily blinded, he almost tripped forwards into the nightmare room but his hand shot out and grasped the doorjamb. He instantly winced with pain, having gripped it with his damaged hand, but the pain was enough to force his eyes back open. He was hit by a whirlpool of emotions and the memories that assailed him threatened to pull him into the room and drown him with its unrelenting undertow.

The thing which anchored him in place was the *thing* that was reclined in Elsie's bed.

His hands shot up to his mouth where he stifled a shriek before crumbling to his knees, as if he were a puppet that had had its strings cut. He collapsed hard in a haphazard stacking of limbs, his eyes never leaving the abomination that was laying in her bed.

He screamed the hideous, guttural cry of a wounded animal into the room.

"No... no.... no..." he murmured over and over.

Positioned on the bed, as if she'd just fallen asleep were Elsie's muddied clothes.

He began to crawl into her room, his head downcast as he followed the muddied footprints to the edge of the bed. He lifted his gaze and realised that what had been positioned on the bed were her filthy grave clothes, the ones he'd interned over the course of the last twelve years, as if she lay in eternal slumber atop her dusty bedsheets. The sight made him fall prostrate on the ground as he sobbed at the violation of her graves and defilement of her room.

CRRRREEEEEAAAAKKK.

He paused in his sobbing.

It was the sound of rusted bed springs.

Something was shifting its weight on the bed.

He slowly lifted his gaze and sharply scuttled backwards across the floor.

Hanging over the bed was one tattered and muddied leg of a trouser, soon another fell down to join it, the hems all torn and thick with grime. Under the bed, through the legs of trousers he observed a deep bulge, the mattress was sagging, whatever those clothes housed had weight, which soon shifted.

His eyes rose to witness her soiled clothes sitting up from the bed, but her body remained absent, just a hollowed-out impression of her had been formed in crinkled, wet and muddied clothes. It had no legs, no arms, no hands or feet, there was no body to hold her clothes up; but they remained there all the same. Frozen with fear he observed her shirt expanding and contracting, the fabric pulling at the remaining buttons as if the *thing* that wore them was breathing.

Although there was no head and therefore no face; he could tell it was looking at him, it had agency and he felt paralysed under its intense, malevolent glare.

"Elsie... it's.... it's...." Henry stuttered, but the rest of the words failed to come when he saw an arm which had hung uselessly at its side shift and begin to move in his direction.

Henry watched on raptly as it slowly extended towards him, the cuff of the shirt hung open, there was no hand or arm to permit such a movement but it came forth nevertheless and he watched it rise with an aching despair as brackish water dripped slowly from the cuff.

The limbless fabric stopped rising and stuck straight out from the body as if it had hidden scaffolding within. He watched on mesmerised as the fabric rippled in the air as if it were battling with a wind that wasn't present. There was the flapping noise of clothes hung out to dry, which to Henry sounded like many whispering voices.

As the arm hung out over the floor between them, Henry couldn't help but notice that the dangling limb had a certain weight to it, as if there were actually an arm hidden within the flapping garment, because it was solid, it didn't billow and flap around, it remained resolute in its position.

He suddenly realised the arm wasn't just hanging there idly, it was communicating something, and he slowly began to crawl away from the forgiveness he'd been desperately cantering towards moments before. He came to realise that the missing arm was attached to a missing hand which pointed a missing accusatory finger at him from the emptiness of that cuff; which as he crawled backwards looked evermore like the opening of a noose than a garment.

Henry stumbled backwards onto his arse as Elsie's voice tore through the room like a banshee.

"YOU DID THIS TO MEEEEEEEEEEEEEEEEEEEEE!"

He was crawling backwards, feet slipping against the muddied floor as he desperately tried to put distance between himself and the *thing* before him, which he now knew was Elsie.

"I'LL MAKE YOU PAY!" Henry noted the sagging mattress return to normal as the clothes shambled into a standing position and it was coming towards him. It moved swiftly and in a disjointed fashion, its arms flailing around in the air like one of those inflatable men you'd see at a car dealership.

Henry managed to turn, get to his feet and run hell for leather for the door.

He peered behind him as he neared the safety of the hallway, Elsie's soiled clothes were billowing in the chase, her legs almost gliding across the floor, but he could hear her feet hammering after him.

He burst into the hallway, turned back and reached into the room gripping the mud-covered handle. He was half-expecting it to slip from his hand as it had in his dream, but he found purchase and pulled, slamming it shut at the onrushing Elsie.

Whatever he'd trapped in that room threw itself at the door.

Thump. Thump. Thud. Thud.

With each strike Henry felt the door handle shaking within his grasp, then he felt the distinct vibrations of hidden fists pummelling the door on the other side.

"You sicken me," the thing beyond the door bayed.

"You need a doctor!" it howled.

Henry thought the ghastly vision was repeating what Kiera had said, twisting the knife in further than his wife had managed; but he soon realised they were his words, spoken from so long ago.

"Why are you doing this to us, all we've ever done is care and love you, and now you bring this shit to our door. You're our little girl... you'll always be our little girl and if you want to continue living under this roof, that's what you'll stay... our little girl..." Elsie's voice dropped to a whisper. "If you don't like it, I hear the gutters got plenty of room!"

Henry suddenly realised that the pounding had subsided. Pressing his ear up to the door he heard the *thing* inside padding slowly away from the door and so he relinquished his grip on the handle.

He turned around and rested his back and then his head against the door and breathed deeply.

The bed springs creaked their displeasure and he imagined Elise was back on the bed reclining as she was before. Then she started to sob and the sound lanced his heart, as it reminded him of how she was towards the end; when her life had become unbearable, a thing to be endured rather than enjoyed and Henry knew the sorrow-filled tears that wet her pillow each night were all shed because of him.

Elsie's voice trickled under the door.

It was the same phrase on repeat.

The words he'd said and wished he could've taken back.

Words no father should ever utter to their child.

"I wish you were dead..." he felt his legs go weak.

"I wish you were dead..." he slid down the door.

"I wish you were dead..." he sat in the mud of the carpet, a stain of his own creation.

"I wish you were dead..." he pulled the phone from his pocket.

"I wish you were dead..." typed a message and sent his distress signal into the world.

"I wish you were dead..." he bowed his head and dropped his phone.

"I wish you were dead..." his eyes filled with tears as the hellish refrain, tore his heart and the last of his resolve asunder.

"I wish you were dead..."

CHAPTER NINE

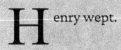enry wept.

CHAPTER TEN

Josh didn't know what to expect when he raced over to Henry's after getting a one-word text from him in the early hours of the morning.

All it said was: HELP.

Knowing Henry wouldn't ask for help if he was on fire, Josh knew instantly that his friend needed him, something was terribly wrong; his thoughts on the drive over had quickly turned to suicide as they so often did in moments of high anxiety and stress.

He imagined getting to Henry's, gaining entry to his property by breaking a window or kicking down a door only to find his friend swinging two feet above the bottom rung of the stairs; the cord he'd used to hang himself imbedded deep within his neck, his body swaying and the sound of the cord creaking lazily through the house as if someone were reclining on a porch swing. Or even worse, he'd find Henry taking a dip in a crimson-coloured bath with his wrists sliced open. Henry was a messy sonofabitch, and therefore Josh presumed his suicide would match the squalor he'd chosen to live his life in.

What greeted him when he arrived was even worse than his imaginings.

The front door was unlocked and so he let himself in – already a bad sign.

He wandered into the house calling out to his friend, but no one answered: *that's another bad sign if ever there was one* he mused darkly. He noted however that Henry wasn't hanging from the spindles of the stairs – *thank the Lord.*

Spindle, I still need to pick one of those up from the hardware store, Josh mused; it was an odd thing to fuss over given the circumstances, but he was desperately trying not to think of the bathtub upstairs where he might find a body, Henry's body, all pale and floating in cherry-coloured, ice-cold water.

He called out a few more times, working his way methodically through the ground floor, clearing each room he passed. When he reached the kitchen he found, to his surprise, the back door leading out to the garden had been left open. It was freezing in the house and this provided him an explanation for it, rather than what he'd initially thought; Henry failing to keep on top of his bills. Josh glanced outside to see if Henry had been taking in the early morning sun with a beer and a cocktail of prescribed medication. Happy there was no body sprawled out on the lawn, he dipped his head back into the kitchen to search the house some more. Glancing down as he closed the door on the frigid morning, he discovered the filthy footprints snaking their way in through the kitchen. He followed their path and they passed right under his feet, and when he turned, he stared in wide eyed fascination, because they led back the way he'd come, to the foot of the stairs and he had no idea how he'd missed them.

Following the footprints to the foot of the staircase, his mind began to run away from him: *Henry what have you done?*

Pausing at the bottom of the stairs, he shouted out to Henry again, but his friend didn't reply; through choice or circumstance Josh couldn't be sure.

Josh stared at the dried mud for some time, weighing his options.

In the quiet of the house and with those muddied prints ascending higher and higher, leading him somewhere, Josh couldn't help but think that his friend, shocked and appalled by the startling realisation of what he'd done; which had been cemented by the visitation of his daughter last night at the séance, had lost his damned mind. Or what there was left of it to lose anyway. *The crazy bastard had gone grave digging.*

Instead of burying something in her memory and to atone for his confirmed part in this tragedy, Josh feared that his friend had brought something back with him and that thought made his heart rise into his throat.

What Henry might have removed from Elsie's many graves, Josh hadn't the mind to ponder as he tried to swallow his heart back down to its natural resting place; but he was sure that whatever he'd find when he climbed those stairs, all the way to the top, would chill his bones, but he had to ascend, and so he did.

What Josh discovered once he'd finished clambering his way up the staircase was everything he feared and more.

Henry was before him; a heap on the ground, a muddied, bloodied, lifeless mess. Josh ran towards him and as he neared he noticed the muddy puddle his friend had collapsed in, which was also complimented by the stench of piss and shit. He couldn't place the foul smell at first, but wrinkling his nose at the reek and covering his mouth with his hand, so he didn't – god forbid – taste it, he pondered the possibility that his friend's bowels had given up when he drew his last breath, because he still hadn't moved and there were no signs of life.

As he bent down to touch his Henry's wrist, to check for a pulse, any sign of life, he recalled where he'd smelt that sickening miasma before. It smelt like flyblown meat; the same smell which was present at Rowen's flat – during the séance.

As his fingers touched Henry's arm, he almost pulled his hand back. His skin was cold and damp. Josh peered up at that moment, not wanting to look on the fate of his friend any longer and noticed the stains which besmirched the door Henry's body was crumbled outside. There was a piece of paper tacked to the face of the door which had curled at the edges over time, scrawled on the paper in a child's handwriting were five letters and they denoted this room belonged to Elsie.

The door was covered in bloodied and muddied hand prints, the handle had something brown hanging down from it, but Josh also noted cracks in the plasterwork around the doorframe which fractured out and away from the door, spreading across the landing wall.

Josh jumped out of his skin as Henry's hand shot out of his crumpled form and grabbed his outstretched hand which was still searching for a pulse. He'd become distracted by the door and the signs of structural damage around it, his thoughts consumed by wondering what the hell happened here.

After letting out a shriek, Josh glanced down at the broken man before him. He could see in Henry's eyes a defeated man, and he knew intimately what that felt like, because he had that same look in his when he stared into the mirror on the morning of his scheduled suicide; hopeless and without a shred of life left in them, dull orbs that only reflected pain.

The sight of those eyes in Henry's head pained him gravely.

Because they meant his friend was circling the drain of life.

But the words Henry uttered next chilled him to his very core.

"She came back, Elsie; I trapped her in there," Henry slowly shuffled himself upright, banging his head against the door, to emphasise the '*there*' of his statement, although it was pretty self-explanatory to Josh at the time.

Josh needed to get them as far away from that hellish place as quickly as possible and so he helped Henry to his feet. Hoisting Henry's arm over his shoulder, pulling him tightly to his side, he half-carried, half-dragged his friend down the hall and away from that nightmare of a room.

Josh's words, which came as they started their slow descent, sounded meaningless to him in the moment, but it was the sentiment they conveyed which he believed counted. It was all his addled brain could think of to say, and he hoped it would reassure his friend that he was there for him.

"Let's get you on the sofa. I'll make us a coffee and we'll talk it all through."

Henry nodded in agreement and let his friend carry him down the remaining stairs.

HENRY WAS SITTING ON THE SOFA.

He'd not moved an inch since Josh placed him down.

Josh shortly entered the room, two steaming cups of coffee in his hands; his was black, Henry's was milky with four sugars, he couldn't remember how his friend took it, but felt Henry needed the sugar boost.

As Josh navigated his way to where Henry sat, he noticed afresh the slovenliness Henry had been wallowing in.

Like a pig in shit, he mused, placing Henry's cup on the coffee table, brushing some half-eaten sandwich out of the way to make room; as he leant forward to do so he caught a whiff of alcohol on his friend's breath, it was strong and heavy, like he'd splashed it on as aftershave. *He's been at it again*, Josh thought.

Josh turned away and sat in the fireside chair opposite Henry. There was a throw over it and he wondered as he collapsed into the seat what stains covered the upholstery below? *Enough to chuck a throw over it*, he thought as he nestled into the seat.

As he reclined, he clasped the warm cup in his hands because the house was still as cold as a witch's tit. He glanced across the expanse of detritus between him and his friend and took in Henry's sorry form. He appeared to be in some type of fugue state, staring ahead into space, completely oblivious to Josh's presence in the room.

Josh took a sip of coffee and regretted it instantly. The molten black-lava of his cup scalded the roof of his mouth. He winced and took a sharp intake of breath and could feel a piece of skin flapping loosely from the roof of his mouth and his tongue instantly started inspecting it. He placed his cup on the floor and when he looked up, Henry was still staring into space. Josh followed Henry's vacant gaze across the room.

He seemed transfixed by a picture which had fallen to the floor; glass and wood splinters decorated the carpet, but the picture itself was laying up against the wall, a family affair and from where he was sitting Josh could see the beaming smile of – what he assumed to be – an eight-year-old Elsie, complete with missing teeth, her blonde hair in a short pixy-like haircut.

When he glanced back to Henry he noticed his friend was shivering.

His coffee remained on the table, untouched.

"Get it whilst it's hot man, you look colder than a well digger's belt buckle," Josh offered cheerily, opting for Henry's humour, anything to drag his friend out the pit he'd fallen into. "What's with the temperature in here anyway?" Josh offered as he peered around the room.

Henry remained silent but reached a trembling hand out for his coffee. *A breakthrough,* Josh thought. Henry took a slurp of his drink, his lips smacking together as he placed it back down on the table.

Henry's eyes then rose to the ceiling, his bottom lip began to quiver, his brow knitting together in anguish. Josh knew what was above them. It was Elsie's room. Josh coughed and Henry flinched, his eyes shooting to Josh instantly where he fixed him with a cold stare. *He's ready to snap under the strain,* Josh pondered.

"Heating's working fine," Henry uttered quietly. "It's been like this since I woke up at – six. After–" Henry couldn't finish his sentence and Josh watched on as his friend's eyes slowly returned to the ceiling again.

Josh observed his friend more closely now that he wasn't under his penetrating, cold gaze. Henry's hands were caked in mud, one of which was badly cut; his clothes were soiled and he had muck all over him, on his face and in his hair, it looked like he'd been dragged through a muddy field backwards. He knew he had to ask the question because the muddy footprints which snaked through the house and the current state of the man opposite him only had one answer, in Josh's mind at least; only one rational explanation was to be had and that was: he'd been to Elsie's grave again.

But he couldn't ask outright, he had to dance around the question.

"You wanna tell me what happened?" Josh said, his voice startling the somewhat distracted Henry.

"What?" Henry replied, his eyes returned to Josh from whatever he was imagining in that room above them. Henry's face was screwed up, as if he'd not heard the question.

"You're scared, covered in dirt and there's muddy footprints all through the house, also your back door was open, I closed it; is everything okay? You doing okay? You can talk to me you know, about anything." Josh reclaimed his coffee from the floor and blew on it, he watched the steam roll off the top like an early morning mist dancing over a field.

Henry glanced down, his eyebrows raised at his sullied-self as if he'd only just realised the state he was in, the mud and the blood; his eyes returned to Josh's and now they were wet, but the tears which threatened to fall were still locked away.

"It all happened after Kiera showed up..." Henry's eyes drifted over to the photograph against the wall.

"She was here? Why? I didn't think you guys were, you know, on talking terms anymore."

"I talk, she doesn't listen, anyway... she left," Henry was still fixated on the family portrait.

"No shit Sherlock, I didn't find her helping herself to your biscuits back there–"

"No." Henry's eyes shot to Josh. The tears he'd held back were slicking his face now. Josh wanted the ground to open up and swallow him whole in that moment.

"She left," Henry continued. "Like literally left me for good. They're moving away, she said she couldn't do this any longer, that I was putting a strain on their relationship. I didn't even call her this time..."

Henry paused and Josh took that afforded moment to process what he was hearing.

She'd left him, for good.

Josh observed Henry fiddling with his wedding band, his thumb flicked at the metal before he began to turn it around his finger with an almost frenzied fussing as if he was desperate to remove it but he couldn't get it over his knuckle. Josh was still musing over Henry's words when he suddenly realised Henry's hands had grown still, he'd stopped worrying with the ring; lifting his gaze, he noticed Henry was deep in thought, biting his lip, fear had carved him a new face in the wink of an eye, one which had been hewn by anger and pain.

"I didn't call her!" Henry spat angrily. "She thinks I put someone up to it... but I... you didn't do it did you?" Henry stared at Josh, he was awaiting an answer.

"Called...Kiera?" Josh asked incredulously. "I don't even know her number," Josh placed his cup down on the table, leant forwards and rested his elbows on his knees. "I have no idea what you're talking about, you need to explain it man, so I can help; she thinks you got someone to call her? What did they say?"

"Sorry," Henry said sheepishly, his eyes flitting down to the table in front of him. "I had to ask. I knew you wouldn't have done it, but... I... I think I'm losing my mind." His eyes flicked quickly to Josh but then returned to the table.

"So, who was it? What did they say?" Josh pressed.

Henry sat there for a moment, slowly turned his head to peer out into the vacant house beyond the threshold of the lounge as if he'd just heard something or he was checking to see that no one was eavesdropping on their conversation. Josh thought his movements odd, because he knew they were the only two souls in the house, he'd checked the place himself but what Henry said next made him question that very notion; because he'd not checked everywhere, he'd not peered inside Elsie's room.

"It was Elsie, she made threats to Kiera and her family, said she was going to enjoy making us suffer!" Henry's shoulders heaved and he began to sob uncontrollably.

"Elsie? But she's—" Josh started to say before Henry cut him off.

"She's... she's... back... Josh... she's... trap-ped... in her... room... I... di-d this to... her... it's... all my... fault."

"What do you mean she's back? Was it like last night? You heard her?"

Henry was able to gain a little composure, so he sniffed and hawked something in his throat before swallowing it down. Josh watched him calm himself with a few deep breaths before he had the nerve to continue. Josh didn't know how long this break in sobs would last, but he'd wait it out if need be, he needed to know what the hell was going on.

"Yes. Kiera had a recording of her."

"A recording?"

"Yeah. She'd recorded it from her answerphone... she thinks it was me."

"Why would she think that?"

"Because I'm the monster, Josh. You know I've called her before, said stuff I wish I hadn't said, usually when I've been drunk. I've blamed her for what happened, threatened her before... I've said some terrible things from a place of pain... it's not an excuse. I'm not looking for pity here; I know I shouldn't have but I did. But this time it wasn't me, I promise you it wasn't, you gotta believe me, because I'd never say the things that were on that recording... it was crazy what they were saying, what she was saying. I might be a prick, but I'm not evil!" Henry was shaking with anger now.

"I believe you, I do, but Elsie? You're sure?"

"Positive. It was her, older but her, and so are the clothes in her bedroom if you wanna go up there and check. They're all laid out on her fucking bed man, the clothes I buried – it's proof... she's back."

"You didn't–" Josh couldn't finish his question, partly because he didn't want to ask it, but their dance was coming to an end.

"What, dig them up?" Henry replied incredulously.

"Yeah."

"Of course I didn't dig them up, what do you think I am some kinda weirdo?"

"Have you seen yourself? It ain't a far stretch of the imagination, you're literally covered in mud and there's muddied footprints all through the house. If you did, just tell me, I wanna believe you but what you're saying is crazy."

"Go up and check if you don't believe me, they're all laid out on her bed like she's sleeping. I promise you, I *never* put them there, they just appeared, like she'd climbed out of her many graves and dragged herself here. Go on check, or are you chicken?"

"I believe you, *if* that's the truth."

"Of course it is, I ain't going to lie to you, especially about Elsie... she's too important for that."

"So, there was the phone call and the clothes, anything else?"

"She came after me."

"She came after you?"

"The clothes, she wasn't there but she was if you know what I mean. The clothes, they were sentient almost, they fucking stood up and walked towards me," Josh stared at Henry in disbelief. "I swear man, she's back and she's pissed."

"And you're sure it was her voice, on the recording?"

"Yeah, I'm positive, it didn't sound like the Elsie I knew, her voice was older like I said; but it was her, the same voice we heard at Rowen's. There's no mistake it was her on the recording, because it knew things, personal things that no one would ever know but her. Also, it sounded as if Elsie, her spirit or whatever it is we brought back last night, has been watching Kiera and her family."

"You're a hundred percent positive it was her voice, it couldn't be someone playing a sick joke?"

"It was the same voice Josh. The same fucking voice that came out of Rowen's mouth when... when... when Elsie possessed him."

"Possessed?" Josh screwed his face up at the word.

"You don't think what we saw last night was a possession?"

"No, I can't believe that."

"You can't believe it or you're choosing not to believe it? It was as plain as the nose on your face, you saw it, I saw it; she was there, in that room with us and now she's loose."

"Was she there with us or did we, and when I say *we* I mean *you*, just believe she was – because you wanted more than anything to see her again?"

"Why you being such a prick about it? Is it because if you entertained it for a second, you'd be forced to admit to yourself that this *Heaven* you've built your recovery on is just a sham? And if it was a sham, Amanda's out there somewhere too, in that other place, lost, alone and–"

"That's enough Henry," Josh spoke with enough authority to drive out a demon.

Henry sipped his coffee, staring coldly at his friend over the top of the mug.

"It would destroy everything you believe in, it'd make a mockery of this Heaven you believe so ardently in; that's why you won't admit it to yourself isn't it?You're still holding out hope that you'll see Amanda right, in Heaven?" Henry paused, a villainous, vulpine scowl took over his face. "I got news for you, there's no hope. Not for you, not for me, not for Elsie or your precious Amanda... from dust we come and to dust we return, there's no Heaven Josh, all of this proves it."

"All of what? What proof do you actually have?" Josh replied, trying his damnedest not to show his anger because he knew his friend was hurting and that everyone, even those closest to you, were fighting battles you knew nothing about, and this battle wasn't against flesh and blood; it was a spiritual battle, one wrapped up in wickedness, suffering and long-held guilt.

Henry opened his mouth to respond but Josh stilled him with a cold glance and the raising of his hand.

"I'm not done. I think you saw what you needed to see, heard what your heart's yearned to hear for the last twelve years, you believed in it so much that you even had me believing what was happening. Rowen just gave you a platform, or we gave it to him, whatever it was it wasn't real, it can't be... what you're talking about Henry, it only exists in fiction and cheap horror films. She's dead Henry, there's no power on earth that can reverse what's happened to her, and if there was, I doubt it would have been bestowed on some emo looking guy who struts around in band T-shirts and lights a few candles." It was harsh but Josh knew that to entertain the madness they'd witnessed last night any longer than necessary would only fuel his friend's delirious obsession all the more.

"You're scared, aren't you? Scared to open your mind up to the possibility that you're wrong and I'm right... you've always gotta be right, don't you?"

"It's not about being—"

"You're scared man; scared that if Elsie's out in the dark, Amanda ain't too far behind her."

"Enough!" Josh shouted.

Henry only shook his head, stared at Josh as if he were a pile of shit he'd stepped in.

"What? You on your period or something?"

"Just had enough of your wild theories."

"Theories? You've certainly changed your tune," a smirk crested Henry's lips at his utterance, savouring the words he'd soon speak.

"What's that supposed to mean?"

"You've just changed your tune is all. You couldn't have gotten out of that place fast enough last night. If it was all the mumbo jumbo, smoke and mirrors bullshit you seem to think it is, then why'd you belt out of that place so fast? You dragged me across the fucking floor or did you forget that? You heard her voice, you saw what happened... and I don't believe you didn't, so quit trying to persuade me that I'm the one who had it all wrong."

"I did, you're right, but instead of going home last night and pickling myself."

"I didn't–"

"I can smell the reek on you from over here. Don't bother trying to deny it. Like I was saying; instead of going home and pickling myself, I thought it through, all of it, the voices, the strange goings on, everything... even the part of us getting the hell out of that place."

"You were screaming like a little bitch," Henry uttered and it was the first time Josh had seen him smile since he'd arrived, the thunderclouds which had been lingering were slowly rolling away.

"I think that was you... screaming like a big sissy!" Josh replied, matching Henry's smirk.

"You might be right about that..." They both laughed and their sudden unity felt like a tonic, the way the drizzle after a fierce thunderstorm feels on your face. It eradicated the temporary wedge that had formed between them, dulled the harsh words shared by dear friends. Josh couldn't help but chuckle inwardly that all it took to be back on the same page was one crude comment, but he knew they weren't truly on the same page, because Henry believed his daughter was back and Josh was leaning towards it being some sick joke that had gotten out of hand, a joke being played at his and Henry's expense.

"What I can't understand is why you aren't on my side about this." Henry said.

"I'm always on your side man. I just can't reconcile what I saw with what I believe... the reason I ran like a bitch, as you so eloquently put it, is because what I saw in that place wasn't good, it was evil, and it goes against everything I believe in... it scared me, I only went blindly into that place because of you, I wanted to be there for you, I still do."

"Pussy!" Henry said before chuckling at his own insult.

"Exactly, I ain't afraid to admit it. It scared me, but it wasn't what happened at Rowen's as such that scared me, although I confess it was batshit crazy, he put on one hell of a show; it's what happened to you, what I saw on your face that scared me most."

"And what was that?"

"Unbridled hope."

"Is that such a bad thing?"

"If it's built on a lie it is; and I think it was."

"We ain't ever going to agree on this are we? This *I believe that, you believe this* bullshit. But now you got me curious, why do you think it's a lie?"

"It just felt forced, I can't really explain it... Rowen comes out of nowhere, you shared some personal stuff in group with him and then all of a sudden we're back at his house and Elsie's supposedly there with us, in that room. It just seemed too... too..."

"Convenient?" Henry offered.

"Forced, is what I was going to say, but convenient, sure, that works too."

"But it worked Josh, all what happened, I didn't imagine it; last night's séance, the message Kiera got, the clothes from her graves, even that thing I trapped in her room, it's still gotta be in there if you wanna take a look?"

Josh could tell his friend was hurting and he was looking for hope in all the wrong places. Henry had been through something tonight which Josh could hardly comprehend and now wasn't the time to shatter Henry's hopeful illusion: it was time to be a friend, but the time would come when he'd need to cut the lifeline of hope Henry was currently clinging to, because to not, was to make him suffer unnecessarily.

"I believe you buddy, I'm here aren't I? But I just can't willingly let you walk down the dark path Rowen's put you on after last night without testing the ground it's built on, without first exploring all avenues, making sure that bridge between you and Elsie that appeared last night won't just collapse the moment you take a step on it towards her."

Henry nodded before Josh continued.

"Whether it's the smoke and mirrors bullshit I believe it be or the truth that you desperately want it to be; whatever's waiting at the end of it for you, whatever you hope to find in all this... look I'm just scared that if we don't test it first, you might discover something that you're not going to be able to come back from."

Henry glanced down at his hands. It was quite clear to Josh that Henry felt uncomfortable about what he'd just said, not because of the content, but because it was said with love and Josh knew that Henry was a big believer in love being between a man and a woman and that there was no grey area regarding that notion, period.

Josh braced himself for the scathing response which was bound to follow, something about him being queer, a derogatory statement about his manhood or lack of it, but it never came. Instead he observed Henry lifting his damaged hand in front of his face. Josh could see him scrutinising the cut on his palm; his face was suddenly a mask of misery and his eyes grew grotesquely wide, resembling two hard boiled eggs.

Henry dropped his hand into his lap and his horrified gaze fell on Josh.

"We gotta go back." Henry said suddenly.

"What?"

"We gotta go back to Rowen's... now!"

CHAPTER ELEVEN

"What you two want?" The sudden, sharp voice made both men jump.

Josh and Henry were standing in the squalid hallway of Rowen's tenement, where they'd been for the last few minutes, knocking at his door to no avail.

No one had answered yet. Or had they?

Where did that voice come from? Josh pondered.

He stepped back from the door and glanced down the filthy corridor which stank of piss and despair; but no one showed themselves, the coast was clear and so he turned back to the door and the task at hand where Henry was thumping the door loud enough to raise the dead.

Maybe he will? Josh pondered wryly.

Josh assumed there was no answer because Rowen, like them, must be feeling a little worse for wear given last night's exploits.

Must have taken it out of him, bloody charlatan, Josh thought as he bit down on the words, swallowed them whole before they tumbled from his mouth, he'd only just got Henry on side, he didn't want to have to start over again.

Josh glanced at Henry – who'd changed out of his bloodied and soiled clothes – as he continued to hammer at the door like a madman. He still looked like the bedraggled mess of a man he'd found outside his daughter's bedroom, you could change your clothes after all but you couldn't change your countenance, and Henry's was heavy and troubled and that stuff got engrained in your skin.

Josh considered that he probably didn't look far off from crazy himself.

If Rowen was inside; suffering from sleeping off last night's séance, Josh couldn't blame him because he knew he'd rather be tucked up in bed right now, himself. Sleeping off the hangover or hang-ups from last night in a sated ignorance; if Rowen had decided to do just that, forget everything that had happened last night, it was a feeling Josh could relate to.

If Josh wasn't allowed to forget last night then neither could Rowen.

"Hit it again," Josh said.

Henry nodded and jackhammered his fist against the door using the heel of his hand.

"Open the fucking door Rowen, it's…" Henry began to shout through gritted teeth. The tendons in Henry's neck were so tight and pronounced Josh thought he could pluck them and play a tune if the mood called for it.

"I said… over here!" the voice came again, louder now.

Josh turned in the direction he thought the voice had come from. The corridor seemed to stretch out forever in some optical illusion, a dark labyrinthine space of squalor like a tunnel all the way to oblivion.

There wasn't a person in sight.

Josh turned away and the voice came again.

"Over here," it whispered.

Josh turned and stepped towards the voice.

"That's it, closer, closer..." the voice uttered, but still they remained hidden.

Josh inspected the doors and noticed a crack of amber light, possibly from a lamp, cutting the squalid hallway in half. He approached slowly, following the whispering voice that begged him to come closer; it led him to a door which stood ajar, three doors down and on the opposite side from Rowen's.

Josh flinched when he noticed the pallid face which stared back at him through the crack. A hand quickly appeared through the gap and a gnarled, arthritic finger curled backwards and forwards, beseeching him to come closer and Josh couldn't help but heed its call.

He still couldn't clearly make out if it was a man or woman, the voice was weak, the appendage all liver-spotted and wrinkled, but as Josh drew closer, as if he were a fish approaching a wriggling worm on a hook, he was left in no doubts that the person who owned that finger was a wrinkly old man.

As Josh approached, the man opened his door wider to reveal a husk of a person, the dressing gown he was wearing hung open to reveal his hollowed-out chest, all ribs and skin, but as Josh's eyes moved downward he noticed the man wasn't wearing any under-wear. It was an unforgiving eyesore; one which Josh couldn't look away from. Because the old codger was hung like a Shetland pony, his junk all hung low atop a thatch of greyish pubic hair.

Josh noticed that the carpet matched the drapes in that aspect, because the man was still clinging on to some of the hair on his head, it was grey too but thinning; not through old age, but through some medical poisoning. *Chemotherapy*, Josh mused before his mind flashed an image of Amanda in place of the man, her hair all tufty and patchy on her head like a threadbare rug thrown over her skull. His wife was staring back at him through the crack in the door as if she were peeking at him from Heaven and he almost said 'I'll be there as soon as I can my love' but as the words trickled up his throat, the vision was lost as the man who's flat it was coughed up a chunk of something then spat it into a hanky.

Josh was now only a few feet away and watched on as the man inspected what he'd coughed up. Josh peered back the way he'd come, Henry was still hammering at the door.

"You the police... detectives?" Josh turned back to the figure at the door, able to see him more clearly now as the man had opened the door wider to peek a look at Henry. A lamp inside bathing the home owner in a weak amber light, which only served to make his skin appear more jaundiced and waxy too, like the skin of an apple. His face was a collection of crude angles; as if a tanner had run out of skin but had one last thing he needed to cover and so he'd made do with what he had on hand, which appeared to be barely enough to cover this man's angular and disturbing face.

"Excuse me for saying, but the mouse is out of the house." Josh nodded down at the open dressing gown. The man glanced down and grabbed at his robe.

"Oh my godfather's, sorry about that." The man said as he wrapped the material around himself and fastened the knot tightly. When his modesty was covered the man peered back at Josh.

"Well then, you the pigs or not?"

"We might be, why?" Josh offered, wondering if his tone would inspire the man to confide in him or slink back into his room to slowly die, people had a love hate relationship with the police and some even loved to hate them.

The man coughed again before his fingers blindly felt for something that was hanging around his neck. He found it after a while of fussing and lifted a yellowing plastic tube to his face; he hooked the tubing over his ears first and then affixed the tube to his nose. Once that was done he lowered his shaking hand to his side where Josh noticed an oxygen cylinder on a wheeled contraption standing by his leg which had been covered by his billowing dressing gown up until that moment.

The man turned the lever on the side.

Josh heard the hiss of an escaping substance, followed by a pleasing groan from the old man.

"Did you see something, Mr.?" Josh offered, trying to move things along whilst also trying to sound official, he'd decided there wasn't really any harm in letting the man believe they were the police.

The man raised a quivering hand into the air and held out a finger as if he were reprimanding a child, Josh waited patiently as directed, the sound of Henry still pounding away at Rowen's door echoing in the hallway behind him.

"LaFaro..." the man uttered before inhaling another lungful of fresh oxygen. "Mr. LaFaro... but you can call me Pat, seeing as you're the coppers an-all."

"Nice to make your acquaintance Mr. ..., sorry Pat, do you know–"

"You here about the noise? I did call it in last night or early this morning, can't quite remember when," Pat lifted his arm, glanced down at the withered appendage; Josh did too. The man's watch hung from his arm like a loose bangle, Josh noted that it was on its tightest clasp but still it was too big for the man's stick thin arms. "Shoot, is that the time? It was about thirteen hours ago I guess... it's almost time for my corned beef sandwich and my lunchtime tablets."

"Sorry for our delay, we're very overworked at the moment, we got here as quickly as we could..."

"Don't doubt it son. Got your time cut out for you with all those bloody delinquents out there; things never used to be this bad in my day. If you stepped out of line you got a clip on the ear, you said something wrong, you got a knuckle sandwich... but I guess you can't do that now can you? Rights and all that... people get offended easily nowadays."

"So, the noise you heard, Pat. Could you describe it to me?

"I already told the call handler everything I heard."

"I understand that, but it helps if we can get a statement, for our records, you know straight from the horse's mouth – so to speak."

"Right, okay, I can see that, sure... so it started at about–" Pat stopped talking, inspected Josh closely.

Josh peered down at himself, wondered if he had something on his clothes; he half-expected to find mud on top, or blood or maybe a bit of both. He returned his gaze to Pat; the ill looking specimen of a man was stooped, breathing slowly, his raggedy chest heaving with each laboured breath as the tank next to him hissed out its oxygen like a snake.

Pat stood there resolute in the awkward silence waiting for something and when it didn't come, Josh spoke up.

"Pat? Are you okay?" He offered, waving a hand in front of Pat's face.

"You can stop all your waving, I ain't having a stroke and my cheese ain't fallen off its cracker yet neither. You said you was taking a statement..."

"That's correct, so if you'd like to continue, then my colleague and I can get a shuffle on and you can get back to whatever it was you were doing before our interruption."

"You ain't got any notebook?"

Ain't no flies on this old bloke, Josh mused.

"Left it in the car... but don't worry I've got a great memory... I'll jot it all down later, please continue, it's important."

"Well it was about two or three in the morning," Josh exhaled, knowing they were in the clear as he'd dropped Henry back at about one-thirty after they'd fled. "Could have been later; there was a godawful racket coming from that flat." Pat pointed through the door at the flat Henry was outside. "Sounded like someone was turning it over."

"Turning it over?"

"You know, looking for something. There was smashing glass, things being broken, shouting; there was so much bloody shouting it woke up the woman's dog next door, then there was barking too... I couldn't get to sleep for hours, not that I sleep much anymore anyway, up all night pissing, but you get the point."

"Could you tell what he was shouting about?"

"Argument it was, but I couldn't make out a word of it, they were going at it like an old married couple, back and forth, back and forth–"

"They?"

"Yeah, the two of them, shouting and screaming like it were some type of contest. I've never quite liked that guy, seems a bit odd, peculiar like... bit of a loner. He's always given me the chills whenever I've bumped into him in the lift, his eyes; it's like you don't know what's going on in his head, who knows maybe he doesn't even know."

Pat cleared his throat again before carrying on.

"I don't like the cut of his jib, something in my gut says he ain't who he claims to be, and my Mable; she used to say that your gut is something you should always trust and pay attention to, unless you had a Chicken Korma from 'Shazz's Cottage' down the way – then that's probably just food poisoning, have you shitting through the eye of a needle that filth she serves and has the audacity to call it India cuisine."

"You're sure there were two people?"

"I'm telling you he had company; female for sure. I don't know if it was some street worker he hadn't paid, or some crackhead he'd swindled out of some gear. But what I do know is that she was as pissed as a lion with a toothache; well she was before she started crying that is, she was bawling her little heart out towards the end... then she wasn't."

"Did you see her leave?"

"Nope, but he left about an hour before you guys started hammering on his door."

"And you've not seen anyone come or go since he left?"

"I couldn't be certain, I don't stand at this peephole all day and night you know... but the walls are thin and sound travels. If she'd left, which I don't think she did, I'd have heard the door slam shut. You don't think she's dead, do you?"

Josh hadn't a clue, but something strange was going on and they'd get some answers soon enough.

"That's why we need to gain entry Pat, to do a wellness check, but as you can see, we're struggling to–"

"Silly me, I've been jabbering away while a poor girl could be dying in there for all we know. I got a key for the flat in my drawers."

"And how did you come by that?"

"Previous tenant, she'd left me a key so I'd water her plants when she'd go away for a naughty weekend, she never took it back; then she moved out and that waster moved in. Wait right here and I'll go grab it for you." Pat shuffled away from the door, dragging his lifeline with him, the squeaking of the wheels grew weaker as Pat disappeared from view.

Josh turned and Henry was staring back at him.

"He's got a key," Josh said in an excited but hushed voice.

Henry stuck his thumb up, peered over his shoulder, checked no one was coming.

"Hurry the fuck up," he whispered back.

Josh turned back to the door as the wheels of Pat's oxygen tank announced his impending arrival.

"Here you go," Pat said as he peered around the door, holding out the key, which Josh noticed was attached to one of those lucky rabbit's feet key-rings.

Josh made to grab it but Pat pulled it away at the last moment.

"You ain't the police are you?"

He's on to us, he's been on to us the whole bloody time, Josh mused darkly.

"Sir, please, you're impeding our–"

"Whatever you say officer, here take it," Pat uttered, a mischievous, knowing smile gracing his skull-like face. "Just make sure you return it after your *investigation.*"

"Thank you," Josh replied as he snatched the key.

"Mum's the word!" Pat whispered before winking and tapping the side of his nose.

"You've been a great help, Pat; thank you," Josh said before walking away from the door. He heard the wheels of Pat's oxygen tank behind him, he glanced back and the walking skeleton was halfway out his flat peering down the corridor at them.

"Just make sure you slip that there key under the door when you're done. I'll be sitting down watching my shows and this body ain't what it used to be, I get tired, I don't wanna have to get up again once I'm down."

"Roger that Pat, I'll make sure to slide it under the door when we're finished with our... investigations."

"You do that," Pat uttered before bursting into a phlegmy, wet, wheeze of a laugh. "*Investigations*; that's a good one... just behave yourselves in there and make sure you bring back my key, mind. I ain't got another one."

"Will do," Josh said with a tip of an imaginary hat, but the gesture was lost on Pat as he'd already retreated into his house, the door slamming closed behind him.

Josh hurried back to Henry holding up the key.

"Rowen's apparently out. Don't know how much time we've got but we know what we're looking for right?" Josh glanced at Henry who nodded but remained silent.

Josh placed the key in the lock, turned once more to Henry.

"We get in, we get out; right?" Josh said.

Henry nodded and Josh opened the door.

THE PLACE LOOKED LIKE A BOMB SITE.

The curtains were in shreds, what remained was hanging from their poles, billowing in the breeze that blew unimpeded through the open windows, but they weren't open, they were shattered. Josh remembered that the crystal which had hung from the ceiling had smashed at least one, but as he took in the twinkling glass across the floor and felt the frigid fingers of the breeze tickle his skin, he noticed that every damned window in the flat had been smashed.

Henry bustled past him. He had the look of a home invader, Josh mused that *maybe they were*. They had a key, they hadn't broken in, but they were uninvited guests however you looked at it.

Josh watched on as Henry went about his task like a man possessed.

Henry's boots crunched down through a pile of wood and glass, what it had been before was anyone's guess but his friend wasn't standing on ceremony, he was ploughing through the detritus with a steely determination.

Henry flung a variety of broken pieces of furniture out of the way, desperate to get to the floor beneath it all. In his bullish burrowing, Josh heard glass shattering under Henry's feet; wood snapped, things were dislodged and other rubble tumbled into the spaces vacated of broken things.

Henry reached down suddenly and began heaving something heavy and large from the floor. He eventually flipped it over and pushed it away, not giving it a second thought; but Josh had. It was the table where they'd been sitting last night, minus the legs.

"It's gotta be here man," Henry's voice was panicked and threaded with anger. Josh thought Henry sounded like an addict who'd lost a bag of Charlie in a blizzard.

"Where is it?" Henry roared, throwing one of the chair legs from the table across the room which smashed into something unseen before he started digging through the rubble again with a renewed urgency.

With Henry as busy as a cat burying its shit in a sandbox, Josh moved slowly across the room, towards the table. He'd seen something which wasn't there last night. As he stumbled over a few broken bookcases and plasterboard, the scarred surface of the table came into view. The gouged letters were still there, the alphabet, the numbers, the yes and the no, but there were letters which appeared burned into the table; letters that made up words, words which made a sentence, a sentence that would have repercussions if Henry were to chance a look in its direction.

I KILLED HER, YOU CAN NEVER HAVE HER BACK

Josh grabbed the edge of the table and wanting to spare his friend any more pain, pulled it towards him so the words faced the floor and slid it across the ground, burying that message from sinking its teeth into Henry. Josh would tell him, in time; but now wasn't that time, because finding what they'd come for and getting the hell out of there was the only thing on Henry's mind and that's what Josh wanted. His friend focused and present.

But as Josh cast his eyes around the flat, their task seemed impossible.

Finding what they'd come for would be akin to finding a needle in a haystack given how small it was and the sheer state the flat was now in. *That's if it was even in here*, Josh mused. But he didn't have time for indecision, not now, not when the wolf could be at the door at any moment. So, he got stuck in.

He sifted through chair cushions, broken crockery, and smashed picture frames. He hefted a few drawers which had been pulled from a dresser dumped in the vicinity of where they'd sat last night. There was a mattress there now, well part of one anyway, it was eviscerated, its guts hanging out; Josh took hold of it and heaved it from its final resting place and launched it over towards the table, adding more litter to keep that haunting message hidden.

When he turned back to the space he'd made he noticed on the wooden floorboards three capsules, two had been broken, quite possibly underfoot, the other was whole. Josh crouched down and picked it up, he lifted it to the light.

"You find it?" Henry called out hopefully.

"No, just some capsule, looks like a tablet or something."

"Well if it ain't what we're here to find, it's not important!"

Henry shouted back as he lifted a sheet of plasterboard which had fallen down from the ceiling and began rummaging beneath it.

Josh examined the capsule once more. There were no markings on it, no printed letters, so it wasn't medication. *What the hell are you?* He pondered briefly, but instead of throwing it away he gathered the other broken shells and slipped them all into his pocket. He had no idea why, but there was something stirring in his gut which told him they were important and as Pat had just told him, the gut must be listened to at all times.

"It's not here," Henry shouted again.

"Keep looking, it'll turn up."

"What you think I'm doing, twiddling my fucking fingers over here. Why don't you go check over there," Henry flung an arm in the direction of what Josh assumed was the bathroom or kitchen; it had to be one or the other because the bedroom lurked behind him. It was empty, not a scratch in there; not even the remains of a bed frame, if there'd ever been one. The only thing that denoted it as the bedroom was the other half of the mattress that lay in shredded pieces of foam at the door's threshold, the stuffing spilling into the room like an animal's innards, as if it were a carcass Josh had just stumbled upon in the wild.

He stepped languidly across the room, trying to stay on his feet. As he trekked over the assortment of broken things, he tried desperately to visualise what Henry had lost, in the vain hope that it might just suddenly appear in some type of cosmic providence.

The needle they were looking for in this proverbial haystack of rubble was the photo Henry had taken from his wallet yesterday, for use in the séance. Josh remembered it now as he tried to will it into being; it was of Henry and Elsie; she'd been seated on his shoulders, wearing a baby pink swimming costume. He recalled how they'd both been beaming, a glorious candid snapshot in time of when things had been good.

Henry had said in the car on the way over that he wasn't willing to sacrifice that memory for anything on God's green earth. Leaving it there, in Rowen's flat to spoil was sacrilegious to her memory. Josh could see his meaning and didn't blame him for wanting it back, which was the sole reason why he was here, now; sifting through rubble and ruin. Josh knew that if he'd had kids and Amanda had captured a moment like that, a moment of such unrestrained joy and love and acceptance, wild horses wouldn't have been able to keep him away from reclaiming it. A moment like that doesn't come often, and for someone who's lost everything, that snapshot had become, over time; his everything.

Josh peered over at Henry who was still frenziedly burrowing though the rubbish littered around the flat and felt a deep pang of pain for his friend. Because Henry believed unquestionably that the presence of Elsie last night proved he'd lost her for good, and if he had – which Josh doubted, but wouldn't voice completely, not yet anyway – Josh would do his damnedest to help Henry find that photo, to preserve the moment Henry cherished above a lifetime of moments; when Henry had been truly present in Elsie's life, when she'd been his little girl and he'd been her doting father.

Josh stumbled over some of the broken pieces of furniture as he made his way to the room Henry had directed him to. Turning into the doorway, the room revealed itself as a bathroom, but Josh didn't step into it straight away because on the floor, in the middle of the black and white grubby looking tile pattern was a thick circle of bone-white powder; and at its centre was an envelope.

Josh glanced over his shoulder as Henry lifted the remains of a huge television above his head and launched it across the room where it hit a wall-mounted radiator, the screen smashing on impact, the radiator coming loose and hanging askew. Henry turned to Josh as the shattered glass tinkled its way across the room, shrugged his shoulders before diving back into the junk at his feet.

Knowing Henry was occupied and he'd hear him if he ventured this way, Josh slowly stepped back into the bathroom. He paced around the white circle and found various places outside of its powdery perimeter where candles had burnt themselves out, each leaving behind a puddle of waxy residue. He counted five in total and as he crouched down beside the circle and put his fingers to the wax, his eyes darted between the other remnants of candles which had been strategically placed around the circle, remembering something about five pointed stars – pentagrams – being used in witchcraft and hexes.

He'd positioned himself so he was facing the doorway, so he'd be able to move at a moment's notice. He could still hear Henry moving things about in the other room and with his friend otherwise engaged, he turned his attention back to the circle and the thing that sat at its centre which filled him with dread.

The envelope was turned away from him, positioned in such a way that it could be read by whomever came through the door. Josh could see there was one word written on the front, but the chicken scratch was hard to decipher upside down and so he reached out a trembling hand to turn it around, but as his hand crossed the circle's edge he pulled it back sharply.

The air within the circle seemed colder than the rest of the bathroom.

He steadied himself again, put the odd sensation down to the cold air barrelling into the bathroom from the shattered windows in the other room. Taking a deep breath he plunged his hand into the circle, fighting against the chill and retrieved the envelope.

Josh glanced down at the envelope and a shiver ran down his spine.

The scrawled word read: DADDY.

"I found it... I fucking found it!" Henry's words erupted in the eerie quiet that had formed in the bathroom, the sudden outburst caused Josh to drop the letter.

He could hear Henry scampering across the rubble now, heading in his direction.

"Josh, I got it, let's get the hell out of here," Henry's words were closer.

Josh peered down at the letter.

Henry's looming shadow spilled across the entrance to the bathroom.

Josh reached down and reclaimed the letter.

"You in there?" Henry said.

Josh stood up sharply, his eyes staring down at the now empty circle.

"Josh... you alright?"

Josh didn't answer because how could he be alright with what he was about to do.

The toe of Henry's boot appeared at the door.

Josh glanced down at the letter in his hands.

Henry's chest came next.

Josh folded the letter.

Then Henry's swinging arm, hand clutching the photograph of Elsie came next.

Josh moved the letter behind his back as Henry's face appeared around the door.

Josh slipped the letter in his back pocket.

"What you doing in the dark buddy?"

Josh pointed at the circle.

"Found this." Josh said sheepishly.

"Right. What is it?" Henry relied quizzically.

"No idea, it doesn't matter," Josh shrugged, turning his guilt riddled face to the floor.

"You wanna get the fuck out of here or you gunna run a bath and take a soak?"

Henry turned away from the room, scampering for the front door.

Josh swallowed his shame, his deception and his guilt and followed in Henry's wake.

CHAPTER TWELVE

A trifecta of deception, guilt and shame had been running rampant in Josh's mind since he'd left Rowen's house with his stolen goods; which one would win the race and set up a permanent residence was still undecided, the odds forever changing. Those dark feelings cantered like wild horses, each jostling for first place, continuously swapping position over the past week and showed no signs of slowing or going down lame; if anything, they were running faster and harder, chomping at their bits and foaming at their mouths to see which would make it over the line and be declared the winner in a race where there would only be losers.

He'd tried his best to ignore their galloping, and the mocking refrain of their jockeys, but their stampeding feet were persistent, a cannonade of thunder, each hoof churned up the ground in the wasteland of Josh's mind causing every thought to be clouded and tainted by his deceptive, shame-filled and guilt-ridden actions.

Josh had wanted to do anything but face those three demons: deception, guilt and shame; they were the horsemen of his own private judgement. And so, wanting to rid his mind of them he threw himself into his work. Josh had worked his fingers to the bone in the days following their visit to Rowen's, spending every waking moment scrubbing and rubbing, stripping and painting, hammering and nailing.

He even tore things down – a stud wall for example – just to give himself an excuse to build something back up again. In the vain hope that if he could fix a wall he'd just torn down, then surely, he'd be able to repair the damage he'd unwittingly inflicted in his and Henry's friendship.

Surely, he could make all things new, it was his job; his purpose, his God given skill.

But you can't fix what you've done – the jockeys would mock from their steeds.

Inexcusable – they'd chide.

Irreparable damage – they'd sing.

Unforgivable – they'd cackle.

The voices had convinced him that repairing their damaged friendship was a fool's errand; it couldn't – wouldn't – be the same again, and maybe they were right. Josh knew he'd never be able to repair what he'd done to Henry – robbing him from the very thing he'd been searching for over the last twelve years; answers to his daughter's disappearance – without firstly owning up to what he'd done.

Until he faced the music of this lonely waltz, the ugly crack which had formed between them would still remain, its fissures reaching all the way down to the very foundations their friendship was built on. Josh knew that the only thing that could fill that hole and bridge that gap was forgiveness, but he also knew from his constant inventory of Henry's emotional state, that forgiveness was temporarily out of stock; the little supply he did have, nestled on the top shelf in a dank and lonely corner of Henry's resolve, was covered in dust and all reserved under the name of Elsie.

He'd still ask for forgiveness, when the time came; maybe his friend would have some stockpiled somewhere, but Josh wasn't ready to face the music just yet, or the inevitable shitstorm that would follow his admission of guilt; because if he was going to ask for total forgiveness he'd need to finish what he started when he'd pocketed the letter, he'd actually need to read it. Then and only then could he beg for forgiveness, then and only then would he have answers to the various theories floating around his head as to what Rowen's part in all of this was; and he had a great many to work through.

The last five days had passed in somewhat of a blur, even though he'd thrusted himself into his work – the flipping of the house on Petherton Road – to allay the despair he'd felt at pocketing the letter, which had been meant for his friend; his best friend, Elsie's *Daddy*. The blur of that week also contained fractured glimpses of his theories regarding its appearance, and the sudden appearance of this loner called Rowen.

Who are you?
What do you want?
How did you find us?
What did you do with Elsie?
Where did you bury her?

Josh had pondered that last question as he had set about whittling a new spindle for the staircase. It had been a question Henry, his dear friend, had wanted to know above all else; but was still none the wiser. He'd found himself plagued by a pang of insufferable guilt and his mind had gone into overdrive at his deception.

I've literally stolen the final words of Henry's... dead... daughter. He'd mused.

Because she's dead, right? She's gotta be.

You can't be missing for that length of time and not turn up in a ditch.

The horsemen had raised their voices in a burst of devilish teasing.

You stole the final words from her cold dead lips, penned by her long-dead hand.

He'd tried desperately over the intervening days to reason with those demons, urgently attempting to excuse his actions, explaining away his reasons to the empty, dust filled tenement he'd find himself cooped up in. He bawled to no one and everyone that what he'd done had been for Henry's best interests, but the rampaging fiends – of deception, guilt and shame – only cackled back their disdain, their horses neighing and panting, continuing their ever-present stampede in his mind, their thrashing legs threatening to trample him beneath the churning of his psyche, resolve and moral compass. Josh knew it was all wishful thinking – doing it for Henry's best interests – because the reason he'd taken it, pocketed the letter when he'd discovered it within the salt circle; was because he'd wanted to know what was written inside it. Plain and simple.

If what he'd discovered would further his circling thoughts that this whole thing was a ruse, a sick joke played at a grieving man's expense – he'd be right, and he loved being right, especially when it concerned Henry. It was a selfish act of course and one that had eaten away at him with each passing day; but his own selfish desires had overridden whatever tattered moral compass he had left, a compass which apparently now spun in every direction other than true.

He needed to know.

He wanted to know.

Because he needed to prepare himself – and Henry – for what would come next if he was right.

———

JOSH LABOURED UP THE STEPS TO HIS ABODE, SLIPPED HIS KEY IN THE LOCK and opened the front door, stepping inside he felt the cold chill that always accompanied his return to his gutted life; no rest for the wicked, he mused ruefully.

"Amanda, I'm home," he called, a painful ritual he'd keep up until one day, when he opened that door in Heaven and she'd finally respond.

He deposited his satchel on the floor as the silence of the house swirled around him.

Silence always greeted him; but today's silence seemed expectant, weighty, and full of anticipation as if the house knew what he was about to do.

He closed the door and locked the deadbolt before shambling down the corridor.

He tried desperately not to look at the photos which hung in the hallway; there were so many that he'd often mocked Amanda that when they moved out, if they ever did, he'd spend an eternity filling the holes, so much so that the wall would be more filler than plasterboard.

The gallery was a constant reminder of all he'd lost, memories stored behind panes of glass which pained him gravely; joyous moments captured from his wife's short and abbreviated life. It was a torturous affair on most days, but since he'd robbed Henry of his daughter's – possibly – last words, the warm and joyous snapshots of good times had turned into a gallery of judgement, each time he shambled past he felt he was in the docks, hands from the pictures pointing at him and screaming: GUILTY!

Over the last few days especially, as he'd slowly convinced himself to open the damned letter, it appeared that Amanda's once loving eyes had begun to stare despondently at the man she'd once loved, the life in them dulling like a worn penny. Her eyes now pools of scorn, he could almost hear Amanda's judgement; tutting, a laboured sigh which was usually followed with a mocking refrain of: *what have you become?*

Each day since that letter had been in his possession, he'd run the gauntlet, and more often than not, the gauntlet won and his evening would dissolve into bouts of inescapable depression, rivalling those feelings that drove him to the brink of taking his own life. Amanda's disapproving gaze was too much for Josh to handle on the best of days, which currently were few and far between. Her scrutiny of him was a blowtorch held to his skin; if he lingered long enough under it, he was sure she'd make him do the right thing; give the letter back to its rightful owner.

He wouldn't do that though, because he needed to know, he needed to prepare for what would happen next, but more importantly he needed to know he'd been right all along and today he'd find out, today he'd finally open the letter of a dead girl.

And so, as he'd done the last few days he returned to his empty house, kept his head down and loped ever-onwards, desperate to flee the gallery of suffering and the judgement that poured from his wife's eyes like a never-ending tide which threatened to drown him where he stood.

Josh staggered into the lounge, turned sharply and closed the door behind him, barricading himself inside, away from the disapproving eyes of his wife. He sheltered behind the door for a moment, taking some calming breaths, it was but a flimsy shield from her judgemental and paralysing gaze but he knew it would hold, until he'd done what needed to be done.

He turned and rested his back against the door, head lowered to the ground, but slowly it began to rise and Josh peered across the dimly lit room, ever-hopeful for a reprieve for the guilt he'd suffered on entering his house, but no respite came; because before him, where it had sat idly for the last five days, growing ominous with each day it remained unread: was the letter.

He read the only word on the envelope from where he stood.

Daddy.

The word he formed in his mind wasn't in his voice, it was a chorus of children.

DADDY. DADDY. DADDY. DADDY.

It repeated again and again, rising in pitch, the diabolical cadence of a heartbeat.

Instead of feeling his racing heart beat as he read the word, he felt it flayed in that moment, a deep-rooted ache that threatened to bring him to his knees before he even read the letter. His mind had instantly become a broiling soup of warring emotions; and in the middle of it all – like a crouton that wouldn't dissolve – was the question he'd been pondering ever since he slipped the letter into his pocket: *If Rowen had this letter, then he's involved, he's got something to hide, he's responsible.*

Josh walked slowly towards the table, with each step the word repeated in his mind.

Daddy.

He was three steps away now.

Daddy.

Two.

Daddy.

One.

Daddy.

He gripped the back of the chair as he peered down at the letter, he needed to hold onto something before he was pulled under by the rising tide of shame and guilt. He slowly slid the chair out from where it had neatly been tucked under the table and collapsed into its welcoming embrace. He sat with his hands in his lap, the courage to pull the letter from its place and tear it open, spilling its long-held secrets still remained an elusive action; he wanted nothing more than to rip the plaster off, but once he did, once he discovered what was inside, there would be no way of putting it back. And so, he waited.

However long he sat there he didn't know, but as he peered at the letters once more, tracing each one with his eye, mouthing the word they spelt – Daddy – he realised that the room had grown dimmer, that night was slowly strangling the day. He'd much rather birth these secrets whilst there was still a semblance of light, albeit a purplish-hue in the sky outside his window. He needed to act. He needed to discover if Elsie's words would give any clarity to the swirling thoughts he'd held about Rowen's authenticity ever since the night of the séance.

He raised a quivering hand from his lap and reached for the letter.

Snatching at it. Pulling it towards his other hand.

The first thing Josh thought as he held the envelope in his hands was how heavy it seemed, as if the words of the dead and the secrets they'd unearth were weighted, as if once he opened the letter, everything would be altered, one way or the other, for good or for bad.

He traced the word on the front with his finger: D–A–D–D–Y.

The writing had been done in biro, the letters slightly embossed, small grooves carved into the paper by the nib of the pen and as Josh's finger flicked off the end of the Y he wondered if that was the last mark Elsie had ever left on the world.

Turning the letter over in his hands, he began to run his finger along the fastening before slowly teasing one corner open. He slipped his finger into the envelope and sawed his way down the gummed fastening; tearing it open like a ragged wound, and depending what was entombed inside – scribbled in a dead girl's handwriting – perhaps it was?

Sliding the letter out, Josh dropped the envelope on the table, opting to keep it face down, a way to ensure he wasn't reminded of his dishonesty at keeping this from Henry, denying him the first contact with his daughter in twelve long years.

Guilt-ridden and shame-faced Josh unfolded the letter and began to read.

Daddy,

To call you that after such a long time feels wrong, as if the word has lost all meaning, because a daddy doesn't give up on his daughter, doesn't send her away, doesn't close the door behind her and lock it so she can't come back, even if she wanted to. A daddy doesn't tell his daughter that he wished she were dead!

So, I'll call you Henry, because you lost the right to be called my 'daddy' a long time ago.

Time away from you has given me perspective, and I've learnt over the years (I'm eighteen now by the way, in case you even cared) that I didn't deserve any of it; your hate and your apathy, your bigoted views and your scornful looks - no one deserves to be treated the way you treated me, but somehow, I let you. Rowen said that how I let you treat me reminds him of how an owner kicks their dog when it misbehaves, how they beat it, choke it and eventually get it to toe the line, always returning to its master's feet with its tail between its legs. You never kicked me or hit me, you let your words do the work of your hands, and those blows landed the hardest, finding the delicate soft spots, time and time again. Rowen's right though in a way, I did always return to you, like a dog does its vomit, because I held out hope (how wrong I was) that you'd eventually learn to love me for who I was and what I was. But Rowen's words are true. As I pen this letter, I've realised: I was always and forever will be, the mutt at your feet.

It wasn't just you though was it, it was Mum too. But she gets a pass, for now, because I've only enough time to write one letter, and I wanted it to be for you.

For years you made me feel less than I was. Even after all the years I've been away I still find finger-prints of your hate on me when I look in the mirror, your hate is a gift that apparently keeps on giving. How can I love myself when I keep seeing your words staring back at me, as those hateful words of so long ago are forever tattooed on my skin?

In a way I hope you die a miserable, lonely death... a death you truly deserve.

It's taken me this long, four long years, to realise I had worth, but I had to be away from you to discover it; and Rowen has shown me the way to love myself, to love who and what I truly am.

I needed to be around the right people to find that worth, to be surrounded by loving, accepting people who didn't judge me like you did, people who didn't call me a diseased little tramp or yell that, the sight of me sickened them.

I found belonging, Henry; something you'll never have.

I found that I could love myself and be loved for who I am; the terrified little girl who you disowned, the child that you let walk away. I'd hoped as a child hopes, that you'd come after me, that by the time I'd gotten to the end of the road you'd have been sprinting after me, but when I looked back, there was only the lonely path I'd walked alone.

When I'd got to the park, at the end of our road. I waited. I waited for you to come for me, but you didn't.

I'd got into a fight with a group of kids from my school, they'd hurled insults at me too, but not nearly as hurtful as yours, but I didn't care because as they slung their insults, all I saw was your face instead of theirs, I hurt them, I made them bleed, I pictured you and savaged you, I only wish it was you. I ran after that, left my bag and hightailed it out of there.

I hitched a ride to Glastonbury, from there I went to Cornwall, from there I made my way to Brighton, but still it wasn't far enough from you and that hate-filled house or your disgusted and sickened face (which I still see each time I close my eyes). I knew I'd never be coming back, and that part of my life, my childhood was over before it had really ever begun.

You've been dead to me a long time now Henry and I've had a great many years to mourn your loss. You, Kiera and that house; that godawful home of torment and abuse, are just things that resemble a dream, a recurring nightmare from a childhood I long to forget.

Rowen told me to write to you. Forced me to, because if I'm completely honest I wouldn't have bothered, but he thinks it's only right you should know, seeing as you brought me into this world.

Rowen said that without saying what needs to be said, without me saying goodbye to the past properly, I won't be able to rid myself of the strangling hold you still have on my life and I won't find peace, when I do what needs to be done - because even now, four years later; I feel you, see you, hear you; I know it's not you, but it is you in a way, your hideous face projected everywhere I look. Every scornful expression and utterance of hate; each flinch from the slightest contact with me once they know what I am. Each push or punch and mouthful of spit directed at me by strangers is from you; because they wear your face, speak your words, use your hands and feet and phlegm. Every sliver of hate I've had to endure in my life has your face behind it; that menacing, mirth-riddled, devilish grin you flashed my way when I left.

You preside over it all, you orchestrated the destruction of me, piece by piece.

So, now's the time to say goodbye.

There's no acceptance in this world, I've discovered; only a thinly held tolerance and that fact saddens me gravely.

Rowen told me that after today, I won't be able to speak to you again, because it's time, time to say my last goodbye.

He's going to kill me Henry... daddy dearest... he's going to kill me, he wants to put me out of my misery, the misery you caused, the misery you caused my heart to become polluted by. Rowen's been nothing but protective of me, wanting the very best for me since he appeared in my life all those years ago, he's the one I ran towards when you kicked me out and he accepted me with arms wide open. I hope that stings, because instead of isolating me as you'd hoped, you only pushed me towards the person that's only ever wanted me to be happy, truly happy with who I was and free from you.

I hope you choke on that.

Rowen's become persistent over time about ending my life, his desire to end my life, to end my pain has become slowly my desire too - he's very convincing as I'm sure you'll find out. Because for me to truly heal, to be at peace, to escape your voice and the disgust you impregnated me with, that lays bloated like a worm in my stomach - I have to die.

Rowen seems to think that's the best way to escape it all.

But don't worry, Henry; I won't be alone, Rowen will be holding my hand the whole time. He loves me. Loves me more than you ever did, or ever could, because his love is based on the acceptance of who I am.

And for me to be happy and content and finally at peace, I need to die.

So, this letter is my goodbye, my long goodbye it would seem.

I don't know why I'm writing it, because I doubt you even care. I also have no idea if you'll ever read it; but I hope you do, I pray unceasingly that you do, because I want you to see what you caused.

I'll make sure Rowen gets this to you somehow, even if it takes him years to track you down or carry out my last wishes.

I want these words to find you and when they do I hope they sting. I hope they cut you wide fucking open and your life dissolves in ruin around you. I hope you can't face living knowing that you caused this, all of this!

But before I go, I want you to know that I did find acceptance in the end and a place to belong and call home. I found peace and love and hope and belonging. And I did all of that to spite you...

Rowen is coming now, he's told me I have to say goodbye, but I don't want to.

Not because I don't want to say it, but rather I feel you don't deserve it.

If you're right about me, about where I'll end up if I kept up my delusions,

I'll see you in Hell!

Elsie

A smile crested Josh's lips as he processed the contents of the letter, which was an odd emotive response he mused, given the words he'd read from Elsie; this strange suicide, death pact she'd made. He tried to rubbish the glee he felt, opting for a more sombre outlook, but he couldn't, the smile stretched more broadly and he nodded his head as he placed the letter onto the table because he'd been right all along and the letter proved that.

Rowen's involved. He killed Elsie.

As that thought crystallised in his mind, his smile faltered as realisation set in.

Elsie *was* indeed dead; as Henry had believed her to be, and also as Henry believed wholeheartedly, *he* was to blame for it all. He wasn't the one that had gotten his hands dirty carrying out the atrocious act, although Josh thought Henry's hands were pretty dirty all the same – given the letter Josh had just read; but the person that was responsible: was Rowen.

Josh had been secretly holding out hope the events of the séance had been an elaborate hoax all along, that it had been Elsie attempting to get back at her father for all he'd done to her; how he'd shamed her for being – what Josh could only assume from the letter and the small morsels of information he'd gleaned from conversations with Henry – part of the LGBTQ community.

Josh knew that Elsie wouldn't be making an appearance at the eleventh hour, as he had once pondered; she wouldn't be stumbling into another séance or a group session with the COCS screaming 'I GOT YOU!' with Rowen in tow.

Because Elsie was dead.

The letter on the table was her last goodbye, one that Josh had robbed Henry of.

Dead.

The word was an anvil, crushing him where he sat. He knew he'd have to give the letter back, own up to taking it with albeit good intentions; but now Josh knew something that her own grief-riddled father didn't know: Elsie was dead.

The thought almost floored him, his deception suddenly a shotgun blast to his soul.

How can I face him tomorrow? Josh thought.

When Henry finally found out his daughter was dead, Josh believed the news would only further perpetuate his friend's grief-spun delusion that what had transpired at the séance was real, regardless of how Rowen had been involved in her death as well as her sudden appearance from the hinterlands of death.

Josh still couldn't fully work out if the events of the séance had been faked, because how does one even fake something like that? Make it seem so real.

Elsie is dead, maybe it was real? he'd questioned, and the question muddled him, because if it was true, what did that make of his beliefs in Heaven.

A JOKE IS WHAT IT MAKES THEM! His subconscious answered.

Amanda soon loomed large in his thoughts and he couldn't help but acknowledge her briefly or the question she posed by her sudden appearance, now; as he pondered the question of life after death.

If Elsie's spirit was real, and the letter proved she'd passed, that she'd gone to wherever it was dead things go, what did that mean for Amanda?

Josh couldn't breathe suddenly, it felt as if a huge weight were crushing his chest and so he pushed his wife away; now was not the time to get distracted, or lose hope, he had to cling to his belief that he'd see her soon, in Heaven. He knew if he didn't force those thoughts away right this instant, he might as well give up, drive himself out to the place that still called to him on lonely nights and finish the job he'd started all those years ago.

Now wasn't the time to mope, now was the time to work out how he could sit in a room with Henry – and Rowen if he showed up – knowing what he knew now, because there'd be no feasible time to broach the subject of Elsie's letter with Henry until after tomorrow's meeting. If Rowen did decide to turn up, Josh would have to bite his tongue and bide his time because they didn't need more bloodshed, and if Henry knew what he'd done, he'd guarantee that blood would be spilt, and it wouldn't be the blood dripping from Rowen's hands which was unmistakably Elsie's.

It would be Rowen's as Henry tore him limb for limb.

Josh peered down at the table, at the collected evidence he'd found so far, desperately looking for a way to prove all of this was an elaborate hoax, something tangible that he could lead with instead of the letter because Josh wanted to say his piece before revealing it, because after that letter, everything he'd wanted to tell Henry about how this was some kind of sick joke would be rendered meaningless.

He pushed the letter aside. It would remain exhibit one, the case breaker; it was motive, confession, and irrefutable evidence of the diabolical scheme being played out before them. But he needed more than the letter, he needed to find out information about Rowen; *who was he, where'd he come from, what was his part in this elaborate scheme of deception and what does he stand to gain from the complete destruction of Henry?*

Josh retrieved his mobile from his pocket and unlocked the screen before scrolling through the contacts, it took him a moment to find the one he needed; his finger hovered over the call button. He knew he had to bring someone else into this mess, but they didn't need to know everything, he'd keep those cards close to his chest.

He had to prove Rowen wasn't who he was pretending to be, because by all accounts that mattered – *the last words of a dead girl committed to paper* – it was clear he was a cold-hearted murderer. One who seemed not only to have been intent on killing Elsie from the first moment they'd met, grooming her over time until the day he took her life and made her believe it was a way to escape her woes; but also seemed quite happy to sit back and watch the slow and painful demise of her whole family, starting with her father.

Josh desperately needed information about Rowen and fast, and there was only one person he could think of who'd be able to help; what he did next was paramount to ensuring he had all the available information on hand when he brought the letter and his findings to Henry, *then and only then* Josh thought; *knowledge would win out.*

It would be the only thing to dissuade his friend from self-destructing.

Knowing this was the only way to get what he needed fast, he pressed the call icon.

It rang three times before a woman answered.

"Hello, Sian?" Josh offered.

"Yes, who's this?"

"Josh–"

"Josh who?" Sian replied abruptly.

"From group. The Circle of Caring Souls..."

"Oh, hiya. Is group cancelled tomorrow or something?"

"No, I need you to do me a favour, could you look into something for me?"

"Errr... sure, what is it?"

"Right, I need you to find someone–"

CHAPTER THIRTEEN

Henry was sitting on his bed. One hand holding a near-empty bottle of whiskey, the other clutching the picture of Elsie, which he'd successfully reclaimed from Rowen's house five days previously. The room was a dull affair which matched his mood, he'd opted for his bedside lamp instead of the overhead lights to ease his five-day hangover that was threatening to spill into a sixth, he'd not yet been able to sleep in the dark since Elsie's clothes had returned to sleep in her bed.

His eyes were red and puffy, not from the lack of sleep, although he was bone tired; his eyes were red and blotchy from the tears he'd been shedding all evening. He placed the bottle of whiskey on his bedside table, before turning his gaze to his hand, where he focused through his blurry, tear-streaked vision at the ragged scar which was slowly knitting itself back together on his palm.

After observing its raised and puckered edges, his eyes flitted back to the picture of Elsie, alighted for a moment on the snapshot before they eventually found their way back to his palm again.

He sobbed, a deep wracking sob which caused his body to rise and fall. Snot dribbled freely from his nose and he reached up his arm and rubbed the mucus away with his sleeve. He lifted the picture of Elsie closer, raised his hand too, bringing both closer to his face to obtain a better look at what he'd discovered.

The scar which he made out in the dim lamplight was the perfect shape and size to the birthmark which decorated Elsie's clavicle, a birthmark she'd always hated and had asked her mother if when she was old enough she could have it removed.

Henry had always told her that he'd loved that little birthmark, that it made her different from the rest, that in time, she'd grow to love it as much as he did. But in time it wasn't the birthmark that marked her out as different, it was something else: her sexuality.

Over time, he'd grown to despise everything about her; even that ruddy birthmark.

His focus switched from the picture to his scarred hand again and he couldn't believe the symmetry between the two kidney shaped blemishes. As the realisation landed, a shiver of trepidation ran up his spine as he mused about the night he'd suffered his injury, his maiming; wondering if Elsie's ghost, spirit or whatever it was which had inhabited her clothes, marred him that night she'd visited him in his dream, so he'd never be able to forget their encounter, or the part he played in her no longer being in the land of the living.

He lowered the picture and his eyes darted quickly to the door.

What was that? He thought he'd heard something shuffling in his room.

He peered down at the bottom of the bedroom door.

The landing light was still burning brightly outside, he'd opted to keep that light on too since the night he discovered something other-worldly stalking around his house, successfully trapping it in his daughter's room after it tried to get him. When nothing broke the beam of light under the door, his eyes travelled slowly along the darkened wall of his room, all the way to the corner where he believed the shuffling sound was coming from.

He half-expected to see Elsie's clothes huddled in the corner waiting to crawl towards him, to clamber up his bed and finally end him.

CREEEEAAAAKKKK.

The slow creak of a door swinging open resounded through the quiet house and sent another fresh batch of chills running down his spine.

He knew now that the sound came from outside his room, but the rusted lament of hinges didn't put his mind at ease, if anything it put his addled mind on edge, because the exact sound he'd just heard had been tattooed on his mind; it was Elsie's door.

He quickly swung his legs out of bed, shuffling his weary bones over to the edge of the mattress and placed his feet on the hardwood floors, if he was going down, he wouldn't be going down whimpering on the ground like before, he'd go out swinging. As his bare feet touched down, he almost pulled them back up instantly; as it had been the night when Elsie's clothes appeared and her muddied feet had stained the carpet throughout his house, the floor beneath his feet was freezing to the touch.

THUD. THUD. THUD.

The sound of footsteps boomed in the landing as they slowly approached his door.

Reaching over to his bedside table, Henry picked up the bottle of whiskey. He necked the remaining amber liquid in a few large gulps before upturning it, holding it by its neck. He felt a small, momentary relief wash over his fear, because now he had a weapon and if whatever roamed his house decided to gain entry to his room, he'd club it with his glass mace and if that broke, he'd set about slicing his assailant with the shards that remained, and if it was what he feared lurking outside his room, he'd shred every piece of clothing that dared set foot in his fucking room; to hell with the memories.

THUD.

The thing was right outside his door.

Henry peered down at the bar of light.

It was now split into three separate beams and two shadows.

The thing was standing outside his room.

His eyes found the doorknob in the dim light of the bedroom.

He sat poised, his feet had melted away the signs of frost on the ground, he was ready to run at the door at the first sign of the handle moving. But it didn't. He almost willed it to move, to have an excuse to release the tension that was building in his chest and threatening to house him in. He glanced down again and witnessed the shadows – the feet – move slowly away from his door; first one, then the other, the thing venturing further, deeper, into the house.

THUD. THUD. THUD. THUD.

He glanced down at the photo still held tightly in his grasp.

Elsie smiled back at him.

He placed the picture in his breast pocket before taking a deep lungful of air, the kind of breath someone takes when they have to do something they'd been putting off for weeks, but Henry had been putting this particular task off for the last twelve years.

Do or be damned he had to go to her, had to tell her he was sorry; even if all she was now was a bundle of soiled grave clothes.

Before he knew what he was doing, he was up and walking, moving gingerly towards the door, hyper-vigilant of each of his foot-falls. He could still make out the steps of his nightly visitor moving away from his position as his hand gripped the doorknob, which was also ice cold to touch.

THUD. THUD. THUD. THUD.

She was heading downstairs.

Henry slowly turned the handle and the door clicked open.

He cursed the noise as he peered through the crack, assessing the staircase beyond but he could only see partway down, the energy-saving lightbulb wasn't strong enough to penetrate the dark that swarmed in the depths of his house. When nothing rushed up at him from the darkness, called by the subtle click of the door, he opened the door the whole way.

Keeping his eyes on the darkened depths of his house through the spindles of the staircase, he stepped into the hallway on shaky legs.

He glanced down suddenly because his foot had come into contact with something that felt out of place, it felt like sand. It reminded him fleetingly of the picture in his pocket, of that blessed day at the beach with Elsie, when he was her doting father and she was the apple of his eye.

When he glanced down he discovered his foot was in a trail of white granular powder. His mind recalled the circle of white at Rowen's house, in the bathroom, that strange circle which appeared to have no reason for being there.

Leaning against the door with his shoulder, as he didn't want to relinquish his weapon to the ground, he lifted his leg, awkwardly resting it on his other knee and brushed at the white that had got stuck to his wet foot.

His palm, which was sweaty from fear, seemed to collect some of the crystals and so he brought it closer to his face once he was back on two feet, as he peered at the remnants of white, it appeared to be plain old salt.

"What the hell," Henry uttered quietly as his gaze followed the trail, one way; to the top of the stairs. He glanced over the top step and discovered a white line leading all the way into the darkness below.

His focus returned to the line at his feet and followed the white line in the other direction, towards Elsie's room; her door was open.

He felt a sudden surge of panic, she was loose.

Her room was still bathed in darkness, so he couldn't tell if her filthy clothes were still reclining on her bed. He wanted desperately to step back into his room and close the door. Hide out in there and face all of this crazy in the cold light of another torturous morning. But sunup wasn't for a good few hours, and the thing might come back when he wasn't ready or when sleep possibly took him, and so instead of retreating into his room, he stepped boldly towards her bedroom.

One aching step at a time.

His head whipped backwards and forwards.

Bedroom. Stairs. Bedroom. Stairs. Bedroom.

He was at the threshold of her room now. He glanced down and his eyes followed the line of salt as it continued into her room before being swallowed up a few yards in by the vacuous black, where nothing existed apart from the absence of everything.

He reached into the room, once again his arm broke out in goose-flesh as it did the first time he groped blindly for the light switch. He found it this time with much more ease and prepared himself for what would soon be revealed before he flicked the switch.

CLICK.

She was gone.

The clothes were no longer in her bed.

But instead, in its place was a pile of salt, a cone of the stuff, had to be at least three feet high, positioned directly in the centre of her mattress. He glanced down at the road of salt he'd followed to her door, it led all the way up to the bed, where a small pile had formed. He stood there stunned by this most recent development, but that feeling soon changed and he felt crushed by sadness, because Elsie's room was once more vacant of her spirit, she'd upped and left him again.

He followed the pillar of salt from her bed to the floor, across her room, out the door and into the corridor; it suddenly hit him. The salt was a trail, if her clothes had miraculously gone, it only meant one thing, she'd got up and walked the hell out of here, leaving a trail for him to follow. He wracked his brain trying to think of the significance of salt, but stopped his musings instantly, when a noise made him jump out of his skin.

BANG! BANG-BANG! BANG!

The noise had come from behind him and so he turned sharply in its direction.

He edged slowly along the corridor, following the path of salt.

He stood at the top of the staircase when the sound came again.

BANG! BANG!

Whatever the noise was it emanated from downstairs because it was louder now.

He peered into the dark at the bottom of the staircase which swelled like a body of murky lake water. The sight filled him with dread because he knew that soon enough he'd be dipping his toes into that frigid, dark world and he'd most likely be disturbing whatever lurked within its folds.

Henry stepped down and followed the path of salt.

As he descended the stairs he wondered if he'd find Elsie at the end of it, her body all withered and sucked dry of moisture like a slug. He shuddered at the hideous vision as he continued down the stairs, nothing would stop him now, because whatever lay at the end of this path, it was clear it was a path he was expected to follow and soon he'd discover what waited for him at his journey's end.

He stepped down onto the ground floor and instinctively reached for the light switch. He flicked it on but nothing happened. He glanced down at the floor and noticed the trail of salt disappearing towards the kitchen, his eyes searched the pregnant darkness ahead, waiting for a new horror to be born.

"Hello?" Henry called out.

BANG. BANG.

Henry flinched at the sudden noise, a shriek escaped his throat.

It was as if the shadows ahead of him were answering his call.

He tried the switch again, frantically clicking it on and off. Nothing.

He glanced up at the landing high above and the light of that floor seemed so far away, as if he were in some subterranean level of the earth under his house, where dark things crawled. *It can't be a power outage*, he mused because the light still burned up on the landing. *Maybe it's a fuse?* He glanced up at the bare bulb in the corridor.

But there was no bulb.

Where the hell? Henry thought as he glanced down at the floor, half-expecting to discover twinkling shards of glass as his eyes roved over the carpet.

BANGBANGBANGBANGBANG.

He spun back to the kitchen, thrusting the empty bottle out in front of him as if to ward off whatever would no doubt soon to be coming for him. He imagined Elsie's clothes shambling out of the dark towards him, her body moving without any discernible structure; as if all the bones in her body had been broken.

Henry shuffled gingerly along the corridor towards the kitchen and the noise. At the door he paused, there was just enough light to notice the white line turn to the left and disappear under another door, this one led to the garden. He inched into the kitchen and no sooner had he left the safety and sanctuary of the hall, the back door flew inwards. Henry staggered backwards, tripped on something on the floor and stumbled into the fridge, frantically swiping at the air in front of him with the bottle, somehow, managing to remain upright.

BANG. BANG.

He suddenly realised his eyes were pinched closed with fright. Opening them quickly he discovered the source of the noise. The back door was swinging freely, open and closed. It hit the cupboard behind it when it blew in, and when the wind sucked it back it slammed against the door jamb.

Henry slowly lowered the bottle, not wanting to let his guard down so soon.

Stepping closer to the door as it swung open to bang against the cupboard once more, he reached out and stopped it. Peering down at the ground he discovered the salt trail turned right, running down the side of the house towards the garden; he was about to step into the night and follow its lead when something glinted in the corner of his eye.

He stopped dead in his tracks.

In the lock were a set of keys.

Keys that had a faded Rolling Stones keyring on it, the one with the tongue and lips; black on red.

Henry removed the key from the lock and held it in his hand.

He was puzzled because the only people who knew where this particular set of keys were, were him and Elsie. They were the set they'd hidden together in the garden for use in an emergency. He'd sworn her to secrecy over their location, because Kiera had told them under no circumstances were they to leave a set of spare keys in the garden, however well they intended to hide them: *'That's just asking for us to be burgled!'* she'd said.

Seeing the keys in his hand shocked him, because he'd forgotten until now that they'd ever existed; but what shocked him the most as he stood there pondering their sudden appearance, was that the key wasn't on the inside of the door, but the outside.

If Elsie's clothes had gotten up and walked themselves out of the house like Henry had imagined: *How come the door was opened from the outside?*

It was that little needle of doubt that gave Henry pause but also made him feel like a fool because there was something going on here that not even he could understand, a cruel joke being played at his expense.

Who the hell let themselves into my house?

He couldn't help but picture Josh's smug face in his moment of enlightenment. Henry had known all along that Josh had his doubts about Elsie ever appearing at the séance; he knew too that Josh had even doubted she'd been in the house the night he'd found him cowering outside her door, her soiled clothes only feet away on her bed, but he never looked inside her room, because Henry knew he didn't believe a word he was saying – they'd argued about it, that he certainly did remember.

As he stared at the keys again he felt he was losing what little of his mind he had left.

I didn't dig her clothes up, did I?

Surely, I'd know if I dug her up, if I brought her home?

He smiled wryly as he thought about Josh's desire to always be right, especially about matters of the heart and the stranglehold grief has on the griever. Henry smiled now though because he knew Josh was wrong; about one thing in particular and it was a big fucking deal. Elsie *was* here with him and she always would be. When she left the house twelve years ago, she never truly left, well not all of her anyway. The impression of her short life had infected this house like a disease, the echoes of her joy, her sadness, her pain and suffering had seeped through this house like a deathly pathogen, bleeding all the way into its very foundations; she'd never truly leave this place, if he couldn't trust anything else, he could trust that truth.

"I'm right!" Henry shouted in the night, the fear that had gripped him and silenced him up until now had crumbled away.

"She never left this place Josh... never... you hear me?"

As his shouts died down, he thought that maybe Josh was right too?

Maybe I've been seeing what I wanted to see all along; her clothes, her phantom each year on her anniversary? Is it all some kinda grief-riddled-alcohol-induced-delusion? Am I losing my fucking mind?

He pocketed the keys and glanced down at the ground, the salt track he'd momentarily forgotten about called out to him again. He decided the only way he'd discover what was at the end of it was if he kept trudging forward. Whomever or whatever had stolen his daughter's clothes might be waiting for him at the end of that white line, and so he stepped forwards and raised the bottle above his head, ready to swing at whatever came stumbling out of the dark at him.

Man, woman, child or laundry.

"You better be gone!" Henry shouted as he shuffled forwards. With each step he took, the line stretched further ahead; there seemed to be no end.

"I mean it, I swear to God, if you're out here and I find you, you'll be wishing you were dead by the time I've finished with you..." Henry staggered on, his feet now treading the dew-covered grass.

Up ahead the salt ended abruptly in the middle of the lawn.

He slowly inched his way towards it; bottle raised, heart racing.

As his eyes slowly adjusted to the dark and what was before him swam into focus the bottle tumbled from his grasp and hit the grass with a dull thud.

He took another step forward and paused.

His jaw hung open as his eyes grew wide and terror carved him a new face.

The salt he'd been following didn't just stop: it fell away into the nothingness of a freshly dug grave in the centre of his lawn.

The darkened hole yawned open before him as if someone had cut a rectangle out of the very fabric of the world; the darkness which resided in the grave called him onwards as the wind howled through the trees and the grass rippled across the ground as if it were water.

Something in the growing clamour whispered for him to take a peek.

He edged closer in increments.

With each faltering shuffle, the grave grew deeper, longer, wider. The walls of it were as dark as obsidian, sheer and smooth, at any moment Henry felt as if the ground would crumble beneath his feet and he'd slide down the depth of those walls and discover what lurked in wait for him at the bottom.

He cast his eyes around the grave, on the muddied ground before him, footprints skirted their way around the clay-like mud which formed the mouth of the grave. He followed a particularly deep set of tracks which led their way to what Henry assumed was the head of the grave.

There was something situated opposite him.

The longer he stared, the more it came into focus.

It suddenly grew in clarity, as if it were a leviathan rising from the deep.

The object only stood four feet high.

But the fear it commanded was severely disproportionate to its meagre size.

Henry was staring across the grave at a crudely hewn cross.

Two planks of broken fence panelling had been tied together with twine.

He couldn't help but recall the twelve graves he'd dug for Elsie.

Each accentuated with a cross crafted in a similar fashion.

The words which graced the crossbeam, painted in red – which could easily have been blood in this light – were still wet. Henry noticed that the paint had run, it hung in crimson tears from the bottom of the wood before they were whipped into the night by the wind.

His blood ran cold as he finally deciphered what was scrawled on the wood beneath the blood-red streaks of paint.

HERE LIES HENRY CLARK

The wind blew hard, almost sending Henry tumbling into the grave. He planted his feet firmly in the ground as the bottle rolled across the grass and tumbled into the dark. He strained against the wind, his eyes watering, stinging; searching within the streaks of red to decipher what was beneath his name. Then it hit him.

DIED

23 / 11 / 22

The date was two days from today and the discovery brought Henry to his knees.

He had to look in the grave, to discover what lay at the bottom. He willed it to be his own lifeless body in the ground, because if it was, this was all some fucked up dream and he'd soon awake in his bed, the bottle of whiskey tucked neatly in the crook of his arm like a sleeping baby. The picture of Elsie resting on his chest.

He didn't wake, this nightmare was his life and now his lot.

He placed his hands on the lip of the grave and pulled his weary body ever-forward until he found himself staring down at the tattered remains of Elsie's clothes; salt covered them as if someone had sprinkled them with lye.

He imagined her fabric arms suddenly bursting out of their meagre covering of salt before pulling her sunken, torso-less, body from the grave. He imagined her skittering and clambering up the sides of the grave using her finger-less hands, dragging her filthy, boneless, limbless, body-less form towards him. Finally, when she'd make it to the top she'd wrap her fabric arms around him and drag him down into the depths of the grave, to be with her forever.

Her clothes never moved and Henry's vision never came to pass but it didn't comfort him none, because Henry now knew that in two days, his body would be in the ground and Elsie, or whoever was doing this to him would finally have their reward.

CHAPTER FOURTEEN

When sleep finally came for Henry it was fitful at best.

THE YAWNING GRAVE APPEARED FROM AROUND EVERY BEND AND CURVE.
Every door he forced open in the darkened corridors of his mind,
opened before the stygian gaping mouth of the grave.

He stood before a door now, one at the end of a long corridor,
muddied handprints and smeared grime adorned the face of the
door like a child's attempt at rendering a Jackson Pollock. He'd heard
feet tiny feet rushing from behind him, the thud of each foot echoed
around him; moving from the floor, to the wall, then to the ceiling.
They were gaining ground and so he reached out his quivering hand,
flung open the door and stepped into the room away from the
onrushing thing that stalked him. But no floor rushed up to meet his
foot, and he tipped forwards and began to plummet into what he
discovered was his patiently waiting grave; because death he'd muse
later, on waking – was nothing but patient.

As he tumbled into the great, dark nothingness, his hand shot out reflexively and gripped the doorknob just in time. He felt his shoulder snap and a fire instantly bloom in the joint, hot, white and all consuming. His body had been thwarted of its quick descent into what would have been his certain demise by his outstretched hand and clinging fingers; as the fire spread rapidly up his arm to his hand and down his body, dancing up his neck and fanning out over his chest, he pondered just letting go, letting death take him; he even willed his hand to relinquish its hold, but it had grown sentient and obdurate and wouldn't obey the simplest of commands.

Just let go.

As he hung from the door, his pendulous weight caused the door to slowly swing him across the cavernous grave. He felt somewhat like a fish on a hook as his legs ceaselessly kicked and wriggled; desperate to build some type of momentum which would carry him over to the grave's edge, where he could then scamper away from the thing that pursued him. He peered back at the hallway, the thing which had been chasing him had vanished for the time being at least, but he knew they'd be back, they were inevitable.

Lowering his gaze Henry stared down into the oblivion below his dangling, thrashing feet, and he wondered if the dark rippled like water and if his frantic, terrified movements would attract something from down there, something with sharp teeth and a hunger to be sated.

His weight was swinging him back towards the hallway and he glanced up again at the doorway and the corridor beyond.

As he swung closer, the end of the hallway seemed to stretch further and further away as if someone had plucked the edges of this new reality and set off running to the horizon. It went on for an eternity, each wall was lined with numerous doors, some were already open – the ones Henry had already tried to escape through – but as reality ran away into a point and the doors which lined the walls got smaller, a thought entered his addled mind.

Hanging over his own, onrushing death and the cold bed he would sleep in eternally; Henry wondered that if he ever did manage to climb out of here, open all of those damned doors, search each one for a possible way out, would they still bring him back to this exact spot: hanging over a grave which would soon swallow him whole?

Darkness, it so happens, does ripple like water and something would soon be drawn from it by his flailing legs, panting breath and the pain-filled whimpers which crawled into the silence from between his clenched teeth.

Partway down the corridor, a door creaked open on rusted hinges.

CCRREEAAKKkkkkkkkkkk

Henry tried to swing his other arm up, to gain purchase on the doorknob, because if he could make it – which was a slim chance at best – he thought he might just be able to get enough momentum to swing himself closer to the edge of the grave, giving him a way to flee; but as he stretched for the brass doorknob, the pain shooting through his shoulder convinced him not to try again.

His gaze turned back to the hallway. From within the door which had just opened like a long-sealed crypt; something began to crawl out. In the dim light of the hallway the hideous writhing *Thing* began to expand from its crouched position. It was accompanied by a chorus of snaps and wet pops, as if limbs were finding their way back into the sockets they'd been torn from previously. Henry couldn't look away as the *Thing* – to call it anything else seemed wrong – twitched and juddered and writhed like a snake trying to shed its skin, before it slowly began to rise and spread out. It was similar to a butterfly unfurling its wings, Henry thought; escaping its long gestation and transformation in its cocoon, testing its wings for the first time. But where its wings should have been, this *Thing* had arms; long fabric, appendage-less arms which spanned breadth of the hallway. The fabric arms fluttered as a sudden wind tore through the tunnel-like corridor, carrying the stench of blood-soaked loam and mildew. Its body continued to unfurl and grow more ominous until it stood erect, its face-less head staring directly at him: it was Elsie.

"YOU!" Elsie bellowed from her non-existent mouth, but existent or not, the stench of her breath soon prickled Henry's nose as it was carried to him on the cold currents of the breeze; the foulness of rotting meat.

Elsie's grave clothes stood before him, her body hulking, her chest heaving; she was breathing, contemplating, judging.

The clothes took a lumbering step forwards and the sound boomed down the corridor and hit him as if it were a physical thing, the door vibrating in his outstretched hand. Before he knew what was happening Elsie was now running towards him; arms and legs flailing in a spasmodic, joint-less gait as she desperately cantered towards him.

Henry screamed and flailed all the more, he was definitely a fish on a hook, the bait to lure the monster. Regardless of how much he thrashed and jerked there was nothing he could do to escape, and he remained utterly helpless against Elsie's approach.

She rushed towards him as an apex predator would its prey. Elsie thundered down the corridor and Henry could feel each footfall rattle the teeth in his head.

Just fucking let go!

But still his hand ignored his plea.

Maybe you're right? Henry pondered; *maybe the devil we know –* Henry glanced to the wraith-like Elsie *– is better than the devil we don't –* glancing down at the cavernous grave and imagining whatever evil waited for him in that fathomless hole; things that had adapted to a life in the dark.

The clothes were almost upon him now, three steps away.

Two steps away.

One step away.

Henry closed his eyes, prepared to be hauled into the great unknown as the flailing, stampeding clothes leapt from the hallway, latched onto him and dragged him all the way down into his private and seething hell.

He scrunched his face up, prepared himself for impact.

Nothing came; no sudden impact, no surge of pain, no scream

and no freefall into the great unknown. He knew what he had to do, he had to open his eyes.

Slowly cracking open his eyes Henry flinched and the sudden movement caused the pain to bloom in his shoulder again; he didn't know what was worse: the unbearable, insufferable pain in his shoulder or the hideous image that presided over him.

The clothes were hunched at the open door. Elsie's shoulders were rising and falling, she was bull-like as her foul, warm breath streamed from her nostril-less face where it hit Henry face with force and tousled his hair.

A cuff was rested on her knee, and if she had hands – which she didn't – Henry mused he'd see the fingers of that hand clutching its knee right about now, as she silently observed the pathetic specimen that dangled before her; nonchalantly deciding what she would do next and how she'd ruin him. Her other arm was outstretched, reaching up another invisible hand to clutch the doorframe, the collar of her shirt suddenly dipped to the side and the fabric of her top crumpled around it as she tilted her head to the side. Henry remembered his daughter doing such an action when she was faced with a taxing problem; she remained that way, head cocked to the side, her foul breath washing over him for an achingly long time, scrutinising her father's wretched existence.

Henry knew what she was doing: Elsie was contemplating how she would end him.

And he didn't have to wait long to find out how.

One of her arms quickly shot out across the divide.

Henry observed and heard the fabric of her arm flapping in the wind like a flag, he wished it could have been a white flag waving above him, because he'd have given anything in that moment to surrender. The arm extended further, reaching towards the doorknob, and his aching fingers. He watched its passage before feeling something cold alight on his hand. Staring at his tightly balled appendage which hung resolutely from the doorknob, he noticed the skin on the back of his hand dimple in five places.

There were no fingers on that appendage-less arm, but he felt them nevertheless, watched them investigate and probe his ironclad grasp on the only thing that kept him from tumbling into the dark pit beneath him.

Suddenly he felt Elsie's fingers take hold of his little finger and he remembered as a toddler how she'd done the same thing whilst they cuddled on the sofa and watched her cartoons; but this was a different feeling, it was done with menacing and cruel intent, she pulled hard and prised his digit away from the doorknob, loosening his grip slightly in the process.

"This little piggy went to market," Elsie's voice from the mouthless bundle of clothes crooned.

Henry watched on in wide-eyed terror as he shook his head. Elsie pulled his little finger back in one sickening, bone-breaking motion; the pain was transcendent, but still his hand hung onto the door for dear life, when all he wanted to do was fall away and sink into the welcoming dark of the grave.

"Funny isn't it, I only learnt later that the market he'd gone to wasn't a market where he'd buy nice things, it was a fucking slaughterhouse," Elsie began to laugh, but there was no humour in it.

Her fingers quickly returned to pawing at his hand as her cackle subsided. Her fingers danced coldly over each of his remaining digits as she set about deciding which one she'd tease free next.

They tugged and prised his ring finger free.

"This little piggy stayed at home," Elsie uttered tonelessly.

Henry peered at her face-less head, shook his head vigorously.

"Please, don't—" he begged before his voice was cut off by the sudden snap and the excruciating pain that tore through his hand and throbbed down his arm causing the fire that already burned there to rage into an inferno.

"This little piggy had roast beef," the voice cackled.

SNAP.

His middle finger snapped back and the bone pierced through his skin.

Henry couldn't talk, he couldn't even scream at the shard of bone sticking out of his hand because he was far too concerned with his two remaining digits. His index finger and thumb, a crude claw which had turned white by the weight and strain of keeping his body exactly where it was, to endure the pain and punishment he deserved.

His mouth yawned open as he watched his thumb being plucked from position; felt the strain on his index finger, felt himself slowly slipping down into the grave, but still it would not relinquish its grip.

"And this little piggy had none!"

SNAP-CRUNCH-POP.

Henry glanced up at his hand and it looked like a dead, flesh-coloured starfish, his fingers all hideously broken and peeled back from their natural positions. Elsie cackled as she peeled back his last finger and Henry closed his eyes.

He felt his body drop and his onrushing fate rise to meet him.

Henry didn't fall.

Snapping his eyes open he half-expected to have awoken on his bed, but instead quickly discovered he was being carried ever-closer to the door by his remaining, hooked index finger. He was then lifted – jerked – higher; the floor of the hallway was near his knees now where before it had been at head height. He could almost lift his leg and skitter across the floor, away from the precipice he'd been dangling over. It soon dawned on him, that he wasn't being lifted to safety, his hand was being pulled towards Elsie's mouth; or where he assumed it would be in that face-less head that presided over every-thing and nothing.

"And this little piggy cried wee wee wee all the way home," Elsie crooned in a creepy, lingering falsetto which echoed all around him, her voice growing deeper and more menacing as it reverberated off the sheer walls of the grave below him, chasing itself down into the dark. Henry was powerless to stop what came next.

CHOMP.

Henry watched his finger sever at the knuckle before his very eyes, and then it was tumbling past him, blood dripped into his face and as he stared up at Elsie, he saw for the first time something appear in that face-less, head-less space before him, it was Elsie's blood-stained teeth: she was smiling.

He remained there for a moment, observing the ruin of his hand as Elsie smiled on proudly at the carnage she'd dealt; she still held him by the wrist as she leered towards him, those bloodstained teeth growing large and sharp before him, and then she laughed in his face. Henry could feel the heat of her breath radiate from her mouth like an infected wound and it danced over his face before he was suddenly hoisted away from the safety of the hallway; returned to the centre of the pit by Elsie's fabric arm which grew longer and longer.

Henry stared down into the grave below him, he could still hear the deep, ominous, booming refrain of the echo below him in the dark.

"ALL THE WAY HOME, ALL THE WAY HOME, ALL THE WAY HOME."

The finger-less hand shook him hard, like a toddler with a broken toy before she flung his repugnance into the great unknown.

Henry screamed as he tumbled into the dark, towards whatever hellish thing waited for him at the end.

THE DREAM HAD SPOOKED HIM MORE THAN HE'D EXPECTED IT TO AND quickly returned to him again.

"All the way home," he uttered as he stood outside the community centre, watching another little piggy desperately try to clamber free from the driver's seat of its green, rusted out Standard Pennant, failing miserably at the simplest of tasks.

As he stood there watching, Henry mused it would have been a much easier affair if Jacob would just put down the box of pizza – or even the slice, which he held in his other hand – and bloody focus, but he did neither. Instead, with the steering wheel stuck in his gut, Jacob dipped his head lower and stole another quick bite from the slice. Henry thought he looked crow-like, as if Jacob was incessantly pecking at the desiccated remains of carrion on a roadside; his need to fill his face and feed his pain seemed to have more of a pull than a metal spoon with a chunk of heroin does for an addict going cold-turkey.

He knew he should shout out, inform Jacob that tonight's session was cancelled; but he was too busy taking great delight in watching that tubby, sack of meat struggle.

I'm doing you a favour, Henry mused dryly, knowing full well that the strenuous scene which was unfolding – quite literally – before him, would probably be the only exercise the chubby bastard would be partaking in all week; *he could do with the damned workout.*

Henry smiled to himself as he glanced down at the ground.

He was standing in the middle of rushing water which was spilling out from the community centre. Dirty, greyish, drain water spilled around his planted feet before cascading down the few steps that led up to the door, and it stunk to high heaven.

He'd traced the river of filth back to its source which poured from under the toilet door, he didn't venture in though, that task he'd leave to Josh, if and when he finally made an appearance. But from the stench and the things floating in the water, it appeared to have been backed up and overflowing for quite some time.

On further inspection when he'd arrived, the whole place was flooded, all except the hall where the COCS met, but even then, as he'd stepped in the room the carpet tiles squelched beneath his feet; most of the room was sodden and he knew there was no conceivable way they could meet tonight or possibly for the rest of the month, because it'd take weeks to get the damp and the stench out of the place.

He'd come in early and was glad of it, at least now he could turn everyone away, everyone except Josh; because he needed him to fix the leak and then they'd grab a little chat. Henry desperately needed to discuss with him his thoughts on the séance and Elsie and the enigma that have vanished like a fart in the wind that was Rowen; also he needed to tell Josh about the huge, freshly-dug grave, which had appeared last night, right smack dab in the middle of his fucking lawn, not to mention the ominous message painted in blood or paint or a mixture of both.

Rowen. Where the hell are you?

Henry lifted his tired eyes to the road.

Although they'd not seen or heard from Rowen after the séance, where Henry's life had been turned upside down and inside out; he knew the enigma had something to do with all of this, he wasn't just a conduit for Elsie, he was something more. Rowen's hands were definitely the ones pulling the strings, but why? And now threats had been made against his life, Henry was decidedly on edge.

He might just show, Henry pondered; *stay vigilant.*

A car pulled in behind Jacob's. It was Roger's and he appeared to already be preening himself for another of his busybody sessions; he'd be demanding answers to what happened and when it would be fixed, most likely coming out with another of his annoying platitudes as he attempted to smooth over the bother; something like: '*Life isn't about waiting for the storm to pass... it's about learning to dance in the rain*'.

If he said something like that, Henry knew he'd lamp the prick where he stood, right in his little self-serving mouth. *How'd you like dancing in that storm you prick?* Henry thought before chuckling at his own wit.

"Hem-ney, why you, stam-ding out-fide?" Jacob uttered around a mouthful of pizza.

Henry's fists were balled at his sides, ready to strike Roger in his holier-than-thou mouth but as he glanced up, Jacob stood peering up at him, the crust of his pizza hanging out his mouth like a chubby cigar and Henry thought he looked like a portlier version of Alfred Hitchcock.

"What does it look like I'm doing?" Henry fired back as he

glanced down; stamping his feet in the steady stream of water running from the building and trickling down the steps.

"Meeting's cancelled," Henry said as he peered back up at Jacob, who it seems had already inhaled the crust and was already reaching into the grease-soaked box for another delicious slice.

"Right? So, what do I do now?" Jacob uttered before taking another bite of pizza, his expression Henry noted was forlorn and lost.

Henry wanted to tell him 'Weight Watchers' was running at the church down the road – the Catholic monstrosity along Wells Road, which looked more like a Giant's discarded Cavalier's helmet than a church – and maybe he should waddle his fat arse on his tubby little legs down there and pull up a pew, maybe then he'd get to the root-cause of his obesity.

However, Henry bit down on those maiming words, because for whatever reason, looking at the doleful eyes staring back at him, as Jacob's cheeks jostled around and struggled to contain the gargantuan bite he'd just taken of pepperoni and cheese, Henry couldn't help but feel sorry for him.

This place and *this* group were indeed his support network, and without it, Henry realised Jacob was totally and utterly lost.

"Go home, Jacob. Take a weight off and finish that pizza..." Henry offered.

"Go home?" the advancing Roger exclaimed incredulously. "And why may I ask would we do such a thing?"

Jacob thrusted out his half-eaten slice of pizza and Henry noticed a slice of pepperoni fly from the end of it and land in the growing puddle at the bottom of the steps, when he glanced up to Jacob the strain of losing that tiny morsel showed on his face with a grimace.

"Fudded," Jacob offered.

"What?" Roger said as he brushed past Jacob and approached the entrance to the community centre. He got a few steps further than Jacob had bothered to venture, only to stop suddenly when he splashed into the huge puddle which had formed at the base of the steps, hidden by the night and the Tarmac.

Henry watched his nemesis hop back from the shock and peer suspiciously down at the ground. Henry stifled a laugh as he followed the hopping man's gaze to his feet. Roger was wearing a pair of long shorts; his white, bean-pole legs were further accentuated by a pair of white socks and leather strapped sandals. Roger's fashion left much to be desired at the best of times, but what he was wearing now, belied the weather because it was as cold as a witch's tit, and his outfit made him look utterly ridiculous.

"Both of you, just head on home, meeting's cancelled. I'd also change out of those wet socks Roger," a smile teased at Henry's lips. "You don't want to catch your death now do you; am I right Jacob?"

Jacob appeared stunned at being brought into the conversation, as if he'd finally realised his life mattered and he wasn't navigating it alone. He smiled broadly displaying a mouthful of teeth and the mushed remains of pizza he'd yet to swallow. Jacob nodded enthusiastically.

"Good one, Henry!" Jacob said.

Roger glanced up from his sodden socks, placed his hands on his hips.

"Well? When do you expect this to be sorted, it's totally unacceptable?"

"No idea, how about we stick a pin in this until I know the timeframe, I'll call you both in a few days!" Henry said frankly, but he couldn't help the niggling thought at the back of his mind which told him none of this mattered, that he'd never make that call; a timeframe had already been predestined for him, one which was slowly ticking away as he entertained the insufferable Roger and his trivial questioning.

"I guess that will suffice," Roger uttered tersely, but he didn't leave; he just stood there in his wet socks and sandals like some end of days bible fanatic, like the ones Henry would often see hollering in Broadmead about atonement of sins, sermons about the coming judgement and God's wrath being poured out on the sexually immoral.

"I'm so pleased to suffice you," Henry uttered through a grimace.

Jacob was slowly turning away now, his eyes still longed for the pepperoni he'd lost, Henry half-thought he'd scurry back and reclaim it from the puddle, but he was soon waddling away from the community centre, back to whatever semblance of a life waited for him when he got home.

"That doesn't even make sense, Henry." And with his final one-upmanship played, Roger turned and squelched away in his wet sandals and socks.

"I'll call you," Henry shouted, knowing full well he might not get the chance.

Henry watched Jacob reverse as the water continued to stream out of the building; as it trickled down the steps it sounded to Henry like hushed whispers. He turned slightly and peered into the darkened building behind him, the only light present was the small, battery operated camping lantern by the door, its light failing to reach much further than the entranceway. He couldn't see anything lurking in the dark and so he returned his attention to the parking lot.

Jacob was signalling to go left, when Henry knew his house was in the other direction, but then he remembered there was a drive-through up the road and mused it was reason enough for Jacob to head completely out of his way, because all roads would eventually lead home and the tubby git would need something to eat later, to help keep his grief at bay, especially when the ghost of his father inevitably came calling.

Roger pulled his car to the exit and Henry noticed through the driver's side window that Roger was wearing leather driving gloves, his hands never leaving the ten-to-two position on the wheel. *He probably drove his wife like he did his car, painfully slow and with a boring, pedantic precision*, Henry thought before caterwauling into the night.

He was about to head into the building and wait for the others to arrive when a car sped into the parking lot, skidding to a sudden stop in the gravel. It sat there idly, the full-beam spotlighting Henry where he stood; he lifted his hand to shield his eyes from the glare to discover who was sitting behind the driver's seat, but he couldn't tell from this distance.

He quickly noticed the glow of a mobile phone wedged against the person's ear, and he realised it was Sian. She shortly put her hand out of the window and beckoned him over, with a flick of her wrist, it appeared to him then that Sian hadn't been intent on staying for the session even if it was on because she never once attempted to get out of the car.

Lumbering down the steps and splashing into the puddle at the bottom Henry made his way towards her Prius, the car's engine still ticking over. He approached her open window and she turned to face him; Henry went to talk but Sian shushed him by holding her index finger out to him, a *give me a second* gesture.

And this little piggy cried wee wee wee all the way home, Henry mused.

"I know. I'm coming, now. No group's not on tonight, some sort of flood or something." Henry shook his head, bemused at what he'd heard. *How the hell does she know there's been a flood?* He turned away from her, peered at the community centre as she continued to rabbit on next to him. He cocked his head to the side and was still flummoxed because even with her headlights illuminating the building, it was still impossible to tell it was flooded from here.

"Anyway, I gotta go, see you soon." Sian hung up.

Henry turned back to the car, noticed her drop her phone into the centre console where it lit up with a handful of notifications.

"How did you know the building was flooded?" Henry said as he placed his hand on the roof and hunched over to peer in her window.

"Hello to you too by the way!" Sian said with a roll of her eyes.

"Sorry, hello Sian. But how did you know it was flooded?"

"Social media obviously," Sian said with a shake of her head, as if how else would she have known such a thing. "You really should get on that, because if something like this happens again you could just let us know and save us the hassle of driving all the way here."

"But who told you... on social media, that it was flooded?"

"Rowen—"

"Rowen?"

"Yeah, said he'd swung by and the building was all flooded out, so he left."

"He left?"

"What the hell is it with you two?"

"Who me and Rowen?" Henry said incredulously.

"No. You and Josh. You both seem to have a raging hard on for him or something; I'd say you've both got a little man crush, but—"

"What's Josh got to do with it?"

"That's why I'm here, silly. He asked me to..." Sian stretched across the car, grabbed an envelope from the glovebox, when she moved back from reclaiming the letter Henry saw even more messages flash up on her phone, she was certainly a woman in demand.

"Here," Sian said as she passed the envelope through the open window.

"What is it?"

"Something he asked me to look into, can you make sure he gets it; I gotta fly!"

Before Henry could even utter his response, Sian was reversing at speed. She quickly spun the wheel and the car spun around to face the road, sending a scattering of gravel across the deserted parking lot.

Henry watched her screech out of the parking lot before turning and making his way slowly back to the entrance of the community centre, ever-wary that he might be being watched because if Rowen knew the meeting had been cancelled he had to be nearby.

As he reached the top of the steps Henry shuffled towards the lantern on the ground, crouching down he held the envelope up to the dim light, he couldn't see much but through the envelope he could see something typed, possibly a print out of something.

He turned it over in his hands and discovered the flap was just tucked into the opening; it wasn't sealed.

He lifted the letter, placed his fingers to the flap and began to raise it. *Just a little peek*, he thought but quickly stopped his inquisitive fingers and shook his head. He knew he might be a lot of things to a lot of people, but untrustworthy wasn't one of them. He searched his heart and knew that if Josh had been presented with the same enticing predicament, a letter addressed to him, he'd have done the right thing; he was sure of it, and so he stood up and went to tuck the letter in his back pocket.

"Who's the letter for?"

"SHIT!" Henry shouted as he spun around to discover Josh standing at the top of the three small steps. "You almost gave me a bloody heart attack you great lump!"

"Sorry, not sorry!" Josh chuckled and beamed a smile at Henry. "You should see your face right now, anyway who's it for?" Josh pointed at the letter in Henry's hands.

"Oh, sorry. It's for you actually."

"For me?"

"Yeah, Sian dropped it off for you..." Henry held the letter out and Josh plucked it sheepishly from his hand. He watched Josh turn it over, run his finger over the loose flap at the back before Josh's gaze returned to his, his eyebrow raised questioningly.

"I didn't peek, none of my business. What you two get up to in your own time is... well you're both consenting adults."

"It ain't like that," Josh said as he stepped closer.

"Whatever man, you don't need to explain anything to me," Henry uttered with a sly smirk.

"No seriously, I just asked her to look into something for me."

"Right..." Henry uttered slowly as an awkward silence grew between them.

Henry desperately wanted to chat with Josh about what had

happened last night, but he didn't know where to start, and in the silence, as he observed Josh, it appeared his friend also had something to say too; and the way Josh was nervously tapping the envelope in his palm, Henry wondered if it had something to do with the letter and what was inside.

"So, what are we doing then?" Josh broke the silence as he stepped up to the entrance of the building and his feet splashed in the steady stream of water rushing from within.

Henry was grateful for the interruption because he hadn't a clue of how to break the silence, all he could think about was; the grave, Rowen, the séance and the loss of his sanity.

"Well I told the landlord that I knew a guy." Henry said jovially as he pulled up alongside his friend.

"Oh, did you now?"

"Yep, said I'd get you to take a look at it and if you can fix it, we'll get the next few months off from paying rent; I already turned the power off, you're welcome by the way." Henry nudged him in the ribs.

"You do know we pay a pittance for this place, right? Is that how much you value my workmanship?" Josh said with a smile.

"Yep, but what else you gotta do tonight anyway?"

"Good point," Josh said as he peered into the darkened hall.

"Also, when you're done I thought I could bend your ear about something?"

"Y-eah, su-re..." Josh stuttered and Henry noticed his friend's cheeks flush red, the distinct colour of shame and guilt and he knew then that Josh was hiding something from him too.

"Good, I feel it's been long overdue, a catch-up I mean, what with everything that's been going on around here."

Josh nodded and Henry noticed his Adams apple working overtime, he glanced down at Josh's hand and noticed his hands were shaking; *he's nervous*, Henry mused.

"Right, you got another one of those?" Josh uttered sharply

pointing at the lantern, and it appeared to Henry his friend was desperate to get away.

"Well, I got a torch from the storage room, and these," Henry bent down by the door, picked up the torch and a metal tool box before returning and holding them out for Josh to take. "I went to the liberty of getting you the community tool box too; Godspeed!"

"You ain't coming with?" Josh questioned as he took the offered items.

"No. I wouldn't be much help, I don't know my arse from my elbow; plus, someone's gotta be here to turn away any latecomers, then we can have our little chat in private."

"Sure. Yeah, no problem," Josh shook the torch in his hand before clicking it on. "Shouldn't take me too long," he said as he began to walk into the darkened mouth of the building.

"Good because we've got a lot to talk about," Henry said to Josh's back.

He noticed the slight pause in his friend's gait at his words; it was a small stutter and then his friend was moving again, but in that temporary pause, Henry knew something was deeply troubling his friend. What it was though, he had no idea, but he'd find out soon enough.

As Josh disappeared down the corridor as if the mouth of the community centre and the darkness within was swallowing him whole, Henry turned back to the parking lot where tiny slivers of broken glass flickered like eyes in the night with each passing car; and he couldn't help but feel he was being watched.

And he knew unquestionably that Rowen was out there somewhere.

CHAPTER FIFTEEN

He knows. Josh pondered darkly as he splashed his way down the corridor to the source of the foul-smelling river he was currently wading through.

The place stunk something rotten, and he couldn't help but recall his research into suicide and his incessant need to keep his death as clean as possible. He'd read that after the body has ceased to exist, everything, *everything* becomes loosed; what was inside, slowly worked its way to the outside, one way or another.

Nearing the toilets, where the stream was steadily flowing from, he pondered if after today, after what he had to confess and explain to Henry, if this building and more importantly the COCS would cease to exist; their group pronounced dead at the scene. Maybe it already was and the decrepit building knew of the deceit in his heart and was finally giving up, succumbing to a slow and agonising death, its bowels emptying themselves of all the suffering which had been deposited and stored in its stomach all these long years.

Why does he want me alone? Josh mused as his boot came down and mushed something soft underfoot. He paused and glanced down, unsure of what he'd stepped in. Lifting his boot, he discovered something brown and pancaked beneath, he didn't even need to entertain what it was because it quickly became apparent it was shit as he watched it break apart and birth a piece of sweetcorn which was soon carried further downstream.

He splashed deeper into the darkened hallway and as the water rushed across the ground and crashed up against his feet, it sounded like many voices prattling on at the same time.

He wants you alone so there's no witnesses...

You betrayed him...

You stole his daughter's last words...

He's going to make you bleed...

He's going to k–

"STOP!" Josh shouted.

He lifted the torch and pointed it up and down the corridor; glancing back the way he'd come, the beam picked out Henry who was right down at the other end, staring back at him inquisitively, most probably drawn by his exclamation.

"YOU OKAY?" Henry shouted.

"YEP, ALL GOOD BUDDY!" Josh hollered back and lifted a thumb he doubted Henry could even see, and so he turned the torch down to the floor, illuminating the river beneath his feet. He took a deep calming breath before stepping closer to the frothing, greyish water which surged from under the toilet door.

He pushed the door with his shoulder but it wouldn't budge.

He tried it again with a little more strength and the door succumbed a little, the water rushing out of the small gap he'd been able to create. With one final push and a little run up he pressed his shoulder to the door and it opened slowly and a torrent of drain water rushed out in a wave and soaked his boots, socks and the lower portion of his trouser legs.

"Fucking great," Josh whispered as he rolled his eyes and stepped into the dank, dark and filthy toilets.

The conical beam of the torch cut through the darkness inside, revealing the utter squalor of the place: the tiled walls were covered in graffiti, three of the four mirrors above the four sinks were cracked or either scratched to buggery, a few of the ceiling tiles were missing and Josh also noted there were a great many balls of tissue stuck to the ceiling, wetted and thrown there by mischievous children but now dried hard like cement.

Lowering the torch, the beam highlighted three toilet cubicles across the room. The first one's door was hanging askew and Josh pondered about fixing that too once he'd found the source of the flooding, but rubbished the idea as soon as it took root.

"You can't make a silk purse out of a sow's ear," he mumbled to himself, knowing the place needed knocking down rather than being built back up again.

The other two doors were damaged but intact, the one nearest the wall had a few dents in it, placed there by fists and the wood was scarred with a few hastily drawn dicks; some had big, hairy balls and others had smiling happy tear shaped come spraying out of the top. Pulling the beam of his torch back he directed it to the floor, beneath the middle cubicle the water flowed in a never-ending, urgent stream.

"Gotcha," Josh said with delight at finding the source of the flooding so quickly.

He made his way across the slick, linoleum floor and clattered the toolbox against the door where it swung open unimpeded, banging loudly against the partition inside, the sudden noise made Josh flinch and the toolbox rattled in his hand. Pointing the beam into the stall revealed the shit-speckled bowl and cistern of the toilet; whoever used it last Josh mused, had a severe case of projectile diarrhoea.

He stepped into the stall and placed the toolbox on the ground which aided in keeping the cubicle door open. When he stood up his eyes followed the beam from the torch which still illuminated the filth-encrusted bowl. Peering inside he discovered brackish-coloured water; a few brown chunks spinning lazily around the reservoir of water trapped within the toilets lip, dancing in some strange whirlpool-like vortex.

He kept his feet firmly planted where they were and bent forward at the waist, shining the beam directly into the bowl. At the bottom – only just discernible because of the things floating in the water – he noticed something blocking the pipe.

He reached for the flush, wondering if one more yank and the additional water pressure afforded by it might just force the blockage free. His hand swiped for the flush but he struck nothing but air; glancing up, confusion creasing his brow, he shone the torch to the handle. There wasn't one; just a snapped piece of plastic jutting out from the hole which disappeared into the cistern.

He quickly jostled the torch under his armpit, training the beam before him so he could have use of both his hands and set about removing the cistern's lid.

Pulling it free was easy and he placed it on the ground before returning to peer inside. He was shocked to discover there was no stopcock, it too had been snapped off; *vandalised* Josh thought, *but why?*

"That explains it then," Josh said to himself, before talking the problem that had presented itself over in his head. *Without the stop-cock the cistern's been continuously filling and running into the bowl, then we've got the additional blockage, so my guess is the damned things been overflowing for days; right, first things first.*

He turned back to the toolbox and crouched down on his haunches.

Taking the torch from under his arm he directed it at the assortment of tools at his disposal, it was a pretty drab affair, nothing like his own treasure-trove of tools at home: there were an assortment of screwdrivers, a plethora of random nuts and bolts, a few wrenches and a ball-peen hammer; all pretty much useless for the task at hand.

Josh let out a tired breath and shook his head before reaching for the long-handled screwdriver. Holding it in the light of the torch he knew it wasn't long enough, and he'd soon be getting his hands dirty after all. Remaining on his haunches he crab walked himself over to the still overflowing bowl of the toilet. With one hand holding the torch aloft – directing the beam into the swirling filth of the toilet – he plunged his other hand, the one holding the screwdriver into the toilet, his arm eventually disappearing into the water up to his forearm.

He shuddered not from the coldness of the water but from the noisome stench that erupted once his hand broke the surface, churning the water inside with his desperate attempts at dislodging the blockage. He felt his gorge rise and he choked; his eyes were watering and his mouth was suddenly full of thick saliva. He paused a moment, turned his head away from the stench and swallowed everything back down before taking a breath, the air was still tainted with the smell of death but it wasn't as strong and he felt the sickness trying to escape him subside, albeit momentarily.

Reluctantly he returned to rummaging in the filthy water.

Peering inside he realised the chunks which had been obscuring his view were gone. He quickly checked his arm to make sure they hadn't attached themselves to him like leeches but none presented themselves in the dim light. He peered down to inspect the floor, not wanting to kneel in one if he had to get down on his knees and haul whatever was blocking the pipe free. The chunks of shit weren't on the floor, instead they were slowly crawling their way down the outside of the toilet as if they were thick, brown slugs in search of a leaf.

Thrusting screwdriver into the blockage once more he managed to successfully pin whatever it was to the pipe and slowly he began to drag it free; little by little the waterlogged thing began to shift and the water level in the toilet began to sluggishly reduce. With one final tug, he pulled the blockage free, sending a wave of water crashing over the toilet bowl as Josh was sent sprawling backwards onto the sodden, filthy floor of the cubicle.

"FUCK!" He shouted as he splashed down on his arse by the toilet's door, the torch had flashed every which way, carving through the darkness of the room like a cheap laser show and the screwdriver had flown from his other hand into the darkness that swarmed outside the cubicle.

He sat there for a moment in the shit-tainted water with a face like thunder before the sound of the gurgling water leaving the toilet gave him a momentary comfort and he smiled despite his current predicament. He'd done it, stopped the flooding for the time being at least, but he knew that in all honesty all he'd done was stick a plaster on a festering wound. He knew the building would burst its seams again and when it did he wouldn't be rushing to its aid.

Josh thought he resembled a drowned rat and so he didn't even bother to stand when he headed back to the toilet, he just crawled across the sodden floor on his hands and knees; because time was of the essence, he still needed to pull the blockage out of the toilet in case it got sucked back down the pipe and he'd be back at square one with nothing to show for it but a filthy-golden-shitty-shower.

Shining the torch inside the bowl revealed the water level one would expect to find in a toilet, but what resided inside it was far from normal. Josh screwed up his face at the discovery; resting part-in and part-out of the water was something large and curled and covered in what looked like fur. Whereas Josh thought he resembled a drowned rat, a long, thick and bloated one.

Josh couldn't take his eyes off the grisly thing.

In the next cubicle, the one he'd not peered inside: something stirred.

Josh reached into the toilet with trepidation, his fingers soon closing around the soggy thing, pulling it from its resting place. He was first taken aback by the sheer weight of it, then by the mushi-ness of it in his grasp, as if it were trying to dribble through his fingers.

Water poured from the waterlogged, bloated thing in Josh's grasp in a steady stream, splashing loudly into the toilet bowl. As the water dribbled noisily into the bowl, Josh failed to hear the two feet step down with a splash from the toilet seat in the next cubicle to the puddle-like floor.

With only eyes for the wet thing in his hand, he also failed to noticed the water rippling below him, as water does when someone throws a pebble into it, announcing a disturbance; but this wasn't a pebble, it was two feet slowly wading through and then out of the cubicle which had hidden them until now.

The feet stopped in their methodical and lackadaisical stride at the entrance to Josh's cubicle. Unhurriedly the person reached down into the toolbox by the door and withdrew a wrench before standing, hefting it in their hands before waiting patiently for Josh to turn.

Turning the rat-like thing over in his hand, Josh soon realised it was a child's cuddly toy. As the bloated thing rocked backwards as Josh shook it in his hand, two ears peeled back from the face and slapped wetly against his knuckles; revealing two button eyes. It was a rabbit, a muddied, creepy looking thing that had seen much better – and happier – days. He recognised it, but couldn't place where from. *Wait till Henry gets a load of this,* Josh mused as he stood – gaze still firmly on the drowned rabbit in his hand – and turned towards the cubicle door.

He felt something shift in the air in front of him and lifted his eyes from the rabbit to see what had caused it to stir in such a manner; a hellish, ghost-like vision stood before him but he only had a moment to process it before he was sent staggering backwards by a sickening blow to his head.

His arms pinwheeled around him and he dropped both the bunny and the torch; there was a sodden splat – the bunny – followed by a clattering sound as the torch bounced and splashed on the ground before coming to a stop. Josh too came to a sudden stop as his body hit the back of the cubicle and he collapsed awkwardly in the corner, becoming wedged between the toilet and the partition and felt the warmth of blood snaking its way from a wound near his temple and trickling down his neck, blanching out across his shirt;

he wanted to touch it, inspect the damage but was frozen in place by the thing that stood opposite him.

The torch's beam was trained on the lower portion of the door, revealing two feet.

"You stole something from us, and we want it back!" The voice was unmistakably Rowen's but it sounded different, as if every word had to bubble its way up and out of his throat through phlegm and mucus.

A wrench dropped to the floor next to the feet with a clang and a splash.

So, that's what hit me. Josh mused, his brain slowly clouding with the onset of a concussion.

"It was for daddy," it was another voice now; female in tone but spoken from the same phlegmy throat.

"Shut up! I didn't give you permission to talk!" Rowen bellowed.

"But he still doesn't kno–"

"I said be quiet! We still have time..." Rowen's voice came again.

Josh observed the feet at the door step closer and he instinctively pulled his feet closer to him, desperately trying to protect himself from his vulnerable, grounded and groggy position.

"So where is it?" Rowen spat.

"I don't think he has it on him," the female voice intoned.

"I don't... I don't know what you're–" Josh began to utter.

"LIAR," Rowen's voice bellowed and Josh felt the cubicle wall vibrate with its force.

"What do you want?" Josh shot back.

"We want what's ours and you took it from ussssss..." Rowen's sibilant voice crooned.

The feet stepped closer before a hand reached out from the shadows and reclaimed the torch from the ground. The beam was quickly swirled around to face Josh, who lifted a hand to deaden the effects the light had on his eyes and the headache which was quickly building in his head like a swarm of angry bees.

"And who the fuck is us when they're at home?" Josh fired back defiantly.

The torch began to rise slowly, leaving Josh for the shadows to claim. He followed the arc of the beam as it climbed the wall he was resting against before it spread across the ceiling and began to lower once more, revealing the person standing at the door, inch by excruciating inch. When Rowen was fully illuminated by the beam, the sight was nothing but jarring, because it was Rowen, but his hair was bleached blonde; his eyes ringed with black eyeshadow as if he were a lead singer in a heavy metal band.

What jarred Josh the most was the voice which tumbled from Rowen's mouth, because it wasn't his; it was female and sad whilst also pained and they appeared to be in distress.

"Please... please give it to him, you don't know what he'll do if..."

"Stop interfering bitch," Rowen roared, his head snapping violently to the side.

Josh stared on transfixed as Rowen's head jerked back the other way as if he'd been slapped.

"Give it to him," the girl's voice again.

Snap.

Rowen's head swung back the other way.

"I'll take it from you," Rowen uttered and stepped forward as his head recoiled to the side again.

"Do what he says, please. We don't want to hurt you... only daddy." The girl's voice was laced with fear and as Josh processed what he was hearing, it suddenly fell into place, because Josh had never heard her voice before.

"Elsie?" Josh uttered quietly and instead of the head snapping the other way, Rowen's head swivelled front and centre, he almost looked like a hawk, his nose a crude beak as the torchlight rendered his features hideous things made of light and dark; he pinned Josh where he sat with an atrocious, murderous scowl.

"Elsie is that you?" Josh ventured as Rowen continued to observe him; a smile fluttered across Rowen's face but it held no joy, just a mild-disgust at what was on the floor before him. The corner of Rowen's mouth lifted in a sneer, baring his teeth as saliva dribbled in a thin, gelatinous rope from his now snarling mouth, salivating at the prospect of what was to come Josh assumed as fear took up a steady beat on the drum which was his heart.

"Elsie's not here anymore, but that doesn't mean she won't return. We don't like Elsie, we never have! We only let her speak when we need something from her, we use her for our means. She's a little bitch that girl, always has been, weak and pathetic, but we showed her a way out, a way to leave everything she was behind... and she gladly took it."

"Bullshit, I know what you are; you murderer!"

"Ahh... so you did take our letter," Rowen stepped closer before crouching down in front of Josh, one hand rested on the lip of the toilet and Josh noticed the black nail varnish was still present, but there was also something spattered over his hand which Josh thought looked like red paint.

"Where... is... our... letter?" Rowen intoned slowly.

"I don't have it."

"Liar!" Rowen roared again.

"And if I did have your stupid fucking letter, you must be more stupid than you look, especially if you'd think I'd just hand it over to you!"

Rowen laughed. It sounded to Josh as if there were many voices in his throat.

"Silly... I wouldn't ask you for it, I'd just take it from your cold dead hand!"

Rowen's head snapped viciously to the right.

"Tell him, he'll kill you... like he did—"

Rowen's head whipped to the other side.

"I said stay out of this BITCH!" Rowen screamed as he spun around to reclaim the wrench from the ground. Josh knew what was coming and began awkwardly trying to get to his feet whilst Rowen had his back turned but he couldn't summon the strength; his legs didn't feel his own and the concussion was bricking him in one brick at a time.

Come on! Josh was desperately trying to will his legs to cooperate.

He stared down at their uselessness and utter defiance of carrying him to safety.

Rowen turned back towards him sharply and with a maniacal look of glee on his face. Josh noticed the wrench in his hand and the fight left him. This was the end; and so he just peered up at Rowen who loomed over him.

"You thought you were doing something noble didn't you? Taking the letter," Josh went to reply but the approaching Rowen cut him off.

"Ssshhh... we're talking now. All you did by taking that letter was move our plans forwards, forced our hand. You made me show myself too soon, it was supposed to be a long, drawn-out affair; we'd planned a great deal of pain for Henry, and in that pain, we'd have found a semblance of pleasure in his suffering – but you ruined it with your meddling!"

Rowen's head snapped up to the ceiling and Josh noticed his throat swelling, a voice was rising from within which he was desperately trying to fight and swallow back down.

"Don't hurt him... we were only supposed to hurt daddy!" Elsie screamed and she sounded out of breath, as if it had taken her all her energy to expel those few words.

Rowen's arm swung out and the wrench imbedded itself in the stall wall.

"DON'T YOU DARE INTERRUPT ME AGAIN!" Rowen roared before yanking the wrench free and returning his focus to Josh.

"Ple-ase, I d-on't ha-ve it..." Josh uttered, his voice trembling with fear and he hated the way he sounded in that moment – scared and afraid.

"I'm not going to hurt him Elsie," Rowen said demurely before continuing.

"I'm just going to smash his lying, deceiving, little face in."

Rowen stood to his full height and Josh noticed the wrench swinging beside his leg like a metronome, back and forth it swung, counting down the last seconds of his life.

"Any last words?" Rowen intoned as he lifted the wrench high above his head.

Josh pondered what to say, what legacy his final words would leave or serve.

"Well?" Rowen asked, poised to strike.

Josh smiled back.

Slowly opened his mouth and lungs and heart; and screamed.

"HENRY RU–"

Josh's last words were instantly silenced by the swinging wrench, which continued to find the soft and hard parts of him long after he'd slipped into unconsciousness.

CHAPTER SIXTEEN

Henry was still on guard duty in parking lot but no other COCS had arrived since Sian sped out of the drive and into the night, leaving behind a letter for Josh.

He'd been waiting patiently for the stragglers to show their faces, leaning against the wall of the centre as the water continued its unrelenting rush down the three steps from the open doors. He was a sniper in a guard tower waiting for a sorry soul to step out from cover and wander into his crosshairs, and when they did, he'd deliver the bad news – the cancellation of tonight's session – like a well-aimed bullet to their heads or chests; a shot delivered without remorse, and all the while he'd have a pitiless look on his face because if there was one thing he enjoyed most, if there was one thing he was good at, it was hurting people's feelings and being the bearer of bad news.

Tearing his eyes away from his sentry duty, he glanced fleetingly at his watch. Their session should have started fifteen minutes ago, and so any latecomers deserved getting shot he mused darkly, because if they were here – him and Josh – there was no conceivable excuse he could think of for others not to have bothered showing up or at the very least, letting them know of their absence.

His thoughts turned to Josh; probably elbow deep in piss and shit and how he'd been working dutifully and diligently for the past thirty-five minuets trying to fix the leak, doing all in his power to help the group get back on track sooner rather than later. *The man's a bloody saint.* He peered over at the steps and at the foul, greyish-water which was still pouring out into the night; *Okay, he might be a saint but his plumbing skills leave much to be desired,* Henry quipped.

Peering at his watch again and then scanning the vacant car park, Henry couldn't help but think the absence of the latecomers and the absconders was a slap in the face not only him, but Josh too: *Ungrateful bastards.*

He crossed his arms, drummed his fingers on his forearm, tapped the toe of his boot on the ground, and peered longingly up to the open gates and the darkened street beyond; almost daring someone to show their ugly face, just to give him an excuse to unload on them. Henry couldn't stand a lot of things, homosexuals were at the top of his list, but what ran it a close second was tardiness, it was something he couldn't abide and if he had to be someplace, he'd get there an hour or so before he needed to be.

He slowly began to curse those who'd still not shown their faces, or sent their apologies, *how hard is it to send a goddamned text message?* It didn't matter to Henry that the meeting was cancelled anyway because of the leak, because to him they should've been here; come rain or shine. *What else do they have to do in their boring, grief-riddled lives? What's more important than group, than being here for each other on a Tuesday night?* He nodded his head agreeing with his internal diatribe. He mused further on the matter, that he and the group – those who'd already turned up and been sent away – deserved better; *those late fuckers treat this place like a bloody hotel, coming and going as they damned well please, no fucking respect, no respect at all for the time and effort this all takes, Josh has probably got his hand down a fucking u-bend right now, sifting through their shit, and they can't even call me to tell me they aren't coming or even turn up on time.*

His anger broiled inside, like a pot left on the stove, as he ran an inventory about who was actually missing. His anger began to subside, albeit slowly, as dear old Ethel's face swam into focus and he couldn't help but feel a pang of regret at the anger he'd directed towards her.

He decided to give her a pass; *daft bat probably can't even remember her own damned name, let alone remember what day of the week it is,* Henry mused. He remembered her growing fragility and failing memory over the past month. He smiled and turned his head back to the open doors of the community centre, he couldn't see inside, into the meeting room because a few feet inside the doors was as dark as pitch and matched his mood entirely. He guessed a few weeks – afforded by the flooded-out building – of Josh not having to wipe up yellowy-deposits from Ethel's seat was a small blessing and Henry considered it was probably payment enough for his friend, who was still; it appeared – given the still rushing water cascading down the steps – diligently working at stopping the flood free of charge.

Although he pardoned Ethel, Harriet was a different matter entirely; the grieving widow who'd suddenly become a nymphomaniac.

Henry let her have both barrels as he turned back to the vacant carpark. She'd always been a stalwart of the group, and she should have been here now, if only for him to turn her away again. The more he thought about it, her absence tonight did seem completely out of character; but instead of thinking something unexpected or bad could have befallen her, he took it as another slap in the face of all he'd given of himself to the group over the years. He'd offered them a place to come and not be alone in their grief, giving them a safe space, comrades in arms to journey their lonely paths of grief together – *ungrateful bitch.* But again he couldn't stay mad at her for long, because there was someone else who'd not shown up who was more deserving of his wrath, but he put them out of his mind for the time being, pondering Harriet's absence further. *Maybe she lost herself in a tryst, got herself tied up in her duvet with her battery-operated love machine between her legs; her cuckolded dog watching on with the pained eyes and spirit of her late husband, staring aghast at her flagrant infidelity in their matrimonial bed, slicking her sheets with her ecstasy and sweat.*

Henry laughed into the night at the vision of Harriet's dog watching on disapprovingly as she rode her plastic lover's-lance all the way to O-town; but his laugh quickly died when his mind recalled the most recent addition to their number, the apparent demon in angelic form, who'd still not shown themselves this evening but apparently lurked somewhere in the dark that swarmed in around him: Rowen.

He was about to turn back to the building to check on Josh's progress, when a figure shambled towards the community centre from across the road, hunched and hooded.

Rowen, Henry thought immediately. He pushed himself up from his casual leaning position before making his approach to the entrance of the parking lot; the suspicious looking character continued in their shambling, staggering gait, appearing to be making a beeline for Henry.

He braced himself, not knowing how he would handle the enigma once he showed his face. He wanted nothing more than to pin him up against a wall, threaten him, choke him with a well-placed forearm across his throat; demand all the answers to the many questions he'd had since his life had fallen apart, since the séance. How is Elsie back? Where is she buried? Why's there a grave dug in my lawn with that ominous declaration of my own death hanging over it?

But above all of those questions, the one he wanted to know the answer to the most was why Rowen was so deeply involved in all of this? *He has to be involved,* Henry thought. *Ghost or spirit or whatever Elsie is now, don't need keys to get in my house, they'd just walk through the bloody walls; ghosts didn't dig graves in your fucking lawn, they didn't bring dirty laundry and place it on your daughter's bed, they didn't leave muddy footprints and paths of salt – Rowen did it... but why? What's he got to gain from it all?*

The figure shambled closer, Henry balled his fists, ready to beat a confession out of Rowen if need be. He didn't want to get too physical on the guy, just rough him up a bit, show him who's boss, demand some answers from the pernicious punk. If Henry thought he was hiding something, like the whereabouts of Elsie's body, only then would he use his fists, he wouldn't think twice in making the sorry sack of shit bleed if it meant he'd find his daughter.

Henry stepped out of the darkened parking lot and approached the figure which continued to shuffle towards him with their head down. He was only a few feet away when the hooded figure sensed his presence and lifted their head. Henry stopped in his tracks. It wasn't Rowen, it was a young girl; her face was riddled with sores, her eyes two dull pennies and he could see that the hair which escaped her hood was matted and greasy. She smiled at him, flashing him a mouth of gums with a few corn-coloured teeth jutting out here and there; her tongue darted out of her mouth and licked at her chapped and herpes encrusted lips.

"You looking for a good time mister?" she offered, scratching at her concealed arms and chest. Henry knew the look of an addict when he saw one.

"No. You're all good; I thought you were someone else."

"I could be someone else, anyone you want?" She looked him up and down.

"I gotta get back to something, you have a good night." Henry went to turn.

"I could come with you, over there, if you want?" Henry turned back to the girl before following her outstretched arm which was pointing to a darkened area of the car park at the side of the building, by the bins and where he'd parked his car. "A quickie, I could get on my knees, swallow what you give me, wouldn't cost you much, just whatever you got on you."

"Thank you, but I'd rather not, I'm waiting for someone."

"Look mister, I need to score, I'll help you pass the time. You can do anything you want, put it anywhere you like, if you really want to..." The girl came towards him, placed a hand on his arm. Henry glanced first to her hand, wondering what diseases she might be passing onto him and then he lifted his gaze to her face. She was a lot younger under the patina of a hard life lived fast, of turning tricks and shooting heroin in alleyways, she was just a kid. "I can call you daddy!"

Henry felt a sudden revulsion. When he blinked the girl's face was suddenly Elsie's and he snapped his arm away from her clutches and pushed her away.

"Get away from me!" Henry screamed at the girl who now wore Elsie's face like a cheap Halloween mask. She stumbled backwards and fell to the ground. Henry quickly back-pedalled into the parking lot, all the while Elsie stared back at him from the floor and he wondered if this was a premonition of what had happened to his daughter? Was she also turning tricks to survive the cruel hand she'd been dealt at his expense? And if she was, did that make him her pimp?

"Fuck you old man!" Elsie screamed.

"No... it's not you... it can't be you!" Henry shouted back. He pressed the heels of his hands into his eyes until he felt pain, he needed to feel something other than utter shame in that moment. He applied even more pressure until white spots appeared on the black canvases of his eyelids.

"What the fuck's wrong with you?" The girl who wore Elsie's face shouted but he didn't dare open his eyes, instead he heard her scrambling to her feet, cursing him under her breath.

Henry pulled his hands away from his eyes and the girl was back, Elsie had vanished once more, replaced by another scared little girl. She eyed him cautiously as she edged past the entrance to the carpark. From this distance Henry could see she was shaken up, her legs were trembling along with her hands which were currently braced to fend off a further encounter. Henry stepped forwards as he dug in his pockets for change, he wanted to offer something, anything in ways of an apology.

He only made it the one step before the girl reached into her tatty handbag and pulled out a knife where she proceeded to thrust it at him, the blade trembling ever so slightly in her hand. Henry stopped his approach and his search for money and slowly removed his hands from his pockets and lifted them into the air, palms out, in a *'no trouble here'* gesture.

"I don't want your money, this ain't a mugging. But I swear, you take one step mister and I'm gunna stick you with this and then I'll cut your useless fucking balls off, don't think I won't. You're crazy, you know that? Crazy..." she lifted the blade higher, pointed it directly at Henry's face, fixing him in place.

"Don't you move," she said, as she backed away gingerly, ensuring she kept Henry in view at all times. When she'd got sufficiently far enough away, the girl lifted her other hand and stuck up her middle finger before turning and rushing into the night beyond and towards the tricks she'd be forced to perform to feed her habit. Henry watched her go, observing that every few paces she took she'd crane her neck over her shoulder to make sure he wasn't pursuing her.

Once she'd finally disappeared from sight, Henry turned back to the community centre.

He'd only made it a few steps when he glanced up at the camping lantern which was nestled on the wall outside the centre. In the dull glow he noticed that the water, the frothing tide which had been tumbling down the steps had finally stopped.

"Josh, you bloody genius." Henry uttered into the night as he hastened his way to the entrance.

He picked up the lantern and began to plod up the steps, his feet splashing loudly in the standing water. When he got to the door, like the young girl he'd just assaulted – pushed to the ground – he peered back over his shoulder, eying the dark for Rowen. He waited a moment and when he failed to show he turned back to the darkened doorway and stepped in to another darkness altogether.

"Josh!" Henry shouted, lifting the lantern in the direction his friend had gone, hopeful to see his beaming face staring back at him around the toilet door. There was no answer. *That's odd.* He mused before taking a few faltering steps down the lamp-lit hallway, he took a few strides down the wet throat of the corridor before his blood ran cold and he pulled up like a runner with cramp, instantly swinging the lantern back the way he'd come, in the direction of the noise.

"DADDYYYYY!" the voice warbled as it echoed down the corridor.

Henry peered into the gloom ahead of him. He couldn't see far and so he lifted the lantern and extended it before him. Its arc of light only reached so far, illuminating nothing of interest, giving him no explanation for the sound and so he assumed it was his addled mind or the wind blowing through the open front door and travelling down the corridor. He swung the light to the right where it picked out the edges of the doorframe leading to their meeting room, but the inside of the door appeared as dark and as bottomless as the grave which he'd discovered in his lawn.

"DADDYYYYY!" the voice came again; Elsie's pleading voice calling to him from the room.

Before he knew what he was doing Henry found his feet inching towards the alluring call. He kept the lantern extended before him in hopes that it would ward off what lingered in that room and called him onwards. The light slowly bled into the room, carving space in the oppressive and all-consuming dark as if it were a physical thing that threatened to press in on all sides, snuffing out the light and crushing him in the process. He stepped across the threshold remaining within his ring of light, each footfall was accompanied by the squelch of the sodden carpet-tiles beneath his feet; peering down he observed the water bubbling up and wondered if it contained the tears of sorrow that had long-since been shed and bled into the carpet by sorrow-filled and grief-riddled souls.

The room was cavernous in the dark and Henry couldn't help but think of it as a cave. Moving the lantern to the right revealed the bottoms of the walls, he half-expected to see cave drawings, something sinister and menacing bedaubed on the wall in mud or blood or the red paint which had been present at his grave. He felt a shiver play its way down his spine at the thought; the lantern trembled in his hand, the light quivered and danced around him like a guttering flame, one he prayed would not blow out or run out of juice.

"Over here..." Elsie's voice, but also not Elsie's voice crooned.

Henry swivelled back to the sound, the lantern swinging in his outstretched arm. He stepped in the direction of the voice and slowly something began to swim out of the darkness and into the soft pool of orange light that puddled around him. A solid shape began to form. Approaching it slowly, inch-by-painstaking-inch, the final shape of the object was revealed as if it had been birthed from the darkness that swarmed at the lights edge.

He took a sharp intake of breath because before him was a vacant chair.

That's impossible, Henry thought because when he'd come in earlier, as night strangled the light out of the day, there'd been no chairs set out, the room had been completely clear.

Someone or something had put it there.

"Sit," the voice intoned, the sweetness of its alluring tone had vanished.

Henry lifted the lantern in the direction of the voice, the feeble spread of light revealed another chair – well, the two front legs of a chair – and two grubby looking Converse trainers, someone was sitting, waiting patiently for him to take a seat opposite them in the dark.

"I said sit!" the voice commanded.

"Rowen?" Henry offered sheepishly. Lifting the light higher, Henry watched it begin to reveal the hidden stranger in the dark. He stretched his arm higher and the glow from the lantern revealed a black T-shirt with an AC/DC logo emblazoned on the front. He held the lamp aloft and flinched when he saw movement from the figure opposite him. He knew it was Rowen, it had to be, but what presented itself by dipping its head into the light was an oddity he'd not prepared himself for.

"Do you like what we've done to our hair?" Rowen offered.

Henry couldn't take his eyes off the peculiar man before him, his hair was no longer black; it was blonde, like Elsie's used to be. Rowen's eyes were heavily made-up, ringed like a raccoon with black eyeliner and equally black eye shadow, and as Henry peered at the pale face before him, drawn to those inquisitive eyes like prey to an angler fish's lure in the darkened depths of the sea; he couldn't help but feel an odd sense of recognition, because Rowen appeared to be looking at him with Elsie's eyes, looking on him with the glare that had graced his skin twelve long years ago, eyes full of utter scorn and devilment.

"What's the matter daddy, does my presence challenge your comfort?" Rowen said with Elsie's voice.

Henry wanted to pull the lantern away, send Rowen back to the dark which had recently birthed him, but he held the light resolutely aloft, allowing it to pool around them both. However much he didn't want to observe this cruel amalgamation of Rowen and Elsie, he preferred knowing exactly where it was, for now at least.

"Cat got your tongue? That's very unlike you daddy, you always have something to say," Rowen offered with a flamboyant flick of the wrist. The voice was still Elsie's but it seemed to be warring with another voice in his throat.

"Stop calling me that!" Henry offered, pointing a challenging finger in Rowen's direction.

"What... daddy, daddy, daddy, daddy!" Rowen chided with his daughter's voice, a look of maniacal glee plastered across his face.

"STOP IT!" Henry bellowed. Rowen stopped his teasing instantly, sat up straighter in his chair like a reprimanded child before a parent. Henry watched him slowly raise a hand from the shadows his body had cast around him from the high angle of the lantern. Rowen lifted his manicured hand to cover his mouth before half-heartedly stifling a giggle.

"Aww, daddy's upset with you Elsie, maybe you should go away for a bit and let the adults talk. We've got a lot to catch up on..." Henry observed Rowen snap his head to the side, and when it returned his face appeared pained, different, scared almost; the voice which issued forth from his mouth was not the one Rowen had been speaking with before.

It was unmistakably his daughter's, it was Elsie's.

"I don't want to go back in the dark, not again," she uttered. "Please don't send me back!"

Rowen snapped his head to the side and Henry heard it crack with the force and speed of the movement. Rowen's head hung backwards for a moment, blonde hair covering his eyes before slowly he lifted his head, peered at Henry through the follicle curtain. Again he could have sworn they were Elsie's pained eyes locking hold of his, but the mirthless grin on Rowen's face vacated any resemblance in an instant, because it was Rowen seated before him now.

"You will do as you're told, YOU RECALCITRANT LITTLE CUSS!"

Henry had seen and heard enough, his legs were shaking and his heart was pounding, the hand not holding the lantern balled into a crude club at his side; prepared to fight and end this torturous act, this performance, this sick joke at his expense. He stepped boldly into the fray, towards the seated Rowen, ready to bludgeon him where he sat.

"I wouldn't do that if I were you," Rowen uttered and wagged a finger at him.

Henry pulled up short when Rowen raised his other hand, bringing with it a wrench he'd secluded by his side in the dark; the end of which was a deep red, which dribbled something wet onto Rowen's jeans as he brought it across his lap and twirled it like a baton before him.

Henry observed the cruel gloss and his thoughts turned instantly to Josh.

"Josh? What have you done?" Henry snapped.

"Wouldn't you like to know?" Rowen chided, giggling further.

Henry half-turned, ready to run out of the room, slip and slide his way down the flooded corridor, desperate to discover what Rowen had done to his friend but Rowen's voice held him in place as if he were suddenly shackled.

"I'd sit down if you know what's good for you. If you want to know where your daughter's body is, that is? I know you got our message... the grave and the headstone... but a message outside of context is just a clanging cymbal in the dark, it holds no meaning, just confusion – Josh stole your meaning, he took something that belongs to you... but I'm sure we can cast some light on the clock that's ticking."

"You're talking out of your arse and I don't like what I'm smelling!"

"Say what you want, but Josh stole something that was destined for you; a letter from me, penned by your dear daughter Elsie... he took it when you broke into my house, did you think I wouldn't notice?"

Henry stood there in a quandary. He could leave now, find his friend and get the hell out of there; but there was something that kept him in place, as if his feet had grown roots and secured him to the floor. It was the swirling thoughts of doubt which were holding court in his mind; because when he cast his mind back over the last week, Josh had been distant since they'd broken into Rowen's, it'd been very unlike him in many ways.

What was in the letter? Why did Josh take it? Why did he keep it from me? Henry pondered as he cast his gaze back to Rowen, his thoughts of saving his friend put on ice temporarily.

"Ahhh, so you stay? Good, good. That's an excellent choice indeed because *we* know Elsie's whereabouts and if you step out of line again, if you try to leave this room before *we* permit you to do so, you'll never know where she is. We'll see to it she remains lost forever... do you understand?"

"If you've hurt him–"

"Josh? He's just taking a little nap... but we had fun with him whilst he clung to consciousness. So, it's in your best interests not to prolong this any longer than necessary, because head injuries can be a trifle serious, if you dilly and dally he might slip into the endless sleep there's no waking from, the one which awaits us all at the end–"

"You bastard, I'm going to–" Henry roared.

"You'll do no such thing!" Rowen spat. "Sshhh… I notice you still have a habit of losing your temper don't you… Elsie told me about that, how you shout and curse and threaten. But let me tell you this for free Henry, if you lay a single finger on me, you'll be pulling back a stump."

"Is that a threat?"

"No, Daddy…" it was Elsie's voice again emerging from Rowen's lips. "It's a promise."

"Elsie?"

"Elsie's gone," it was Rowen's voice again. "And I'll ensure she stays gone if you misbehave. I'll see to it that you'll never find her and I'll also be forced to do something I don't want to do…" Rowen lifted the wrench, pointed it squarely at Henry before raising an eyebrow. "Capeesh?"

Henry nodded in response, even though he wanted nothing more than to reach forwards and crush Rowen's windpipe with his bare hands, feel it crunch as his fingers closed around it, anything to stop the atrocity that was his daughter's voice emanating from that throat.

"Good, because it's not time to end you yet, that's tomorrow if I'm not mistaken? So, please, sit down and we can have a little tête-à-tête." Rowen lowered the tool from Henry's face and directed it towards the chair opposite.

"We've got so much to catch up on." Rowen uttered with a smile.

Henry wanted to rip his deceitful tongue out of his lying mouth, he knew he couldn't trust the delusions of this mad man as far as he could throw him. But instead of doing what his anger wanted him to, he surrendered to what his heart was pleading him to do, to find

Elsie. And so, he backed up to the chair, and lowered himself into it. He reached forwards and placed the lantern on the ground and as he lifted his head his eyes found the wrench and its blood covered tip; a part of his mind instantly began to imagine what he'd find left of Josh in the toilets when all of this was over; the rest of his mind was solely focused on finding his daughter.

"Good. Good, boy!" Rowen uttered as if he were talking to an obedient mutt.

"Cut the bullshit Rowen, what have you done with Elsie, where is she? I know you're involved, but I don't know how or why."

"She's here Henry, with us... don't you see?"

"I don't believe you Rowen. It's all just a game to you, you're just a fucking charlatan like Josh has been telling me all along. I can see that now, the things that have been happening, it's not her... it's you!"

"A charlatan? That's a big word for an ape like you! But I promise you Henry, Elsie; she's here, she resides in me, well part of her does; the bruised and battered soul you cast away like a piece of rubbish... she whispers things to me, sometimes she even sobs her broken little heart out to me."

"I don't believe you..."

Rowen shot forward in his chair, his face looked like a badly fitted rubber mask, baggy around the eyes and fixed Henry with a murderous scowl. Henry watched on in horror as Rowen's eyes began rolling back in his head, like a shark about to bite down, his mouth opened and a sudden, bloodcurdling scream burst from his lungs and throat and mouth.

"DADDY!" Elsie's voice or what it would have sounded like if she'd been allowed to grow old hit him; Rowen jerked in his seat violently and Elsie was gone again. Henry watched on transfixed as Rowen's body shook, his arms and legs spasming, his feet thudding and squelching out a steady tattoo on the carpet tiles, it appeared to Henry as if Rowen were in the throes of a seizure but after a moment it subsided, his body relaxed in his chair and his eyes found Henry in the gloom once more.

"She's persistent, I'll give her that; she had a lot of fight in her, until she gave it up to me along with her ghost." Rowen reclined in his chair and crossed his legs at the knee; *like a cat that's got the fucking cream* Henry mused.

"What did you do to her? Tell me!" Henry pleaded.

"Nothing she didn't want. She welcomed it in the end."

"Welcomed what?"

"Release from a life lived in bondage. I offered her a way out, she knew she couldn't deny me any longer. It was, what shall we call it... inevitable."

"You killed her?"

"Well if you want to put a label on things, yes!"

Henry shifted in his seat and Rowen instinctively lifted the wrench, reminding Henry who was the boss in this situation and that he still had a means to end him if it came to that.

"Don't." Rowen uttered before lowering the wrench's business end into his bloodstained palm of the other hand.

"I don't believe you."

"Oh, well that just hurts our feelings; *big bad daddy* doesn't believe us Elsie."

"If Elsie's spirit or soul or whatever the hell it is you're pretending to talk to; if she's in there, inside you, then let me talk to her?"

Henry observed Rowen squirm in his seat and he knew he had him, recognised in that small tell all of which had gone before: the séance, the voices, the clothes, the footprints in his house; all of it was a lie, a deception, a sick and twisted joke played at his expense. With the sudden realisation flooding his brain, he felt the room spin around him, the darkness which had been kept at bay by the lantern throbbed and pulsed towards him, pressing him in on all sides. From the gloom, the leering face of Rowen edged closer, scrutinised him where he sat with a look as if he'd tasted something which had disagreed with him.

"You doubt us? After all we've shown you, after all you've seen?"

"I know, Rowen." Henry offered.

Rowen raised his eyebrows and pouted his lips, the hand holding the wrench rolled it in the air between them as if he were a Goblin King requesting his subject to elaborate.

"You killed her, you've said as much yourself. You took her from me. I know it's you and not Elsie that's behind all this smoke and mirrors bollocks...you've been putting on a show, but now's the time for the show to end, just tell me where she is."

"We never did anything she didn't want us to do, she begged us in the end to stop her suffering, we didn't kill her per se, we just helped with her passing."

"I know you've been in my house."

"Like you have mine, naughty, naughty. Now wouldn't you say we're even?"

"It was you who brought her clothes, you who dug up her graves, planted things around my house. I know it was you Rowen because you left the keys in the door, the set of keys that only Elsie and I knew where they were—"

"She gave over their location freely, I can assure you we didn't hurt a hair on her head," Rowen lifted his hand up to his own hair and began twiddling a section of his fringe between his grime encrusted fingers, turning the blonde hair a muddied, bloodied brown.

"It was you who dug the grave in my lawn, you who called my wife."

"Ex-wife—"

"Semantics at the end of the day, but I know It was you all along, wasn't it?"

"YES! It was us."

"But why?"

"We are working for Elsie's end... she told us she wants you to suffer, and we'll make you suffer because I can't be free of her until we've destroyed you, until we've ended your miserable, sorrow-filled, pitiful existence. Your abuse runs deep Henry, like a bruised piece of fruit. Elsie looked okay on the outside, but if you peeled her open, like we have; examined her gooey innards, you'd notice that beneath her beautiful, blemish-free complexion, she was ruined all the way to her very core. Her heart, the one which beat for you once before had become a withered, necrotic thing in her chest, poisoned by the words you took great delight in destroying her with."

"I don't believe you... she wouldn't want this... LET ME SPEAK WITH HER!"

"As you command, ask her anything you wish, test us if you must; but I'll be listening and I'll end her drivel in an instant, I've done it before, I won't hesitate to do it again."

Rowen's head snapped viciously backwards then lolled forwards as if his neck were broken where it lolled limply on his redundant neck. Henry was about to approach, to see if the man was still breathing, but as he shifted in his seat he heard a gentle sobbing reach him; a child's whimpering, a weeping he knew all too well, one which had been tattooed to his bones. It was Elsie's and the soft whimpering soon turned to gut-wrenching sobbing.

"Elsie?"

Henry noticed Rowen flinch in his chair as if his voice had scared him.

Elsie's sobbing ending almost instantaneously.

Slowly his head began to lift, revealing Rowen's face, but it was Elsie's countenance which was present, the same look of utter disdain and anguish she'd sent his way more times that he could count. The black makeup had run thick, black fingers down Rowen's face; displaying tracks of dirty tears. From where Henry sat and in the dim light, it looked as if fingers were reaching out of Rowen's eyes, widening them to reveal the person who apparently lived within; the person who'd possessed the man before him: his daughter.

The sight filled him with doubt once more, *could it be?* He pondered; because staring back at him from Rowen's eyes, were his daughter's, as if she'd never been away. Her eyes were here now, in that sickening face, worms hadn't been burrowed into those succulent orbs that rotted somewhere in the ground.

She was present, she was here and she stared at him as if she wanted to maim him.

"Elsie? It's Daddy–"

"I know who you are PIG!" Elsie spat. "Rowen said you wanted to talk to me?"

"Elsie, I don't know what to believe any more. I don't know if this is real or all some fucked up joke that's gone too far – is it you or is it Rowen? He's sick... deluded..."

"Don't!" Elsie shouted from Rowen's mouth, her eyes which were in Rowen's face scanned the room, checking that they were alone. "He'll hear you, he hears everything, don't make him angry... just ask your question before he comes back and I have to go away again."

"Okay, listen. I need you to tell me about the photo in my wallet, you know which one right?"

"The one with me on your shoulders, at the beach?"

It was the right response, but even Rowen knew that small detail; it'd been the one he'd presented at the séance, the one they'd broken into Rowen's flat to reclaim.

"That's right. But you see Rowen also knows about that photo, and I need more than anything to know it's you in there Elsie. What I need you to do is tell me what I said to you just before that photo was taken, I know you remember. If it's you in there, if this is real, if you've come back; you need to tell me what I said, okay?"

"That's an easy one," Rowen smiled broadly as Elsie's eyes sparkled in the lantern-light.

"Then you won't mind telling me, will you?"

"You told me you'd die for me."

The words hit him like a thrown axe which thudded home in his chest, cleaving his heart in two.

It's her. My Elsie.

Henry almost couldn't comprehend what he was seeing, his daughter, her soul, her eyes staring back at him from the face of the monster who'd taken her; who'd abducted and killed her and whose body she now possessed – it was an abomination. Henry was about to speak, but the words that tumbled from Rowen's hideous mouth, spilled from between his sinful lips was his daughter's voice; each word pulled the axe free from his chest only to find purchase somewhere else, those five words dismembered him, piece by stinking piece.

"But you lied, didn't you?"

Henry couldn't speak, his voice had left him as conflicting thoughts swirled around in his head, now believing the séance *had* brought Elsie back to him; but why was she using Rowen as her hands and feet, her mouthpiece. He wondered if it was because a ghost had certain limitations, they couldn't touch a person after all.

"You said you'd die for me, but still, here you are..."

"I tried Elsie." he spluttered.

"And you failed, like you did as a father... and a husband. I know mummy left you; you're continually letting people down aren't you; but your time is almost–" Rowen's head snapped to the side, the action stealing her last words.

"Elsie? Elsie? Come back please... please... I'm sor–"

"Save your snivelling, Elsie's gone. There's only us now and it's almost time for you to pay the piper isn't it?"

"What, I don't understand, bring her back... now!"

"Tut... tut... tut... he still doesn't understand, but we'll make you... soon enough."

"Let me speak to her, one more time, I need to tell her I'm sorry... please."

"All in good time; you'll be able to speak to her tomorrow... at your funeral. But I fear if we don't hurry this along, we might have to dig another grave beside yours to bury your dear, dear friend Josh... I can sense he's not long for this earth. So, you've a decision to make;

him or me? Your friend or your daughter's murderer? Because now it's time we say our farewells, until tomorrow that is... you could try to stop me from leaving, but I'd advise you strongly against that... because if I die, Elsie; well she'll die with me and you'll never get the closure your heart and soul needs before the end."

Rowen quickly slid out from his chair and stepped away from the lantern and the darkness seemed to reach out stygian arms and welcome him back home, they enfolded around him, stealing him from existence once more.

Henry bolted to his feet, reclaimed the lantern from the floor and began waving it before him, beating back the dark in small arcs, the light only reaching so far into the room until the darkness fought back, swallowing the beam like molten tar.

He spun around quickly as Rowen's voice emerged from behind him.

"I can't wait to end this, rid myself of the remnant of that snivelling, weak, pathetic thing you called a daughter. That persistent ache in my core, the piece of her you broke apart and then forged back together with your words of hate – it's obstinate and tenacious in its need for retribution. It's attached itself to me for far too long, she's a parasite; her will, her need, her hankering for closure have stopped us moving on, because without ending you, without her laying the ghost of you to rest, there will never be any rest for me from that sliver of her soul that won't just die."

Rowen's voice moved around the room and Henry followed it with the lantern.

"You see, sometimes a spirit, a soul even; attaches itself to someone whose character is compromised... and well as you can see, she's found a home in me, but with you out of the picture, I'll finally be able to lay the ghost of her to rest."

Henry stepped towards the sibilant voice, waved the lantern ahead of him and with the light's encroachment he heard retreating, squelching footsteps, slap across the room in the opposite direction. The darkness keeping Rowen embroiled within its garments. Henry spun around as the voice erupted from the far corner of the room, furthest from the exit, if he wanted to venture into the room he'd have him cornered, but instead he raised the lantern, stretched his arm to its limits, but the light never travelled more than a few feet, it was a pointless affair, but he stood there resolutely, willing the beam to reveal something, anything.

"When we're done, when she's finally said her piece, she'll cease to exist; every piece of her will be gone; mind, body, spirit, soul. All of it. Her existence completely eradicated at my hands...and she'll become someone you used to know, a memory."

Rowen began to laugh, a chuckle at first but soon it sounded like a deafening chorus of the damned.

Henry turned from the sound, made his way to the door, heading towards what waited for him when he opened the toilets.

"I'll finally rid myself of the bitter taste of shame that's coated my tongue for all these years," Rowen uttered to Henry's back and it felt as if he was being flagellated by each word. "The shame you made her feel for what she was. *We* can finally be whatever *we* want to be; free of her, free of you... because when we're finished with you, when Elsie has her say; and she will have her say, she'll never be silenced by you again. After tomorrow, she'll finally be unshackled and ultimately free.

Henry continued squelching his way to the doorway, he was at the threshold now; he didn't look back, didn't want to acknowledge the stinging words or his part in Elsie's suffering. He was now in the corridor, but Rowen's wounding words still managed to find him.

"Knowing you'll be in the ground will be a cathartic release for her and for me. The beast of her past finally secluded in the dark where things like you belong; abominations of fathers, disgraced husbands, bigoted monsters of men, destroyers of innocent children. Once you're dead, and we'll kill you Henry, mark my words. Once we end your miserable life, you'll rot or burn, depending on your religious leanings of course, but either way *we* will win; I win, Elsie wins... you on the other hand will lose. So, you'd better run along now, drag the remains of Josh out with you; get some sleep if you can, because tomorrow's a big day for you, for us. Tomorrow's the day you die at Elsie's hands, or rather, she tells me she killed you all those years ago, but someone forgot to bury you. Fear not: after tomorrow, we'll actually finish the job she started... we'll see to it you're interred for all time, like you deserve."

Henry splashed his way down the corridor, running from the thing in the room, running from his daughter's judgement. He turned back briefly, cast the lantern in the direction of the black void to ensure Rowen wasn't rushing towards him with the wrench raised high. When Rowen didn't reveal himself, Henry turned and ran faster.

He hurtled down the corridor, splashing through the standing water; hit the toilet door hard enough to almost lose or smash the lantern, all in a crazed desperation to help his friend.

The door flew open and Henry skidded to a stop.

"No... no... no... no... no..." he whimpered.

The lantern cast only a sliver of light, but it was enough to see his friend collapsed on the floor, the water trickling across the ground no longer grey but muddied: bloodied. His feet were hanging out of the stall at one end and as he approached, he raised the lantern and the light gradually climbed up Josh's forlorn body. He inched closer, the light now illuminating Josh's chest; his shirt was bloodied, his arms which lay redundantly at his sides were marred with cuts and abrasions, dark welts of bruises already blooming: defence wounds, Henry mused.

He staggered the last few steps to the door of the cubicle and the light spilled in to reveal the worst of the damage. Josh's face was busted wide open; one of his eyes was grotesquely hooded making his eyelashes look like stitches on a wound that was about to rupture, his nose was broken and two deep lacerations marred his forehead whilst his lip was split and his face looked as though it had had golf balls implanted beneath his skin.

Henry rushed into the stall, stepped around his friend's broken body. Pulling the toilet lid closed it fell with a loud CLANK and he placed the lantern atop it, giving him light to see the carnage and manoeuvre his friend with both hands free.

"JOSH... JOSH, CAN YOU HEAR ME?" Henry shouted as he gripped Josh's shirt and hoisted his torso up from the wet floor, dragging him onto his lap. Henry pressed his fingers to Josh's throat, desperately searching for a pulse in the puce coloured flesh of his neck. He paused, trying to lower his own racing heart, then he felt it, a soft THUDTHUD-THUDTHUD under his trembling fingertips.

"It's okay buddy, we're going to get you–" Henry stopped.

Peering down at the ground he noticed his daughter's bunny. He shook his head, wondering how it had gotten there. He noticed its soggy, bloated form; the water still bleeding out from around it and he came to the startling realisation that Rowen had stuffed it in the toilet. *Rowen had planned this all along, isolating the both of us*, Henry mused.

Suddenly Josh grunted in his arms and his focus returned swiftly to his friend.

Josh's good eye was open and staring at him. He tried to open his mouth to speak but pain kept him silent for a moment before a mumble of vowels tumbled into the air.

"OUAIUEE UOOOO EAEEEE"

"Don't try to talk buddy, I got you, you're safe now... we just got to get you out of here."

Henry reached an arm around Josh's back and began to lift him from the ground. Josh moaned in pain as he was unceremoniously hoisted to his feet. Henry wondered briefly if Josh had any cracked ribs, but his need to get him out of there, to safety, trumped any discomfort his efforts caused. He pulled him tighter to himself and dragged him towards the stall's door; Josh winced again as pain wracked his body.

"Ro-wen, he's..." Josh's panted.

"Don't talk buddy, I know, it's okay he's gone... we gotta get you to the hospital man."

Josh shook his head, tugged at Henry's shirt.

Henry stopped dragging Josh's dead weight and glanced at him.

"No hospital..." he shook his head, no.

"I got to man, you look like someone hit you with their car and then backed over you again just for good measure."

"Probably still look better... than you!" Josh offered, Henry could see Josh's split and swollen lip trembling, the tiniest glimpse of a smile in a face of ruin.

"You're probably right, but I got to take you..."

Josh pulled himself away from Henry's grasp, stumbled into the door of the cubicle which stopped him from collapsing to the ground.

"No!" Josh shouted.

"Okay... okay, how about I take you back to your place, fix you up there?"

Josh nodded and Henry rushed back to him before he fell down. Shoving his arm around his friend again he pulled him close, Josh winced once more, took a sharp intake of breath and they began to make their way to the toilet door, leaving the lantern where it was; soon they were shambling down the darkened hallway, shuffling and splashing frantically for the exit.

"I'm sorry..." Josh's words were a whisper.

"Don't you be sorry, I'm the one that should be saying sorry, I put you in this mess."

"Not about that..."

They were stumbling down the stairs of the community centre now, heading for Henry's car which was parked at the side of the building near the bins. Henry scanned the area, looking for Rowen, but he was nowhere to be seen.

"I... I..." Josh stuttered, Henry didn't know if he was about to lose consciousness or the ability to speak given the obvious head trauma.

He opened the passenger door and carefully lowered his friend into the seat. He was about to pull away, close the door and rush to the driver's side when Josh's hand shot out and grabbed his arm.

Henry peered down to Josh's hand, his grip was like a vice; then slowly he lifted his gaze to Josh's face and watched as a tear fell from his good eye.

"Elsie... she's dead... Rowen... he killed her!"

Henry wanted to question him, ask him how he knew such a thing, for certain; but as he stared down at the broken man before him, he decided it could wait.

"I know," Henry uttered, lowering his eyes before placing a hand on Josh's chest.

"I'm sorry Henry, I should have... I shouldn't have... I-I-I–" Josh was squirming on the seat in pain and discomfort, and Henry wondered if it were the words he was trying to say, the confession he was trying to voice which caused him the greatest discomfort of all.

"It's okay Josh, relax. I forgive you okay, whatever you did, I know you did it to protect me. Let's just get the hell out of here okay?" Josh nodded.

Henry pulled away and closed the door. Making his way to the driver's side of the car all he could hear were the dulled sobs of a broken man and a broken friend.

The cries of the best damned friend he'd ever had.

CHAPTER SEVENTEEN

Josh peered at himself in the bathroom mirror; he didn't see the difference between the damage caused by Rowen and which had been inflicted by the wrench, he didn't even pause to acknowledge the broken nose, split lip and new dental work, or the eye which was now grotesquely hooded and fit to bursting. All he could see staring back at him was the man beneath the blood and the grime, a man who'd stolen the last words of a dead girl; and the deceit of that act had carved him a new face. One he didn't recognise as his own.

He could hear Henry in the lounge: the sound of cupboards being opened, two glasses chiming together as they were placed on the counter, quickly followed by the sound of a bottle being uncapped and then the unmistakable glugging of whiskey from a bottle.

Josh finished washing his hands. Watched the grime and blood and quite possibly excrement – as only an hour ago he had his arms elbow deep in a toilet – flow down the plug hole, carrying his ruin into that black hole which stared back at him. He half-wished he would be able to climb down there too, float away into the great beyond, anything to avoid what was coming: his omission, his guilt and his shame. There was no escaping his fate though, it was something he'd need to face head-on, but he feared the repercussions and lasting damage it would cause.

Stepping out of the bathroom, he heard the glasses touch down on the coffee table in the lounge before hearing a chair give credence to Henry collapsing into it, followed by a tired huff. He stilled himself in the hallway, but it was once more a torturous affair as the eyes of his wife found him as they often did. The gallery of snapshots had morphed once more, causing her eyes and countenance to become almost penetrative; he could feel them burrowing into his flesh, examining his very soul and discovering the deceitful, wretch of a man he'd become.

Josh glanced up timidly, only to catch Amanda's head shaking side-to-side in the photo he'd taken of her at the beach in Weston-Super-Mare, but as his eyes drifted from that mocking photo he noticed the same action being carried out by all the photos along the wall; her utter disappointment at what her husband had become made him want to flee, but there would be no comfort to be found in his escape, because he knew he would only be jumping from the frying pan and into the raging inferno which waited patiently for him in the next room.

Hobbling into the lounge and feeling worse for wear given his bludgeoning by Rowen and the penetrating, soul-wearing stare from his wife, Josh soon discovered the ball of fiery fury seated at the coffee table where the two tumblers of whiskey were placed upon it as if it were some sacrificial altar awaiting a burnt offering. Stepping closer, when all he wanted to do was shrink away from the heat of Henry's stare, Josh approached the table; in full view of Henry were the fruits of Josh's recent labour: the capsules he'd taken from Rowen's, his scrawled notes and the letter – the letter addressed to *Daddy*.

"I think we need to talk," Henry uttered, his eyes darting to the letter on the table and then back to Josh.

"Henry... I... I..." Josh started to speak but his shame kept his words at bay.

"Sit." Henry said sternly and Josh could tell from the timbre of his voice that it wasn't a request it was a command.

Josh limped ever-closer, drawing alongside the sofa Henry disappeared from view and Josh was momentarily glad that Rowen had sealed his eye closed with the wrench because it meant for the briefest of moments he was out from under Henry's glowering stare; he half-wished Rowen had blinded him though as he shuffled slowly around to face Henry once more. He slowly reached into his back pocket and the movement caused him to wince from the subtle twisting of his torso; the pain from his suspected broken ribs flaring as if he'd been lanced before it spread across his chest like a heart attack, cutting short his breath. He slowly removed the letter Sian had dropped off for him, the one Henry had passed on without opening – even though he could have, because it wasn't sealed – and as he held it in his hand, he felt the judgement of Henry's stare hit him like a freight train as Amanda's mocking voice sounded loudly in his mind like its whistle.

Henry didn't peek at your letter, did he?

Josh's eye flicked from the letter which trembled in his hand to the one on the table.

That's because he's your friend and friends don't steal from each other, do they?

Josh slowly lowered his battle-worn body into the chair opposite Henry, all the while keeping his cyclops gaze on the letter in his hand for fear of what he'd see if he glanced up.

He loves you. Cares for you. Wants the very best for you and you treat him like scum!

Josh edged forwards, moaning sharply at the ache which once again bloomed in the soft places between his ribs as he placed the letter on the table. His eye darted to the other letter. *DADDY*. Once he'd deposited it Josh gingerly edged his way back before placing and pressing a comforting hand to his sore ribs; but comfort was just a word in that moment, holding no meaning whatsoever because he knew he'd soon be forced to look at Henry and face whatever judgement his actions deserved.

Amanda didn't give him a chance to get comfortable as her voice instantly chided him again, her words a well-aimed jab to his solar plexus which caused all the breath in his lungs to leave him instantly and leaving him gasping for air. She was nothing but persistent in her assailment of him, he was on the ropes, waiting for someone – anyone – to throw in the towel, but the only soul in the room was someone intent on watching him squirm and suffer.

All you've ever wanted to be is right, isn't it? Right about this, about Rowen and Elsie? Right about my cancer and diagnosis? Right about every damned thing... well I can tell you without a shred of doubt.

Here comes the knockout, Josh mused.

You were wrong about this Josh and I'm ashamed to have ever married a man like you.

Josh wanted nothing more than to scream at the taunting voice of his wife, but as his eye lifted to reveal Henry sitting opposite him; his face stern, his jaw clenched, his anger broiling beneath the façade he was simmering in, any and all objections he'd wanted to say to his wife were swallowed into the pit of his shame-filled stomach.

"What's all this then?" Henry said with a nod to the table.

"It's... look Henry, I'm sorry. I never meant to... I was just trying to... to..."

"Spit it out goddamnit, you retarded or something? That knock on the head messed up your internal wiring?"

"I was just trying...to protect you—"

"I ain't no kid and I sure as hell don't need you protecting me, I'm big enough and damned sure ugly enough to look after myself, what I needed in all of this was a friend... and well, I guess..."

Henry's words felt like a blowtorch aimed directly at his face, he'd done the unimaginable and deserved the consequences. Shame ate what little resolve he had left and he knew things would never be the same again, but he could try to say his piece, even if it took him the rest of his life to make *this* better, to rebuild that trust, fix this friendship, he had to try and he'd gladly walk over burning coals to do it: he'd even lay down in them.

"I–" Josh started before Henry cut him off.

"I haven't finished." Henry reached forwards, picked up his whiskey, took a large gulp of the amber liquid. "Looking at all of this, and looking at that," Henry extended his index finger of the hand which held the glass, pointed it at Josh's face. "Looks like I've gone and found myself one of the very best friends a guy could ask for."

Josh felt his body twitch, before he was even conscious of what was happening he was bawling into his hands, each jerk of his body brought with it an internal suffering from his various injuries, but he welcomed it all, he deserved it all; the one thing he felt he didn't deserve but which was being offered freely was Henry's grace.

"You do-n't kn-ow... how mu-ch I need-ed... to hear th-at right n-ow." Josh's voice was a broken thing.

"So, as I said, what's all this?" Henry shifted to the edge of his seat, peered down at the assortment of things on the table. Josh wiped his eye with the back of his hand and also shuffled closer, wincing in pain as he reached out to pick up one of the broken capsules on the table.

"Evidence. It's all evidence that proves Rowen's having us on. This for example."

Josh held the capsule aloft and Henry peered at it.

"This, I found at Rowen's house, when we went back to get that picture of Elsie. It's not what it seems, I thought it was some type of pill; I don't know, like some schizophrenia medication or something. But when I smelt it, it's like one of those joke pellets, a stink-bomb or something... here." Josh extended his arm across the table, groaning once more at the simplest of actions as pain erupted in his ribs and lit a fire in his chest. Henry reached out and took it from him.

Josh shrank back, drew his arms closer to his body to ease the ache and watched as Henry moved the capsule to his nose, sniffed and instantly recoiled from the smell as if he'd been struck before shaking his head at its foulness.

"Bloody hell, that stinks... smells like—"

"Rotten meat, right?"

"Yeah, but why?"

"I think it's all part of the show, you know I didn't think the séance was real to begin with, well this proves it; the smell which filled the room when Elsie came, when she spoke through Rowen that first time, it was caused by these, he must have broken a few of them... a ruse, to make us believe something of Elsie had come back from wherever."

Henry shook his head, disbelievingly.

"Look, Josh. I know you don't believe a word he's said or that Elsie actually came back, but tonight, I tested him, tested them. I asked him something only Elsie would know... and she damned well answered me. It's her, in there with him, don't ask me how, because I don't have the foggiest how that can be; I'm as confused as you are... I've had my doubts but after tonight, after what she said, I know it's her in there, and we gotta get her out – before it's too late."

"Too late?"

"You're going to think this is crazy, but hear me out; someone dug a fucking grave in my lawn yesterday—"

"A grave?" Josh fired back disbelievingly.

"Yeah. A great ruddy thing... but that's not the worst of it, there was a cross too... it had my name on it and the date I'm going to die."

"What?"

"Listen. I've been ping-ponging backwards and forwards on this for a few days now, but it feels good to talk it out, so just humour me for a moment, please." Josh nodded. "Good, right; so, I truly believed she appeared at that séance, and I know you think I was a fool to believe that, and maybe I was. Then there were her clothes, and her footprints and a whole load of other freaky things which helped to cement that belief she'd come back, but I also know that I've been fuelled with alcohol too, which makes me see things."

The first step to freedom is acknowledging you have a problem, Josh mused.

"But recently; recently I've been thinking there's no conceivable way that the things that are happening could *ever* be attributed to her: the grave for instance, how and why would a ghost dig a fucking grave." Henry scoffed. "Also, someone let themselves in to my house with a set of keys; what entity have you ever heard of that uses a bloody key, just walk through the fucking door right? Whoever it was also removed Elsie's clothes, there's a fucktonne of other stuff too man... like the phone call to Kiera? I can't reason it away with what I know about spirits, but I also can't forget what Rowen, what Elsie said tonight."

"Man, this is crazy, but let me backtrack; what was the date on the grave?" Josh asked.

"Tomorrow. But we'll get to that soon. Look, this evening when I turned up at the community centre, I was convinced it was what you've said all along: a ruse. A sick game being played at my expense; but there's no way Rowen could have ever known what I asked of Elsie tonight, no way! It's gotta be her, trapped somehow in there with him and we gotta get her back... maybe if we can find out what he did to her, find out where she is, maybe that will help to drive her spirit, her soul, out of him."

Josh wanted to scream at Henry, tell him how stupid he sounded, but the look in Henry's eyes was one of dogged determination and utter belief in the madness he was espousing. All Josh had were the facts, the little undeniable – in his mind – truths scattered on the table before him. He reached for one now, reclaiming the letter Sian had dropped off and opened it. Scanning the contents briefly Josh peered up at Henry, although it stung to do so, he couldn't keep the smug smirk from his split lip.

"Just as I thought," Josh uttered as he held the limp piece of paper out for Henry to take.

"What am I looking at?" Henry fired back as he snatched the letter and gulped down the last of his whiskey.

"I asked Sian to do a little digging into our friend, who better to snoop into Rowen's social media than the woman who's constantly plugged into it? As you can see, there's limited social media presence for Rowen, just this one account, which also only appears to have emerged online about a year ago; which for someone of his age is very odd indeed, peculiar even, like he's got something to hide."

"I don't get it." Henry said as he continued reading the sheet of paper.

"Well, it shows he appeared somewhat overnight, one moment he wasn't there, the next, BANG! Where's he been all these years? Also, who's to say Rowen's who he says he is? He could be any Tom, Dick or Harry. Sian couldn't find out anything else about him, no other profiles on any platforms... just this one account and also it's pretty telling that the only friend he has on there is Sian – why just her?"

"Access? To the COCS?" Henry offered.

"You're probably right there buddy, the game is most definitely afoot isn't it? Also, Sian's information aside, there's been something which has been playing on my mind since the séance, I know I should have said something sooner, but I didn't want to rock the boat."

"We'll you're rocking it well enough now, so why don't you just tip us over?"

"The thing I've been wondering about since that night was how did he know your surname?"

"What?" was all Henry could offer as his face screwed up with confusion.

"Rowen, at the séance; as far as I can recall you never told him your surname, but when he called on Elsie's spirit, or whatever fucked up sleight of hand he was doing at the time, he called her by name – Elsie Clark. He used her name man. Your name. This wasn't some random act as we've been duped into believing it was; this was all planned from the very start."

Josh could see Henry was pondering the new information, his eyes roving over the assortment of items on the table.

"You wanna know what I think?" Josh offered.

"I've a feeling you're going to tell me." Henry replied as he lifted his gaze from the table and fixed Josh with cold stare.

Josh leant forwards, one hand holding his ribs in place whilst the other reclaimed the letter addressed to *Daddy* from the table.

"You're gunna need to read this." Josh said as he tried to pass the envelope across the table to Henry. It hung there between them as Henry eyed it warily, as if Josh were handing him a snake. He watched Henry's eyes trace the writing on the envelope. *DADDY.* Josh waved the letter in his hand again, trying to get Henry to take it, but instead of reaching forwards Henry placed his empty glass on the table and shrank back into his seat, folding his arms across his chest protectively.

"I don't want it." Henry uttered, shaking his head, no.

"Take it," Josh reached further across the table, felt his ribs scream out their protestations of his actions; Henry flinched back from it, fearful, as if it were a snake which would soon pierce him with its fangs.

"I DON'T WANT IT!" Henry roared and Josh instantly pulled the letter back and held it between his trembling hands.

"It's from Elsie," Josh offered.

"No shit Sherlock, I *can* fucking read it says *DADDY* on the bloody envelope. Just tell me what it says," Henry tilted his head, peered at the underside of the letter. "I can see you already opened it."

Josh felt his face prickling with shame.

Henry had turned the blowtorch to white-hot in an instant.

"I really think you should–"

"Just give me the CliffsNotes."

"You're sure?"

"Just tell me."

Josh opened the envelope and pulled the letter out.

Scanning the chicken scratch, he wondered how to surmise her last words, how to phrase the letter which was bleak at best, filled with words and sentences crafted to maim instead of bringing any comfort. Josh peered up at varying intervals at Henry, who glared at him pensively. Josh paused, read the words in his mind before attempting to speak them. He swallowed but his mouth was dry, his tongue sticking to the roof of his mouth. Picking up his whiskey, he took a large gulp before returning it to the table, shook his head at the words he'd just read, *nope they won't do*. He scanned further down the letter, noticed the paper shaking in his hands, hoped that Henry couldn't see the tremor.

"Well," Josh started, before clearing his throat with a cough. "Turns out that Rowen, well… he was… he…"

"Killed Elsie," Henry spat as he quickly sat forwards in his chair, resting his elbows on his knees and lacing his fingers together so his hands hung between his legs. Josh didn't answer Henry's statement, he didn't know how, but the confusion which must have been etched on his face said everything he wanted to say: *How did you know?*

"Rowen told me as much tonight," Henry answered the unspoken question. "You told me too; but I guess you must have forgot given the crack you took to the ol'noggin."

"He what?" Josh uttered.

"In a round-about way he told me he killed her, and that I'm next, some bollocks about her spirit needing me dead so she can finally be free. He said her spirit had attached itself to him because he was compromised or some bullshit, and if he killed her as he said, then he's compromised, wouldn't you say? The only thing that will set him free and for him to be free of Elsie… is me dying. I don't know how it works, before the séance I thought all this was some mumbo-jumbo bullshit, but he's convincing, I'll give him that, apparently I'm tethering Elsie from moving on, it's me that's keeping her from being truly at peace."

"He told you he killed her?" Josh chimed in.

"Yeah. And I'm sure that letter talks some truth into that too, don't it?"

"Well, yes it does. But it's a letter written by who we presume was your daughter, but him telling you that in person, him confessing that to you, its admission to the crime; we gotta go to the police man!"

"We're not going—"

"Henry! This guy's dangerous, we gotta go to the police; look at what he did to me, the threat he's made to you, he even told you he'd killed Elsie, we gotta report it."

"WE'RE NOT going to the police."

"But we've got evidence, look at all of this," Josh fanned his hand out over the table before waving the letter with a renewed vigour at Henry.

"We've got shit... that letter, who's to say Elsie even wrote it... yeah it says Daddy on the front and what's in it pertains to me, it's all circumstantial. You're telling me you wanna walk in there with a few stink bombs, some half-arsed reconnaissance carried out by a civilian who's probably seen one too many true crime documentaries and this letter; which by the way doesn't even look like Elsie's handwriting, or not the handwriting I remember her having, anyway." Josh observed Henry peer down at the cut on his hand as he started to trace the craggy skin with his finger.

Henry peered up again after his moment of silent contemplation.

"It could have been written by anyone," Henry said brusquely. "Also, Rowen could just as easily deny he'd said anything to me, deny he's had any involvement; it's not like I bloody recorded him, or have his confession on tape."

"But it's all here, look at my face! Look what he did to me! He's unhinged..."

"And you think the police will listen to us, we look like two winos who've been given a good going over? They'll laugh us right out of the police station. You really think they're going to take us seriously when we start telling them about the séance, Elsie coming back, possessing Rowen, the clothes, how this guy murdered my daughter, the letter all of that? I'm not willing to risk it."

"Risk what?"

"Rowen said he'd tell me where he buried her, that I'll get the answers I've been craving since the day she disappeared. You think he'd give those up willingly if the police took him in... Josh we're so close to finding her." Henry's voice was full of hope. "I'm so close to getting the closure I need, and if I have to die in the process, if that grave and the marker are right, it's a fate I'll gladly take; I at least have to do something right with my life for Elsie... no one is going to stand in the way of that."

"But–" Josh wanted to intercede, tell Henry that it was sheer lunacy what he was planning, what might unfold if he allowed his friend to walk willingly into this madness.

"I know, I know. Don't even try to talk me out of it... if you've not already noticed, I'd gave up living my life a long time ago buddy, I'm just surviving and I'm tired... the day she disappeared, died; I died too, but they haven't buried me yet."

"It doesn't have to end this way Henry, come on, what you're talking about is insane! You can't seriously believe this is going to work. It's got to be some sick joke... come on... don't do this man, there's got to be another way."

"If it's a joke then I'll be called a fool, but if it's not; and you can't tell me you're one-hundred percent right about this, I'm not willing to risk losing her forever because I didn't believe – I thought if anyone would understand that, it would be you!"

Henry's words struck true and deep and Josh felt instantly ashamed. Henry had given him a tough time over the years for his beliefs about Heaven and seeing Amanda again, but not once was he cruel about it, not once did he try to push his own views on the subject, however deluded he thought Josh was.

"I'm sorry, if that's what you wanna do, if chasing this down gives you comfort, I'll be standing beside you all the way..."

"Good, I'm glad you've seen what a dick you were being. And

you owe me." Henry didn't have to tell Josh what he owed him for because he knew: the letter, the deception, the guilt and the shame.

"You're one crazy sonofabitch man. We won't contact the police, yet, but if shit starts to turn sideways and it turns out this is nothing but some scam, if Elsie's not at the end of the road for you, you know I won't hesitate if I need to do all I can to protect you, and that means calling the police... you mean more to me alive than you do dead, you understand that right?"

"Don't go getting all quee-" Henry paused, rephrased his words and it was telling to Josh that he'd opted to drop his intended slur, *he's trying to be better, for Elsie,* Josh mused. "Don't go getting all sentimental on me. Also, why don't you tell me something I don't already know; I'm as mad as a box of frogs, that's why you love me right?" Henry circled a finger around his temple before continuing.

"I've been thinking about it and there's a way we can do this man, without involving the police, and on our terms. A way we can get to the bottom of it all... find out if he's been lying all along, like you surmise; or if he's telling the truth as I believe he is. If we do things my way, we can hopefully set Elsie free or at least find out where he buried her, he'll never see it coming, if we act quickly that is, because the clock's ticking right?"

"And how do suppose we do all this and stay within the law?" Josh replied sceptically.

"Who said anything about staying within the law?" Henry uttered as a wicked smile spread across his face. He shifted in his seat and began rummaging in his pocket, found what he was looking for, pulled it out and held it up to Josh as if he were a magician pulling a sleight of hand trick.

It was a key.

The key to Rowen's flat.

"I thought I told you to give it back?" Josh said.

"Looks like we've both got something to repent for now doesn't it?"

263

"I guess we do." Josh uttered as he glanced down at the letter on the table. "So, what's the plan?"

"We go and pay him a little visit," Henry said.

Josh glanced up, saw Henry's smile widen as if someone had just slit his mouth with a razorblade.

"You're serious?"

"Deadly."

"Look, I know this is all crazy and trust me I'm not trying to talk you out of it, although I should be because what you're proposing is sheer lunacy, but the man's threatened you, in no uncertain terms he's said he's going to do it tomorrow... he's dangerous man, look at what he did to me, you think he's just going to sit there and let us have a little heart-to-heart with him?"

Henry just waved the key in Josh's face as if that was the answer, when Josh remained quiet, Henry elaborated.

"He won't be expecting us, we've got his key right? We just go and let ourselves in, tonight–"

"Tonight?"

"Why not? He ain't going to suspect a thing. He sure as hell won't expect you to be up on your feet already. If anything, I'd assume he thinks we've gone to the hospital... but he doesn't know you like I know you, that you're as strong as a bloody ox... although currently you look more like something that fell out of a cow when it was giving birth..." Henry winked.

"And then what?"

"You still got that fixer-upper on Petherton Road?"

"You know damned well I do."

"Well, we're gunna need it."

"Look Henry I don't mind helping but–"

"Stop being such a pussy, we just need to take him somewhere, away from his place... isolate him, scare him. Then we'll ask him a few questions; you have my word, if shit turns sideways at any point, we'll call the police, I'll take the rap for anything that happens, tell them I threatened you to help me."

"So, let me get this straight. You want to break into his house."

"We won't be breaking in we've got his key!"

"Semantics really. But I'll rephrase it, you want us to *unlawfully* gain entry to his house, kidnap him and then take him to an isolated location and do what?"

"Ask him some questions."

"And if he doesn't want to answer those questions?"

"Leave that to me."

"That's what I'm worried about; what if the answers you get aren't what you want to hear? Like I said, what if it's all some sick joke played at your expense? What if he doesn't tell us anything, you're just going to let him walk out of there?"

"He will."

"But what if he doesn't, Henry? What you're planning, what you're asking me to do... we can't just let him go afterwards, you know that right? He'll do what *I*, what *we* should have done the moment we learned of his involvement in Elsie's death and disappearance."

"And what's that?"

"He'll go straight to the damned police!"

"Well, we'll just have to make sure he doesn't."

"And how do you propose we stop him doing that?"

"Don't worry about it, I can be pretty persuasive at times," Henry's devilish smile was back. "You still got your toolbox in the trunk?"

"Henry?"

"Do you, or don't you? It's a simple question."

"Yeah."

"Good..."

"Henry, just think about what you're planning here... there's no going back from this, you realise that right?"

Henry reached into his back pocket, pulled out his wallet and riffled through it. After a moment he pulled out a piece of paper, glanced at it admiringly before turning it over and holding it out to Josh.

It was the photo of Elsie on Henry's shoulders, the one they'd reclaimed from Rowen's previously.

"This is why we're doing this Josh."

"Henry, I understand but what you're asking me to do..."

"You know what I told her just before this photo was taken?"

Josh's eyes flicked to the photo and then back to Henry.

"I told her I'd die for her... so if it's my time to fulfil that long overdue promise, I'll do it gladly."

"Cut the bullshit man, what you're talking about is torturing someone who's quite clearly mentally ill."

"Well, he should have thought about that before he started fucking with the one thing I still care about. It's taken me twelve years to realise that, twelve long years of heartache and pain and suffering to realise I was wrong. I loved her with an unceasing love, even when I despised everything about her. Hell, I still love her. I'll never truly understand her, what she became, what she was all along. I'm not even sure I could love that part of her that tore us apart, but I could try, right? This, what I'm proposing, this is how I make it right. Listen, you don't have to lift a finger, I'll do all the heavy lifting, I'll be the one getting my hands dirty."

"I can't let you do this by yourself, you and I both know that..."

"So, you're with me then, wherever this ends up?"

Josh glanced once more at the photo, saw the love between a father and daughter and felt the full force of the purest of promises made so long ago and it almost crushed him beneath its weight.

"Does a rocking horse have a wooden cock?" Josh said.

"Good," Henry got to his feet. "Make sure you bring the keys to the place on Petherton Road, we better get a hustle on, time be a wasting. I'll meet you in the car, I got to check the toolbox, make sure we've got what we need."

Henry walked across the room, turned at the doorway to face Josh once more.

"You got a plastic bag and duct tape?"

Josh nodded.

"Good, grab those too."

"DADDY, I'M SCARED..."

The sound of Elsie's voice in the back of the car chilled Josh's bones.

"Please, Daddy! Why are you doing this to me... Josh help me, tell him to stop... he's crazy... please make him stop, he's going to hurt me... again... please stop him."

Josh was desperately trying to ignore the scared little girl in the back of the car as he turned the car on to St. Philips Causeway.

The night aided in secluding their cargo in the back, her voice however was like a radiation leak, slowly poisoning him where he sat.

"Daddy... he's hurting meeeeeee!" Elsie screamed, but her voice soon cut off as if someone had slit her throat, there was a moment of gurgling before her pleading voice was replaced by something altogether more sinister.

"I'm going to enjoy ripping her piece from stinking piece, until there's not even a remnant of her soul left, you fucking pig!" It was Rowen's voice, full of venom and spite and if Josh could have seen his face in that moment he was sure his teeth would have been bared and ropes of saliva flying from his mouth in rage.

All Josh could see as he peered up into the rear-view was the plastic bag which enshrouded his head, secured around his neck with duct tape. A small hole torn near the mouth to permit him to breathe, a hole which Josh had been insistent on adding; Henry had been keener on seeing the bastard suffer and suffocate.

Henry hit Rowen with a swift elbow to the jaw. Josh heard his mouth clop closed like someone hitting a home run from the front seat. He peered up at the mirror and observed Rowen's head rock back before it lolled uselessly on his neck, the bag rustling noisily with each pendulous movement as Josh hit the indicators and turned onto Bath Road. They were ten minutes away from the house, which couldn't come soon enough.

In the momentary silence and as Josh neared their final destination, he recalled how easy it had all been to abduct someone, and his thoughts turned briefly to Elsie and how it was possible to snatch someone without causing a scene.

He kept his eyes on the road and pondered about how they'd gained entry to Rowen's flat, surprising him whilst he slept amongst his squalor, like a junky strung out on their recent score. Once they approached him though, he hadn't come as easily as Henry had thought he would, there'd been a scuffle, Rowen had almost made it to the door before Josh had to get involved, felling the fleeing Rowen with a rugby tackle which left him in excruciating pain as his possibly broken ribs ground against each other in his chest, but he'd held on nevertheless as his breath was slowly stolen from his lungs; only relinquishing his grip once Henry had scrambled over the rubble and broken furniture, getting in a few licks to momentarily stun Rowen long enough to slip the plastic bag over his head and secure it with the tape, which muffled his caterwauling long enough to get him in the car, where Josh had torn the hole in the bag for him to breathe.

"Daddy... please don't hurt me..." Elsie's words turned to maddening sobbing.

Josh couldn't help but think there were two people trapped inside that plastic bag, warring personalities, but one would overcome the other soon enough. There was suddenly a choking, coughing and spluttering sound. And then Rowen's voice came again.

"She doesn't love you Henry... all that sobbing's just crocodile tears, she tells me that she hates you, that she wishes I'd ended your miserable life sooner... but there's still time, the hour of your judgement has yet to pass."

Josh tried to filter out Rowen's words and so he peered intently around the deserted streets and was instantly glad they'd chosen this late hour to make their move, their abduction. Glancing in the rearview again, checking that there wasn't a late-night police car behind them, he noticed Henry sitting next to the hooded figure as casually as you like, as if they were going on a picnic somewhere. Josh however couldn't take any solace from that thought because he knew this wasn't going to be a walk in the park or a bloody picnic, this was going to end in bloodshed and torture and however much Henry had promised him his hands would remain clean in this whole sorry affair, he knew that by the end of the night they'd all have blood on their hands – no one would leave the house they were travelling to in the dead of night unbloodied or untroubled.

Although Josh had filtered out the taunting voice of Rowen, the bag was another matter, the rustling that accompanied each laboured breath was putting his teeth on edge, a disconcerting sound which caused him to grip the steering wheel tighter. He wanted to put the pedal to the metal, get the torturous act over with, free himself from the rustling of that damned bag sooner rather than later. But he'd opted to keep to the speed limit; if only to ensure any late-night bystanders wouldn't be drawn to observe the hurtling car and its peculiar cargo.

Josh felt that the roads were also against him, desperate to keep him a prisoner for as long as they could, because as he turned onto West Town Lane he remembered that the speed limit dropped from 30 to 20. He slowed, not wanting to be pulled over by a parked or passing police car for being in excess of the speed restrictions; especially given their current predicament: on their way to torture someone in an abandoned house.

Explain that one away, Josh mused.

Peering down at the speedometer revealed he was still travelling over the speed limit and so he tapped the brakes. Rowen rocked forward in his seat, his bagged head rustling with the sudden shift in his weight before the seatbelt snapped tight and locked.

"Hey, driving miss Daisy, you wanna put your foot down?" Henry chided from the back.

Josh was about to reply when Rowen spoke again.

"It doesn't matter Henry, we'll get there when we get there and when we do I'll see to it that you die... maybe earlier than expected, which is a shame as I've enjoyed our torture of you, but what other choice do I have other than to move your death forwards."

"And how do you suppose you're going to do that dickhead?"

"We have our means... but I won't have to touch you, to kill you, will I?"

"So, how do you suppose you're going to kill me if you don't touch me?"

"I'll bury Elsie once and for all, somewhere where you'll never find her, I'll send her pathetic life back to the dark, bury her so far down that she'll never come back... that I'm sure will be a death enough for you... never knowing where she is and that a piece of her will always be out there... suffering!"

Rowen coughed again and Elsie's voice screamed from beneath the bag.

"Daddy!! Please... I don't want to go away again... please..."

Another phlegmy cough and the voice morphed again back to Rowen's.

"Ahhh, the weak, pathetic child speaks... well Daddy dearest make the most of it, because I'll silence her soon enough!"

"Shut the fuck up!" Henry yelled.

Josh heard the swift crack of Henry's fist finding Rowen's bagged head.

There was a sniffling in the car now.

A wet smacking of lips.

"I had to kill her. And now because of your actions I'll have to end her, you understand that, right? None of what she was can remain... it would be a fool's errand for you to try and stop me."

"I said shut up!" Henry roared before directing his frustrations at Josh.

"Does this piece of shit go any faster?"

"To let her soul, continue as it is, to leave her as you made her, stripped of her identity, seen as sub-human in your sight, is not an option we can allow!" Josh peered up into the mirror and watched as Rowen turned his bagged head to Henry, addressing him directly now.

"You still think I'm to blame for all of this? Which is laughable really, I know you've both read *our* letter, you both know Elsie died at my hands, that much is true... but it was your words that chopped her up into little pieces. It was your tyrannical rule and your bigoted views that desecrated her very soul in the first place, deformed her from the inside out. It was you who made her feel less than she was, time and time again. You made her run away, you wished her dead... it was you that destroyed her, it was you that caused her to find a way out of her suffering and it was *me* that ushered in her death. She was such a beautiful little girl, so full of life and love and hope; it was YOU who failed HER, it was YOU who failed to love the person she wanted to–"

"I said shut your filthy, lying trap!" Henry hit Rowen again. Josh heard the thump of a fist connecting, followed quickly by the thud of Rowen's head as it connected sickeningly with the window. Josh half-expected to turn and see the glass spiderwebbed.

"Henry... shit man, lay off him a bit, we need him awake don't forget."

"Keep out of it, just you keep driving... let me worry about what state he'll be in when we get there."

Rowen grunted and Josh peered fleetingly over his shoulder, observed the bagged man pulling himself up from his slumped position against the door. Josh glanced back to the road before flicking up to the rearview, he desperately needed to keep tabs on Henry, because his desire to destroy Rowen and get the answers he craved; *a dead man can't talk,* Josh mused. *We need answers not a bloody corpse at the end of all this.*

Josh observed Rowen in the back.

The bag was now one flesh with his face, stuck tightly to his hidden features by sweat and blood. In the dim light Josh noticed something dark leaking from the breathing hole he'd punctured in the bag and when they passed a streetlight, it was clear the substance was blood.

Josh peered once more at the road and then back to the mirror, watched on as Rowen turned his face once more to Henry, defiantly so; almost willing him to strike him again. Josh knew if this madness went on any longer they wouldn't be escorting someone into that torture chamber of a house that awaited them, they'd instead be carrying a body from the car and out to the back garden, and burying them in a shallow grave.

Josh put his foot down and the car lurched forwards just making the lights which led onto Hengrove Lane. *Four minutes, four bloody minutes and we're in the house*, Josh pondered before Rowen started baiting Henry again.

"You wouldn't leave a wounded dog in the state you left your own daughter, the only good thing to do was put her down. But I guess you just didn't care did you, she was always a mutt to you wasn't she? Whining at her master's feet, something you could kick and feel good about it... just to make you feel better about your insufferable, bloated existence. But Elsie kept coming back didn't she? Kept thinking you'd love her... that you'd accept her for what she was. She didn't know you were obdurate to change, unable to love someone you couldn't understand, she deserved better, and she found it when *we* revealed ourselves to her, when we helped her navigate death into a new life. Do you want to know a little secret?"

Josh turned left onto Petherton Road.

Tapped the wheel with the palm of his hand.

We're almost there.

"What?" Henry spat.

Josh could see the house now but the further he travelled down the road, the road seemed to stretch out into infinity before him, taking the house with it.

All he could hear was the sound of the plastic bag rustling, expanding and contracting. Josh peered up into the rearview, watched as Henry turned to face the bagged Rowen.

"What? Tell me!" Henry said again as his hand shot out from the darkness and gripped Rowen by the throat.

"Henry! Cut it out!" Josh shouted as he peered over his shoulder, the car swerving momentarily before he turned back to the road.

"We're here, just let him go, let's get him inside!" Josh shouted over the sounds coming from the rear of the car, but Henry didn't hear him.

"Tell me!" Henry raged.

Josh shot a glance to the backseat again, noticed Rowen's bagged head loll to the side. Henry was bearing down on him, the bag tight against Rowen's gaping mouth. The rustling of the bag was suddenly louder and Josh saw Henry thrashing Rowen's head from side to side like a dog with a ragdoll before he had to turn his gaze back to the road.

"She cried... when she knew she'd never see you again, as she once was... because she knew... she knew you were a liar... because she knew you'd never die for her... she knew that you wished she was dead for what she was... and even now..."

Rowen's words were cut off by Henry's vice-like grip.

Josh reached an arm over into the back, tried to pull Henry away. He managed to grab a handful of shirt, which loosened Henry's grip slightly; briefly allowing Rowen to gasp a much-needed breath, the shirt soon tore from Henry's thrashing and the grip Josh had was lost.

Free of Josh's grasp, Henry once more returned to Rowen and began bearing down on his throat but Rowen had drawn enough air to splutter what Josh was thinking would be his last words.

"Even now... you... won't do the right thing... and just die... like we planned... like you promised–"

Josh turned the ignition off and was reaching for the handle about to rush to Rowen's aid when he heard a choked, strained voice come from the bag which paralysed him where he sat; because it wasn't Rowen's.

It was Elsie's.

"You're hurting me daddy... please... stop... you're... you're killing me... you're... killing me... all over again... stop... sto...st...s."

CHAPTER EIGHTEEN

Henry was thinking about how close he'd come to ending
Rowen's life.

I would have.

I could have.

If it wasn't for you.

Damn you Elsie.

Elsie's voice, which had snaked its way weakly out of the plastic
bag obscuring Rowen's face had saved him; her words formed from
snatches of breath as he'd choked Rowen *were* the only reason Henry
had stopped when all his hands wanted to do – to feel – was the
crunch of Rowen's windpipe beneath his fingers. But he'd stopped,
just as Rowen's body had slumped into unconsciousness and Josh –
dear Josh – had pulled Henry free from murdering the bagged man
where he sat.

They'd carried him from the car, unconscious but still alive.

Now, I'll get my answers, Henry mused.

"Right!" Henry said, clapping his hands together.

He glanced over to Josh who was seated at the bottom of the
staircase, watching everything unfold from a distance. He didn't

interject or even move to intercede. If he had the strength to do either of those things, Henry knew he'd be in no fit state to stop him. Josh was still clutching his ribs, his face dripping with sweat, his mouth – hung wide open and he was panting like a dog. His injuries were now taking their toll on him.

And with that small glance, he knew the fight had gone completely out of his friend and so Henry rose from his haunches and approached the man duct-taped to an old dining room chair with a bag for a head.

<hr />

Josh had slung Rowen's arm over his neck, had pulled him tightly to himself as they pulled him from the car. Josh's other hand held fast to the toolbox, which contained the instruments they'd need to pick the lock of the room Rowen had been able to keep secured all this time, and in that room, they'd find the answers they craved, and with any luck they'd also find Elsie. It was Henry however, who took the bulk of Rowen's weight as they shuffled up the path because he knew Josh was having a hard enough time shifting his own weary and battle-worn body himself, each subtle movement he made was accompanied by winces of pain and the screwing up of his face.

Rowen's bagged head hung limply, and Henry had smirked at the sight: *Dead man walking*, he'd mused. But the smirk had faded quickly, because he wasn't walking, he was being dragged and Henry hated more than anything being this close to the thing that had killed his daughter, who still wouldn't tell him where she was buried.

They'd approached the door and Josh had to let go of their sick-ening-cargo to get his keys; as he did so, Henry took hold of Rowen's full weight and his bagged head had rolled towards him, coming to rest on his chest. He'd felt his gorge rising being that close to his daughter's killer, it had felt somewhat intimate – something a daughter might do to her father when she'd been dumped, left broken-hearted – and he'd shuddered. It had been a torturous moment for Henry but soon the door was opened.

Josh had gone inside to drop off his toolbox and flick on some of the 'KINGAVON' halogen lamps before returning; they'd decided to do what they needed to by the glow of those portable lights because if anyone were to peek through their curtains, discover someone in the house, they'd think Josh was pulling an all-nighter and not torturing a murderer. Wincing once more, Josh helped take Rowen's weight and they finally dragged him into the house.

Once inside they'd dropped Rowen to the ground.

They'd needed a chair and Henry had sent Josh in search of one as he stood guard over the crumpled body of Rowen, although he'd not be going anywhere anytime soon in his condition. Henry had been adamant about the type of chair they'd needed and dismissed the first two which Josh had procured from the lounge; a dusty, dark room which contained all the furniture – covered in a variety of sheets – which had cluttered the house when it had come into his possession. The third chair Josh had struggled to remove from under a Spiderman duvet-cover was the charm; an oaken monstrosity with thick, strong arms and with equally thick, sturdy legs.

They hauled Rowen's dead weight from the ground before unceremoniously dumping him into the chair. Josh had winced when they'd deposited Rowen and Henry observed his friend pull away sharply; a hand swiftly moved to clutch his ribs, where he held his side tightly, as if it had sprung a leak, one he was desperately trying to apply pressure to, determined to do all in his power to hold the onrushing waters of pain back.

Henry had waved him away. '*Take a pew I got this*' he'd said, and Josh had shuffled over to the stairs, lowered himself gingerly and sat on the bottom step where he rested his head against the wall and watched the proceedings from a distance. Henry had realised then, that his friend was in serious pain, his pale and clammy face said everything without him having to say a word; it was clear to Henry that Josh's internal injuries were more severe than first thought, previously dulled by adrenaline, which had now worn off. He was in a bad state and getting worse with each passing second, he needed medical assistance.

That can wait, man's as strong as an ox, what's a couple more hours, just hang in there Josh. Henry had pondered.

Because one thing that couldn't wait was Rowen.

He'd turned back to Rowen with renewed vigour and set about securing Rowen into the chair by wrapping thick shackles of duct-tape to his wrists which he'd looped around the arms before turning his attention to securing Rowen's ankles tightly to the legs of the chair with grey, duct-taped manacles.

Once secured, Henry stalked back across the room, turned and crouched down onto his haunches. His eyes drifted from the shackled Rowen and had fallen to the toolbox, where he pondered the many tools at his disposal, wondering which one would pick the lock to the door behind which Rowen kept his secrets.

HENRY APPROACHED THE STILL UNCONSCIOUS ROWEN, THE LIGHTS IN THE room were all directed squarely at him and cast huge, dark shadows behind the chair and the body slumped in it. Henry reached out and placed his hand against Rowen's hanging head and began to push it up; soon it approached a tipping point and Henry gave it a little shove where Rowen's bagged head fell backwards and came to rest against the back of his chair.

Rowen's neck was suddenly exposed under the knot of the plastic bag and Henry couldn't help but think how easy it would be to reach into the toolbox and remove a Stanley knife, click it open and slit the man's treacherous throat.

But if you do that you'll never know, and you need to know.

His mind was the voice of reason he needed in that moment – and given Josh, who usually acted as his moral compass, was incapacitated, it was a welcome voice of calm in the raging storm of his mind – and instead of reaching for the blade, his hands began pulling at the plastic bag, frantically tearing it open.

He tore pieces of the bag free and soon the godawful face which had been concealed up until that moment appeared; bloodied, bruised and slicked with sweat and congealed blood. The bag was wet on the inside, covered in beads of condensation which had been formed and warmed by Rowen's shallow breath.

Henry continued to tear at it and the bag began to perish between his fingers as he frantically tore ribbons of this peculiar second-skin free – because in places it had adhered to Rowen's flesh, formed like the crinkly charred dermis of a burn victim.

Casting his eyes up to his shadow which prowled behind Rowen's chair, spreading itself across the wall ominously, Henry couldn't help but think his shadow-self resembled a beast with large talons – *his fingers* – pulling clumps of flesh – *the bag* – from a carcass to get at the gooey innards within.

As Rowen's face emerged, Henry couldn't help but feel he was tearing open an amniotic sac, birthing some unholy abomination once more into the world. A persistent piece of the plastic bag had adhered itself to Rowen's face, obscuring his eyes like some hideous birth caul. He reached for it again, his fingers slipping off its slick surface but eventually he found purchase and peeled it away, revealing the closed puffy eyes of his daughter's murderer.

"Time to wake you up, you sorry sack of shit." Henry said as he turned towards the kitchen. "You got the water on?" Henry asked in the direction of Josh, who was still hunched over on the bottom step, squeezing himself tightly.

Josh only nodded, his words trapped in the bear trap his ribs had become.

"Good. Keep an eye on him, I'll be back in a jiffy..." Josh nodded and Henry continued on to the darkened kitchen, picking up a discarded pasting-bucket from the floor on his way. Placing the bucket in the sink he began filling it with cold water, a moment later he was strangling the taps off, and he remembered briefly those same hands around Rowen's throat in the car. He shook the memory off and lifted the bucket from the sink before hauling it into the dining room where in his haste the contents sloshed up the bucket and spilled on to the recently buffed and polished floorboards.

He paused before the cretinous Rowen in the chair.

One hand held the bottom of the bucket, the other the handle and he set himself. The bucket trembled in his hand, but it wasn't from the exertion of holding it aloft, it was the apprehension for what was to come, the answers that would soon spill from Rowen's mouth like the water from his bucket. He calmed himself and prepared to throw the bucket of cold water over Rowen, ready to wake him from whatever dark places people like him tread when they're not with the living.

"In for a penny..." Henry uttered as he threw the bucket of water over Rowen.

Instantly Rowen awoke with a huge intake of breath.

His head snapped quickly forwards and his penetrative, hawk-like eyes found its prey. Henry stood there defiantly for a moment, drinking in Rowen's disdain before he cast aside the bucket where it clattered to the ground and rolled against the far wall.

Rowen lowered his gaze, peered down at his hands, discovering each of his wrists were secured bound around the chair with duct-tape. Henry observed him flex his fingers, each hand opening and closing like two dying, fleshy, spiders. The tips of Rowen's fingers he noted, were still crowned in black, chipped nail varnish.

Rowen slowly leaned forwards, as far as his binds would permit and glance down at his feet; jostling them slightly, grunting with his efforts to free himself. He also attempted to pull his arms free, shifting them wildly, straining against the binds, desperately trying to free himself, but there was no give.

His eyes slowly rose from his bound ankles, glanced briefly once more at his bound wrists before lifting his gaze to meet Henry who smiled back at him.

"Are we sitting comfortably?" Henry chortled.

"Let me out of this chair..." Rowen replied coldly.

"I didn't hear the magic word." Henry said before cocking his head over his shoulder. "Did you, Josh?"

Josh grunted back, Henry took it as a no.

"I didn't think so," Henry said as he stepped closer.

"LET ME OUT OF THIS FUCKING CHAIR NOW!" Rowen screamed, the chair's legs rattling on the ground due to the full-throated exhortation and his desire to free himself from the chair; the veins and sinews in Rowen's neck appeared like corded ropes as he lurched forwards.

Henry didn't waste a beat and his hand flew out and connected with Rowen's face; it wasn't a punch, it was an open-handed slap which sounded out like a dry twig being snapped across a knee. Rowen's head snapped to the side and blood dribbled from his mouth. Rowen kept his head to the side for a moment, let the blood trickle from his mouth to the floor before he licked his foul lips, slurped up the dribbling blood, which disappeared into his mouth like a kid sucking in a strawberry lace. Henry noted him pressing his tongue into his cheek, moving it around his mouth as if he were savouring the taste of his ruin.

He turned slowly, defiantly, back to Henry.

"Mmmmmm... delicious!" Rowen uttered as a rictus grin spread across his mouth. Henry watched on as Rowen's smile widened, revealing a mouth which appeared to have far too many teeth, all of which were bloodstained; he ran his tongue over his many fangs, smearing and mopping up the dark-red treacle from his teeth.

Rowen's mouth then yawned open, revealing the full extent of the cavernous bloodied hole, and from within something slick and coated with tacky blood emerged; he let his tongue flop out of his mouth like a panting dog, presented the blood covered organ to Henry, as if for his approval. When no approval came, because the sight disgusted Henry, Rowen slipped his tongue back inside and groaned in a crazed form of ecstasy, his bound body squirming and shivering in delight.

He sat there for a moment, oohing and aahing before smiling balefully at Henry.

"She tastes so good your daughter... your little Elsie." Rowen said before cackling.

Henry stepped closer and Rowen stopped laughing immediately, shrinking away as much as his restraints would allow, but it wasn't far enough and Henry grabbed Rowen by the chin, his fingers biting into the man's face and pulled Rowen's despicable face towards him.

"I'll end you if you don't tell me where she is." Henry said sternly.

"I've already told you, you pathetic pig!"

Henry's fingers clamped Rowen's jaw harder, securing him in place whilst he cocked his other arm.

"Tell me. I've had enough of your silly games—"

"Games? This isn't a game, this is life... this is death..." Rowen offered.

"The fuck it isn't a game. You've tested my patience long enough, you had me half-believing I was losing my mind, I almost believed your lies...but, unfortunately for you, I've seen the truth, you're nothing but a fraud, and my patience has long since run dry. So, I'll ask you once more... don't test me Rowen; where is she?"

"Hen-ry... don't... you..." Josh's voice came to him in pained gasps.

Henry peered briefly over his shoulder.

Josh was trying to stand. Henry could see his arm was outstretched, his hand trembling as it gripped tightly to the bannister, but as he began to haul himself up he let out a yelp of pain and collapsed back onto the stairs; his arms instantly and defensively curling back around his sides, desperately trying to hug the pain away. He rocked there for a moment, like a boy sent to the naughty step by a parent for playing with matches; Henry wanted to go to him, check he was okay but before he could move, Rowen's sibilant voice weedled its way from his bloodied, gargling, spluttering mouth and found Henry like a snakebite.

"Elsie's here, with USSSSSSSSSSSSS..." Rowen crooned.

Henry turned instantly back to Rowen, ready to thrust his fist

down his conniving little throat, force him choke on a knuckle sandwich as he tore out his tongue; but what he discovered as he faced
the thing before him caused him to stagger away in disgust and fear.

Rowen's eyes were rolling up towards the top of his head. His
body was twitching and jerking in the chair. His torso twisting and
bending and thrashing. Suddenly he stopped whipping his body
about and began pulling up against his restraints, arching his back,
his head – like his eyes – rolled backwards over the lip of the chair-
back, as if a hand had reached from the shadows nestled behind him
and was slowly pulling him home.

Henry didn't know what to do, but he took another step, not
towards the thing in the chair but away from it and stared in abject
horror as Rowen began writhing again.

"HE'S HURTING ME DADDY!" Rowen screamed in Elsie's voice.

Rowen continued to squirm in the chair as if he were a snake
trying to slip out of its skin. The chair protested all the while against
its wriggling inhabitant, creaking and cracking from the sheer force
of Rowen's desperate movements. Henry wondered how much
longer the chair could withstand and hold its shackled hostage;
glancing down at Rowen's wrists, Henry noted the skin – which had
turned a whitish-blue – around each restraint had become bunched
up and Henry wondered if Rowen might deglove his own hands in
his desperation to escape.

"Help... him...Hen-ry..." It was Josh again, imploring from his
felled position at the bottom of the stairs. "If... he... dies..." Josh
continued but the pain cut his words short as the bear trap
constructed of broken bones snapped closed in his chest again.

Henry turned from the bucking – and now – foaming at the
mouth Rowen, beseeching his fallen friend. Henry's hands were held
at his sides, palms open in an '*I don't know what to do*' gesture.

"If he die-s... we'll nev-er... you'll nev-er find... her–"

Henry turned back to Rowen and his mouth and chin were
covered in a beard of bubbling pink-foam. He was sure the sick sonofabitch was having a seizure and he knew if he didn't do something

soon, Rowen would likely choke on his own tongue or vomit or whatever the pinkish stuff was that bubbled and dribbled from within.

He stepped towards the toolbox, opened it and peered inside.

Pulling the Stanley knife free of the toolbox and quickly thumbing the blade out, he turned back to Rowen whose head now thrashed side-to-side; foam and blood and spit flinging from his mouth in gelatinous ropes like a St. Bernard shaking its head.

Henry edged forwards, crawling across the floorboards on his hands and knees, the blade clasped tightly in his scarred hand, ready to cut Rowen's binds. He was a few feet away now, and stopped dead in his tracks as Rowen's head snapped forwards, the chair clattering loudly on the ground with the sudden weight shift and almost upended before finally settling back down on all four legs.

Rowen was staring directly at him, with a godawful smile on his blood-smeared face.

"Hello daddy," it was Elsie's voice.

"I... I..." Henry tried to speak, shaking his head at the visage before him.

Rowen's head snapped up to face the ceiling and his arms pulled desperately at the restraints, his exposed neck seemed to swell with the force he was exerting on his binds, struggling against something unseen.

"GET BACK IN YOUR HOLE!" It was Rowen's voice once more.

Rowen shivered and then began to slowly lower his head towards Henry.

Rowen was trembling, whatever was happing took all his willpower to overcome.

His eyes found Henry again.

"NO..." Elsie's voice barked. Brave and defiant. It reminded Henry of the day she left.

Rowen's head snapped to the ceiling again and his voice roared into the room.

"YES! YOU PATHETIC LITTLE RUNT, YOU RECALCITRANT PIECE

OF GARBAGE… WE WILL TELL YOU WHEN TO SPEAK AND WHEN TO STAY QUIET AND MORE IMPORTANTLY WHEN IT IS TIME TO SAY YOUR GOODBYES TO YOUR PATHETIC FATHER."

"STOP IT!" Henry roared as he quickly staggered to his feet.

Rowen's face lowered itself from the ceiling and Henry noted that there was no sign of his daughter's countenance in it now, just an abyss of evil intent and suffering; the vacant, dead eyes of the monster that had stolen Elsie from him stared back at him.

"You want to stick *us* with that don't you?" Rowen said as he nodded to the blade in Henry's hand. Henry raised it, he'd almost forgotten he'd been holding it and as he stared at the blade, he pondered Rowen's question: his heart answered *YES*, but his mind convinced him *NO*. If he did, he wouldn't get the answers he needed.

"Go on, slit our throat with it… I know you want to… do it… do it… DO IT!" Rowen goaded.

"Bring her back… or I swear to God—"

"SLIT OUR THROAT!" Rowen wailed.

Henry rushed forward instantly, grabbed a tuft of Rowen's blonde hair and pulled it back, exposing his neck and silencing Rowen's goading instantly.

Henry hadn't realised what he was doing, it felt as if someone else were moving his body and when he peered down, he noticed the blade resting against Rowen's throat. Henry noticed his hand was shaking, observed a tear of blood bloom from under the tip of the knife which dimpled Rowen's neck. The tear of blood slowly snaked its way out from under the blade and ran down Rowen's smooth neck, disappearing beneath the collar of his T-shirt.

"DON'T HENRY!" Josh shouted behind him and instantly winced.

"TELL ME ONE GOOD REASON WHY I SHOULDN'T?" Henry yelled back.

"YOU'RE NOT A MUR-DER-ER…" Josh managed before he descended into a coughing fit which wracked his injured body, he spluttered and bawled for a moment, and when he found the strength to speak again his voice was weaker and tinged with suffering.

"You're not like him... don't let him turn you into something you're not!" Henry heard Josh collapse behind him onto the stairs, moaning in agony but remaining in place.

Henry glanced down at the blade again.

"D-add-y?" It was Elsie's voice again and when he glanced to Rowen's face it was Elsie's scared eyes that stared back at him.

Henry pulled away sharply, throwing the knife to the ground.

Rowen continued to stare at him with Elsie's eyes. Henry turned his gaze away and dropped to his knees under the weight of Elsie's scared, pained and confused scowl.

"Were you going to *kill* me?" She asked inquisitively.

Henry couldn't bring himself to look at Rowen, to witness his daughter's gaze and watch her voice come from that sinful mouth was an abomination of the worst kind, she was still in there and he needed to get her out.

Henry kept his eyes focused on the ground and shook his head from side-to-side.

"Were you?" she probed again.

"No..." Henry offered.

"Was killing me once not enough for you?" Elsie chided.

"NO... I wouldn't—"

"LIAR!" It was Rowen's voice again. Elsie had been cast once more back into the abyss.

Henry lifted his head now, knowing his daughter's face and voice had gone and Rowen was once more inspecting him like shit on the bottom of his shoe.

Searching me for a weakness, aren't you? Henry mused.

"Where is she... just tell me where you buried her!" Henry said boldly.

Rowen's mouth turned up at the corners and he began to chuckle. The chuckle turned to laughter and the laughter soon turned to a maddening chorus of gut-bursting chortling.

286

"WHAT'S SO FUNNY?" Henry shouted to be heard over the noise.

Rowen's laughter subsided and he tilted his head to the side before answering.

"What's funny is that you think we buried her!" Rowen threw his head back and when it returned Elsie's voice came from his mouth.

"Silly daddy..." Elsie began laughing at him too.

Rowen's head snapped up again and returned to face him.

Rowen was laughing.

Snap and return.

Elsie cackled at him.

Snap and return.

Nothing. Silence. Henry observed the sinister glare of Rowen as his tongue snaked out once more to lick at his foul lips, glossing them with the blood from his mouth.

"All this time," Rowen began. "You've been asking *us* where she is; and all this time we've been telling you that she's here, with us, in this very room, in this very body..."

"I don't understand? Just tell me... what have you done with her, where is she, where's her body?" Henry uttered wearily, feeling the numbing effects from the chorus of mocking laughter; his daughter, his Elsie – laughing at his incompetence.

"I'll never give her to you, you must know that, right?"

"Just give her to me, tell me where she is and I might even find it in my heart to let you leave this place."

"What makes you think we want to leave this place? The only way we'll be leaving here is when we've stood over your dead body and checked that it's cold... the hour has come has it not?" Rowen peered out of the window and Henry followed his gaze, morning was fast approaching.

Rowen turned his face back to Henry before continuing.

"You'll die today Henry. And as I said before, we won't even have to lift a finger to see that it's done, your own guilt will be your undoing... your own pride will consume you." Rowen's eyes turned away from Henry again and Henry followed the direction they'd travelled; on the floor was the blade.

"You can never have her back, Henry; Daddy-Dearest... she's gone, we killed her!"

"What did you do to her, tell me... please?" Henry was pleading now, his eyes filling with tears as his mind filled with thoughts of turning the blade on himself as Rowen surmised he might end up doing. It took all his strength to turn away from the coward's way out, knowing he'd see this damned thing through to the end, he'd get the answers he craved even if it killed him; if in the end he had to use the knife to end his sorrow-filled life, he knew he'd make sure it was coated in the blood of the man sat before him first: After he'd cut him a new mouth, six inches below his existing one.

"We feasted on her," Rowen purred before licking and smacking his lips together.

Henry got slowly to his feet, stepped forwards and Josh groaned in pain behind him.

"We feasted on everything she was," Rowen continued. "And now there's nothing left, even the remnant of her that remains, which *we've* permitted you to converse with, is now slowly digesting in our stomach–"

"Let her go," Henry said as he stepped closer, tears wetting his cheeks.

"NEVER!" Rowen shouted as he lunged his head forward, his mouth snapping open and closed as if he were a feral dog trying to bite.

"You can never have her back, because she no longer exists... we subsumed her into *us*; mind, body and her dear lost and damaged soul... which had been tenderised expertly by your words and actions and deeds. *We* thank *you*. Because you made her taste delectable; she was so tender, so sweet... so–"

"Let me talk to her, bring her back."

"That's not an option any more Henry... there's nothing left... you failed her again."

"This is your last chance Rowen…" Henry stepped closer-still.

"That's laughable… if anything, this is *your* last chance."

"Last chance for what?"

"To tell her that you loved her… and to thank *us* for ending her miserable existence!" Rowen uttered coldly before winking at Henry and bursting into a fit of hysterical laughter.

Henry couldn't control himself any longer.

He pulled back his fist and let it fly.

It connected with a sickening crunch to Rowen's nose but instead of silencing the man it only served in making him laugh all the harder: and so, Henry hit him again and again. He hit him until his fist had pieces of Rowen stuck *to* and embedded *in* his knuckles, he hit Rowen until he stopped laughing and when he'd fallen silent, Henry hit him some more for good measure.

Henry backed away, panting and out of breath; his fist hung at his side, bloodied and most likely broken. He turned to Josh, who was still at the bottom of the stairs, he was shaking his head, rocking backwards and forwards. It wasn't the pain that had caused his rocking, Henry could tell that by the look on his face; his friend was in shock from witnessing Henry destroy a man right before his eyes and knowing he was utterly powerless to stop him.

Rowen spluttered and Henry turned back to him, observing clods of blood and shards of broken teeth tumble from his ruined mouth.

"Hen-ry… enough… he's suffered enou-gh…" Josh managed to say before moaning and falling silent again. Henry could hear Josh desperately trying to get to his feet behind him, but knew from his scrambling feet and his moans of pain that he had time to act before Josh could make it to him, attempt to pull him away or even throw his broken body atop of Rowen like a human shield. He had time to make Rowen suffer and he still had twelve-long-years of suffering to mete out and Rowen hadn't suffered enough yet and Henry would see to it that Rowen suffered greatly, like he had, before he allowed him to draw his last breath.

If I can't have her, then no one can; especially you!

"Hen-ry... stop..." Josh's voice was still far away, still wracked with pain.

I've still got time to kill him; stay down Josh... just stay down. Henry mused darkly.

Rowen slowly lifted his head and Henry discovered the utter ruin his fist had caused and smiled.

"Tell me..." Rowen started to say before he coughed and a clod of blood tumbled from his mouth.

"Tell you what?" Henry snarled before grabbing a fistful of Rowen's shirt.

"Tell me..." Rowen coughed again and covered Henry's face in droplets of blood.

"What?" Henry shook Rowen by the shirt, cocking his balled and bloodied fist.

"Tell me how much you love me–"

~~Henry let his fist fly.~~

It landed with a *CRUNCH*.

"TELL *US* WHY YOU ALWAYS HURT THE ONES YOU LOVE!"

His fist connected with a wet *SPLAT*.

"Tell me... how much... you love... us?"

Henry hit him again, this time with a sickening uppercut that clattered Rowen's teeth together and sent his head whipping backwards. The chair rocked back, raised on to the rear two legs momentarily before it clattered back down, flinging Rowen's head forwards where it hung limply, blood dribbling from his face into his lap.

Henry thought he'd knocked him out but Rowen began to chuckle again.

He grabbed a fistful of Rowen's hair and flung his head back up where it rolled around on his weak neck, the mushed remains of what once was his face stared blankly back at Henry. The hideous, deceiving hole of a mouth yawned open and Rowen's laughter bubbled wetly from his throat. Henry thought he was actually enjoying his destruction. Welcoming it. *But why?* Henry pondered; *what's he got to gain from all of this?*

"Love *us* like you did..." Rowen's voice gurgled from his mouth.

Henry grabbed Rowen's shirt again.

He could hear Josh finally staggering closer, but he wasn't close enough to stop what was to come next.

"Love us like you did... when we were on your shoulders!"

Henry hit him again and felt Rowen's orbital socket crack on impact. Henry didn't relinquish his grip, he held Rowen up, making sure he'd witness his own end head on.

"*She*..." Rowen whispered.

Henry bent his head lower, brought his ear to Rowen's hideous, lying mouth.

"She's never... coming back. This time... you've lost her for good."

"I lost her twelve years ago you evil son of a bitch, you took her from me... you killed her, all I ever wanted was to give her a decent burial, lay her to rest. Grieve at her graveside like any father should have the right to do; however much they may or may not deserve that right. You took that from me... my right to atone, to make things right... and now it's all too late."

"Maybe you'll get the chance one day..."

"What the hell's that supposed to mean?"

Rowen began laughing again, his mouth opening wide, displaying his new and macabre dental work; broken shards and cracked teeth glistened wetly in the halogen light.

"What's that supposed to mean? You know where her body is don't you... tell me, do one decent thing before I *KILL* you!"

Rowen's laughing ceased.

"You still don't understand do you, she's gone... there's only us now. Kiss me Daddy."

"Hen-ry don't... list-en to him... he wants you to... do it." Josh's voice was closer, Henry peered over his shoulder and discovered his friend lumbering closer, one arm tucked securely around his ribs the other outstretched to the wall, keeping him upright.

Henry still had time and turned back to Rowen to hear the last words of a soon to be dead man.

"The best thing you could do right now is take that knife," Rowen nodded to the knife on the ground. "Take it, and slit your throat. You see, once you're dead, you'd have fulfilled that veiled promise you made to your daughter so long ago..."

"And what was that?" Henry said as he pulled Rowen closer.

"You said you'd die for her, so why don't you do the right thing... *we* beg you to. Because only by you dying can *we* become what was intended all along. With you in the ground, peace will finally be found for a ravaged soul. She was ravaged by the one person in her life whose only job was to love *his* daughter for who she was... not vilify her for what–"

"IF ANYTHING, SHE FAILED ME..." Henry roared.

"And still you can't see–"

"SEE WHAT?"

"How a father's love should be unconditional... but yours was only offered with conditions and outdated notions... you don't deserve her. You never have. And now all you'll remember of her is us... your daughter's–"

"Murderer–"

"I'd prefer the term salvation... because that's what we were to her, we were Elsie's salvation... from a gutless father and a life of living under your shadow and ruin... you should be thanking us for ending her life, for enabling her to transcend, to be free!"

Henry couldn't stop himself.

He hit Rowen again and again and again.

"STOP!" Josh cried.

Again his fists found their way to Rowen's face.

"HENRY YOU'RE GOING TO KILL HIM... STOP..." Josh yelled.

Again, and again and again Henry's fists tenderised the meat of Rowen's face.

"ST-OP... HEN-RY... DON'T!" Josh was panting, closing in.

Henry continued hitting Rowen until he became a wet pulp beneath his knuckles.

But however hard he hit, Henry couldn't end Rowen's baying laughter.

Henry stepped back before swinging a haymaker. It connected with Rowen's temple and sent him, and the chair he was strapped into, toppling over to the side.

There was a loud THUD as the chair hit the floor and somewhere on the way down there was a sickening THUNK as Rowen's head bounced off the wall-mounted radiator. Henry stared down at the felled figure on the ground and the silence his ravaged soul craved swarmed around him; because Rowen's laughter had finally ceased.

Henry stood defiantly over Rowen, transfixed by the crimson which quickly pooled around his head like a ghastly halo of vermilion.

Henry could hear Josh's wailing now, but in the enormity of the moment, as Henry observed Rowen's life ebbing away in red on the polished wooden floorboards, Josh's cries of anguish appeared muted, as if they were miles apart but in the same room.

It wasn't the possibility of killing a man in cold blood that had rocked Henry to his very foundation; it was the startling realisation that Elsie was once more lost to him.

Forever and for all time.

CHAPTER NINETEEN

B lood. *There's too much blood.*
    "What... have... you... done?" Josh said laboriously as he hobbled closer, slowly drawing alongside Henry who was muttering to himself.

"Die you piece of shit... die... die..." he was a record stuck on repeat.

Josh grabbed Henry's arm; stifled a cry of pain which threatened to escape his throat, caused by the throbbing ache in his chest, which once again teased with flooring him by the simplest and subtlest of actions.

He bit down on the pain, determined not to let it have another victory and shook Henry hard, trying to jolt him awake from the fugue state and the monotonous babbling he'd descended into.

Josh needed to bring him back – and bring him back quickly – from whatever dark corridor of his mind he'd been wandering down and become lost in; because he couldn't do what needed to be done by himself. It'd most likely kill him, and then there'd be two corpses instead of one to contend with; three if Henry followed through with Rowen's previous goading and took his own life.

He might, he's impulsive. Josh thought darkly.

But Josh also knew, hoped, that there might not even be a corpse if he could get Henry to return to himself.

"Hen-ry, there's st-ill time. We'll fix this... Hen-ry... wake the fu-ck up!" Josh panted.

Josh relinquished the pressure he'd been applying to his ribs with his other hand and slapped Henry across the face with it; the slap was hard and loud and Henry's head rocked to the side but returned quickly to the body on the ground, completely oblivious – it seemed to Josh – that he hadn't been struck at all.

Josh peered over his shoulder, the puddle of deep-red was still expanding.

He slapped Henry again.

After contact he felt something shift and stab him in his side... no that was wrong... it felt as if something had stabbed him *inside* his chest. The pain he'd been keeping bottled up was suddenly uncorked by his impulsive movements and agony reigned like a vicious and conquering dictator; it flooded his core with heat and stole his breath, making his legs suddenly redundant and he felt himself crumbling to the ground.

But he didn't hit it.

Glancing up as he hung in the air he discovered that Henry had caught him.

His friend's arm was tucked around his side and Josh ground his teeth against the pain caused by it, but slowly Henry lowered him to the ground, a few feet from Rowen and the ever-expanding puddle of blood.

Josh waited a moment, tried desperately to get his breathing back to somewhat resembling normal. He needed to speak and needed more than anything to use what words he could muster to convince Henry to help him save a life instead of taking one.

"You've got... to he-lp him..." Josh managed to utter between laboured breaths.

"I wouldn't piss on him if he was on fire, you're joking right?"

Josh shook his head, no.

"You're serious?"

Josh nodded, yes.

Josh wanted to scream: *You're not a murderer Henry, you're a troubled man... deeply troubled, but a murderer you ain't, don't let Rowen turn you into that, because that's what he wants, to ruin you.*

But all he could muster were three words.

"Please... for me..."

"I ain't touching him, no way. I'm gunna stay right here and watch him empty himself all over your floorboards."

"Please—"

"He killed Elsie... you heard him, right? He butchered her, consumed her – whatever the hell that means. He's dead already in my book."

Josh glanced over at Rowen, his body was still strapped in the chair and the pool of blood around his head was vast; Josh had never seen so much blood, he didn't even know a body could house so much of it.

He could be dead Josh mused; *but he could still be alive. We can still make this right... somehow.* Josh gripped his ribs, applied pressure and the ache subsided enough for him to talk.

"If you can't do it for me," Josh uttered, turning back to Henry. "Do it for Elsie."

"Don't you even dare use her as a bargaining tool—"

"Okay then, tell me how you're go-ing to find her if you're in prison?"

"What?"

"If he dies, which he will... if we don't do any-thing. You'll go to pris-on man." The pain was returning but Josh gritted his teeth, pressed his hand tighter to his side and continued.

"Ab-duction and man-slaught-er, that's as serious as it gets man. Hell, I'll be keeping you company in the next cell too if we let him die... we can't let him die Henry... if we do, that's murder, that's life... you're not a murderer."

Josh coughed and pain fired through and around his body like an electrical charge from a faulty plug socket, a sensation he'd become intimately familiar with over the years. He steadied himself, applied more pressure to his side, felt something grind within and drew a pained, shallow breath before continuing.

"If we can save him, there's a way we can spin this–"

"What, we just turn around to the police and tell them we're sorry?" Henry offered sarcastically.

"I'm not sure what it looks like yet, but we gotta try… if he dies… it's all over."

Henry was shaking his head at Josh's words of truth.

Josh tried to make eye contact with him but Henry wouldn't look his way; he only had eyes for the carnage he'd caused and the life he'd wrecked which currently lay dying, emptying, a few feet away. Josh slumped to the side and in this newfound position it felt as if a crushing weight had been lifted off his chest and he could suddenly breathe freely again. He filled his lungs – unencumbered by pain – with air and his agony gradually subsided with each inhalation and he found he was able to talk clearly and unrestrained.

"Listen to me, Henry. All of this… everything we've done and found out; his coercion, his threatening phone calls, his stalking, his assault of me, the threats on your life, the murder of Elsie. All of it, all of the evidence and motive for his sick and twisted ends will mean jack shit if he dies. You'd be no better than him. If anything, he'd be better off, because he'd be dead and not able to answer for his crimes, whereas me and you, will be the ones facing the judgement he should be facing… we'd be murderers."

"You never touched him, it'll be me who goes down, and I'm more than happy to take the fall–"

"I'm complicit Henry, whatever way you slice it, I enabled you. Just help me."

"I can't–"

"YOU CAN." Josh shouted. "You're better than him Henry, there's still good in you, don't let him take that. I'm imploring you, please; be the better man here–"

"I'm better than he'll ever be... ALIVE OR DEAD!" Henry roared, scowling at Josh.

"Then prove it. Because all I can see from here is a stranger. A bastard of a man who's lost their goddamned mind... what you do now, what you choose to do now, will define the rest of our lives."

"I don't have to prove shit to anyone... especially you."

"What about Elsie?"

"Don't, Josh. I've warned you... and anyway, you're forgetting she's dead, gone–"

"I'm talking about her memory and her body. She's still out there, somewhere. We can still find her... we can try to find her at least... but we can't do that if *he* dies."

Josh observed the penny drop.

Henry's eyes grew clouded revealing the storm brewing in his mind.

"Help me save him Henry... please–"

"Fuck-sake!" Henry huffed, got to his feet and stalked towards Rowen.

Josh couldn't stand but he could crawl and so he followed in Henry's wake; dragging himself inch-by-painful-inch towards the chair which held their dying captive.

Henry reclaimed the Stanley knife from the floor and moved with menacing intent towards Rowen, the blade twinkling and winking at Josh in the glare from the halogen lights. Josh was about to scream for Henry to stop but realised quickly as Henry lowered the blade to the duct-tape, that his intentions were pure and not as savage as Josh had first thought – dicing Rowen up into smaller, disposable chunks.

Henry severed the ties which bound Rowen to the chair and his body slumped before sprawling out across the ground.

Josh watched on as Henry dragged the body from the puddle of red and dumped Rowen callously in the centre of the room, his already damaged head bouncing on the floor. Josh crawled in that direction now, towards the lifeless man at Henry's feet, and as he approached Henry backed away once more, wiping his hands clean of the mess he'd caused and the part he'd played, bloodying his jeans with the red from his hands and knife.

Josh pulled himself closer to Rowen's body, pawing at his clothes, grabbing at his limbs, desperately hauling himself closer to Rowen's head; all the while gritting his teeth against his own pain, his own inner torment, desperate not to let it incapacitate him.

He was soon level with the pulped remains of Rowen's face. And Josh mused that the house always won, Rowen had walked into their lives, played the cruellest of games and as he gazed upon what once was a face, he realised Rowen had lost in a big way; but he also knew there was still a possibility that everyone would lose, if Rowen died.

Josh placed his hand to Rowen's neck, felt for a pulse.

"Come on," Josh whispered. "Where the fuck are you?"

"He's dead man, good riddance is what I say, we should be digging a grave instead of–"

Josh turned his head slowly to Henry and fixed him with a 'not now' stare.

Henry shrugged his shoulders and leant back against the wall nonchalantly.

Josh returned to the task at hand, pressed deeper, closed his eyes to help him focus and he found what he was looking for, he felt it throb weakly below his finger.

"He's still got a pulse," Josh exclaimed and turned to face Henry. "Help me."

"You're on your own, I ain't touching that sack of shit."

"I can't do it all by myself, we gotta do CPR, my ribs; I don't have the strength to–"

"FUCK!" Henry exclaimed as he pushed himself off the wall and shambled forwards.

"Thank you," Josh offered.

"I ain't doing this for him, you realise that right? I wish the bastard was dead, but I can't stand around and watch you kill your-self trying to be a hero, now can I? I ain't burying you too. What do you need me to do?"

Henry knelt down beside the body as Josh shuffled up onto his elbows by Rowen's leaking head. Josh tilted Rowen's besmirched head back, whilst his fingers pushed his chin back the other way, opening his deceitful mouth along with his airway; where he suddenly realised the extent of the trauma Henry had inflicted on him. His gums were full of broken shards of teeth, and those that remained looked like the broken headstones of a neglected graveyard in hell.

He felt his gorge rising with the prospect of what he had to do.

"I'm going to blow, and you're going to pump."

"That's what she said," Henry offered wryly.

If it wasn't for the seriousness of their situation Josh would have found it funny, but a life was hanging in the balance; three lives for that matter.

He glanced up at Henry as if he'd not said a word.

"Cut his shirt off, use that," Josh nodded to the knife. "You're going to need to locate the centre of his chest and pump it for as long and as hard as you can, right?"

Henry nodded and lifted the blade, bringing it closer to the throat he'd almost slit.

Josh noticed Henry's hands shaking and could tell his friend was still battling the desires to follow through with slitting Rowen's throat and being done with everything.

Josh lowered his head towards Rowen's gaping mouth.

What will be will be, he mused.

He paused for a moment, swallowed back the bile which was clambering to escape and placed his mouth over the moist, bloodied, foul orifice of Rowen's; and began breathing life into him.

Josh heard the cutting of fabric.

He lifted his mouth from Rowen's, waited a beat and breathed again into his mouth.

Come on, come on, don't die on us. Josh willed.

The fabric was tearing now, the knife cast aside for quicker access.

Josh lifted his mouth again, waited; and then breathed into Rowen again.

He was still emptying his lungs into Rowen when he heard a sudden commotion, a scrambling of feet and thumping of hands on floorboards, the knife being knocked aside and spinning away from them. And then he heard the shriek.

A sound he was sure he'd never be able to unhear for as long as he lived.

Wailing so atrocious that it should never have been permitted to exist.

It sounded as if the gates of Hell had opened and all of its interned, tortured, inhabitants had cried out at once.

Josh pulled his mouth away from Rowen's and his eyes found Henry.

The hellish noise was coming from his open mouth.

He'd scurried away from Rowen and now his back was up against the wall; his face was deathly pale and his whole body was shaking, rocking actually as he hugged his knees. It was his eyes and not the abominable banshee cry which frightened Josh the most; they were bulging out of their sockets, white and wide with fright and fear: he'd never seen someone look so scared.

"What? What, is it?" Josh shouted.

Henry had stopped screaming.

He shook his head violently from side-to-side and rocked himself back and forth.

Henry opened his mouth to speak but all that emerged was the deep, guttural cry of a wounded, dying animal. Josh noticed that Henry's eyes were transfixed on Rowen as saliva began to fall from his open mouth as tears rolled down his cheeks.

"Henry?" Josh offered.

"It's... it's..." Henry mumbled as he lifted his hand, stared at his palm.

"What?" Josh said.

"YOU'VE GOTTA SAVE HER," Henry shouted, his eyes still locked firmly on his hand.

"I know. We will... but first we've got to save—"

Henry snapped his head away from his hand, his sad, imploring eyes found Josh.

Henry extended his arm, held out a shaking hand and pointed a trembling finger towards Josh, but Josh soon realised he wasn't pointing at him, he was pointing to the right of him, towards Rowen.

"It's... it's... it's..." Henry stuttered.

Josh turned his attention back to Rowen as Henry continued to stutter.

"It's... it's... it's..."

Josh's eyes wandered down from the pulped remains of Rowen's face, where they quickly discovered Rowen's now exposed chest. Josh frowned at the discovery of scars marring the smooth plains of the skin of Rowen's torso; two crescents, eight inches long, made up of pinkish-purplish scar tissue which ran under Rowen's pectorals: *surgical scars*, Josh mused.

It should have been enough for him to realise what he was looking at, but then he noticed the birthmark; the kidney shaped blemish on Rowen's collarbone, the same brown smear which was present in the photograph in Henry's wallet.

That's when the bottom fell out of Josh's world as he realised who lay bloodied and broken on the ground before him.

Rowen *was* Elsie.

Or more accurately, Josh thought; *Elsie had* become *Rowen*.

Josh turned his face back to Henry and words failed him as they stared at each other over the expanse of the room and Josh wondered if he'd ever be able to reach his friend again, but he didn't have to wait long to find out, because Henry dragged himself back into the fray, scrambling in desperation across the floor towards them.

"Tell me what to do man, we gotta save her–" Henry paused, corrected himself. "We gotta save him, WE'VE GOT TO SAVE MY BOY!" Henry bellowed and Josh felt his heart tear in two at Henry's words and confession.

Acceptance. Finally. But at what cost.

"You pump his chest," Josh said. "You can do this Henry!"

Josh observed Henry lifting his shaking hands, interlocking his tremulous fingers and preparing himself to start compressions. Josh descended once more to breathe into Rowen's mouth; after five strong blows, pausing after each one inflated Rowen's lungs, he lifted his head. He'd been expecting Henry to have dived straight in, already doing the compressions; but all he witnessed before him was a petrified man, broken man who had his daughter's – his son's – blood on his hands and who was staring at them despairingly.

"You can do it Henry!" Josh encouraged.

"I can't... I can't touch him..." Henry was shaking his head, no.

"You can, because you must, if you want him to live you'll pump his chest as if your life depended on it, and it does... so do it!" Josh shouted.

Henry nodded. Mumbled something inaudible before slowly lowering his hands.

Josh could tell touching Rowen's desecrated body, defiled by Henry's own hands; fuelled by his hate-filled heart was a fate worse than any death imaginable and it was something Josh knew would stay with his friend for all of time. Henry would recall this memory on cold and lonely nights when dreams were something he chased but would never come, only nightmares would await him, where he'd feel his dying son's warm body growing colder beneath his frantic fingers.

Henry, finally and almost begrudgingly – although he had no choice – lowered his hands to Rowen's chest and started compressions. As his hands touched his son's flesh he moaned uncontrollably and unreservedly into the room, it was the sound of a father realising their child had no hope and it chilled the marrow in Josh's bones.

Rowen's body jerked up and down with each heavy compression. Checking Rowen's face for signs of life, Josh noticed with each downward stroke delivered by Henry only increased the flow of blood from Rowen's head wound.

"I'm sorry... Rowen... I'm sorry..." Henry murmured as he kept thrusting down on his son's chest.

More blood spread around his head.

There's too much blood. Josh thought.

And he knew it was too late to save him.

"Come back to daddy, please, I need to tell you..." Henry's words were quickly feasted upon by his sobbing. When he started speaking again he was pleading, begging, imploring and remorseful, everything the man had never been before. "Please, don't leave me again... I'm sorry. I'm sorry I didn't see you, that I couldn't see you, that I refused to see you. This whole time you've been standing right in front of me and I failed you again, like I did twelve years ago... come back to me please, I see you now... and I'm sorry... COME BACK TO ME!"

Josh lifted his hand, palm out and Henry stopped his compressions.

He placed his fingers to Rowen's neck, knowing what he'd feel.

The absence of a pulse.

He moved his fingers, pressed deeper into Rowen's neck.

He glanced over at Henry, his eyes stared back at him, wide with a father's hope.

Josh felt nothing. Glanced down at the body before them on the ground, he couldn't bear to do what he had to do looking into his friend's beseeching, expectant eyes.

Josh shook his head ruefully and heard the immediate eruption of Henry's suffering.

"I'm sorry, Henry. I'm so sorry but he's-"

"DON'T SAY IT!" Henry roared.

Josh found himself suddenly pushed away. He fell backwards and peered up at the scene before him; watched on as Henry reached out his arms and hauled the lifeless body of Rowen off the cold floor and into his lap. Josh crawled backwards, holding his ribs tightly, hugging himself like Henry now hugged his child.

"Rowen, I'm..." Henry began to mutter as he ran a hand through his son's bloodied hair and rocked him in his arms, cradling him like a newborn child, and Josh mused Rowen was in a way; he was the son Henry had never known existed.

Josh dragged himself upright and reclined against the wall, watching Henry father Rowen in death in a way he'd not been able to father him in life: unconditionally.

"I'm sorry. I'm sorry. I'm sorry... forgive me... son..." Henry voice tapered off.

Josh stared at the scene before him and realised that their lives would never be the same again and he realised in this second – finite – death; the desires of a vengeful child, seeking retribution for a life-time of punishment and derision, squeezed into fourteen painfully long but short years. Inflicted by a vindictive, bigoted father's abuse towards what they truly were, had struck the mortal wound they'd intended to deliver all along.

Rowen's prediction was right, Josh mused darkly.

The graveside message had come to fruition at the allotted time; because as Josh stared across the room he saw not one, but two dead people and one of them was staring back at him.

"What have I done?" Henry tears ran from his eyes like poison from a wound buried deep inside of him, one that had festered with hate for twelve long years and was finally rupturing.

Josh couldn't answer because the words he wanted to say wouldn't provide Henry any comfort, if anything they'd strip him of the solace he was seeking; the forgiveness he was begging for from the lips of his dead son.

And so, Josh stayed silent, hugged himself tighter, hugged the pain away whilst he watched the last moments of a son, finally returning home into his father's open arms.

"I've always loved you…" Henry muttered as he pawed at his son's bloodied face.

Henry rocked Rowen as if he were preparing to sing him a lullaby.

"You're perfect." Henry blubbered as he kissed his son's head.

Josh felt tears cresting in his eyes.

"I'm sorry it's taken me up until now to realise that… to tell you that."

The tears were falling now and Josh continued to watch through his corrupted sight.

"I'm sorry I never allowed myself to see you before. But I do now, I see how brave you were, how wrong I was… I'm sorry for what I did goddamnit…"

Henry hugged his son tighter.

"You left me as a daughter, but returned to me as a son…"

Henry choked on his words, steadied himself once more and continued.

"I love you."

His body twitched and he brushed his son's face again, looked on him with awe.

"I love you because I love you because I love you."

Henry hauled his son from his lap, rested his head against his neck, held him close in a fatherly embrace. Josh could hear him whispering; all of his regrets, his pain, his suffering, his apologies and his petitions for forgiveness tumbled from his trembling lips.

He pulled Rowen away slightly, peered into his son's vacant face once, returned it to the crook of his neck before nestling his own face against his son's where he began pouring out his heart once more in words and sobs.

Henry held his son like he'd never let him go.

He held him and loved him unconditionally.

Henry wrapped his arms around Rowen, rocking him into gently into the next realm and the sight of it filled Josh with hope.

Rowen had wanted acceptance all along, and now he had it.

But the price he'd paid for it was catastrophic.

As Josh contemplated everything that had transpired and led them to where they were now, he pondered what would be waiting for them once they'd left this house of slaughter; and as he observed the wreckage before him, the broken remains of a family torn apart by denial and rejection and hate.

He realised that *love*, was the most divine healer of them all.

But the cost of finding that love...

...for Henry,

...for Elsie,

...for Rowen,

...for Amanda,

....had proven fatal.

ACKNOWLEDGMENTS

First and foremost, my heartfelt gratitude goes out to my dear friend and supremely talented, Josh Malerman, to whom this book is dedicated.

Thank you Josh for being so generous with your time, expertise and encouragement during the writing of this book. Your crazy idea of writing books at the same time and swapping first drafts every 10k paid off greatly (*I can't wait for people to discover your novel 'Incidents Around The House*). It would be remiss of me not to mention the fabled and famous '*Malerman Momentum'* here, which you've spoken of regularly. It is that momentum which pulled me kicking and screaming through this whole process, and made me a better writer in the process. This book wouldn't be what it is today without your guidance, friendship and never-ending support before, during and after that crazy writing session of 2022... let's do it again sometime!

Clash Books (*Christoph and Leza*) thank you for your enthusiasm for this book. When I wrote '*I Died Too, But They Haven't Buried Me Yet*' I knew it needed a publisher who *got* the book and who *got* me. It needed a publisher who was brave and progressive, whilst also being intelligent about being progressive and I found that in you. I'm thrilled to be part of the Clash community of authors and truly humbled that this book found a home with you. Thank you for all your dedication, support and encouragement in bringing 'I Died Too...' into the world.

Tyler Jones, your insight regarding the first few chapters of this book were inspired – *iron sharpens iron*. I am forever grateful for your input and delighted to call you a dear friend, onwards and upwards my good sir.

My thanks also goes to Joel Amat Güell for his wonderful cover art which is both subtle and eye-catching, and the perfect foil for this soul crushing story.

Brett Petersen my heartfelt gratitude for your work in polishing this manuscript, your editing was sublime and I enjoyed the many comments of how I destroyed you along the way... especially that last one.

As always, a huge portion of my thanks goes to my darling wife Anna and my beautiful children Eva and Sophie. Thank you for being my constant, thank you for loving me, thank you for always allowing me to share my ideas with you (*however peculiar they may be*), and thank you for your unwavering support and encouragement of all that I do, and am yet to do. Eva, at long last the idea I told you about when it was just a few scrawled passages in a notebook is finally in print. When you're old enough to enjoy it, I hope it's as good as that discussion we had about it. The look of awe on your face when I explained it to you was priceless. With the three of you in my life I am truly blessed.

And thanks to you, dear reader, for picking up 'I Died Too, But They Haven't Buried Me Yet' - I've more nightmares percolating, so it won't be long until I horrify you all again.

So, until then...pleasant dreams.

About the Author

Ross Jeffery is the Bram Stoker and 3x Splatterpunk Award-nominated author of The Devil's Pocketbook, The Juniper Trilogy (Juniper, Tome & Scorched), Only The Stains Remain, Beautiful Atrocities and Tethered.

Ross lives in Bristol with his wife (Anna) and two children (Eva and Sophie). You can follow him on X here @RossJeffery_

ALSO BY CLASH BOOKS

EVERYTHING THE DARKNESS EATS

Eric LaRocca

THE BLACK TREE ATOP THE HILL

Karla Yvette

BAD FOUNDATIONS

Brian Allen Carr

BELETH STATION

Samantha Kolesnik & Bryan Smith

THE LAST NIGHT TO KILL NAZIS

David Agranoff

PEST

Michael Cisco

THE ECSTASY OF AGONY

Wrath James White

HEXIS

Charlene Elsby

LES FEMMES GROTESQUES

Victoria Dalpe

CHARCOAL

Garrett Cook

WE PUT THE LIT IN LITERARY

CLASHBOOKS.COM

FOLLOW US

Twitter

IG

FB

@clashbooks

Printed in the USA
CPSIA information can be obtained
at www.ICGtesting.com
JSHW021240101023
49920JS00003BA/3